Harlan's
Race

PATRICIA NELL WARREN

To Neil—
love
Patricia Nell Warren
Montrose Pride 2000

Wildcat Press
Beverly Hills

Copyright © 1994 by Patricia Nell Warren

Jacket design:
Barbara Brown, Jay Fraley, Tyler St. Mark and Patricia Nell Warren

Jacket art, photographs and half-tone illustrations:
Jay Fraley

Book design:
Barbara Brown Desktop Publishing and Patricia Nell Warren

Typesetting:
Barbara Brown Desktop Publishing, La Crescenta, CA

Printed on acid-free paper by Patterson Printing, Benton Harbor, MI.

First printing: May 1994
Second printing: June 1994

PRINTED IN THE UNITED STATES OF AMERICA

Library of Congress Catalog Card Number 94-060438

ISBN: 0-9641099-0-5

OTHER NOVELS BY PATRICIA NELL WARREN

ONE IS THE SUN (Ballantine, 1991)

THE BEAUTY QUEEN (William Morrow, 1978)

THE FANCY DANCER (William Morrow, 1976; reissued by Plume)

THE FRONT RUNNER (William Morrow, 1974; reissued by Plume)

THE LAST CENTENNIAL (Dial Press, 1971)

POETRY BY PATRICIA NELL WARREN

HORSE WITH A GREEN VINYL MANE (Novi Poezii, 1970)

ROSE-HUED CITIES (Novi Poezii, 1966)

LEGENDS AND DREAMS (Novi Poezii, 1962)

A TRAGEDY OF BEES (Novi Poezii, 1959)

ABOUT THE AUTHOR

Patricia Nell Warren was born in 1936. She grew up on a Montana cattle ranch, and worked as a Reader's Digest editor for 22 years. Two of her novels were bestsellers. She has won numerous awards, including a Walt Whitman Award for Gay Literature and a Western Heritage Award from the National Cowboy Hall of Fame. She lives in California today.

For
all my readers and all the bookstores
who have hung in there with me
and
all who helped with this book.

Author's Introduction

After *The Front Runner* became an international best-seller, my William Morrow editor, Jim Landis, was enthusiastic about a sequel.

The new book would answer the question of what happened to Billy Sive's son, described as born in 1977. But dealing with a teenage boy, as I wanted to do, meant writing a book set in the early 1990s. In the late 1970s, this amounted to writing science fiction! After grappling with the story for a year or two, I finally had to tell Landis that I couldn't get a handle on *Billy's Boy.*

Time has brought many changes and challenges to the gay community and the U.S. that track coach Harlan Brown knew in *The Front Runner.* Among other things, AIDS was unheard of when I wrote *TFR* in 1973. Not many Americans of the late '70s saw ahead to how heavily our world of the 1990s would be marked by environmental and economic decay, media power, a resurgence of racism and intolerance, and new Vietnams. Above all, few foresaw the growing social violence, and the need for self-defense.

Starting in 1982, I wrote my fifth novel, *One Is the Sun.* Ballantine brought it out in 1991.

With my thoughts turning back to *The Front Runner,* I realized it was time to write the sequel. And there needed to be another book to bridge between *The Front Runner* and *Billy's Boy.* Titled *Harlan's Race,* this book would answer the question of how Harlan Brown survived the violence and challenges of those changing times.

Patricia Nell Warren

Harlan's
Race

PART ONE

A Question of Innocence

ONE

In the summer of 1990, when I was 55, with so many things coming full circle for me, I went back to New York for the first time in many years. The Gay Games were held then, and I attended — made some new friends, and saw a few of the old ones who were still alive.

"Hi, Harlan, how are you? God, it's been ages. Yeah, we're still together ... hanging in there. Did you know Justin died? And Chen? So, tell us about you. Got a boyfriend these days? Why the hell aren't you down there in the mile run?"

The usual stuff.

Afterwards I took off alone, and found myself drawn to places where I'd spent the Seventies — that blurred time of my own race through life.

I'd always been one to brood on the past. So that old curve of the American earth called me back, to run down a missing clarity. It wasn't going to be any sentimental journey. More yawned in wait for me than mere years. An era had vanished into a holocaust of time — a present-time version of what people like to see as those sunny antebellum days. A point of view had belonged to me, and to other gay men and lesbians, and also to many straight

Americans of those times. It had vanished, without our knowing that it was at risk.

In New York City, I felt the first little shocks. The Village was more dangerous and decrepit than ever, with less reason for a dyed-in-the-wooler to go on insisting it was the best turf on earth. Many businesses and bartenders and bars and bookstores and coffeehouses that I remembered were gone with the wind. Steve Goodnight's apartment, where I'd faced the end of my coaching career and struggled to become a self-supporting writer, was gone. The old brownstone building, and half the block, had been razed for a new apartment tower.

North of the city, all those green reaches of Westchester County that I'd known so intimately in the Seventies, were patchworked with crass new shopping centers. The campus of Prescott College, where my track team sweated for eight years, was now the corporate headquarters for a foreign company. Those woods where my cross-country runners had hurtled along the trails, where I'd scattered Billy's ashes in a remote glen, were being bulldozed to make way for split-level ranch houses. Crashes of oak trees hitting the earth seemed almost as jarring as the gun-shot that killed Billy.

But it was on the South Shore of Long Island that I got the biggest jolt.

In the Seventies, the Great South Bay was still clean. Through the inlet, dolphins came roaming in from the sea. In the fall, millions of monarch butterflies migrated through the area, on their way to Mexico. The warm shallow waters offered a feast of clean food — quahog clams, oysters, and blue crabs. Flooding in from the ocean, to spawn, came striped bass and weakfish.

Old-time bay families were known as "bonnikers", and they'd been there forever. Their men and women went out on the water, and hauled in food with no more regulation than a license to dig and a limit on size. Only the first whispers were being heard about hepatitis in clams that were dug near the mainland creeks. You could gill-net a bunch of weakfish, and eat them without a thought.

Now, as I rented a 19-foot bow-rider in the Patchogue marina, I watched the health inspectors tagging every sack of clams that went in the buyers' trucks.

That lovely bay was dying of pollution, and many bonnikers had gone to wherever people emigrate these days. A few diehards were struggling to build a seafood farm modeled on those of Japan. Two bonniker cops I'd known took me to lunch, and asked me if I'd eaten striped bass recently. One cop said you could only eat striper a couple times a year now — too many PCBs in it. And, said the other cop, it tasted "some different".

When I ate my plateful, I agreed.

That afternoon, when I took the rented boat out, a few sights still looked the same from afar. The ferry, an old PT boat, still plowed a white wake across the bay. But up close, the bay was dappled with sarcomas of red-brown algae. Breezes carried a subtle reek of chemicals and sewage. I drove the bow-rider at a low speed, shocked at the emptiness everywhere.

Along the southern rim of the bay, a strip of barrier beach runs for thirty miles. This is Fire Island, the real reason why I'd come here. A place that was a symbol to me — and to many younger Americans who were both gay and straight — of our belief that love and freedom were ours for the taking. I had lived on the east end of Fire Island. From its tidelands noisy with birds, to its clusters of beach houses on stilts, the "Beach" had been as lovely and remote as some South Sea atoll.

Just looking at that long, low Island on the horizon, with its undulating dunes, made me choke on memory. For months after Billy was shot to death, my mind's eye was obsessed with a picture of his body laying dead on that distant beach, where we'd taken so many walks and runs together. Now I could remember him as alive — his strong arms gripping me, his breath warm on my lips, blue-gray eyes holding the cleanness of Atlantic sky. His curls were like the tumbling sea-foam. His torso was sleek as a wave gathering, muscles playing under his skin like a herd of wild dolphins.

Yes, memory does trick us.

As I drove the boat past the tiny Fire Island community of Davis Park, my mind knew that I'd see the changes wreaked by Hurricane Gloria when she ripped through the island in 1985. Yet my brain believed that the little marina of 1976 was still there.

Just west of Davis Park, as my boat engine idled along, my eyes moved unwillingly, achingly to the new inlet that Gloria had torn through the island.

Right there, where high tide was falling back through the channel, the beach house called "Hotel Goodnight" had stood. That house was my spiritual home for so many years. The Hotel had been one of the many, many houses of love — my loves, the loves of my friends. The sounds of passionate love-making I could still hear so clearly from its bedrooms. The deep kissings and humpings, the urgent groans of men coupling — were stark in the hot golden air, like dragonflies in amber. Now its broken stilts stuck bleaching out of the sand. A few weathered shingles were still blown across the dunes.

On the raw new beach of the inlet, a dead dolphin lay.

So I cut the motor, and drifted in the silence, staring at that carcass half buried in the sand.

Beneath me, the boat rose and fell gently, humped by the passing swells. On the hot, humid breeze, that stench of the rotting meat drifted to my nostrils. I closed my eyes, and remembered my own war to turn the tide of life, to call it back to me.

That life that was ripped from me on September 9, 1976, at the Montreal Olympic Games. The day that Billy died.

TWO

September 9, 1976
Montreal Olympic Games

Of all the things about the day Billy was killed, I most remember that butcher smell on my clothing.

I had run the fastest sprint of my life, to where Billy had fallen, in the closing yards of the 5000-meter run. I was kneeling right on the track, in lane 1. He lay on his back, with his bleeding head in a widening pool. His long legs sprawled out on the track.

People jostled around me. The U.S. team doctor, Parker, an ex-Army medic, who had already told me it looked like a bullet wound. Canadian police and stadium security. My head bodyguard, Harry Saidak, and my young assistant, Vince Matti. Through them, I glimpsed the paramedics racing toward us with the gurney. But I'd gotten to Billy first. I had a right to be there with him. Beyond all the uproar about my relationship with Billy, I was his coach.

"No pulse," Parker said. "No respiration."

"Hang on, hang on," I said to Billy, gripping his hand.

"Come on . . . stay with us," Vince told him, kneeling by us.

But Billy's hand was limp. The glow of spirit was

already fading from his half-shut eyes. His tongue was forced out grotesquely. Parker parted Billy's hair, exposing the tiny entry-hole of the bullet in his right temple. Exiting, the bullet had blown open his left temple. The blood was thick and dark red — the color of deep oxygen debt. His brains were a currant jelly soaking his hair. The smell was a wet, fleshy slaughter smell.

Bits of gray bone had lodged against my gold wedding ring. The matching ring glinted on Billy's hand, now limp on the track.

My lover had always held his head strong and proud, like a young roadrunner speeding free just ahead of a shotgun blast. His brown curls were supposed to be plumes, with the wind of his own speed lifting them. His blue-gray eyes should be open, looking at me with their fierce love of life.

"Harlan, you okay?" my bodyguard asked, gripping my arm. Harry's voice quivered with helpless rage.

"Yeah," I said automatically.

Vince helped me and the others lift Billy to the gurney. My assistant looked dazed. One of Billy's spiked shoes slid off in his hand. In the stands by the final turn, the crowd was suddenly screaming and stirring, as if something had just happened over there.

Then the announcer's voice was echoing through the vast stadium.

"— THE GUNMAN IS IN CUSTODY. HE HAS BEEN DISARMED. WE REPEAT. REMAIN CALM . . . STAY SEATED."

The paramedics were loading the gurney into the ambulance. Legally, they had to do their drill — get Billy to an emergency room. But I knew it was too late. As a Marine, I'd been too young for Korea, too old for Vietnam. But I'd heard the old guys talk about wounds. Nobody can live with half their brain shot away.

"Let's go," my bodyguard said quietly.

He hurried Vince and me off the track. As my assistant and I jogged along, Vince was clutching Billy's spiked shoe against his chest, and tears streamed down his face. He had a tender, young heart, and Billy was his best friend. Mine was the steel heart — it took a while to melt down.

"Unscrew those spikes," I said. "They'll hurt you."

Vince fumbled in his pocket for the little spike screw. He got the spikes out, dropped one, picked it up, and fumbled them into his pocket.

Up there in the stands, the rest of our family were either sitting frozen, or trying to fight through the crowd. Billy's father, John Sive. Betsy Heden, the young lesbian who was Billy's best woman friend. Joe and Marian Prescott, founders of the college that supported Billy's Olympic bid. And writer Steve Goodnight and his lover, Angel. Three more bodyguards were with them.

Outside the stadium, those ambulance sounds were fading away.

At the crowded stadium gate, I saw Marian and Betsy with Harry's bodyguard partner, Chino Cabrera. The two women threw their arms around me and Vince, while Chino gave Harry a quick report. The rest of the family were hurrying to a rendezvous point outside.

"Harlan, aren't you going with Billy?" Marian panted.

Then she and Betsy saw the red mess on my clothes.

"Dear ... heaven ..." Marian murmured, hands over her eyes. She threw her arms around Betsy, who simply uttered Billy's name drawn out to a terrible wordless shriek.

The panicky crowd had us trapped near the stadium entrance. Chino and Harry had planted themselves in front of us. Then camera flashes started blinking off in our faces. Images of our bloodstained little clan would be flashed around the world — by those media who had stalked Billy and me since our relationship was publicized in a tabloid newspaper last spring. An ABC-TV female interviewer pushed briskly toward us, with her mike. A cameraman followed, equipment on his shoulder.

Marian was our media liaison. She moved up beside Chino, and barked, "Be a little kind. Statements later."

"Mr. Brown," the interviewer called to me. "Mr. Brown, would you — Mr. Brown, as Billy Sive's coach, can you tell us how you felt when —"

Now spectators yelled down on our heads, from the tiers above.

"Billy lives!"

"Serves him right!"

And a loud woman's voice trumpeted, "Homos deserve to die! I hope they shoot you aaaaallll!"

Late that night, in our downtown hotel, the family managed to shut the world out. Everybody sprawled exhausted in beds or on chairs, or bathed swollen eyes in the bathrooms. Footsteps and voices shook the corridor outside, where Harry's voice could be heard barking, "Keep the bribe, buddy. Press conference in the lobby tomorrow morning at 8."

So Harry and Chino were returning from the stadium. I wondered what they'd found out.

I was standing at the window, staring out at the glowing skyline of that French-Canadian city. Church spires cut across the city lights. Somewhere, a church bell was tolling midnight.

The bedroom had sheltered Billy and me, on the two nights he left the Olympic Village. It was stuffy, as hotel rooms were in those days when everybody still smoked so much. On the dresser, beside my old Bible, lay the gold medal that he'd won in the 10,000-meter run. His T-shirt was draped over a chair with kid forgetfulness — I could still see him pulling it off, eager to make love, baring his lean torso that rippled with life, like water. The double bed, so disordered after we finally lay quiet, was neat now, under its worn chenille spread. Just an hour ago, I had seen that torso inert under glaring lights in the city morgue. They'd verified a gunshot wound as cause of death. His dad had identified him and authorized shipment of the body home. I was jostled aside. Officially, I did not exist.

Now, barely looking at myself in the mirror, a 41-year-old man who'd lost the only lover he ever had, I noticed something. The bloodstained suit. It was still on me.

From the adjoining room came a TV newscaster's voice.

Moving in a numb quest to understand what had happened, I opened the connecting door.

The room was Harry's and Chino's. But right now, Vince, Steve, Marian and Bruce Cayton were in there, hunched amid blue layers of cigarette smoke, watching the screen. Bruce was an old-school, chain-smoking, skirt-chasing journalist I'd known for years, who by some miracle of sympathy had become one of our staunchest media supporters. Mike Stella was there too, a teammate of Billy's.

". . . of Richard Mech's confession to the shooting," said the newscaster somberly.

News-clips slid before our eyes. A pan-shot of the stands beside the straightaway, as Billy was pulling ahead of Finnish runner Armas Sepponan. The killer had taken advantage of the uproar — people standing up and screaming wildly for or against the queer. A slow-motion zoom showed the dark puff in the air by Billy's head.

Cut to police escorting Richard Mech. It was my first look at my lover's murderer. Mech was about my age, clean-cut. By tonight, police and media already knew from his confession that Mech was an Idaho country boy and an Army sniper in Vietnam.

A guy like me, I thought, *did this to us.*

Steve, sitting beside me, wordlessly put his arm across my shoulders.

". . . U.S. authorities demanding that Mech be extradited back to the U. S. to stand trial," the newscaster went on. "Meanwhile, there are reactions from Canadian and American church leaders, who . . ."

Mike Stella wordlessly squeezed my arm and left. I trudged back to my room. Vince followed, and shut the door. His eyes were bleary, and his handsome face tear-stained. He leaned against the faded wallpaper with Billy's shoe still stuffed in one pocket of his black leather jacket. His silver peace symbol, on its leather thong, was askew.

This tall, rangy youth had exchanged a look or two with me, before Billy and I fell in love. At that time, I still had a rule about not sleeping with my runners, so I had stiff-armed Vince. After I finally let myself love Billy, Vince had

hidden his feelings out of respect for Billy, who was his best
friend. Officially, Vince was in Montreal as my assistant.
Unofficially, he was the other gay, world-class runner I'd
trained — the one who hadn't made the team. The ruined
miler whose stride still gave him the look of a wolf on the
hunt. Now he felt like he wanted to cry on my shoulder.

My shoulders ached with weariness — I hitched them.
Vince hesitated, then came over and rubbed them gently.

"You should . . . like, get out of those clothes," he said
hoarsely.

I knew he wanted to show caring. But touch was something I shunned right then, so I walked away to the closet.
Billy's brown velvet suit was hanging in there. Just last
night it had clothed his living frame, at an uproarious cele-
bration dinner. My fingers ran down the sleeve. So soft.
But not warm. A deep wrenching racked my guts. But no
tears came.

Just then, Harry Saidak and Chino Cabrera came in.

"Oooh, it's the baby killers," Vince said with an edged
voice. "Lock up the napalm, Mary."

Vince was 24, and as a college student he'd evolved from
the peace movement into the gay lib movement. But my
peacenik assistant had a hard time stretching his acceptance of gay to include these two veterans.

The two vets ignored him.

They were a colorful pair. Harry was 35, a six-foot Green
Beret, with the Midwestern good looks of a blond Rock
Hudson — except he was missing Hudson's gift for comedy.
He'd been in Vietnam early, and was still the perfect soldier. Chino was 27, Chicano, 5' 10", sinuous and Asian-
looking. He was a SEAL, fresh from the Nam, where he'd
been a scout/sniper, and later an advisor, and he was struggling to adjust. Chino was the one with the humor, though
his power to laugh had been severely strained.

The two had met at a veterans' group, spotted each
other's gayness and hunger to come out, and agreed that a
peacetime use for their skills was in order. With violence
against gays and lesbians on the rise, they figured they'd
get some business from the gay community. So Harry and

Chino had settled in West Hollywood, the gayest part of
L.A., and started their own small firm — H-C Security
Service, Inc.

But gay celebrities and gay hoi polloi had a passion for
living on the edge. "We shouldn't have to be protected,"
activist George Rayburn told H-C indignantly. So the two
men, who'd had millions spent on them in uniform, often
wound up working for beer money as bouncers at gay clubs.

During that long Montreal day, our two Mary marauders had lost a little spit-polish — boots dusty, jeans sweaty.
They wore no holsters — Canadian authorities wouldn't let
them carry arms. Chino didn't like packing a gun anyway,
because he was still too afraid that he'd over-react.

"Okay, everybody . . . time to talk turkey," said Harry.

Wanting to listen, Bruce, Marian and a hollow-eyed John
Sive pushed into the bedroom too.

Billy's father, a civil-rights attorney, had an angry expression that reminded me I'd ignored his advice on bodyguards. Before the Games, worried by death threats, John
and I had agreed that we needed our own security — gay
brothers whose loyalty was beyond question. John hadn't
liked my hiring H-C. Combat vets are too trigger-happy, he
said. But few big-name protection services wanted to protect any famous faggots, whereas H-C was eager for the job.
John and I had had a big fight — our first.

Harry looked at Bruce. "Not a word in print till you
hear it from the police," he growled.

"I know the drill," said Bruce coolly.

Harry looked around at all of us.

"So," he said, "sniping got a shot in the arm in Vietnam.
Makes the JFK hit look a little primitive. Now the thinking
is coming home, and other people are using it. Mech and his
partner are that kind of sniper."

My whole body jerked, with a volt of nervous energy.

"Partner?" I said. "More than one?"

"Professionals usually work in pairs," Chino told us. "The
boss and I just looked at some footage from the security
cameras in the stadium. The techies zoomed us as close as
they could. Mech was with this bearded guy on an aisle

near an exit. They were talking. Then the bearded guy left. Mech had a clear shot down the aisle, about 40 yards, to Billy's head. A shooter and his spotter. I can feel it."

"Convenient of Mech to get arrested," said John.

"Yeah," Chino agreed. "I can't believe he thought he was going to retreat from that position. Maybe he wanted to be caught, so he could make a statement."

"So you're saying the spotter got away in the confusion," said John.

"Yeah," said Chino. "He let his buddy eat it. Weird."

"Did the police get the gun?" I asked.

"It's a custom .22 rifle disguised as a crutch," said Harry. "Slick little job. The round was probably a .22 Magnum."

That slaughter smell surged in my memory, and I retched.

Harry lit a cigarette, adding to the blue reek in the room. My non-smoker eyes were burning.

"Well," said Chino, "if they don't catch this second guy, he's still a possible threat."

Meaning the next target could be me.

"Are the police looking for him?" said Marian.

"Oh, they say they're checking all leads. The usual shit," said Harry.

"If I was him," Chino added quietly, exhaling, "I'd try again."

Harry, Bruce, Marian and John left. Vince and Chino stayed, staring out the window. Suddenly I remembered my bloody clothes, and headed for the closet again. Steeling myself, I moved the velvet suit aside and grabbed clean clothes. Just then, a hand gripped my shoulder. I looked up into Chino's eyes — into his combat stare.

While other young gay men were dancing their brains out in discos, and fucking their brains out in bed, Chino was isolated from them behind a wall of blood. He'd come back from the carnage with only one overriding passion — caring for his own, and making sure they stayed alive. A few years ago "his own" were his men in the jungle. Now his own were us. Coming out had estranged him from his Chicano *familia*, so we were all he had. Billy wasn't just a "client" — Chino had adopted him with a family fierceness that surprised us.

"Harlan," said Chino hoarsely.

"Yeah?"

"I . . . feel like there was something we could have done. I've been over it a million times in my mind already. But I don't know what it is. Except not let Billy run."

His light-gray eyes held mine — strange eye-color in a Chicano. For a moment, their expression was strangely young, vulnerable. One of his own, someone under his protection, had just been murdered. He was devastated.

"You guys are not to blame," I said in a stifled voice. "We all knew there was a risk. Billy knew."

"Sure, Harlan," Vince said harshly from the other side of the room. "Turn the other cheek."

Vince stood with feet braced, his long, uncombed hair wild around his face. His own love and protectiveness for Billy, a more sexual kind, now exploded in resentment.

"Let's face it," he provoked us. "The two nelly Lt. Calleys here . . . they fucked up."

For a moment, it seemed like Chino had spun on his heel toward Vince in one deadly blur. Harry had told me how Chino shot on pure instinct. As a sniper, he could set up a hit with silent speed. Chino never talked about his skills, or showed them off. I'd seen his lonely figure in a gay bar there in Montreal, watchful, protective, standing by the smoky dance floor with that lethal move trapped inside him like a scorpion in amber, while Billy and Vince and a hundred other young men were boogying down, deep in their own kind of shooting.

But I must have dreamed the move, with my exhausted eyes open. Chino just stood there with his brown fists clenched.

Then he relaxed his hands.

"Hey, sister," he said pleasantly, "you spit a brick that big, it might fall on your nelly toe."

Rage at Vince's lack of sensitivity ripped through me.

"Kid," I said to him, "you don't have anything to say to these two guys. They risk their asses for you, too."

Vince turned on his heel, and walked out of the room.

"Well," Chino said to me, "you'll need our help through the trial. Personally . . . I'm yours for as long as you want me."

I was shucking my trousers. A little blood, now dry and black, had soaked through onto my boxer shorts. Shocked, I stared down at it. An old part of my mind screamed that I had done wrong to love Billy, that his blood was on me forever.

Chino stared at my shorts too. He'd seen miles of black stains like that, but I think he read my mind.

"We'll talk about it tomorrow," I whispered. "I need to be alone."

Chino went into the next room, sliding his glance over everybody, checking out the rest of "his own". Betsy sat in a wing chair, staring at the turned-off TV. She and Billy had been as close friends as lesbians and gay men ever get, and she was in shock.

Hunkering down by her, Chino took her small hand in his, and started talking to her. Betsy eyed him warily — she was another fey liberal.

I showered to get the smell off me — changed clothes, roamed the room in helpless numbness. Desperate for some consolation, I picked up my Bible. Through years of struggling to hold onto my faith, I had doted on the few passages about love. They bloomed like wildflowers among all those thistles of hate that seemed to crowd scripture everywhere.

This time, however, the dog-eared book fell open to *Ezekiel 28: 6-7*.

> *Because thou hast set thine heart as the heart of God,*
> *Behold, therefore I will bring strangers upon thee, the terrible of the nations:*
> *And they shall draw their swords against the beauty of thy wisdom,*
> *And they shall defile thy brightness.*

Was it God who sent Richard Mech and his partner against me and Billy? Or was it human fanatics, drawing their sword?

Angrily I slammed the Bible down on the dresser.

From across the street, bright-lit offices of a glass tower stared into my window. If the spotter was hiding over there, he could study me with an infrared scope. I yanked the curtains shut, made sure the door to the corridor was locked. The next room was quiet, but Chino and Harry were there. They were buddies, not lovers, but they stayed tight.

Billy had run his race. Was this my race, from now on? Would I have to live behind barred doors, hiring guns to protect my family — in the land of the free and the home of the brave?

Long after that distant church bell tolled 2 a.m., I finally surrendered to exhaustion, and crawled into that cold bed. On the pillows, I could still smell the faint fragrance of Billy's after-shave.

Dreams swallowed me. Vince was hovering there, asking if he could sleep in my bed for the night. He looked so young, like a kid who'd been scared by a horror movie he'd seen and wanted to bunk with Dad for the night. He crawled in beside me, wearing sweaty jeans and T-shirt. Around him was a feeling of pot, poppers, unwashed sex, and all the wild partying since his own running career was destroyed. That sweaty, desperate nestling against me was strange — his body was a man's, not a child's.

Then Vince was swept away by a storm of cheers and curses.

THREE

Twenty months later
May 1978

The voices hammered my ears as microphones were thrust in my face. Flashbulbs winked off. Conservative U.S. and Canadian media had soft-pedaled the murder trial, but today the sentence had come down, and restraint was out the window.

"Hey, Harlan, do you think justice was done?"

"Har! Hey, Har! Give us a photo angle."

"Vince! This way!"

"*You* should be locked up!" one man bawled. "Not the hero!"

To the reporters who called me "Har," I snapped, "It's *mister* to you."

Richard Mech, now 44, had just heard his sentence in the Montreal courtroom, and his braced neck was disappearing down another marble corridor as Canadian marshals escorted him to prison. With Harry just ahead of us, and Chino just behind, Vince, John Sive and I strode down the main hallway toward the entrance. Once again our two vets were unarmed, by police order. All of us wore vests

18

made of Kevlar, the new miracle fabric used for body armor.

John, 54 now, burying the loss of Billy in his work, looked dreadfully tired, trudging with his heavy briefcase. We were being dragged down by a pack of yammering wild dogs.

"Mr. Brown, what are your plans?"

"Harlan! Hey, Har!"

"Mr. Brown, why do you think the Canadian and U.S. governments aren't interested in the conspiracy theory on this case?"

Outside, there were cars, buses, squad cars, Royal Canadian mounted police, riot police, demonstrators, media and spectators. Lovers of justice in both countries knew that the verdict was a litmus test on the future. Were governments and peoples willing to honor the lives of their gay citizens? Canada had its own gay-rights movement — indeed, Billy's slaughter had been seen on TV all over the world, and jarred gay men and lesbians everywhere. Activists — Vince Matti among them — had demonstrated throughout the trial. Today, people's emotions were out of hand. One placard said in English, BILLY DIED FOR FREEDOM, right next to several in French Canadian. Other signs read GIVE MECH ANOTHER MEDAL and DEATH TO SODOMISTS.

Loving hands of gay and lesbian demonstrators reached out to touch me. Numbly, I squeezed hands back.

Vince stood right behind me, his handsome face dark with anguish. Always a pacifist, he had marched against the Vietnam War when he was 15. But Billy's death had shaken him with change, deep as an earthquake. Lately he'd growled about a tooth for a tooth — the death penalty for Mech. I had disagreed, feeling that a lifetime in prison was worse than death, for a country boy.

But the law was clear. The Canadian government had refused to extradite Mech, and the death penalty was outlawed in Canada. Police had made no further arrests in the case — the man glimpsed by the cameras seemed a ghost. The defense seduced the jury with Mech's clean country look and war record.

"Yes, I acted alone," Mech had insisted. Deep moral outrage at Billy and me had driven him wild, he said. He had not lived through hell in Vietnam, he said, so that deviates could enjoy freedom too. He wept in the dock. Canadian conservatives were no different than the American variety — they might harden their hearts to the tears of a black child or a battered wife, but they came unglued at the tears of a war veteran. For the most public murder of a homosexual in the history of North America, Mech got ten years.

Our little party paused for the expected statement on the courthouse steps. Several dozen microphones aimed at us.

"All right," I said in my locker-room voice. "Listen up."

The media people quieted. Though the Canadian court had tried a news blackout on the trial, a changing U.S. had followed any news avidly on TV. American religious zealotry was finally drawing its sword on the new sexual freedom of gays and straights. Florida politician Anita Bryant had had her own things to say to the media, against the brightness and beauty of gay life.

Now a spring breeze played with my tie, and fanned my feverish head through my crew cut. On a day like this, Billy and I had made love for the first time, two years ago. In my worst nightmares, I couldn't have seen myself standing here — or Billy's ashes scattered in the woods near my home.

I cleared my throat.

"People ask me about justice," I began hoarsely.

From that seething sea of heads, thousands of eyes met mine. Some eyes were crying. Some looked away, or looked down. Some eyes blazed with incredible hostility.

"There are those who say that Billy deserved to die," I went on. "I was raised in the kind of home that these people come from. That Mech came from. I served in the same uniform he did. Their cruel and cold-blooded America is not the country that I stand for. It all starts with words of hate. Words turn to bullets. Maybe a courtroom can't bring to justice all the people who murder with words. But history will."

I turned away from the mikes.

"Vince!" "Mr. Matti!" "Vince!"

Vince was the picture of defiant leftist — rock 'n' roll mane and tattered bell-bottom jeans. His peace medal was conspicuously missing. He leaned to the mikes and shouted:

"I have nothing to say to a corrupt society that killed my best friend."

As he made a Panther fist in the air, cheers went up from the nearest gay radicals in the crowd who could hear him.

Then, between our bodyguards, John, Vince and I pushed along the narrow aisle of barricades, towards the curb, where our limousine waited. It was an old black Cadillac limousine with bulletproof windows, that John had hired. Corky had the engine running, with Jemal riding shotgun. From both sides the crowd leaned on us, cursing us and blowing us kisses, past Royal Canadian Mounties towering on their horses.

"No further comments," John Sive was yelling at the media.

"Shame!" a woman shouted at John. "Faggot fathers are the worst scum of all!"

A chant started. "Free Richard Mech! Free Richard Mech!"

"J'aime Beelee," cried a young French Canadian man in my ear.

Out of the corner of my eye, as Chino pushed me into the limo, I saw riot police dragging some young passive resisters towards a police van. One woman was still clutching a sign — I caught the word LOVE.

In another minute, we were shut tight in the limo. Faces friendly and unfriendly pressed against the windows. A dead cat bounced off the hood. Trying to even the score, a little band of French Canadian activists threw flowers at us. Then we pulled away, leaving the uproar behind.

We drove through the city streets in silence.

Finally Chino passed his pack of Tiparillos around and tried to lighten things up. "Not very nice, were they? They didn't even offer us a drink."

Everybody lit up, even Vince and John. I, the long-suffering non-smoker, opened the window beside me. The vets had carefully checked the limo for bugging devices, so it was safe to talk.

"Well?" Harry asked John. "Are you guys going after the second shooter? Get a conspiracy investigation going at home?"

John opened his briefcase, and took out a fat file of hate letters. There were three from a correspondent who had cut out words and letters from newspapers and magazines, and laboriously glued them to a sheet. His style was now familiar. The newest one read:

YOU WILL REGRET THE DAY MECH GOES TO JAIL. YOU WILL LEARN TO FEAR MY NAME.
LOVE,
A SECRET ADMIRER

"Did you show this to the FBI?" Chino asked, reading it.

"Yeah," John said. "They flipped through the file. Standard celebrity stuff, they said. Harlan's paying his dues, they said. They've got bigger fish to fry. Watergate. The Mafia."

John shut the file, and put it away.

Now we could scream and yell, picket the FBI and the New York attorney general's office. But compassion, like blood, is hard to squeeze out of a stone. At that moment I made the decision that so many gay men and lesbians make when they can't get justice — I'd tough it through on my own. And who knows — maybe a miracle would happen. Hadn't the peace movement gotten us out of Vietnam? Weren't civil rights moving ahead on other fronts? Maybe things *would* get better. Maybe Billy's death, and all the more anonymous deaths, and all the misery of centuries, wouldn't be for nothing.

"Well, Harlan, if there *is* an extremist group behind Mech," said Chino, "the boss and I can sneak and peek for you."

I stared out the window, letting the fragrant spring breeze buffet me. A terrible lump swelled in my throat, but wouldn't come up and be tears.

"Well?" John prodded me.

"Look," I said in a stifled voice. "Nobody has proved there was a second shooter. I'm sick and tired of living behind a cyclone fence —"

Hauling off the armored vest, I flung it on the seat next to the vets.

"You're crazy," John barked, in his best cross-examination voice. "And when things go bad for you, it'll be me cleaning up the mess!"

"— Prescott hired an associate coach," I barked back, as if I hadn't heard, "because I've been away so much. My psych is shot —"

"You don't need a psych, Harlan," Vince interrupted me, lounging on the opposite seat. His lean thighs were spread insolently apart. "You need —" He let the rest go unsaid.

Vince and I glared at each other. Lately, the old attraction between us was stirring again. Vince was volatile, impulsive, with a reputation for being passionate. I'd always had a weakness for passion. A few weeks ago, Vince blurted that he loved me. He'd tried to kiss me. But part of me was still choosing duty over desire. So, I'd held the young hellion off. He had slammed away in frustrated rage.

Now his eyes said, *Coach Brown, you don't have the guts to love me.*

"I have to get out of the public eye. Make a living," I said softly. "Get my life together."

As the limousine headed toward the Montreal airport, I stared at that city skyline of church spires, and brooded about my life.

Athletes need a "psych" — a picture in the mind that gives them a mental edge. For me, it went further. The psych was my armor against all loss.

Ever since I was young, I'd go clipping through life at my planned pace, thinking that a level track lay ahead. All of a sudden I'd stub my toe. Before I knew it, the hard earth would slam me. It was the kind of good hurt that reminds a runner he's alive. It was also the kind of hurt that cracks your psych like a mirror. For the 16 months that I'd had Billy, he'd been my psych. Running through my mind with his feathery stride, he was a symbol for me. So his death was the worst fall ever. If I'd been suicidal, or suffering from some disease, it would have been easy to let go of life, and join Billy. But I was only 42, in good health, no quitter.

If I just made the effort — I believed — I could slap a Band-Aid on my psych, and jump back in the race.

The need for an iron psych started in 1936, when I was born into an Irish-American family. They were Protestant, Bible-reading, conservative, blue-collar, patriotic, military. Dad was a Marine lieutenant, wounded at Guadalcanal during World War II. I loved and feared my dad, and tried to live by his belief. Like so many military men, his language brimmed with scorn for faggots and pussies. "Only a real man," he said, "can take a hill."

So I wasn't exactly thrilled to discover that I was gay.

From an early age, I was a highly sexed kid. Like some boys, I had the high-school flame, Chris Shelbourne, who set the first brush fires of passion in my heart. Chris had his own problems — his family was even more puritanical than mine. White heat of sex with males, and our hunger to know it, had our knees shivering in our jeans, and our spirits frying with guilt. I desired a lot, and dared very little. In high school, in college, I was curious about women, enough to bumble into fatherhood and marriage. But women were a quiet moon-glow — too quiet. They couldn't outshine the sun-heat of men.

As a top college miler, I had my own Olympic dream.

But my dad's dream for me was the Marines. By the time I was 10, he had pushed a .22 rifle in my hands, and sent me out to plink at rabbits. Dad was furious when I shrugged away an appointment to the Academy. I loved my country, and wanted to serve Her. But I was a feisty, abrasive, stubborn kid, and a hitch as a common jarhead was all I'd agree to. It was the first time I crossed my dad, and he never forgave me. My mom backed him up.

The only hills I took in the Corps were the Marine track team, and my last efforts to choke down the hunger for men. They hammered it into my head that my rifle was my friend. I was the fighting machine — followed orders to shoot, knew I'd shoot before "they" shot me — but knew I'd cry inside as I did. Scuttlebutt told us of court-martials for men caught bare-assed with men. Of course I sneered at faggots myself, in self-defense.

Back home, the Olympic dream died. Dad was ailing, the

family needed help. Tangled in marriage, I slaved as a sports-writer, went to night school for the credits to teach phys ed — and wound up with the plum job of coaching track at Penn State.

One desperate night in New York City in 1964, at age 28, as America was fracturing into the "now generation" and the "establishment", I finally chucked my dad's morality, and had sex with a man for the first time. My mouth tasted the wild joy — and also the loss, like blood from a split lip. Loss of conservative illusions about America. Loss of career — Penn State unloaded me on suspicions that I was gay. Loss of my parents' love. Loss of my two sons — my wife divorced me, and got custody.

The last thing that Dad ever said to me was, "If you'd been a real Marine, this would never have happened."

I moved to New York, and came out.

With Vietnam happening, guns couldn't hurt me worse than the baseball bats of gay-haters who prowled the streets. Child acceptance of "biblical authority" exploded into a quest for my own authority. I was the glowering crew-cut stud, flaunting his star-spangled cock, carrying a stick inside his denim jacket. I'd learned stick-fighting in the Marines, and God help the baseball-batter who messed with me.

But neither generation was my home. I was no flower child. I was no hard-shell either — the kind who said that long-haired kids should be shot. In 1970, when Kent State students were ripped by killing machines in National Guard uniform, I shuddered to think I might have been one of those machines.

In the 1970s "the gay community" was born. It was a span of outlawed viewpoints, that shared a hunger for po-litical muscle and pride. Yet even when little Prescott College offered me a coaching job, and the chance to be an openly gay faculty member, part of me still saw being gay as a cross to bear. When I met Billy in 1974, his self-acceptance lured me because I had so little self-acceptance of my own. Youth like Billy and Betsy and Vince, so glory-ing in their queer nature, were a different breed.

Now, with this trial over, what I hungered for was not

sex. I hungered to sit in front of a window with shades pulled up, and enjoy the sun and air, and not worry about me or my own being shot at.

I hungered for a "normal life".

Was it possible to get back into personal running? The AAU had a new over-40 masters' division. Just four months ago, I'd braved the screams of "Kill the fag!" to win the masters' mile at Madison Square Garden. The victory had felt wonderful — I wanted more.

Could I believe in something? I still attended a gay church in New York City. But my critics swore that Billy was now writhing in the flames of hell. It was time to decide if I should go on taking the Bible seriously.

Could there be family life?

Years ago, my ex-wife had barred me from seeing my two boys. Before Billy's death, he and I had wanted a family. Gay parenting was still a new thing. But Betsy Heden had loved us enough to help us with it. After Billy's death, she did insemination from a frozen semen sample, and became the mother of my lover's child. The unwritten agreement was that Billy and I would have custody. John William was born eight months ago, on September 2, 1977. Because of our notoriety, we'd kept the baby's parentage a secret. Only Vince, John Sive, the Prescotts and I — and Cal Jacobs, the gay doctor who'd helped us — knew the truth.

With Billy gone, Betsy now wanted to keep the baby. I felt responsible for John's getting born, and wanted to live close to him and his mother. Maybe even marry her — if she was willing. But she'd already been so alarmed at the death threats, that she'd had Doc Jacobs destroy all the medical records relating to the baby's conception. And she'd never acknowledged Billy's fatherhood on the birth certificate.

C hino's gritty voice pulled my mind back to the present.

"I think you're wrong," the Chicano was saying to me. "I can feel that second guy out there. Maybe he wants to get even for his buddy going to prison."

"Somebody's money was behind the operation," Harry added in. "Custom rifles cost."

"There are vigilante groups," Chino pointed out, "who are heavy into paramilitary stuff."

"They'd off you because you're a symbol," said Harry.

"I know, I know," I said.

But the two of them pounded away at me. "The next target might not be you," said Harry. "It could be Joe, Betsy, Vince . . ."

They didn't mention the baby, because they didn't know the family secret.

But I dug in my heels, and told them:

"Effective today, I'm giving you guys your notice. Please don't think I'm ungrateful. But I don't want anybody babysitting me, or taking a bullet for me. I'll be my own goddam bodyguard. School is out in a week, and I'm going to disappear . . . let things cool down."

"Where?" John Sive demanded.

"Fire Island. Spend the summer with Steve Goodnight."

Vince laughed with raunchy glee.

"You call Fire Island *disappearing?*" he wanted to know.

The two vets let their eyes rest briefly on Vince's magnificent crotch, as if it was a Vietcong booby trap.

"Don't worry," I said. "I'll manage."

"Steve isn't exactly invisible," added John. "Not after all the uproar about his last book."

"I'm going to look at the water," I said, as if I hadn't heard them. "Do some writing. I used to be a sportswriter . . . remember? I'd better have a back-up profession. What if Prescott fires me? What other school is going to hire me?"

"Better take your .45," Harry told me.

"Sure," I said recklessly. "The cops are pretty liberal in his part of the Island. They won't like the idea of a nut shooting at summer people. We'll be okay."

Harry shrugged. "I hope we don't have to say I told you so."

John's lips were pressed shut. His eyes were angry, remote.

Only Chino's eyes lingered on me, with a haunted anxiety.

"If you need us, call us," he said.

Letting the bodyguards go did make me feel naked. A sniper had every advantage on his side. But my plan to disappear was all worked out.

"Well," said Harry, "that's it, then. John, you heading for San Francisco?"

"As fast as I can," said John crisply.

"Vince, where are you off to?" Harry asked.

"New York City," said Vince.

"I hope that means you're getting a job," I said.

"Got one already," Vince shot back.

"Doing what?"

"Ram signed me for a film," he said, just a little defensively.

"A porno film," I said.

"Yeah."

At this news, the other three men kept their faces expressionless.

"A year ago, you turned Ram down," I said.

"I'm flat broke. I'm only going to do it once."

"They're giving you top billing, I hope?" I couldn't hold back the sarcasm.

"I'm the star."

"You majored in TV film production. What's a bright kid like you doing in front of the camera with no clothes on?"

"You're not my mom," Vince growled.

"Mother knows best. And before you go, give me Billy's shoe."

"Fuck you. It came off in *my* hand."

Chino shook his head, and lit another Tiparillo. Harry looked like he wanted his shot of bourbon. But they wouldn't drink on duty. They'd get blasted on the plane to L.A. John leaned back in his corner and closed his eyes — he needed a nap. The last two years had aged Billy's dad by ten years.

We were crossing a city square, where thousands of pigeons were flying around a few old people feeding them. I could see the set of the porno film, probably somebody's penthouse living room, shades down, hot lights, camera moving in for the extreme close-up. Many years ago, I'd donned a black-leather mask and made a film myself. Just once, for groceries.

The Bible was right about one thing — not throwing the first stone.

Back on campus next evening, around 9 p.m., Betsy and I were lounging on her downstairs window-seat. She occupied a small faculty house not far from mine. I'd gotten so worried about endangering her and the baby that I seldom went there now. So this was a rare visit by the "old friend" and "ex-coach".

My wild idea of proposing to the mother of Billy's child was not one that I'd discussed with anyone. So my knees quivered a bit. Would she see my reasons?

The spring night was a little cold, so a bright fire crackled in the fireplace. We were bundled in clean sweats, with a huge patchwork quilt around us. The baby was crawling in the joint lap that our knees made. I was trying to feel cheerful, putting that courtroom defeat behind me. The evening was off to a good start.

Betsy and I were having one of our friendly arguments about runners. She'd been a top NCAA sprinter, and was going to coach the Prescott women's team in the 1978-79 school year. Betsy was like a hummingbird — small, feisty, and hard to catch. So we liked to get each other going.

"Go on," Betsy scoffed, "women runners *can* compete with men."

The baby was gung-ho to crawl off the window-seat. We kept grabbing him.

"Aw, Bets," I said. "Look at the spread between men and women in short distance. Look at the 60-yard dash, for chrissake. Women will *never* come close to the men's world bests. No matter how hard they train!"

"Aw, yourself!" she laughed back. "Look at long distance. Women are beating men one-to-one in the 100-mile races."

Holding the baby in one arm, she used the other to bat me over the head with a sofa pillow.

Happily I defended myself with upraised arms.

"Only a few women can win a hundred miler," I said, taking the baby from her. "Exceptions prove the rule."

The kid was eight months now — all that was left of my lover. Alert, he stared at me boldly, waving his fists. Half of his chromosomes were Billy's — how many would dominate? His blue-gray baby eyes — were they going to be Billy's eye color? Would his black hair change color, like so many babies' did, and go light brown, like Billy's? His strong little feet felt more gifted at karate than running.

I had heard the hippie talk about reincarnation, and wondered if it was possible — if Billy's spirit was back in this tiny body?

The baby grabbed my nose.

"Holy jeez," I exclaimed, pulling back.

"I can hardly wait for him to start walking," Betsy said dryly, taking the baby back.

"He's like a little falcon. He zooms in and nails things."

"A falcon? God, the Irish poet in you comes out at the weirdest moments."

"Well, that's how falcons hunt. Good nickname for you, kid."

Falcon suddenly squalled with hunger.

"Right now, he's hunting me," she said, sticking his head under her T-shirt, so he could nurse.

His kicking feet quieted, and soft suckings floated in the air. Studying her lamp-lit figure, her smiling face bent over the baby, I felt that emotional foliage stirring in me that was still photosensitive to women's moonlight. All the bitterness toward my ex-wife, and some negative attitudes about women in general, hadn't killed it.

"What're you looking at?" she said, blushing a little.

"Oh . . . you and Falcon."

Shyly, she pulled her T-shirt farther down over the baby.

I shook my head. "You act like I'm going to grab your tit."

"Now and then I catch this vibe from you," she said, coloring.

"Some guys never touch women. I wasn't one of those."

"Oooooo, the Neanderthal is talking bi."

Now I was running backwards, trying to lighten things up. "I'm not going to chase you."

"You couldn't run a hundred miles anyway," she leered puckishly.

The subject needed changing.

"How much were you with guys, anyway?" I asked.

Betsy shrugged. "Oh . . . a couple of times, in high school. But it wasn't home."

"There's all kinds of home."

"What do you mean?"

"It might be a good idea if we got married."

Mouth open, she stared at me. *"What?"*

"You heard me."

She touched the gold ring on my hand. "You're already married."

"More safety for you and Falcon. Legally, socially. And just on general principles. Unless you want to live with your own bodyguard."

"But nobody knows he's Billy's kid. I always let on that I don't know who the father is."

"Supposing people find out? Like that guy who writes the hate letters?"

"So . . . you're proposing a passing marriage? No sex?"

"Yeah. Strictly camouflage."

"What about you and Vince?" she asked.

"I'll have to decide. I have a bad feeling about Vince."

"He really loves you."

"Vince isn't my type. We'd drive each other nuts."

She shrugged.

"And supposing *I* want a lover? I'm getting ready for the butch of my dreams to take me home."

"We can both have lovers."

"Great idea on paper . . . complicated in real life. Especially if the media hears about it."

"Sure you won't consider it, Bets?"

"No," she said flatly.

Sliding from under the quilt, she carried Falcon toward the baby room. He rode quietly under her shirt, asleep now.

"Every kid needs a father," I said to her retreating back.

At the door to the hallway, she turned and stared at me.

"Bullshit," she stated. "Your father wasn't there for you.

And neither was mine, when he beat me up and threw me out. And neither of us had any trouble figuring out who we are."

While she put the baby down to sleep, I sat staring at the fire, feeling myself at a crossroads. Okay, my plan to disappear for the summer was definitely a "go".

Betsy came back, and picked up the lesbian magazine *Ladder*.

"Listen," she said suddenly, "you're not going to try to take him away from me, are you? I mean . . . I agreed to give him to you and Billy. But we never signed any written agreement, and —"

"What kind of a heartless S.O.B. do you think I am?"

She seemed to relax a little.

"Just wondering," she said. "Seems like all I do is worry about John . . . okay, Falcon. Now that you're back, I hope somebody doesn't fire-bomb the house, or . . . shoot through the window . . . or something."

"Don't worry. In a few days, I'll be out of sight, and gone."

Had anybody bugged her house, and heard us talking about the baby? But Billy's killer was in prison, and it was all over, wasn't it?

The depression that came over me was so heavy, I almost couldn't get up off the sofa.

FOUR

M y clam-boat had her blunt prow into a light breeze, and she rose and fell gently on the swell. In the silence, the noise of the water slapping and gurgling along her sides was almost music.

Holding a nautical chart of the Great South Bay, I leaned against the boat's cabin, trying hard to feel the magic of teeming life all around me. Down in the clean green water, silver-gray shapes of sea trout swarmed past. Half a mile away, where a fisherman was hauling in a full gill net, hundreds of sea gulls wheeled in the air. I'd always seen my runners as birds, free of flight, running the gauntlet of hunters' guns. Billy was down, floating dead in the water. Vince struggled to spread his magnificent wings. I was a bird too, driving my wings desperately, feeling the gun barrel leading on me.

The hour was past noon. I'd just cut the engine here, to try a new spot.

South of me, along the horizon, the low, tan silhouette of Fire Island ran from east to west, disappearing into haze at either end. Locals called it "the Beach". North was the green skyline of Long Island's South Shore. Fewer clam-boats were out than two hours ago. Most everybody had his catch on, and was going home. Only a few pleasure boats dotted the distance, and the tiny ferry heading for the South Shore port of Patchogue. So far, my rake had come up empty.

But I wasn't worried. The main thing was — I was finally alone.

Past visits to Fire Island had given me a look at the clammers who'd worked these waters for centuries. They were loners, independent as cowboys. Some were dropouts from elsewhere. Putting into practice some tricks I learned from Chino and Harry, I'd surfaced on the South Shore with no name, a beard, longer hair, the right kind of sunglasses and old clothes and rubber boots and fish knife, and an old truck. A classified ad led me to a Bellport boatyard, and a good boat that a clammer had left to be sold. She was old and weather-beaten, built broad and flat-bottomed to stand the chop, with a cabin just big enough to stand in. For a month I'd been staying in Patchogue at a rundown motel patronized by fishermen.

Today I'd see if the coast was clear — to start visiting Steve Goodnight's house on the Beach.

Time for a little music. The previous owner had fitted the boat with a good stereo, to deafen himself and girl-friends with rock music. Marijuana seeds still lurked in the cabin corners. I pushed in one of my own tapes. I couldn't stand rock 'n' roll, but I liked B. B. King.

To dig clams, you didn't need a high-school diploma. You needed a strong back, and the ability to work like an ox, day after day. The only piece of paper needed was a shellfish license in the name H. Brown. The chart gave an idea of the shallower bottoms, where beds of quahog clams might be found. I'd watched where other boats worked, and steered clear. That was the bay code of manners, and the cue that you didn't like company. My well-oiled gun rode in the cabin. It was a battered holster with the old-model Colt .45 auto-matic. I'd bought it after Billy and I started getting death threats, but never fired it except at a pistol range.

Time to stop lollygagging.

To work at the new depth, I re-adjusted the long metal-tube handle of the rake, with its heavy cage-like basket and digging teeth. Then I got up on the flat prow of the boat, and heaved the business end of the rake over. It hit the water with a deep echoing plunge, and went down. As the iron teeth dug into the sandy bottom, I went into the clammer's dance, pulling with rhythmic jerks on the rake handle. You had to time the pulls to the gentle pitching and yawing of the boat. Good thing I was fit. With time, a clammer grew impressive arms and shoulders.

As the breeze pushed the boat, those iron teeth dragged slowly through the sand below, picking up whatever they found and feeding it into the basket.

The sun poured down.

I was barefoot, naked to the waist, dark as a pirate, crusted with sweat. An old boonie hat I'd found at the army-navy store shaded my brain. My busted-out jeans stank of shellfish and seaweed. But no matter how hard I worked, my mind never stopped digging through the past, raking up all kinds of pictures. You don't forget. Harry had told me that.

The rake felt heavier than it had all morning.

When I finally pulled it up, it was full of stuff. Old oyster shells, one blue crab, and quite a few clams. Mostly big ones — chowders and cherrystones, the cheaper grades. Better than nothing. I dumped the grab on the deck, and started culling. It was the law that seed clams, less than one inch at the hinge, got tossed over the side. I didn't want trouble with the conservation cops — they could board you and inspect without permission.

Some clams and the crab were put aside, for dinner.

B. B. King's voice floated over the water.

Resting with a beef sandwich and some tea from my flask, I squatted in the cabin shade and closed my eyes. Right away, my hungry mind dug up Vince's image. I'd catted around with the best, but always thought I'd be monogamous if I ever found true passion. Billy was monogamy, while he lived. It had been 21 months since he died. Even straights said that a year was long enough for widowhood. "Serial monogamy" would be a more honest description of me. No harm in fantasizing a little.

When I first met Vince, he had been an exciting but conventional sports-world figure, owner of the third fastest U.S. mile. He had a killer kick — watching him surge to the front gave me the chills. Meet directors and AAU officials had wet dreams about Vince bringing drama back to track. But all that ended in 1976, when his closet door was blown open at Oregon State. Along with Billy and Jacques LaFont, who were also fingered in the gay witch-hunt. We had hoped that Vince would join Billy on the 1976 Olympic team. Ironically, it was greed, not gay, that blitzed Vince out of athletics — he'd taken under-the-counter money from meet directors. So the AAU tore up his card.

Now, at 26, Vince was no boy, but he still had a vulnerability, an odd kind of innocence, that made him so deeply appealing to me. He even got me feeling goddam protective. Now he faced life baffled, lonely — running career destroyed, best friend murdered. He was running wild, lost somewhere in the gay bars and back rooms of Manhattan, where he'd plunged after Billy's death. We'd been out of touch since Mech's sentencing. I had no idea if he was still in New York, still single.

My hand unzipped my jeans and pulled it out. Closing my eyes, I felt the sun on me. My hand was Vince's — his mouth, his heat against me like the sun. How I wished I'd done this with Chris Shelbourne, my high-school love. It was amazing how deep the pain and guilt still was, of that stillborn passion of my youth.

By mid-afternoon, I was tired as hell, my shoulders hurt, and I had four bushels on.

Screw this. Time to quit.

As the boat thrummed into the Patchogue marina, one buyer's truck was still parked on the quay. A clammer was already there, selling seven bushels of little necks at $30. The buyer's helper was bagging clams for the truck. I tied up and unloaded my own modest haul. Buyers had me pegged as a beginner, because I always came in light.

"One chowder at $10, two cherry at $15, one neck at $30," the buyer said, and slapped $55 cash into my palm.

I wasn't kidding myself that I'd survive at this line of work. But never had a bit of money seemed so sweet. Grabbing a water hose, I cleaned my boat.

Then I walked into the marina parking lot, grabbed my truck and drove into town. Nobody looked at me with any idea that they'd seen my gnarly unshaven face on the TV news. A dime into a pay phone told Steve that I was coming. By evening, I had checked out of the motel and was back at the marina, with a sack of groceries. At the pump, I spent the last of the $55 to gas the boat. As the sun set, I was heading out past the breakwater again. The ten-mile trip across the bay could be short if I pushed full throttle on the 150-horsepower engine. Yet I was still so hungry for aloneness that I didn't hurry the trip.

It was dark by the time the boat neared that long barrier beach, with its dunes showing in the moonlight. I slowed the engine to a crawl. Ahead was Davis Park, that small marina and community of beach houses. Windows glowed with gentle gaslight or kerosene lamps. People in this part of the island liked to live primitive.

Off to the west, a lone glow in some wind-bent trees was the house of my friend, Steve Goodnight.

To me, that 30-mile sandbar was one of the most beautiful spots on Earth.

Carved by the sea, Fire Island once belonged to a few tiny communities of smugglers and whalers. In the 1930s, fey folk of the arts and theater started renting beach houses here. Cherry Grove became the world's first gay and lesbian town, followed by The Pines. Meanwhile, straight freedom-seekers were clustering in Davis Park and Bayberry Dunes. By the 1970s, Fire Island had become a beachhead of the sexual revolution, and lived out its courting rites like some South Sea society that Margaret Mead was there to study.

Here in Davis Park, some weekenders wanted family fun. But most were single, looking to party and do drugs, and find true love. Failing that, they'd settle for screwing anybody of the opposite sex. All this made Davis Park a trading-floor of disease. But didn't antibiotics fix almost everything? Nine miles to the west, similar partying — minus children — went on in The Pines and Cherry Grove.

Steve had chosen Davis Park because he swore he did more writing here than in The Grove. He also hated the idea of living in a gay ghetto, and carved a toehold in the mainstream. The straight visitors, who tended to be liberal, had learned that the recluse writer was not a stereotype sally, but a prickly Texan whose shadowy young companion was not a lover but his adopted son.

Stomach churning, I shut off my running lights, and nosed the boat silently into the small cove at Steve's house.

Was a media stake-out waiting?

The shingled house sat by itself, on a neck where the island narrowed to just 100 feet. Realtors had warned Steve that the ocean could break through here. But Steve loved the privacy. The front deck faced the ocean. The back deck led to a small dock by the cove. Amidships was a two-story tower where gaslight glowed in the upper windows — Steve's studio. Over the door was a twist of driftwood lettered HOTEL GOODNIGHT. From the security standpoint, this site was very exposed — easy to watch, and shoot at. But so was every other house on the Beach.

As I eased the boat into the boathouse, I wondered how long I could quietly come and go from here without being noticed. City weekenders didn't pay much attention to the working boats. But the local people, some of whom had houses on the Beach, knew every single clam-boat by sight, even the generic ones like mine.

"Hi," said a voice out of the dark.

Nobody was there but Steve's familiar figure, sturdy and broad-shouldered as a hawk, with unruly hair and half-breed look.

"Coast clear?" I asked.

"It's been quiet. Guess our media friends decided the cold war is more important."

He wrapped his arms around me, and hugged me hard. It

felt good. I was so hungry for even the most minimal intimacy with males. Even with this long-time friend who was so close to me that I'd never considered sleeping with him.

Steve pulled back and studied me in the dark.

"Don't think I'd recognize you on the street, buddy. What's that new cologne?" He sniffed my fishy aura. "Channel No. 5?"

"Don't complain," I said, handing him the burlap bag of seafood.

Another shadow came forward — Steve's companion, Angel Day. Angel was around 18.

"Hi, Angel," I said.

As usual, Angel said nothing, stroking their big black cat who sat on his shoulder. He had gotten very thin, but moved with his usual languid energy as he helped us carry in the food. The cat weaved adoringly around his ankles.

In the glow of gaslight and warmth of the Franklin stove, living-room curtains were drawn so that no one could see in. Marian and Joe were relaxing there with glasses of wine. They had come quietly on the ferry, also disguised, after some maneuvers to throw off any tails. They got up, and we had more warm hugs and exclamations about my new cologne. Joe had a look of deep exhaustion, and his cigarette cough was worse than ever. All the heat he'd taken for supporting Billy's Olympic bid, as college president, had cost him.

The clams went into spaghetti sauce, and the crab into boiling water.

While spaghetti cooked, Steve said the fatal words:

"I've got some good news and some bad news."

"What?" I asked, feeling uneasy.

"The good news is . . . Vince is out here for the summer. At The Pines."

"This is good news?"

"I thought you'd be pleased."

"Only if he's calmed down a little."

The mere mention of Vince's name sent emotion rushing through my nerves. "What's the bad news?"

"Later," said Steve.

Over dinner, Steve and Marian chatted about visiting

the gay towns the next night. The Prescotts had wanted to get closer to gay life. But now Joe said he'd be too tired to go. I filled my belly with pasta and listened, and wondered if I should go with them and look Vince up. Later, after Marian and Joe had gone to bed, Steve and I sat up in the Tower Room talking, and he gave me the bad news.

"Vince is trying to organize a gay revolutionary front," he said. "He's talking violence . . . revenge for Billy."

Shocked, I stared at Steve. What had happened to my peacenik boy?

"Where's Vince staying?" I asked.

"In some yuppie's house. A guy named Mario Vitti."

"Doesn't sound very radical."

I could blow off rumors of gay revolutionaries. By 1978, America had been boiling with radicals and revolutionaries for more than a decade. On many campuses, there had been Students for a Democratic Society — SDS. There'd been Abbie Hoffman and his Yippies, who disrupted the 1968 Democratic convention in Chicago. There'd been Weatherman, who went underground and violent. The Chicano movement, and the Black Panthers, and the American Indian Movement — AIM. The FBI had hounded all these movements. I could even blow off a rumor of Vince starting the Gay Panthers. But I couldn't blow off jealousy of Vince's sexual adventures. The feeling was like stepping on a stingray in the surf. You didn't die, but the pain was paralyzing.

"You going to see him?" Steve pursued.

"I don't want to live in a graveyard. But . . ."

"Yeah," said Steve. "Always the but."

He sat thinking. "You going to keep on clamming?"

"I'll stay here nights, and some days. But I need the time alone on the water."

In my room, I unpacked my gear.

Steve was a thoughtful host — he had put me in the North Room, where I'd never slept before. But the pine furniture, antique kerosene lamps — all reminded me of the East Room that I'd shared with Billy in '76. This window looked onto the back deck. Just 25 feet away, the cove waters riffled in a night breeze.

On the bedside table went my colorful collection of tools.
My faithful .45 and hardwood stick. My fish knife. Unpack-
ing a cardboard box, I set up a desk on the table. My clunky
old Remington Office-Riter, a dictionary and thesaurus, the
Bible, a desk lamp, and office supplies. Carefully I stood
Falcon's christening picture on the windowsill.

Then I stripped and looked in the mirror.

Many gays are no smarter than straights about maturity — you're over the hill at 30, dead and buried at 40. I
was 42, and young guys still hit on me, mostly because of
my "fame". I tried not to wonder when the hitting would
stop, and worked to stay looking good. Flat-muscled as a
young man, today I was on the lean side of "ripped" — as
with many runners my training now included free weights.
Clamming would keep me hard. As a licensed athletic
masseur, I knew how to use almond oil on my skin, so the
only wrinkles were a few lines on my forehead, and squint
lines by my eyes. A gun-metal sheen showed in my crew cut
and body-hair. The dark tan was a good touch.

My fingers caressed the old tattoo of a Leo on my left
shoulder. Billy had worn the Virgo sign on the same shoulder. The touch led to other things, before I dropped off to
sleep.

Next morning, no clamming. Instead, I hauled on old
running shorts and a ragged sweat shirt. A workout
might help me decide yes or no on Vince. The stick went
into the sweat-shirt pouch, in case I met trouble.

"Catch you later," Steve called, seeing me leave.

Outside, a sandy path led through the beach grass. The
black cat, Horatio, passed me with a songbird in his mouth.
He was a muscle-bound animal with balls as big as his
paws. We had jokes about how Horatio was hot, hung and
heartless.

Eroded by winter storms and littered with driftwood,
the shore curved away both east and west, into misty distance. Tire tracks in the sand showed where the police Jeep
had cruised by. Waves eased in, to stroke the sand like

after-love caresses. Nearby, Marian and Joe were strolling arm in arm, talking.

Here, the memories ambushed me.

Billy and I had taken training runs on this shore — walked with our arms around each other, had a serious fight or two, worried about what was ahead. His image had held everything sane in my world — everything sacred, and clean. Now my Front Runner was a ghost who moved with endless, eerie bounds just ahead of me. I was the shattered kicker, trailing behind his shoulder. Try as I might, I couldn't kick hard enough to pass him, to get on with my life. He was burning my kick to a cinder.

Vince lived in a body that could still be touched.

Billy, I asked that image within me, *I was a jealous man when you were alive . . . more afraid of losing you than losing my life. Will you be jealous if I am with Vince?*

The image replied, *You decide. It's your race, Harlan.*

At my feet was a piece of green glass, smoothed by waves.

God, what is Your truth? Is it the terrifying things written in Your book? Or is it what I feel in my heart?

God didn't say a word. Only the gulls were mewing.

I picked up the beach glass, and slipped it in the pouch of my sweat shirt.

First, a few minutes of stretching. Then I broke into a gentle run, and headed east along the shore.

I was an easy target for that second sniper, if he was sitting in the dunes right now. Then . . . *screw the crosshairs,* I thought. Nobody was chasing me except my own mind. Yes, that was my race. Trying to kick past Billy's ghost. His image had become a monster that symbolized the hate of the gay-hunters, the pain of loss. I had to get ahead of the monster.

Two miles out, I turned back where the ribs of a wrecked clipper ship poked from the sand. On the way back, somebody's Doberman snarled at me. A whack of the stick, and the dog ran home.

By the time I saw Hotel Goodnight just ahead, the sun was high in the sky.

Steve and Angel were on the beach waiting for me. My writer friend wore his favorite beaded belt with his jeans. He had a towel in one hand and a highball glass in the other. The two whiskeys that he nursed all day were what he called "typewriter cleaner fluid".

Steve had been described by the *Advocate* as looking like a gay Will Rogers. His mix of English and Comanche blood had left him homely and ironic. As a young no-name journalist writing gay porn between *Village Voice* assignments, Steve had a hard time getting anybody to go home with him from a gay bar. So he spent lonely years making love to his typewriter — hand-jobbing his craft till a sentence cried out with life. These days, Steve was immune to flashes from his growing public. He had found his great love in Angel Day.

Now, looking at them both in the daylight, it struck me that neither of them looked good, somehow.

Steve tossed me the towel, while Angel hunted for beach glass along the wash. The shore was so rich in weathered bits of glass, from centuries of shipwrecks, that people collected the stuff.

"Vince is really on your mind, huh," Steve said.

"A relationship with him is logical."

"Uh-huh," Steve agreed.

"But it's not very sensible. He's —" I made a frustrated gesture in the air. "You know, when Vince came to Prescott with Billy, he was this warm-hearted, gutsy kid. Everybody liked Vince. Yeah, he was hot-headed. But it was never a problem, except when he sassed the race officials. But he has really gone nuts after . . ."

My voice broke.

"This Gay Panther thing," I shrugged. "Are you sure about it?"

"George Rayburn told me. You know George. He's way to the left, but he draws the line at guns."

"So George hoped you'd talk to me."

"Yeah. And I hope you'll talk sense to Vince. Where is he going to pull this revolution from? Who'll join him? Gays have always been non-violent. Some of us are *too* passive. Face down, for the straight prick."

"Sounds like too many people already know about Vince's thing. Every Mary south of Riverdale."

"George said just a few people know."

I stood staring over the ocean.

"Vince is going to be a handful," I said. "Drugs. Wild sex. Who knows what disease he's got now?" I was glumly rubbing my hair dry. "I'd have to clean him up."

"You sure don't sound like a hopeful swain," Steve laughed.

"Hard to feel hopeful about a promising lad who turned into a slut."

Steve stared at me, his eyes like two gun barrels. "Nobody was a bigger slut than you, Harlan."

I glared at him.

Steve laughed again. "It's easy to get your goat, my friend. You're such a puritan queen. Why can't you just let people be?"

"I want to keep my love life in some kind of sensible balance with my career and family."

"Screw sensible," said Steve. "Are you in love with Vince?"

My fists clenched in the towel.

"Vince goes back before Billy," I said.

The towel around my neck felt like a hangman's knot.

On the southern horizon, a few thunderheads were piling up. Studying the clouds, my friend drained his highball with a clink of ice. Then he said briskly, "Well, if I were you, I'd go down to The Pines and drag him out of there."

The thought jolted me. I could do it today. With some luck, that hot young guy would be in my bed tonight.

"And," Steve added, "you're what stands between Vince and trouble. The FBI has been looking for fag conspiracies ever since the Fifties. They would love to find a real one."

Angel had found a hunk of amethyst glass. Proudly he held it up to the sun. As Steve admired it, his head and Angel's bent together. The boy's long chestnut tresses brushed Steve's hands.

No one knew Angel's real identity. Maybe he'd been a kidnapped child. The same year I met Billy, Steve had rescued him from a S & M pimp, who had the kid on heroin to keep him dependent. Angel was mute from years of sexual brutality. Steve knew the kid would wind up in an institution, so he managed to adopt him and got him on a methadone program. "Angel Day" was a made-up name. Now Angel was a handsome young man with fragile health and the eyes of a refugee, who could say Steve's name and a few other words. Angel clearly loved Steve, but he didn't tolerate any touch. So he and Steve had never gone to bed. Steve was frustrated, but passionately committed, to a platonic love by default.

Steve pocketed the piece of glass. Then he tossed the ice from his tumbler, and walked away with Angel.

Suddenly, at the sight of Steve's noble patience and care with Angel, I felt ashamed. Couldn't I be as noble with Vince? He might be wild, but he wasn't a wreck like Angel.

As I went up the steps to the deck, I stopped by the big pottery jar that stood there. It was half full of beach glass. The custom was for Steve's friends to add their gems of joy or sorrow. Somewhere in there, were bits that Billy and I had gathered.

I added my wild jewel, and went in to shower.

"When the jar is full," Steve had often said, "we'll have a helluva party, and empty it into the waves . . . and start over."

E vening was hot, humid and still. The thunderheads vanished as we barbecued steaks on the back deck. Now and then, I broke into a hot sweat, thinking of Vince. Everything that happened in the house slammed me with thoughts of sex and danger. In the bathroom, Steve was jabbing an old syringe into his own bare butt, giving himself a vitamin injection as casually as if he were vaccinating a horse. For years Steve had been a health fanatic, shooting himself with different concoctions.

"That looks like one of Angel's old methadone needles," I said.

"It's the only way I can be intimate with him," Steve grinned.

This gave me a shiver. Recently we'd learned that junkies share hepatitis B virus when they share needles. Doc Jacobs always kept me up on the latest medical news.

"Isn't that kind of risky?" I said, as diplomatically as possible. "Whatever Angel's got, you've got."

As we ate dinner, Joe studied me from his deck chair, noticing my tension.

"Harlan, you okay?" he asked.

Joe had been like a father to me, ever since he'd hired me in 1970. His care and sensitivity had fed an old kid-hunger for father love. At the same time, I wasn't ready to blurt the turmoil about Vince.

"Yeah ... I'm okay," I said.

"You sure?" Joe pressed, and broke into hacking.

Dinner over, Joe was tired from smoker's cough. So about 9 p.m. the rest of us — Steve, Angel, Marian and I — assembled for our jaunt to the gay shore. At the last moment, I decided not to go.

Steve's eyes told me I was a chickenshit.

The three disappeared along the dark boardwalk, toward the Casino, a bar at the marina. They'd catch the beach taxi there.

Joe slumped on the sofa, looking strangely ancient, soaking up the warmth from the Franklin stove. Horatio, in a rare show of domesticity, was draped across Joe's lap. I stirred up the fire and joined the old man.

"What do you think, Joe? You think they're going to leave us alone now?"

Joe roused himself out of his torpor.

"I hope so," he said. "They've won this round. The next move is up to us. The next thing we do that provokes them."

For me, taking a new lover might be that provocative act. Especially taking Vince.

"Do *you* think there was a second sniper?" I asked.

"There'll always be a second sniper," said Joe darkly.

This was not the old exuberant, optimistic Joe.

"I used to believe that education is the answer to everything," the old liberal added. "But you can't educate people who think they already know it all. Especially people who want to kill their own kids if they grow up thinking differently."

Heavily, he got up and shuffled off to bed.

Joe's words left me feeling gloomy and defensive. I locked the doors and windows. Then I went to my room, got the .45, the old King James and a red pen. I had started in *Genesis*, crossing out passages that I didn't agree with. Back at the fire, I opened the book, and some loose pages fell out. That infamous passage in *Leviticus 20:13* was staring up at me.

> *If a man also lie with mankind, as he lieth with a woman, both of them have committed an abomination; they shall surely be put to death.*

Almost breaking the pen, I made red marks through those lines.

Vince's rage was at this belief, and the strangers that it sent to war on our gay beauty. The picture of his hot eyes rose in my mind — the vibrant sound of his young baritone voice. Closing my eyes, I conjured the memory of that night he'd made his move on me — the hard embrace, the not-unexpected four-letter words of pure gay passion.

The fire crackled. Out on the beach, long waves breaking sounded like trains going by. Was the house being watched by unfriendly eyes?

Then the boardwalk vibrated with approaching footsteps. My hand hovered by the .45. But it was Steve, Marian and Angel trampling in, looking disgusted. Steve saw the gun first, and raised his hands in mock surrender.

"The taxi went in some quicksand," said Marian. "The police finally came and pulled us out."

"It happened because you didn't go," Steve teased me.

"Okay . . . okay." I raised my own hands in surrender. "Tomorrow night for sure."

PART TWO

Summer Things

FIVE

These days, some straight and bi Fire Islanders liked to dare the nine miles down the shore to gay turf. Some went to gawk, to shoulder us aside on our own beaches. Others went to drink up the liberated sexual energies. Gays and lesbians hated the tourism, but couldn't lock it out. If you had a boat, you tied up at the Pines or Grove docks. If you were afoot, you rode one of the few vehicles on Fire Island — the beach taxi. Tonight the rusting sedan was piloted by a new driver, Rowdy, who had a joint hanging between his lips. In the back seat, Steve lounged in one corner, with Angel sitting stiffly beside him.

In the other corner, Marian had on pedal pushers, blazer and sunglasses — her one concession to disguise. She looked worried.

Reaching my hand back to her, I gave her a brotherly wink.

"Worried about your first close-up on the Life?" I asked.

She gave my fingers an uncertain sisterly squeeze.

"No. It's Joe . . . the future," she answered.

The window by me was rolled down, so I wouldn't get high on Rowdy's smoke. My clothing was clammer chic — frayed jeans, boots and scuffed bomber jacket. The sheepskin collar was turned up against the blast of salt wind. My limbs were vibrating with expectation like a tuning-fork. Now and then, our tires hit the wash, and a wing of spray flew beside us in the moonlight.

Then the first thunderheads hid the moon.

Thoughts of the second sniper intruded on my thoughts of Vince. Who was out there in the dark dunes, watching us drive away?

A t The Pines, Steve gave Rowdy a tip big enough for an ounce of weed.

It had been several years since police stopped harassing us here. The boardwalk led toward flourishing shops and nightspots in the marina. Tea Dance was over, and houses blazed with light — not many piss-elegant gays forewent the electricity that back-to-the-land straights did without in Davis Park. Singles and pairs — mostly butch men, here in The Pines — crisscrossed everywhere in the dark. They walked hand in hand, shared kisses, wore what they liked — mostly jeans and Frye boots — said what they felt, lived the Life.

At the Pines marina, crowded ferries were still coming in.

We sat at an outdoor table. Steve, Marian and Angel ate seafood fresh from the bay. My stomach was so full of butter-flies that I could only manage half a dozen oysters. Marian was too well brought-up to stare, but she looked thoughtful. Here was the sexual reality that her college had defended. Was my sister having second thoughts?

The dance floor of the Sandpiper Club was packed with Beautiful People. Same-sex couples had won the legal right to dance together. Everybody was moving like a Broadway cho-rus line, in a dance called the Hustle. I gazed impassively at the scene, remembering my own clubbing days in '60s New York. Cold-steel sex in parks and movie theaters. Relentless drinking and drugs. Vice raids on the hustlers' bars and dance bars. Bruises from beatings. Our new freedom was so fragile — if a Richard Mech burst into the Sandpiper tonight with a submachine gun, he could fell a whole field of homosexuals like ripe corn.

Vince wasn't here. The well-heeled Pines was not his taste. More likely he was partying in Cherry Grove, where the crowd was younger.

My wild hair and beard got some frowns — the well-barbered look was "in". Nobody recognized me except activist George Rayburn — the very guy who'd said, "We shouldn't have to protect ourselves." He did a double take, as I pulled him aside. George was an old friend of Billy's father.

"Well, well," he said. "I do declare. Nobody's guarding your precious body tonight. Does this mean I get my chance?"

I ignored his barb.

"Yeah," I said casually. "Off security for good."

George wouldn't leave it alone. "Sweetie, I know you scorn fashion," he said, fingering my beard. "But isn't this going too far?"

"Who's Mario Vitti?"

"His dad owns half of Jersey City. He and Vince are probably getting high at a house party right now. They hit the discos late . . . make a grand entrance."

"How late is chic these days?"

"Around 2. Did Steve talk to you about the other problem?"

"Yeah."

"You gonna put your move on Vince?"

"Politically, I'll do what I can."

"One Vince shooting people will set us back five hundred years. By the way, I need you for a march coming up. We need every gay who is nationally known to —"

"Forget it," I interrupted him. "I need time out from being a target."

"Other people will lose *their* Billys, and their Bonnies, if enough of us don't fight."

"I'll write stuff, do fundraising. Even lick stamps. Anything but the podium."

Rayburn shrugged, and walked off.

Just after midnight, our quartet walked onward into Cherry Grove. In those days, The Grove was smaller than The Pines — gayer, noisier, artsier, more women, more drag queens, more people of color, more of whom were viewed as "trash" by some upscale Pines gays. Grove houses were tinier, homier, funkier, crowded closer together. There wasn't even a police station in The Grove. We checked out the Blue Whale. Then we killed an hour in a small disco, the Monster. Vince didn't show up.

As we walked, Steve and I explained things to Marian. Like the bandanna tucked in right or left hip pocket — a signal for top or bottom.

"And over there, in those trees," Steve told Marian, pointing, "is the Meat Rack. At 4 in the morning, it's like opening day of deer season in there."

As thunder rumbled overhead, flickers of lightning lit that distant maze of trails and brush. There, men who'd been denied the full sex life that every straight male claimed as his birthright would be braving poison ivy and disease to cleave unto each other in wild anonymous sucking and fucking.

Marian looked at me, wondering if I'd ever visited the Rack.

"Not any more," I told her.

Our guided tour made me think how times were changing. For many gay males, there'd been a wistful traditional glow about hoping to love a good man forever. In recent years, this had chilled into new-wave rhetoric about throwing off oppression and restraint. Our looseness separated us from the lesbians, who were more circumspect. In the late '60s, I had tasted my own wild time. Passion was the next visit to the bathhouse or the Rack — the next warm body waiting. The fierce pleasure of anal sex meant that many guys wanted to bottom. As a top, I'd been one of the guerrillas who roved those thickets. But by the early '70s, when I was coaching at Prescott, one warm body too many gave me a double whammy of clap and crabs.

And that was another reason I'd reined in — health. As a campus athletic director, I was a fanatic about health, and knew that sexually transmitted disease was getting out of hand among young people. It was definitely to the wildfire stage with straight "swinging singles". These days, gay doctors were charting the same spike — everything from genital warts to amoebic dysentery. My doctor, Cal Jacobs, kept talking about new diseases that can't be cured with antibiotics, like herpes II.

Steve's voice cut into my thoughts.

"It's almost two o'clock," he said.

As we headed for the Ice Palace, my knees were shivering again.

To Marian, Steve explained, "The Ice Palace is the mother of all discos. The concept started right here . . . in '70, I think it was."

Ahead was the large spotlit clapboard building, with its adjoining Beach Hotel and pool. At the disco door, music grabbed us — that pumping, relentless, rambunctious, high-energy new kind of music. I hated disco as much as I hated hard rock, but had to admit that the driving new beat had become the anthem of our Life.

With the jaundiced eye of a non-smoking non-drinker, I peered in. The mirrored walls that reflected the dancers, the blinking lights and turning glass balls, the massive sound system — such a new idea then — created a lightning storm of sensation. Here, only a few souls were synching out the Hustle — most were hot-wired into the sexier Boogie. To the side, a packed crowd watched a young male who was go-go dancing on the bar. People were blowing whistles and beating tambourines in time to his beat.

"Good heavens!" exclaimed Marian. "It's Vince!"

My sister forgot her manners, and stared. She had never seen a man move his body like that. The Vincent Matti she'd seen around the campus was a young man in the last throes of conformity, with a disciplinarian coach (me) breathing down his neck.

"Isn't *he* a delectable little biscuit," some guy said to a friend behind me.

Vince didn't have the barbered "in" look, but he had taken gay society by storm, because of who he was. Tonight he was barefoot, wearing nothing but thin cotton drawstring pants. In the humid air and bright lights, he was so sweaty that his torso gave off sequin flashes. The wetness made his tattoos stand out — Scorpio on the left shoulder, Lambda of gay liberation on the right. His soaked pants revealed every detail of his lower body — the half-aroused cock, the tan line. Arms high, flexing his spine, snapping and grinding his loins, he drove his lean frame through the moves with hard, edged movements. The pants had slipped so far down that his flanks were bared. In his armpits, black curls were wetted to the skin, as if he'd just surged from a swimming pool. His coal-black mane stuck to his back, then broke loose to whip the air.

Everyone watched him, enthralled. It wasn't just his crass beauty that gripped their attention. It was his rage. Unlike me, he'd been public about his grief over Billy. That rage mirrored what so many gays felt in their hearts. I felt sad — remembering when Vince danced with a joy in life.

Nearby, a trio of well-barbered princes eyed him.

"Hail Mary full of grace," drawled one mustachioed male.

Even as they spoke, Vince's pants worked down another inch, barely hanging on his bush.

"Tsk," the second mustache said. "If I want to see animals, I'll go to the Bronx Zoo."

"Well, he can fuck me anytime," commented the third.

Steve said in my ear, "Look at Vince's eyes . . . he's speeding his brains out."

A dark-haired man, probably Mario, reached a popper up to Vince. Without a break in the motion, Vince cracked the little vial and snorted deep. The carotid swelled in his neck, as chemical energy blazed through him.

My sister was awestruck.

"What is Vince snorting?" she yelled over the music.

"Amyl nitrate," Steve yelled back.

My heartbeat was choking me. What I wanted as much as his body was that ardent spirit, that wounded tenderness and vulnerability, that power of deep affection that he hid from almost everyone. And the fierce loyalty. Once after Montreal he'd yelled at me, "I would have stopped that bullet with my own head so you and Billy could still be together." Many people disliked Vince, because all they ever saw of him was the arrogant stud horse.

Steve caught my eye.

"Marian, darling," he said, "let's find a nice quiet piano bar."

The three of them left.

Slowly I pushed ahead through the crowd. Faces turned toward me, the same stares at my wild look. My encounter with Vince was going to be uncomfortably public. Would my disguise hold? Were the snipers watching? Even here?

Finally I was in the front row of spectators, about 10 feet from Vince.

Now the Ice Palace was vibrating with whoops, whistles and ooooohs — Vince down-shifted into slow grinds. Standing with legs braced apart, he slowly eased the drawstring. One hand barely kept the cloth in front of him. But the loose pants slipped down behind, baring his haunches in the hot lights. Sweat coursed richly down his spine, into the dark curls between his buttocks. When he squeezed into the next slow luxurious thrust, those powerful muscles pressed sweat from between them.

As the males in the crowd went wild, I suddenly had a mental image of some self-righteous redneck shooting point-blank at Vince. A shotgun blast would tear a red rat-hole in that perfect body. I felt myself break out in a hot terrified sweat. Harry and Chino had warned me.

Because thou hast set thine heart as the heart of God . . .

Strangers' hands were caressing his legs. Unsmiling, meeting the strangers' eyes boldly from his Olympian height among the hot lights, Vince turned slowly amid their feels, giving everyone their look.

Then his dionysian stare met my puritan frown.

He wasn't so drunk and stoned that he didn't recognize me. He stopped dead. And he blushed. The flush started at his nipples, and went up his neck, clear to his hairline. It had always amazed me how my frown had such power to rouse his shame.

The pause broke the magic spell. Most people surged back onto the dance floor, like the sea closing over Egypt's chariots. A few men whistled — they were disgusted that Vince held back from nudity. Meanwhile, Mario looked me up and down, then walked away. His pants still held at half-mast, Vince stood there on the bar, chest heaving like a racehorse's. His blush was fading. Now the air between us was bathed in a sheet-lightning of male-male non-verbal communication.

With stoned dignity, he pulled up his pants and slid off the bar. Behind him, the bartender polished away his foot smudges.

Warily, Vince squinted at me like a cornered wolf. Then he lunged at me. His rush carried me a step backwards against the bar. Damn — was he going to break my neck? No. He was embracing me. My nostrils were buried in his wet hair — breathing him was like being in a steam room crowded with fifty men. I crushed him against me, feeling the preciousness of his young life.

People were whooping. Somebody blew a whistle at us.

Then, suddenly, Vince sagged — light-headed. Too many poppers.

Quickly I got his arm over my shoulder. People spent only a few seconds watching the mysterious wild man drag the reigning beauty away. Then they went back to their revels.

Outside, in the cold air, Vince recovered. We went to Mario's house. Vince's amphetamine high was collapsing now. In a few minutes, he had fumbled into a dry sweat suit, running shoes and his black leather jacket. A travel bag was slung over his shoulder.

Ten steps down the boardwalk he said, "Shit . . . I forgot my hair-dryer."

"Leave it. No power in Steve's house."

We barely caught the next cab.

During the long ride, Vince lay half passed-out against my shoulder, his face pressed into my neck.

In Davis Park, as we walked toward Hotel Goodnight, my eyes nervously surveyed the dark dunes. It was past 3:30 a.m., the darkest hour. The night belonged to anyone smart enough to use it. Had the enemy penetrated my disguise?

Was he watching the two of us go in the house together, knowing what this meant?

The Hotel was quiet. Joe had left one gaslight burning in the front room.

Thunder boomed overhead as I closed the curtains in the North Room, then lit a kerosene lamp. A hot shower would warm Vince, and get the disco reek off. Shucking our clothes, we both stood under the steaming spray. He was so shaky he could hardly stand, let alone maintain a hard-on, so he just leaned into me, his magnificent limp cock nudging me. I ignored it, and scoured his shivering body from hair to toenails with a loufa and soap. Rubbing him dry with Steve's luxurious terry towels, I inspected him for crabs, but didn't find any.

What I did find was a fresh needle track in his arm.

"Speed?" I asked.

"Yessir," he mumbled.

While Vince pulled on his sweats again, I made him some camomile tea, to warm him and calm him. Shortly he was in my bed, shivering under the covers. I blew out the lamp, then opened the drapes. Outside the open window, brush hissed restlessly in the storm breeze. My sniper panic and religious scruples were fading. But making love to him when he was so stoned didn't seem fair.

Wrapped tightly in a terry robe, I sat down by him.

"Shit, man . . . I'm really crashing," he murmured. "Sorry."

"Don't worry about it. Just listen up," I said, running my fingers through his wet-sleek hair.

Lightning lit his face, as his eyes tried to focus on me. He looked so unconfident, so undone by feeling. I caught his thought. Billy's death had opened the way for us to make love. We both shook the thought away.

"Two problems," I said.

He closed his eyes. "Uh-oh. Problems."

"Problem Number One. You and me together might piss off the enemy."

"So you *do* think there's a second guy."

"I wish I didn't think so. I've spent a month covering my trail. But it feels like we're being surveilled."

He moved his head to kiss my fingers. "I've waited a long time for this. They're not going to stop me."

"Problem Number Two. I don't want clap, or whatever you have. Monday, we go for tests. Till then . . . I don't trust you."

"So I . . . stay?"

"Would you have come for a trick?"

"Babe," he said, coming to life a little, narrowing his eyes with drunken seductiveness, "you wouldn't trick with *me*."

"Why not? You're the biggest whore on the Beach."

"Jealous, huh?"

"I won't ask what you've been doing. And you won't do it any more. That includes drugs."

"It's a deal." The covers rustled as he settled in deeper, moving his hips ruttishly.

"No more porno films."

"Seal it with a kiss."

I hesitated.

"You are so fucking bourgeois about kisses," he said violently. "I want to know if you're being real with me."

It was supposed to be a short kiss. But his spell was on me — making me ache to feel what he felt for me. As his strong arms tightened around me, with that overwhelming tenderness, his tongue licked into mine, wolf-like. He smelled so clean now, like rain, and his mouth tasted of wild daisies. It turned into a long, long kiss, and reminded me all over again why human beings think of making love as a chance to feel intensely alive. When I felt my restraint fraying and tried to end the embrace, it was like trying to pull two ten-ton magnets apart. Thunder was muttering louder.

"Hey, easy . . ." I said.

"No, not easy." He was falling asleep in the middle of the kiss, mumbling. "Hard. Very hard."

SIX

By morning, the storm had passed. Rays of sun sent fiery flashes of color through the wet cherry foliage outside. That beautiful morning started out as a Fire Island next-morning — one when you couldn't imagine that anybody might want to shoot you.

Late in the a.m., every head at the breakfast table turned as Vince and I emerged from the North Room. Vince had mellowed out, and seemed his normal self. Marian and Joe raised their eyebrows, but didn't seem surprised to see us together. Vince made me a cup of my favorite black tea, and sat beside me. Under the breakfast table, his hand slyly slipped into my shorts pocket to feel me up.

With one hand, I blocked his move. With the other, I gave Joe a letter from the batch of mail they'd brought.

"Hey, Joe, read this," I said.

It was from Jacques LaFont.

Jacques and Vince had been lovers when they arrived at Prescott with Billy in '74. Jacques was bi-sexual, a gifted runner but high-strung. But with America debating us, Jacques couldn't handle the pressure. He dropped athletics and Vince, and married Elaine Foster. Now, at 25, he was a father, and a "new biologist" starting a career in ornithology. His dream was a population study of endangered native birds on Maui. Running was limited to the occasional road race, and he was teaching in his home state, at the University of Illinois. But he still wrote me plaintive son-to-father letters.

Hi Harlan,

Just a short note to say I'm thinking of all of you, and wishing I was back with my Prescott family. Eileen and Ana are fine. I wish I could say the same about my job. There has been some alumni unhappiness that this native son was one of the "infamous Prescott Three". I have been asked to quietly resign my post in the science department. Unfortunately, the grant hasn't materialized yet, for my Maui research. So I am up Shit Creek right now.

Lucky for me, Eileen is being supportive . . . .

Not interested in our talk, Angel drifted out to look around for Horatio.

"Poor Jacques," Vince said, shaking his head.

"When will this country grow up?" growled Joe.

"I'll *kill* the university," Marian snapped. "I'll write them a letter."

"Better yet," I said, "let's give Jacques a job. At least till his Maui thing comes through."

"I'll think how to do it," said Joe. "We're running top-heavy on faculty."

The rest of the mail included another of those cut-and-paste hate letters.

FEAR MY NAME, WHEN YOU FINALLY HEAR IT.
YOUR SECRET ADMIRER

Just then, Angel came slamming in the door, his eyes wide with shock.

"Steve!" he cried out in a strangled voice.

We went running out on the back deck, to see a shocking sight.

Horatio lay dead on the dock, covered with buzzing flies. So friendly and gentle, he had been lured — by a can of tuna, maybe — and caught. Whoever did it had castrated and gutted him, then dumped him there. A bloody trail showed where he'd crawled a few feet toward our door, before he finally expired. The blood was dry and black — he'd died hours ago. The deed must have been done after Vince and I fell asleep, and before daylight.

We all went white.

"Dear ... God," said Marian, closing her eyes.

Angel started to cry, hands over his face.

"Some local redneck?" I asked Steve.

"I don't know," whispered Steve. He was trying to comfort Angel.

"The second sniper?" added Vince quietly.

He looked at me. "Harlan, you're right," he said. "Somebody must be watching us. Last night, of all nights."

After some discussion, we phoned the tiny police station at the Davis Park marina.

"No time like the present to find out if they'll help us," I said.

Police Sergeant Chapman, a middle-aged bay-man, and his rookie Lance Shirley weren't in a hurry — they got to the scene an hour later. They didn't know who I was, and I didn't tell them, but they knew that Steve was a controversial writer, and they weren't as liberal and protective as I had hoped. With an air of going through motions, they searched the area, but said they found nothing. No tracks in the sand, no blood. The perpetrator had walked on the boardwalk, leaving no tracks. Evidently he had smothered the poor animal's head, so the screams wouldn't be heard.

"Any neighbors bring cats out?" asked Chapman.

"Yeah. The Abramsons ... the Millers ..."

"Maybe," said Chapman boredly, "the perpetrator thought it was the neighbor's cat, right? Maybe he don't like your neighbor, right?"

"Your cat killed birds sometimes?" asked Shirley.

"Sure. Like any cat . . ."

"People get some pissed about bird-killing, right?" Shirley added in bay-man rhythms. "Especially people on the Beach, right? They come out here for the wildlife, and I don't mean the sex kind. Maybe your neighbor is a nut for birds, right?"

"Look," Steve said, "you guys know — we know — it's a threat."

"Then you gotta have a bodyguard, right?" the husky young rookie stated. "You gotta."

They weren't going to do more than shrug.

"Pig-fuckers," said Vince hoarsely as he watched them walk away.

Steve was still trying to dry Angel's tears. Angel wanted to pick up the dead cat and hold it, but Steve walked him away. I got a shovel, and buried Horatio under a scrubby tree, well away from the house.

F or the rest of the day, Steve and Marian walked around to some of the houses in that end of Davis Park. They limited their visits to families that Steve knew. Standing in the drifting smoke of barbecues, they asked if anybody had seen or heard anything strange. Some weird-acting visitor or singles drop-in at their Saturday night party? Some redneck with a fish knife who didn't like liberals?

A few people were mildly sympathetic.

Most shrugged.

When Steve and Marian came back, Steve quoted one bonniker householder who said, "There's thousands of pilgrims drift on and off the Beach in a weekend. On the ferry, right? Driving their own boats. Some people don't even put up anywhere, right? They party all night, they get some drunk, they get some laid at somebody's house, they get laid in the fuckin' dunes, they get laid in somebody's house-boat, they even get laid some good in the bottom of somebody's clam-boat. Right? Then they go off the Beach on the morning ferry, and nobody remembers shit about them. Right?"

That evening, our house sat up late and feverishly discussed the killer's motive.

Maybe the deed was aimed at Steve personally, because of the gay realism in his books. Maybe some religious fanatic with a talent for private investigation had found out that Vince and I were there. But was it "the second sniper"? Somehow it didn't feel like his MO.

Vince was high again — on rage and adrenaline.

"I swear," he said hoarsely, "I swear . . . when I get finished with America, man, nobody will *dare* to lift a finger against our people!"

Later, privately, Steve and I talked about calling Chino and Harry. But I was still being fanatical about not living behind a chainlink fence. Steve was fatalistic — sure the two vets couldn't do anything.

"If they're going to get you," Steve said, "they get you."

Finally we decided to hang tight.

For three days now, I hadn't been out on the water, and was already missing the sweet aloneness and safety out there. My boat sat locked up in the boathouse.

T he next day was Monday.

At 9 a.m., I called Doc Jacobs' office and made a late afternoon appointment for the tests. Then Vince and I walked to The Grove. From there, we rode the ferry over to Sayville, where The Grover ferries dock. Near the marina, locked in a garage space that Mario and Vince had rented, was the red Testarossa that Mario had given him.

"Mario also paid for my clap shots," Vince volunteered, as we checked the car for a bomb before gingerly starting it. "So I'm probably clean on everything."

Vince drove the gleaming, racy car with verve down the Long Island Expressway. I brought up the subject of politics, pretending that I didn't know anything about his plans for gay revolution.

"What do you mean by 'getting done with America'?" I asked.

"What any committed activist would mean. Change. Real change. Like ... the attitudes ... the laws that we need to change."

"Sounds like violent change."

"I shouldn't have to ... like ... *remind* you, man ... how violent they've been to us, man."

In downtown Manhattan, at Jacobs' office, Vince bared his arm and pumped his vein. I did the same. Quietly, Doc suggested how to help him handle speed withdrawal. Afterward, going to a restaurant for dinner, we passed a small gay theater where a Casey Donovan film was playing. Vince's film would premier later that summer.

"God, I love movies," he said wistfully. "Me and Billy ... at Oregon, man, we lived in two places. The track and the movie theaters. I want to do the great American film like you want to do the great American novel."

"Then do it. With your clothes on."

Next afternoon, as we drove back to the South Shore, I was at the wheel because Vince was having tremors. By the time we got to Patchogue and stored the car with a new company, his whole body was hurting for drugs.

We took the Patchogue ferry back to Davis Park.

"Mario was copping for me," he whispered on the ferry.

"So that's why you were with him?"

"I'll quit, I'll quit. Just ... help me." In Davis Park, as we walked down the ferry gangway, he said, "Maybe Steve still has some of Angel's old methadone."

"Quit cold. It's better that way."

We walked slowly home along the boardwalk. As the sun went down into smoggy hazes, an edge of conflict was sharpening between me and Vince. He stopped by a grove of scrubby wild cherry trees, and suddenly tried to kiss me among the branches. Blossoms rained down over us. I remember the tiny petals dotting his hair, catching in his eyelashes, sliding down the black leather jacket. His nerveless lips tasted of pollen.

Just as I pushed him away, a straight family came into sight behind us, with their loaded kiddie wagons, like a miniature pioneer wagon train. I hoped they hadn't seen us.

"Don't do that," I said. "This is not The Grove, and I want to keep my nameless clam-digger image. Wait till we get to the house."

We were walking on now, fast.

"You're such a romantic," Vince said disgustedly.

"I've never been good with the Scarlett and Rhett stuff."

"The other night you carried me up the stairs."

"You couldn't walk," I retorted.

Then my discomfort found more words. "I don't love you the way I did Billy. This is different."

His angry eyes misting, he grabbed me by the lapels. "I don't want Billy's place with you. I want my *own* place."

"Quit grabbing me in public, dammit."

Finally, safe behind the dense Hotel trees, we stood with our arms around each other.

"I'm sorry," he said against my neck.

This young bird of mine was a snowy egret, with one long leg caught in a snare, his great sunlit wings beating the air. I was trying to hold his wings down so he wouldn't hurt himself. I was trying to free his leg. But he kept fighting me, thinking that he would get free his own way.

T hat evening, Vince's edge was sharp in all of us.

We were still trying to forget Horatio's death. Everybody was in the warm kitchen, cooking a bouillabaisse and a rich dessert. The James Beard cookbook lay open on the counter. We'd decided to try and put some weight on Angel. Vince was still fighting the withdrawal discomfort. The edge dug in when he insisted on talking about Billy, as he often did. Why was I involved with a goddam kid again? Twenty-six-year-olds seemed like such kids.

"Falcon doesn't look anything like Billy," Vince remarked, chopping a board full of green onions.

"I think he's taking after Grandpa Sive," I said, filleting a sea trout with my fish knife. "He's got Billy's nose, though."

"His nose is the size of a fucking raisin. How can you tell?"

"Oh, just the way it looks."

"Don't forget he's 50 percent Betsy's kid," said Vince. "She's little and dark too . . . ow!" as he almost cut his finger.

"Only a bi would stick up for the ladies the way you do," Steve told him.

"I'm not bi any more," Vince said. He left the onions and prowled into the living room, antsy with drug desires. "I don't want to go *near* anything straight."

"Except for your straight friends in the kitchen?" Marian asked, stepping over to finish his onions.

"Yeah, certain straight friends are cool," admitted Vince.

He yanked at the closed curtains, as if angry that he had to live in hiding. Then he leaned against the wall, pressing his face against the cool cedar planks. He had a sheen of sweat on his face. We all looked at one another, having seen a million students go through this syndrome.

"Why do you want Falcon to look like Billy?" he said to me. "You wanna . . . like . . . fuck him when he grows up?"

Everybody's heads raised from their cooking, and they got very quiet. It felt like Vince had shot me in the chest at point-blank range. The idea had never crossed my mind.

I went into the front room, fish knife in my hand.

"*What* did you say?" I demanded of Vince.

"Well?" Vince pursued. "I mean . . . hey, it's not incest. So why not?"

He stared at the knife trembling in my hand.

"That'd better be the dope talking," I growled.

"Are you being honest?" Vince lashed back. "When you look for Billy in him?"

"You were never robbed of your children," I said. "So a snot-nose like you wouldn't understand."

As Vince slammed out the back door, the kitchen crew covered their embarrassment by busying themselves with cuisine.

"Hang in there, Harlan," said Steve as he dumped the onions in the kettle.

Steve was patient with all the lovers' fights that went on among his guests. He wrote the best ones into his books.

Outside, in the moonlight, Vince was sitting slumped on the dock. Down the shore, rows of lighted houses disappeared into evening mist. Other people's lamp-lit windows always look so peaceful — the only house full of bloody war is your own.

Vince had tears running down his face.

"I wish I didn't love you," he said.

Not wanting to argue when he was so drugged out, I just stood there.

But now Vince launched a tirade at me.

"You are so fucking conservative!" he said, making a fist. "So bourgeois! Sometimes you act like you never came out! You don't really commit. You always ... like ... hold back something. When we were trying to get Billy to Montreal, you made all the right political moves for him, yeah ... and, yeah, you told the press you're gay. But you never once said, *I'm proud to be gay.* You fucking held back. And you held back on Billy, didn't you? What you held back on him was me. Well, I'm not like you, man!"

The words were so cruel, and so true, that I rose to the bait.

"Sure," I said. "Be a kamikaze. Guys like me carry on after guys like you crash and burn."

Vince bounded to his feet, with that cornered-wolf look in his eyes. He went to punch me with his right, and telegraphed the punch so many miles that I blocked it easily. So he threw a left, and my block got him off-balance. I was pissed off now, and hit him a hard jab to the chest. My lover went backward into the water with a tremendous splash.

Streaming and silent, he crawled out on the dock. His slumped shoulders and hanging head told me that he felt humiliated beyond belief. I had just done something to him that was going to change things between us for good.

"If you're going to fight," I barked in my best Parris Island voice, "you'd better learn how."

The following weekend, the Prescotts quietly slipped back to Prescott College. They must have told Betsy about the cat murder, because she moved her oar and put more water between her boat and mine. Now she was hunting for a house off campus. Marian and Joe tried to point out that the campus was safer. But she tightened her lips, and kept rowing.

I was settling into the rhythm of Fire Island life, still trying to stay incognito in Davis Park. My collar-length hair and solid beard had really altered my look. Mostly I hid in our shelter-belt of cherry brush, enjoying the writing and long talks with Steve, and (most of the time) being with Vince. He said nothing about losing our fistfight. In fact, he was quieting down. A couple of times, before dawn, we ghosted the clamboat out of the boathouse, and spent a good day digging together. Vince learned to cull. One day we hit a good spot, and pulled grandly up to the buyers' dock with 6 bushels of neck on. Neck had dropped to $25. I split the $150 with him.

On the following Monday afternoon, Doc Jacobs' nurse called. The tests were okay. Vince's blood work did show traces of hepatitis B. But he was clean on syphilis, gonorrhea, herpes, amoebas.

"Well," said Vince, with a glint in his eye, "bourgeois time is . . . like . . . over."

But I still had some uneasy questions.

"Workout first," I said. I was trying to get him running again.

He smiled slyly. "Whatever turns you on, Mr. Brown."

SEVEN

It was a weekday, so the Island was quiet.

That evening, Vince and I went for a short run, along the 9-mile stretch of empty dunes that lay between Davis Park and The Pines. Two miles at an easy pace — Vince wasn't used to sand yet, and I didn't want to stir up his old knee injuries. It was the first time that he'd felt "unfucked-up" enough for any cardiovascular stress. As we headed out, I was wearing my shabbiest sweats and carrying the stick, as usual. His sleek new sweats looked good on him, but they'd clearly seen little use.

About an eighth of a mile west of the Hotel, in the last light, a bird-watcher was sitting in the dunes. Armed with binoculars, he looked like he was watching songbirds. Suspiciously I eyed his distant figure as we passed. A paparazzo in disguise? Was a tabloid headline going to read SHOCKING SECRET LIFE OF HARLAN AND VINCE IN FIRE ISLAND SEX NEST? Or was he surveilling us for reasons of violence?

Finally we were jogging the last quarter mile, in the dark.

"Where'd you get hepatitis B?" I asked.

"Sharing a needle, I guess."

"How do you stay so squeaky clean on amoebas?"

"I never do much of anything to get amoebic."

Surprised, I looked over at his sweaty profile glinting in the moonlight. These days, so many men and women, straight and gay, had done everything in the book. Even I had tried everything once.

"It's refreshing to find a man who's still a bit innocent," I said.

Vince laughed.

"I wasn't Billy's friend for nothing," he said. "Only I . . . like, translated his philosophy a little different."

At a tense moment in our courting, Billy had said, *I go to bed only with people I love.* One time he had said these same words to Vince. He and Vince had met at a California high-school meet, and Vince was instantly attracted. Billy had rebuffed him in the kindest way.

By now, Vince and I were opposite the empty dunes just west of Hotel Goodnight. It was dark, and the bird-watcher couldn't be seen. Probably he had gone back to his campground, or back to the mainland.

"So . . . how do you translate Billy?" I asked him.

Vince looked over his shoulder at me, with that bewitching grin.

"I only get fucked by people I love," he replied.

He'd insisted he never loved anyone but me. So he meant that no one had ever had him that way. Not quite believing him, I punched him in the shoulder with a scoffing expression.

"I never wanted to," he shrugged. "Had too much fun on top."

"It doesn't fit the picture I have of you."

"You don't know me very well, Mr. Brown," he said, grinning with wonderful insolence. "I'm patient."

"Lazy, maybe," I ragged him. "Or nobody wanted your hairy ass."

When I grabbed at his arm, he evaded me. Our workout dissolved into rough play. It was good to discover that I could kick up my heels again. We ran in wide circles, tagging each other, hot in the impact of our salt-rimed bodies.

"Not too hard . . . careful of your knees," I said.

Vince quickly looked up and down the moonlit beach. It was empty, except for a distant stroller or two.

So he recklessly hauled off his clothes, and sprinted naked into the surf. I was close behind, nude myself — coming up on his shoulder with my own racing kick. Nobody could get good pictures in the dark. Screw the media. Screw the snipers. Screw our notoriety. Wings of water flew from our feet. Vince delighted my eye, plunging forward into the foam, ducking under it. Then he straightened exultantly, with hair sleeked and bubbles draining down his body. Even in the dark, that virginal butt of his shone whiter than the rest of him. I surged up beside him.

We were just getting into a good surf-wrestle when suddenly Vince said in a low voice:

"The fuzz."

From the west, the beach Jeep of the Fire Island police had just come through a cut in the dunes, probably off the Burma Road, which was an unpaved service road, the only one to be found on eastern Fire Island. Now their headlights were jouncing toward us. Our clothes were strewn on the beach, in plain view. The authorities weren't too hard-line here. They winked at heterosexual skinny-dipping if it happened far from crowded family beaches. But we were gay men, far from the sanctuary of Cherry Grove.

"They probably can't see us . . . but let's get farther out," I said, with heart hammering.

Beyond the breakers, we swam quietly with many yards between us. It felt like Greenwich Village of the '60s, with vice cops kicking in the door. Right in front of us, the Jeep stopped. It wasn't clear what they were doing — maybe talking on the radio. But our jock straps lay 50 feet away, like a flashing red light.

Then . . . a miracle. The police Jeep jounced on east, toward Davis Park.

Watching them go, Vince and I swam toward each other.

"God, I peed when I saw them," said Vince, his voice shaky.

The terror had sobered us. Catching the next wave, we body-surfed into chest-deep water. There, we stood embraced. The moonlight bathed our heads and shoulders, while our cold bodies pressed together underwater, getting aroused. His face in my neck, he drew a deep sigh, trying to relax the tension.

"So you're patient, huh," I said.

He laughed, his stomach moving against mine. "I'll tell you when I fell for you. Wanna hear my confession?"

"I'll listen to any lie once."

"The three of us had just been kicked off the Oregon team. We went to San Francisco to talk to Billy's dad. We were all in fuckin' tears, man. John gave us this folder and said, Well, boys, there's this one gay coach. See . . . John'd been . . . like, tracking you . . . ever since he heard why you were fired from Penn State. There was this old interview in *Sports Illustrated,* maybe you remember the one . . . the photo of your face. It was . . . like, something in your eyes, that got to me. Billy looked at the same goddam picture, and he . . . well, he just shrugged. Billy didn't fall for you till later."

I moved my gaze along the beach, watching for more intruders.

"After you blew me off last winter," Vince went on, "I put out lots of good juju, into the universe."

"You prayed, huh?"

"You call it prayer . . . I call it magic. When you said you were coming out here, I didn't have a fuckin' dime for any Fire Island summer. So I . . . okay, I spent my film money to meet Mario and get into his house. When I was dancing at the Ice Palace that night, I was . . . like, really thinking about you, dancing to you. You know? And there you were."

After three years of a student-teacher friendship, I'd assumed that I knew this young man. But the story made me look at him with new respect. On the flip side of the young impulsive Vince, lived a mature Vincent C. Matti who was capable of grand strategies. One for our side. One to equal their best, whoever he was.

"So juju works?" I said.

Vince narrowed his eyes, looking at me through the moonlit beads of water in his eyelashes. He knew his eyes were beautiful, damn him. Vince's real juju was being lovable, and knowing the effect he had on people, both at once. His eyes weren't just "brown". Shadowed by his black eyelashes, those irises looked dark now, but in sunlight they were clear as amber. The intelligent, restless eyes of a young wolf who had roamed far from the den, without an old wolf to guide him.

"Juju always works," he said throatily.

I caught him around the thighs with one arm, and lifted him up. The water's buoyancy made it easy. Towering into the stars above me, he let his body ride against me, buttocks resting on my arm. With my free hand, I caressed those twinned muscles, hard as rounded rocks washed by the sea. Between them, they guarded that orifice, sensitive and mysterious as a sea anemone. As I kissed his wet belly, it seemed like nothing could go wrong. Love, and being with me, would mellow him out and make him forget about revenge. We would have our grand passion, survive the sniper bullets. Maybe even live to be old curmudgeons. Could I be serially monogamous with this polygamous spirit?

"Don't tell me when you fell for me," he said quietly, pressing my face into his navel. "Because you haven't — yet. But you will, Harlan."

"Let's go home," I said.

So many times, I'd fantasized what loving Vince would be like. That first time was passionate, yes — and disturbing.

Vince's mind was like a vast underground cavern. A spelunker was smart not to dare it without a map and a lot of safety lines. His thinking was laced with hidden rivers and drifts of diamonds. One crystal cave led to another, past walls of rainbows and pterodactyl bones, to bottomless chasms that suddenly yawned at the feet. Wrestling as I was with the old Bible mind, I thought of Vince as part of my sinful nature. Vince was bad — something to resist and question. Billy had been good — a passion of light, prayers that worked, Bibles that made sense, glowing warmth, hearth and home, happiness.

Now, as night fell, I had wrestled with this God of Earth, this naked bacchant of pure will. His way was to give love without reserve. Mine was to have it within limits. But I was so hungry for it that I almost lost control. He struggled lovingly against my reason, so he could spawn his hot life into my hand. Feeling his affection against me, then under me, was like trying to stop a speeding planet on its orbit.

Deep within the body, the pleasure of the male organ massaging the prostate gland is the whitest heat of gay love. I had let only Billy have me in that radiant frenzy. Even Vince didn't rate that kind of trust yet. This time, my pleasure was seeing him feel it for the first time. I held us there like two runners at the vastest stretch of a stride — he the front runner, I at his shoulder, pushing him with my explosive kick. He hung there with me, willing it, stride for stride, straining for breath and energy. His eyes were shut, and he was groaning with every breath, till we both hit the electric eye of the finish. He almost fainted.

Slowly Vince opened his eyes, and looked up at me from the crushed pillows and rumpled sheets.

He was so changed by the experience that I hardly recognized him. I must have looked altered too — was trembling violently as I rose up a little. Outside the window, an owl called somewhere in the mugho pines. Through the closed bedroom door, we could hear Steve talking to George Rayburn and another visitor.

We were laying by the large plate-glass window, with the room dark and the drapes open to the moonlight. I figured that no one could see us, and I had wanted to see him as he arched and thrashed under me. I drew myself gently out, pulling a last groan from him. His thighs slid down.

Vince let out a shuddering breath. To my changed eyes, he looked almost translucent. Like the membranes of a jellyfish, his tensed torso had the power to reveal the ribs, lungs, entrails. His pelvis and thigh bones were lit from within. I could see the big strong heart squeezing like a fist, in its veil of irridescent gristle — the left ventricle enlarged from running. His skull was carved from crystal, with rainbows boiling in the brain.

Slowly, my X-ray sight faded.

For a moment, I was aghast, shaken, almost undone at the enormity of what he'd shown me.

My lover drew me down, my belly into the hot slipperiness upon his, my face into the warmth of his breath. He was nuzzling my face tenderly, nibbling at my eyelids, tonguing at my lips like a wolf pup asking for food. I was so close to undone, on the very edge of that abyss of tenderness where I'd plunged so deep with Billy. Why did I feel like I wasn't really touching him, only his image through a glass window?

"I more than love you," he whispered.

When I drew my breath to say something, he put his fingers gently over my mouth.

Moonlight glowed with a gentle blue on our tangled bodies. In the living room, Steve and George were laughing about something.

Suddenly, with a crash of sound, a glitter exploded over Vince and me.

It seemed like a glacier of rainbowed ice had been dynamited over the bed. As intimacy shattered and our naked bodies were startled apart, knives and splinters of light fell on us for what seemed like an endless time. With the clarity of a dying man seeing his life pass before him, I was sure that I'd been shot in the head. Or Vince had been shot in the head.

The window was gone — cold night air poured over us. The bed was covered with broken glass. Our bodies were literally inlaid with knives of glass, razor blades of glass, even glass dust. Glass was slithering and sliding all over us, making sounds like sabers honing together. The entire floor, even part of the bed opposite, shimmered with glass. It was amazing that a single window could have blown its fragments so far. Vince's eyes were briefly horrified — then shut.

Looking down at him, at myself, I saw there was already blood everywhere — down our torsos, over our genitals, down our thighs, spotting the glittering bed like red rain.

It took two hours for Steve and our horrified activist friends to clean us up.

"God," said Rayburn. "Jeez."

In the middle of the night, finding a doctor on Fire Island was hard. The three men tweezed the glass out of our

skin, doctored us with iodine from the house's medical supplies. The injuries were not serious. But our bodies, even
our genitals, were stinging from dozens of tiny cuts. Vince,
laying on his back, had shut his eyes instinctively — but he
had a bit of glass in one eye and got panicky because it hurt
so terribly. While I calmed him, Rayburn removed it with
a magnifying glass and medical tweezers.

By then, Steve had made a search outside. The bay was
silent, shimmering under the moon. Boardwalks were empty.
Beyond our shelter-belt of wild cherry brush, a few lights
shown in neighboring houses.

"Call the cops?" he said dubiously.

Vince and I traded looks. For once, briefly, Vince and I
were in the same throbbing emotional place. There went
my gay dream that we could walk the streets of America
without fear. But a fish knife, and a hitch as a jarhead, did
not equip me for this kind of war. Windows that broke over
me and my lover also broke over Betsy and Falcon, over
everybody I cared about. It was time to swallow my pride,
and call in the experts.

"Fuck the police," I said past the cut on my lip. "Let's
get Chino and Harry."

"Oh, God, not the baby killers again," Rayburn protested.

"You got a better idea?" I was wrathfully grabbing the
phone.

"Yeah . . . world peace," George insisted.

"You call this peace?" yelled Vince, his voice breaking.
He yanked down his briefs, and grabbed his bare iodine-
painted genitals at George.

"Jeez," said George, agonizing, caught in the question.
"We've all had our losses. We're all hurting bad, some way.
But you two guys are both getting waaaaay out there, man.
I don't feel like I know you any more."

George and his friend left, to walk back to The Grove.

H-C Security didn't answer. They must be out on a job.

It took another hour to clean up the bedroom. Behind the
other bed in the room we finally found the thing that had
broken the window. Somehow I'd expected a .22 bullet. Instead, it was a smooth rock, about 1-1/2 inches in diameter.

The kind of rock that anyone could pick up on the beach. Glued on it, in little black letters cut from a newspaper, was one word:

LEV.

The cut-and-paste style was familiar. This thing was from "the secret admirer".

We picked it up in a cloth, and put it in a clean baggie, not wanting to damage any fingerprints that might be on it.

"What the hell is LEV.?" asked Steve.

"A name, maybe," I said.

"Lev is a Jewish name."

"This is different . . . looks like an acronym."

"The period makes it an abbreviation," said my text-conscious friend.

"*Leviticus,* maybe?"

"Why *Leviticus?*" Steve wasn't as Bible-wise as I was.

"Because," I said patiently, "that's the part of the Old Testament with the Hebrew laws in it. The death penalty for faggots, among others."

By the time we got Chino and Harry on the phone, it was 4:15 in the morning, New York time — 1:15 a.m. California time. Harry was a professional — he didn't waste time saying, "I told you so".

"How about an expenses-paid summer on Fire Island, and your time, in exchange for getting to the bottom of this?" I asked wearily.

"We'll replace ourselves on this concert gig we've got. Meet us on . . ." He paused, evidently looking at airline schedules right at his elbow. ". . . United flight 64 arriving Kennedy 11:30 a.m. tomorrow."

In the morning, Vince and I went into New York so that Doc Jacobs could check the first-aid job on our cuts.

Both of us were subdued, brooding. With me, emotions always imploded, staying inside. But Vince was the exploder. When we got back to Hotel Goodnight, he was off on his own tangent again, and started berating Steve and me. He didn't think we were going far enough to deal with LEV. Most likely, the guy had helped kill Billy. Other than throwing more money at bodyguards, we were just taking it laying down, he said. We were chickenshits, always sucking the straight cock, always knuckling under to the terror. It was time to force respect from the pig-fuckers. Etc., etc.

"What are *you* going to do?" Vince demanded of Steve. "*Your* house was violated."

"It's Harry's decision," Steve said.

"Bullshit," Vince barked. "Harlan, if you have any guts, give Steve some."

"You've got a lot of nerve," I said. "You're a guest in his house."

Steve said nothing, just retreated up to the Tower Room. Both of us knew in our hearts that Vince was half right. But if we resisted in the ways that Vince had in mind, straight America would drive Sherman tanks over the top of us.

"They'll break our windows every day if we push it that far," I told Vince.

"Then Steve should move to The Grove!"

"And live in the goddam ghetto forever?"

"Billy was *your* lover. Why am *I* at the barricades?" Vince shouted, jabbing his fingers at his own chest. "Why are you hiding here at a goddam typewriter, letting you and me be shot at? Why aren't you in New York with me? Helping the activists ... doing *something?*"

"Look," I shouted back. "You're talking revenge. I'm talking self-defense. Revenge won't bring Billy back. And it won't change people's attitudes ... just make them worse."

"I don't believe I'm hearing this," Vince said. "And you know what the worst is? Like — the absolute worst?"

I didn't care to ask.

"*I* don't know how to fight!" he burst out. "I gotta say it — you were right when you tossed me in the water. I can't even protect myself!" His eyes blazed. "But, Harlan ... you, like, *know* how to fight! You were a fucking *Marine,* man. And you don't do jack-shit except hire a couple of gay goons to watch our asses!"

His voice broke, almost in a sob. Brusquely, he went into the North Room, and threw clothes in his travel bag. I glimpsed Billy's track shoe — he always carried it with him.

"You're leaving?" I asked him. "After all the I love you's?"

Vince pressed his hands against his temples, as if he were trying to stop an atom bomb from going off in his brain. His eye was still watering, oily, with the antibiotic ointment in it.

"I don't know!" he cried out, in a strange tone that wrung my heart. "Every time something like this happens, I feel like I'm holding Billy's body again! I *refuse* to be this helpless queen! I *will* have justice!"

"Wait till Chino and Harry get here. Let's talk this out." I tried to take his arm, but he pulled away.

"No! Talking won't fix this!" His voice was strangled. "If I'd been a real fighter like Chino or Harry, maybe I could have kept Billy alive!"

Shoving on his sunglasses, Vince brushed past me, slinging his bag over his shoulder, and headed down the boardwalk toward the marina. His strides were purposeful, measured. I hoped he had enough cash to get to New York. At least he had a car.

Loving Billy had hurt sometimes — but never like this. For a while, I sat silent in the front room, listening to Steve's typewriter upstairs. While all the uproar had gone on, Angel was hiding up there with his new cat — a female tabby from the Patchogue animal shelter. Now he was silently helping his lover keep pages in order.

"Hang in there," Steve called down the spiral stairway. "He'll be back."

EIGHT

July 1978

The next day, while Steve kept watch at the house, I drove my rattle-trap truck to Kennedy International Airport. The new look was working — I walked right past a news crew waiting for some celebrity at the terminal, and nobody recognized me.

Harry Saidak and Chino Cabrera came striding up the jetway together, travel bags slung over shoulders. Despite their different personalities, their eyes held that same hard stare. Their caution, as they looked around the crowded boarding area, identified them as combat vets. As they gave me quiet hugs, I was damn glad to feel their strength and expertise in my arms. Especially Chino.

Driving them back to the South Shore, I said:

"I don't expect you guys to take a bullet for me. Just help me stay safe — keep the family safe. And I want to learn more about being responsible for our safety."

"We can do it two ways," said Harry. "One way, we're ghosts. You'll hardly ever see us. The reason is — they'd watch us, to know how to get you."

"On the other hand," Chino added, "this is Fire Island. If

we do the social shooting and looting with you, it might work to let them think our guard is down. They'd try an easy hit, and we'd zap them."

Them. I still wasn't 100 percent convinced that LEV. was connected with Montreal.

We took the clam-boat across the bay.

A fter Chino and Harry dumped their gear in their rooms we spent the rest of the day analyzing the broken-window incident.

First the vets looked at the rock, in its sandwich baggie.

"We know a guy," said Harry. "His name is Julius. He's got access to labs. Julius ought to see this."

Then we left Angel taking a nap in the house, and Harry, Chino, Steve and I walked out to the dune where we'd seen the bird-watcher. Chino read the signs easily, moving along with that quiet command that added inches to his five foot ten. His high-cheekboned face could look European or Asian, depending on the angle of the light, or the mood he was in. Right now, in the strong afternoon sun, Chino looked like an Aztec tracking missionaries who'd massacred his tribe.

"Look," he said, pointing at the trampled sand. "Your birder was laying prone here. You didn't see him the second time because he was down in the brush. He scuffed the marks over. But sand is tricky — he couldn't restore the old crust on it."

Chills rushed down my spine.

We followed the vague tracks across the sand dunes for a hundred feet, to the bay. At the grassy muddy tide-flat, we couldn't go any farther. Chino hunkered down, Asian style, to point out some marks through the wet grass. "Look at that. The fucker was wearing those wide tire-tread shoes that the North Vietnamese wore. You can walk across mud without sucking, and you don't leave identifiable footprints."

"And let's not assume LEV. is a vet," Harry pointed out. "Anybody can learn Vietnam stuff if he pays enough money to guys like us."

Steve and I looked at each other gloomily.

Chino's eyes scanned the bay with their eerie alertness. Despite the clear afternoon, not many boats dotted the water. Right now, a family of four was out there treading for clams, waist-deep in the shallows. Their boat was bobbing gently near them, at anchor.

"He had his own boat," said Chino. "Anchored offshore like that family. Nobody would look at him twice."

"Somebody must have seen him," said Steve. "If they remember the boat's name or license number, we can trace it."

"If this guy is as good as I think he is," Harry said, "he'll have a fake boat registration."

"He broke your bedroom window from the boat too," said Chino.

"How the hell . . ."

"He'd probably been around for a few days. Just birding. Camping in the brush. Saw enough to know which room is yours. Watched you and Vince on the beach. Saw you getting horny and going to the house. Waited till after dark. Came sneaking up on the north side of the house, just outside your cove, and . . . *wham*."

"Why no engine noise?"

"An engine silencer."

"Why didn't he *shoot* the window out?" Steve asked.

"That's the interesting part, man. Probably because he couldn't put his name on the bullet. This is his fucking calling card. It broke the window with a lot of force too. My guess is — he used a wrist-rocket. That's a metal slingshot — a kid can buy one in any sports store. Maybe he customized it a little. Wham and scram. He's saving the bullet for a special occasion."

I was aghast.

"He sure knew the most delicate moment to shoot," I said.

"No shit," said Chino. "You had the curtains open? He was probably sitting out there in the boat using . . . well, it's a kind of binoculars designed for low-intensity light. You can see somebody thread a needle half a mile away."

A slow, hot, angry flush rushed over me.

"I'd say our guy is a kinky latent," added Harry. "He hates what we do, but he can't get it off his mind."

"Somebody is going to a lot of trouble," Steve muttered.

"Yeah," Harry shrugged. "LEV. is either independently wealthy, or he's with a vigilante group that has beaucoup bucks, and you're on their 'A' list."

"You think he killed Horatio, then?"

"Maybe," said Chino. "The cat got it the night you brought Vince home. He's studied you for a long time, Harlan. He knows that Vince is a serious step for you."

Chino stood up and looked directly into my eyes, with those gray eyes of his that had seen everything.

"This guy is not your standard hit man," he said. "Right now, he's playing with you. Taking his time. Lots of foreplay before he tries to fuck you . . . his way. Snipers are definitely top men. If we don't zap him, you may be in for months of this . . . years. You'll have to commit to a different way of living."

The base of my spine went cold.

"Do we call the police?" Steve asked.

"Not yet," said Harry. "They don't care enough about faggots. We might luck into some detective who's a brother. But we might not. Same for the attorney general, the FBI. There'd be leaks. Maybe to the wrong people. Only a few of us need to know. You two, and Chino, and me. And John Sive, if we ever have to."

Vince wasn't mentioned as needing to know details. Sad, but true. We couldn't trust him either.

"If we get our hands on LEV.," I said, "what do we do with him?"

"Depends," said Harry.

"On what?" I asked.

Both vets were scanning the island with their keen eyes. Chino had an eager look. He was the perfect hunter-killer that America had spent millions to train, then flung away with a sneer, like the priceless pearl that Shakespeare wrote about. Now he had glimpsed the perfect war.

"On whether he has a mysterious accident before the cops get to the scene," smiled Chino.

"I'd rather see him stand trial," I said.

Harry shook his head in disgust.

"Yeah, sure," he murmured. "You and John Sive, and your

propaganda victories. I remember you guys talking about how Billy was going to have one of those in Montreal."

Next day, Harry took the boat over to the mainland and sent the rock to Julius by registered mail.

W hen Billy, Vince and Jacques had come into my world, I thought of them as three storm-driven birds. Now two new birds had landed — feathers battered by the winds of war. Saidak was the screaming eagle. Cabrera was the cormorant, at home in the sea.

That night, we cooked up a butch supper of thick steaks and clams fresh from the bay. Chino's dry humor was back in form, and he had us laughing and guffawing. It was not going to be your average screwing-in-the-dunes kind of Fire Island summer.

After dinner, we started making the area more secure.

"Your desert island may be poetic as hell. But it's wide open," said Harry.

H-C Security went on to elaborate. Hotel Goodnight was exposed — no fence, accessible by land or water, easily fire-bombed. Our dock made it simple for kidnappers to grab some-body and make a quick retreat by boat. Davis Park was an incorporated township, so building codes banned fences — they'd spoil the view. No fence meant no guard dog.

"Forget dogs anyway," said Chino. "A .22 pistol with a silencer does a dog." He stroked Angel's new cat, Striper. She arched her back and smiled at him. "We'll watch the cat here. She'll tell us stuff."

"We need to keep bugs off the phone," Harry said. "We need a few Motorola walkie-talkies — always handy to have around."

"We get to know your neighbors' boats, in case we have to steal one," Chino added.

"And we need an alarm system," said Harry. "Is all that okay with you, Steve?"

"Hey — do whatever you need to do," Steve replied.

Operating an alarm without electricity would be a chal-lenge. In that part of Davis Park, a few residents had phones, including us. But most had chosen to be primitives, with gas-lights instead of electric lights. We were among the primitives. Harry proposed a fancy battery-operated alarm system that cost around $6000. But Chino argued in favor of a low-tech system.

So, working at night, all of us rigged a trip-wire system around the house. First we dug a foot-deep, yard-wide trench. Miles of dry seaweed lay in rolls on the beach — Angel's job was to gather armfuls of the stuff. With all that weed, we packed the trench almost full. On top of the seaweed, we laid trip-wires that were connected to tin cans hanging hidden in clumps of brush, or by the house. A layer of sand covered the trip wire.

It wasn't the kind of booby trap that would injure some wandering child. But at night, any footstep on the trench (including a deer's) would sink far enough to rattle the tin cans gently together and alert us. Another wire was set only at night — across the 20-foot-wide entrance to the cove, just below the surface of the water, where any sizable intruder would trip it.

In the boardwalk, the vets pried several boards loose near the house. More boards were jimmied on our dock. These now creaked when anyone stepped on them.

Then we secured the house, replacing standard window-panes with one-way glass and outside screens, to minimize the danger of fire-bombing and rock-throwing. We already had three ground-floor doors for quick exits. The Tower Room became another emergency exit, with windows opening onto the roof. In one place, the dune was high enough that you could safely jump from the roof.

For extra weapons, we fags had baseball bats, pokers, towel rods, barbecue forks, fire extinguishers, and so on. A mighty swat of a tennis racquet across an intruder's face is a good stopper.

As a final touch, we started shuffling bedrooms on a random basis.

"Never set a pattern," Chino kept reminding us. "Always do the unexpected."

I wasn't getting any writing done, and the clam-boat sat in

the boathouse. But it was a relief to be taking some action. Keeping busy dulled the pain of missing Vince.

He didn't call.

N ot till two weeks later, with changes complete, were the two nance commandos ready for a little partying. "Time to prowl and growl," said Harry. "Where's that East Coast action we've heard so much about?"

Since we never left the house unguarded, Steve took Harry up to the gay towns. The next day, on my assurance that he could find a brown boy or two in the gay towns these days, Chino and I jogged toward Cherry Grove. As we passed the spot where Vince had cavorted with me, I had to fight back jealousy. Where was my young hellion? What was he doing? Who was he doing it with? Maybe I should look up my old flame, Chris Shelbourne. It was amazing how vividly I remembered him — the tender, throbbing, guilty, secret boy-love that almost was.

Screw Vince.

As we traveled along, Chino updated me on their lonely life in L.A. Since Montreal, Jemal and Corky had drifted away from H-C. Somebody in the Navy had recognized Chino in Montreal news footage. They couldn't give him the dishonorable discharge now, but a former superior had written him an ugly letter. As usual, bodyguard jobs were few, and poorly paid.

"Fifty dollars an hour for my butt and my gun," said Chino disgustedly. "Shiiiit . . . I could make more money if I just sold my butt," he grinned.

While Chino talked, between breaths, he was running softly at my side. His open windbreaker and green Speedo displayed a bullet-creased torso as supple as the sea snakes in the Asian waters where he'd fought. An ugly scar gnarled one breast. His long, powerful legs were spotted with a few little phosphorous burns. His black hair, short in the Navy in '73, was now long enough for one of the first male ponytails I'd seen. Clean-shaven, he forewent the *cholo* mustache that many Chicanos sported. He was 29 now, and felt older than me.

Chino and Harry — two attractive straight-looking guys, the kind I liked. But I already knew their professional ethics — they didn't fuck their clients. And we were all living with the crosshairs on us. It was no time to think with your dick.

"How's your thing with Vince going?" Chino asked.

"Not too good," I said.

At the gay towns, we passed an exuberant lesbian softball game. Then a strip of beach where gay muscle-boys oiled their hides and showed off their pecs. Finally a strip where cantankerous white clones with money and mustaches were camping. Some Anglo gays didn't like Hispanic gays who came out from the city. Now, several whites noticed my brown friend.

"Latin trash," one of them said as we passed.

Chino's jaw tensed, but he kept jogging.

The next clone yelled, "Hey, spic! This is our beach!"

He went to stand in Chino's way. All Chino did was rivet the clone with those eyes of his, the same eyes that hundreds of Vietcong had seen just before they died.

"Wrong," said Chino pleasantly. "The beach belongs to everybody."

The clone and his buddies took a reading on Chino's eyes, and they got the feeling they should back off. Anyway, fisticuffs weren't gay style. Why fight with a guy if you can make love to him? I wanted to smooth things over, so that Chino could start out on the right foot down here. Hopefully, there was one horny stud in the crowd who would be into tricking with a brown sea snake.

So I said:

"Go ahead, boys. Take my friend on."

They considered my double-edged hint.

"Nah," somebody drawled. "He can take me."

The tension broke, and everybody laughed.

Suddenly a man my age in a black leather G-string recognized me under all the hair. He was hip enough not to say my name, but he couldn't resist a dig.

"Hey . . . what're *you* doing in a mustache?" he asked me. "Trying to hide your stretch marks?"

His name was Bark. He took us to the Ice Palace, bought us drinks, was very attentive to me. Chino silently chugged his shot of whiskey, his back to the few dancers on the floor. He was looking morose and introspective, about to go off and cruise alone, when he saw a young Puerto Rican in a red Speedo standing there gazing at him, awestruck. The boy looked to be in his early 20s, with lovely eyes and long, nappy curls down to his shoulder blades.

All Chino did was hold out his arm. The boy slid under it, nestling against him. Chino left with him, and was back in an hour, looking relaxed, to find Bark and me talking about old times.

As we walked back to Davis Park, Chino was silent now, brooding.

But as we passed that place again where Vince and I had embraced each other in the water, I felt a different feeling this time — a heavy wave of nostalgia and pain for that first time we'd made love. I missed him, missed his body, his smell, his wild giving. Chino had just had a man's body that way, Speedos down, warm skin against warm skin. I envied even that minimal release that my friend was feeling.

Chino must have picked up my thoughts, because he looked over at me. But he didn't say anything.

Around July 1st, Chino and I made a quick trip back to Prescott. I wanted to try and talk Betsy out of moving off campus.

When we got to her house, packing boxes were sitting around. Chino prowled the yard while I went inside. Betsy looked at him through the window, all her own gay liberal anti-war feelings in her eyes. Then she invited me unsmilingly into Falcon's room, where she was putting him down for a nap. His crib was hung with a fantastic array of mobile toys. As she changed his diaper, he kicked his legs, looking lovingly up at her with his soft myopic baby eyes.

Very reluctantly, I gave her an update on Vince and the sniper.

"Yeah, the minute I saw the Neanderthal with you again," she said, "I knew things must be serious."

Feeling oddly remote from Falcon, I put out my hand. The

baby grabbed my thumb in his hot little fingers with astonishing force, talking a blue streak of mah-mah-mahs and bah-bah-bahs. How much I yearned to hear him saying, "Dah."

Betsy's hands were shaking a little.

"For a while, I believed it was going to be over any time now," she said. "I don't want Falcon to grow up in the middle of all this violence!"

It was clear that Betsy was bailing out of my life, taking my lover's child with her. And not a court in the country would uphold my deeply felt claims. Feeling helpless, I let Falcon's hot little hand jerk my finger around.

"I *hate* feeling this way about Vince," she went on. "I mean — he was one of my first gay male friends. Only Billy was closer to me than Vince ... you know that. But Vince has changed. I hardly recognize him any more."

"You're taking Falcon away from me," I barked angrily.

Betsy touched my hand, as gently as if she were putting baby oil on Falcon.

"No," she said. "I'd never do that to you. But will you listen to me?"

Grudgingly, I got myself in hand and nodded.

"Look," she said. "Billy's death pushed us all to the edge. But Vince is over the edge. And now you and Vince are together. So it brings his scariness close to the baby. Don't you understand?"

I didn't want to.

"Is he going to live with you?" she asked. "I mean, at Prescott?"

"If he comes back to me. If we last the summer."

"And you wanted to *marry* me? That's a clear message to the second sniper, if that's who he is ... to anyone out there. They'll want to know why I'm so important to you. All they have to do is bug us, and find out who Falcon's father is. Maybe they know already! Somebody might kidnap Falcon so he's not brought up gay. Billy's parents might find out, and go to court to take him away from me. He could get hurt just by being around you ... a fire-bomb ... somebody shooting at the house."

I knew she was right.

Betsy was inserting Falcon into his giraffe pajamas.

"And if you and Vince live together on campus, and you try to go on coaching, there's going to be more trouble. The college will be under more pressure. And supposing Vince really does the Gay Panther thing? That means the police — the FBI — the media all over us again."

I drew a deep sigh of weariness.

"Living off campus will be more expensive for you," I said. "At least let me help with the expenses. And you shouldn't live alone."

"I can handle it. It'll be great to have my own place."

"You won't have the campus security. You'll be isolated."

"It couldn't be any worse than living next to a lightning rod." Then she smiled. "And . . . I need some privacy. Room in *my* world for that golden lover. That's what Vince used to call it."

In the soft afternoon light I studied her face as she bent over the crib. She wore her helmet of short black hair like a Roman bronze. Her blue eyes, with long curved eyelashes, didn't have a flicker of humor in them. Her delicate cheekbones and jaw were chiseled by some ice-ax of female determination. Betsy was the most loving and devoted mother I had ever seen. But she was also a loner, like me — stoic and embattled.

I held Falcon up, and kissed his tummy, which he loved. That wondrous life-heat of his — her heat, and Billy's — warmed my hands.

"The vets ought to know that he's Billy's child," I said.

"I want as few people as possible to know."

"How can H-C protect him if they don't know all the angles?"

She thought about this. Reluctantly, she finally nodded.

So I called Chino in, and Betsy took a deep breath and told him the family secret. Our war-dog stared down into the crib, as the baby made mighty swipes at the dangling mobiles. He had been there when Falcon was born, but now he was visibly shaken. As he picked the baby up, he showed us that tender, gentle side of himself that he usually kept hidden. Chino felt like he'd been raped by death, and crawled away from it with a desperate desire to protect life.

"Mi'jito, mi vida," purred Chino. *"Qué guapito eres . . . ."*

The baby melted into Chino's shoulder, and took a fistful of his glossy black hair. Next he grabbed the little medal of Mary that my friend wore around his neck.

"Ayyy, mira-mira . . . La Virgencita," Chino said, showing Mary to the baby.

As Betsy watched Chino expertly coaxing a burp out of Falcon, her eyes widened. Clearly he'd been a veteran babysitter in a big *barrio* family. Then, behind Chino's back, she looked at me with a grudging little smile and gave me a thumbs up.

W hile Harry gravitated toward Steve, Chino and I edged toward friendship. I'd coached a few men of color, but never been close with one. He was intriguing, elusive, still a little edgy about our differences, but willing to express them in humor.

War had taught Chino to keep people guessing what his scene was. Let other gay males spread their peacock tails of chic. He lived in clean jeans, work shirts, jungle boots. No tattoos, no bandannas or studded belts, no sassy T-shirts. Besides, belts and earrings were handles for an enemy to grab you by. The medal that he wore, of the Virgin of Guadalupe, was oxidized, so it never glinted — a glint could spell death in the jungle — and it hung on a light chain, easily broken. The only hand-hold was his long hair — and heaven help anyone who touched it. His only display was that dignity and reserve. Emotion lay hidden a thousand fathoms deep in him, like broken ships.

As I got started writing, Chino sat in my room by my typewriter, reading Steve's *Rape of the Angel Gabriel*. I had cut my literary teeth in a busy newspaper office, so having a sidewalk superintendent was not a problem. In fact, his presence was comforting.

When I took breaks, we talked.

"Where'd you get those gray eyes?"

He shrugged. "I'm a California half-breed — Mexican, Spanish, Japanese. Kids in the barrio called me Chino, because

I look so Asian. And my *mamita* was part Chumash, and she raised me the old way. So I'm not even Catholic. I don't know where the eyes come from. Maybe the Spanish side."

About childhood and school, he said only:

"*Mamita* stood up for me — she thought I would grow out of being a *joto*. She wanted me to be the big Latino man. To have respect. But I had to survive. The *vatos*, the gang guys, beat on me all the fucking time, man. I learned my first evade and escape stuff on the home streets. When I was 17, I dropped out of school and enlisted. Mama cried . . . and cried. But the SEALs have a high-school equivalency program, and I made her happy when I finished it. Yeah . . . I had big plans in those days. Things got FUBAR later."

"Fucked up beyond all repair" was all he'd say about Vietnam.

"Harlan, you writing a book too?" Chino asked.

"He's going to write about Billy," Steve broke in. "Tell it with dignity, like I did."

"The hell I am," I said.

As the summer passed, Harry became the kid brother I'd never had. But Chino became a deeper kind of *familia* — my passionate sidekick.

O ne day Steve and I were taking one of our long walks on the beach, where we talked about everything under the sun. Steve said, "You're all sweaty over Vince right now. But you're going to fall for Chino."

"Go on."

"Chino's so crazy he's sane . . . and he's pure gold."

I considered this. "He's the first gay man I ever met who isn't running after romance or fucks. And he's twice as single-minded as Billy was. At least there was room in Billy's mind for two things — love and running. With Chino it's only one thing. Getting LEV."

"Feels good to have him and Harry around, though."

"Especially Harry, huh?" I couldn't resist the dig, as I picked up a bit of beach glass.

Steve ignored the dig. "The two of them confront me with something I've avoided thinking about. Jeez Louise, I remember laying awake nights, sweating, terrified that I'd get drafted for Korea."

"Yeah," I said. "I promised myself I would never be a guy like my dad. I've had this child-like faith in courtrooms, like a lot of us do. We've been fighting back in the courtrooms. But whenever we win in court, they go to their guns. And you can't beat guns unless you think like Chino and Harry."

We were getting gloomier and gloomier.

"Yeah," said Steve. "I used to think we'd win by clicking our magic heels together. Who are we kidding? The straight world is not sending their Dorothys to do us. They're sending their own Chinos and Harrys."

I hurled the bit of glass back into the sea.

Often as I fantasized how we'd apprehend LEV., I wondered why Chino had been so deeply affected by Billy's death — why he tracked LEV. with his own lonely passion.

Late in July, just as Steve had predicted, Vince came back. That morning, we were all on the front deck having coffee, when the boardwalk squeaked. Heads turned. My lover was walking up from the ferry, luggage over his shoulder. The cuts on his face had healed.

"Hiya, Vince," said Steve, trying to keep a straight face.

The vets rose with polite handshakes. Their eyes said that they didn't like Vince any better than before. They didn't approve of my affair with him, and were too polite to say so.

But his eyes, aglow with innocence, now rested on Chino and Harry with a shy new respect. *Real fighters,* he'd called them. It seemed like his thoughts had been moving along the same new groove that mine had. Except that, in his typical fashion, he was going to go off the deep end with it.

Me, I was the paragon of common sense, wasn't I?

NINE

On the back deck, Vince and I had it out, sitting at the cable-drum table. His eyes noted the fortress air of the house, as he brazenly lit a joint right in front of me, then thoughtfully blew the smoke down-wind so it didn't get in my face. I hated seeing him smoke dope, ruining his good lungs and — in my opinion — his brain cells. The *Reader's Digest* would denounce my sexuality, yet they'd support me 100 percent in the efforts to get my lover off weed.

"How's New York?" I asked.

"I stayed with — you don't want to know who. We, uh, did some brainstorming."

Had he slept with this man? I felt a dreadful loneliness.

"I know what you're thinking," Vince said, taking a long deep hit on the joint.

"You're 26 and I'm 42, and you know what I'm thinking?"

"Goddam flaky kid. Now we have to start over. New lab tests, new withdrawal . . ."

"Yeah, I was thinking that," I admitted.

"I didn't run those mile times because I was a flake."

"True."

"I haven't fucked around, I've been running a little, and I've stayed away from speed."

"You're still hooked on pot."

"That doesn't count." He looked at me steadily. "Look — I want to have the summer with you. But then I have to go and do my thing. Get my life going."

I met his eyes. Was he hesitating in his rush to violence? Was this a cry for help? There had to be a way to get his brilliant but moth-holed brain in gear. I had to buy some time till I could think of something to stop him.

"The only way it will work," I said, "is if we don't argue about politics."

"Then I can't ... like ... have an honest difference of opinion with you."

"That kind of difference wears love out."

Vince shrugged. "If it wears out, it wears out. Meantime, we have what we fucking have."

Putting the roach in his pocket, he ran his hand up my arm. "Come on," he said quietly. "Don't be uptight."

In my bedroom of the moment, it was shirts yanked open, bare chests pressing. "Oh God, I've missed you," he said into my beard, into my chest hair. He smelled like a hayfield, but not the agricultural kind.

"What took you so long to come back?" Into his hair, as we went down into a square of bright morning light on the bed. My hand jerked the curtain shut, and his opened knees slid caressingly up along my sides, almost in the same move.

"My fucking pride, and my ... Oh." His head arched back.

"So you want a summer thing," I said against his throat.

"Summer thing, winter thing." He could hardly talk. "Oh God."

I wanted him so much that I didn't care how he smelled.

"Oh God, I love you," he was saying.

We tried to keep quiet, so we didn't drive the other guys in the house crazy. Afterward, exhausted, we slept till early evening, and took a short run in the moonlight toward The Grove.

"Mr. Brown," he said, between breaths, "I have to get you to live in the moment. You live in your head too much."

Was LEV. watching this through his high-tech binoculars?

"Can I try and get you to quit smoking?" I asked.

"Mr. Brown, you can try anything with me," he grinned.

That night, the two vets gave me level looks, but said nothing. They walked Vince through our security routines. With surprising docility, he agreed to do what he was told. He wanted to get in good with them.

As the summer passed, those bedroom times were challenging. The intense college senior that I'd met in 1974 had matured into a highly sexed knothead — like me. With other men, I had always maneuvered to be the one in control, and now I prayed that my control could keep Vince out of revolution. But it was hard to control Vince — his feelings were awakened in a new way, and he was eager to push the envelope of sensation. I wasn't into extremes, or rough sex, so I tried to hold the line. All the while, I kept asking myself "why?" about Vince. I had never asked myself why I loved Billy. That love simply was — like the sunrise is. Yet I was getting as addicted to Vince as he was to dope. Addiction, to me, had always meant alcohol and drugs, so this was a humbling thing to realize.

Outside the bedroom door, Vince courted the vets' trust. I went through ridiculous little secret fits of jealousy. Did he find Harry or Chino attractive?

If it was Harry's turn to relax, our screaming eagle shared Steve's bottle of bourbon and Vince's bottle of burgundy, and told us a thousand and one tales of Vietnam. Vince listened with rapt horror, and the last of his liberal shudders. One day, Harry casually mentioned hauling a dead Vietcong out of a rice paddy, to sit on while he ate his lunch.

"Christ," Vince said, "it'd take me . . . like, *years,* before I'd get that hardened."

"It'd take you 24 hours," Chino said dryly.

Our cormorant never told war stories. When it was his turn to relax, Chino kicked back with his six-pack of beer and told us funny tales of what he'd seen on the boardwalk. Now and then, he got dick-dragging drunk, and left us to pass out on his bed. This was a new thing since Montreal.

"Yeah," Harry said quietly, "Chino took Billy's death very

personally. But his drinking problems started in the Nam. A mission's like shooting speed — afterward you go on a spree to come down."

"What's his history?" I asked Harry. "I've known you guys for two years, and I don't know a thing about Chino."

"I *live* with the guy," said Harry, "and I don't know much. He was one of the last SEALs in Indian country, before we pulled out. Advisor to a unit of native mercenaries. They ran POW rescues."

Vince's eyes lit up. Rescuing prisoners was a noble thing. As a liberal, he could allow himself to admire this.

"I don't think Chino was ever a commie-hater," Harry went on. "He wanted to be a SEAL for manhood, I guess. I get the impression that some of his teammates knew he was gay. But SEALs stay tight — they never turned him in, and he never got caught. He started having questions about the war after he started springing POWs. After they gave him the yahoo medal. I always thought —"

"What medal?" Vince interrupted.

"Navy Cross."

Harry glanced through the bedroom door at Chino's sprawled form on the bed.

"Well," he said, "I always had a feeling that somebody he loved was killed. When I met him after the war, he'd just gotten out of the VA hospital, and he was addicted to morphine from the pain, and half nuts about something. And he resigned his commission. So they never got to throw him out."

Chino's mystery seemed to hold a key to LEV.'s mystery.

Now and then, little threats kept us on edge. Strange clicks in the telephone line. A boat hovering on the bay nearby. On duty, Chino often spent nights outdoors, and Striper often slept with him, like she knew what her job was. One night, Chino was alerted by the cat's sudden stare. Then he heard a faint early-warning of the tin cans from the cove. Something had tripped the wire in the water. Chino was over there in an instant, like a supersonic shadow — and saw nothing.

Meanwhile, word got around The Pines and The Grove that Steve Goodnight and Harlan Brown had hooked up with military animals — the kind that had blood clear to their elbows. George Rayburn, who belonged to the pacifist wing of the gay activists, was hardly speaking to me these days.

"Girlfriend, I'd let myself be machine-gunned to goddam confetti before I'd ever hurt another human being," George told me on the boardwalk one day.

George had been a friend of Billy's, and Billy's dad — another link to the past.

A s I sat at the typewriter trying to capture thoughts, my post-hippie, radical-chic lover was captured by the military mind.

At the Hotel, games kept us sharp, and vented our tensions. Our volleyball and touch football was so noisy that we drove bathers off our beach. Our daily runs were races. Some days, we went out in the boat to see who could dig the most clams. Even our cookouts resolved into who could fillet fish faster. We played at breaking patterns, changing booby traps around.

As Harry and Chino got to know Vince, and he pestered them with questions, their attitude softened. But they took a sadistic joy in keeping him on edge — checking on his self-control and his willingness to learn. Vince was smart enough to know he was being tested. One afternoon, on the front deck, I found the two of them hooting at him. Vince was wearing a G-string and cocoa butter, and trying to learn how to throw knives. The vets were wearing Speedos, sunglasses and cheap tan oil, and they were ragging Vince about the effects of weed on his hand-eye coordination.

"Harlan," Chino said cheerfully, past the little cigar he was smoking, "we are fucking with your pinko pot-head boyfriend's mind."

For a target, they had hauled a big driftwood plank up from the beach, leaned it against the house, and drew a human silhouette on it. I perched on the rail with a Coke, and watched as ... WHACK! ... Harry put his combat knife between the shoulder blades. The board vibrated with a deep *thunnnngggg*. Then WHACK! ... Chino sank his knife right beside Harry's.

Then ... *whunk* ... Vince's throw with Harry's knife bounced off the board and clanged to the deck.

"Whatsa matter, Vincie Wincie?" Harry wanted to know. "Catch your high heel?"

Vince tightened his jaw. His next throw stuck on the very edge of the board.

Steve, Angel, Bark and I started throwing too. I even threw my stick. Angel got surprisingly good. We graduated to the gamut of sharp things from the kitchen drawers. Low-score man had to do the dishes. When Vince finally sank one into the "heart" for the first time, Harry said, "Hoo-ah! We'll make a sow's ear out of you yet."

As days passed, Vince learned to take down and clean the vets' handguns. Party-line liberalism was out the window.

My lover's one counterculture obsession was to grow his own pot on the Beach. Those were the days before marijuana became a U.S. agribusiness, when it was every druggie's dream to plant just a few good imported seeds. By pinching and fertilizing, you were sure to get one super-plant that would send you straight to whatever heaven you believed in. Vince started some seeds in a big flower pot hidden in the brush, where he hoped the FIPD and the National Seashore rangers wouldn't find it, and stealthily went there to tend it. One day he found his plant in wilting ruins, and accused me of having pulled it up.

"There's a deer out there somewhere," I shrugged, "who is in Nirvana."

G uns and knives would be useful to a fledgling terrorist. One day, I finally broke down and told the two vets about Vince's intentions. The three of us walked alone on the beach, and the vets listened, their somber eyes sweeping the dunes as we strolled along. Always competitive, we were skipping stones on the water.

"The kid has potential as a fighter," Chino admitted, hurling a flat white stone. "He's *loco* ... aggressive ... smart."

I skipped a piece of beach glass. It sank near the shore.

"He'll probably try to recruit you guys," I said.

Chino seemed to think this was funny. Harry just frowned.

"What do you want us to do?" Harry asked.

"Help me talk some sense into him. He has a following in the community. All he needs is a dozen other smart, aggressive locos, and he could start a movement that would hurt all of us."

Harry squinted at me. "Where's your pull with the kiddo?"

"I'm too close to home . . . I don't carry any weight."

"So we try to turn Vince," said Harry. "Is that it?"

"Don't tell him I put you up to it."

They both chuckled.

"Oh, we're fairly subtle," Chino said.

"A few things, though," Harry told me. "Once Chino and I go in, you stay out and you don't know a thing . . . unless we ask you in. Understand why?"

I didn't.

"You're in love . . . compromised," put in Chino.

Was this how I looked to them? As their sunglasses stared at me impassively, I had to face the gap between my emotion-racked present and the leatherneck past. In their eyes, my wild feeling for this wild young man made me a discipline problem. I'd hired them, but they outranked me.

Next, my jealous lunacy reared again. Would either of the vets succumb to my lover's charms? These guys wouldn't let sex wreck their work, would they? If they were that loose, they'd have died in Southeast Asia.

Angrily I fired a stone. A breaking wave engulfed it.

"Nobody needs to know but us three," Harry was saying. "Anybody else — Chino and I decide on who."

"How about John Sive?" I asked.

"Not unless we have to."

Chino said, "*Halaaaaa*," under his breath in Spanish and hurled a stone five yards farther than Harry or me.

Harry went on, "We'll have expenses — can you handle that? No questions asked?"

In the name of the greater good, I choked down my jealousy. "Sure," I said recklessly.

The vets' eyes held mine — quiet, narrowed, pondering.

"Hey, sweet thing, what do we call this operation?" Chino

asked Harry, with a glint in his eye. "Rolling Paper Thunder?"

"Oh, something simple," Harry said. At times, Harry was as humorless as me. "How about 'Boomerang'?"

The next day, Harry returned from the Davis Park marina, where he'd used a pay phone for a confidential phone call.

"I talked to Julius," he said. "Lab report on the rock. Our sniper is a genius of the generic. The three letters are common Canadian newsprint, three different fonts, looks like three different newspapers. LEV. might have a job that involves travel — picks paper stuff out of the trash. Common dime-store glue, a brand sold all over the country. The rock is South Shore granite. Either he's a local guy — which I don't believe — or he brought his materials, and made the thing here. A few pollen grains of local plants. But no fingerprints. No hairs or fibers stuck in the glue. *Nada.*"

Harry had also been drifting through mainland marinas — Bayport, Patchogue, Bellport, Sayville. He'd asked about a lone bird-watcher with a boat. *Nada.*

As August neared, and LEV. made no more moves on us, I started feeling a little silly. But Chino and Harry didn't let us drop our guard. Frequently, my lover walked the beach with them, deep in talk. I noticed his pot use was tapering off. He was thirsting for target practice with firearms, but you couldn't do that on the Beach. In the Patchogue army-navy store, he'd found a good knife of his own, and he threw it obsessively for hours.

For a guy whose most lethal weapon had been his hairdryer, it was a change.

The two vets found a few off-duty hours to have their own summer things. When they went home to L.A., they'd probably be standing in line for clap shots.

Harry was sweet on Steve, but Steve was into his platonic thing with Angel, so Harry became the darling of Bark and any other A-list gays on the Beach who were not hostile to warmongers.

Meanwhile, Chino had his Puerto Rican beauty, whose name was Tito. A few times, Tito walked all the way from The Grove to get laid. Chino was kind, but not interested in romance. All he wanted was Tito's beautiful brown ass. Through their bedroom wall, we heard Tito groaning in Spanish. The rest of us wished we understood.

The first week of August, it seemed like Harry was fighting a mild little flu that had gone through the house.

Enough women came and went from Hotel Goodnight that we didn't attract too much unwelcome attention in Davis Park. For a week in mid-July, a lady editor from William Morrow, named Liz Ostling, came out. She worked with Steve on the final edit of *Pollen Kisses,* his autobiography. For Liz, we dropped the bedroom noise levels, and became highly civilized. Then, in mid-August, Marian came out for the rest of the summer. My sis chewed us out about conditions in the kitchen.

"No wonder some of you are sick," she scolded us. We drooped our ears, and scrubbed out the refrigerator with baking soda.

One more summer thing happened. Chino and Marian looked thoughtfully into each other's eyes, and a faint blue lightning licked the air between them.

It was hard to fault Marian — healthy young wife, with ailing old husband. If I were in the same situation, I'd be hungry for intimacy myself. But I had winced at the sting-ray of jealousy, so I wondered how Joe would feel. And I wondered about our cormorant. Was he bi? Twenty-five years ago, I'd traded those same bi looks with Mary Ellen Rache at a senior high-school prom. Two flesh-and-blood sons were born out of that lightning. My ex-wife was now a sworn enemy, believing that I was a child molester. During the Olympic uproars, I got a hate letter from my youngest boy, Kevin. The oldest, Michael, had stayed remote. Had God punished me by taking my sons away?

For the next three weeks, what we saw of Chino's and Marian's "relationship" was a ripple on deep waters.

They never went in each other's rooms. But suddenly Tito didn't come around any more.

Sometimes, on evenings when Chino was off duty, he and Marian walked on the beach, and over to the Davis Park marina. There, the Casino sat grandly on a dune — jukebox music and a straight roadhouse atmosphere. Baymen flocked there, in hopes of getting laid by one of those liberated women they'd heard so much about. Our twosome lounged at the bar, where they were stared at as a "racially mixed couple". They came back with war stories as hairy as any you'd hear in The Grove. Like the one about the girl who did 100 guys in one weekend, for an average of two an hour.

"Gosh, it makes the Meat Rack look a little tame," Harry commented.

In the third week of August, just as I started to think our tight security at the Hotel was a waste of time, my mail was forwarded from Prescott. It included the first LEV. letter in a while. The envelope, a "business reply" thing, had no postmark.

YOU'RE HAVING A WONDERFUL TIME — WISH I WAS THERE — YOU AND VINCE MAKE SUCH A BEAUTIFUL COUPLE — LIKE YOU HAVE NOTHING TO FEAR
LOVE
LEV.

When Chino and Harry read it, they exchanged glances.

"This guy's surveillance is good," Harry said. "Usually it's half obvious if you look for it. You know, the van parked across the street with all the antennas on it. The car tailing you. LEV.'s smooth. He's got good hardware."

"Why do you think he waited so long to write?" I asked.

"Maybe," Chino said wryly, "he has to stop now and then, and make a few bucks. This is his way of saying he's been tied up."

On the next trip to the mainland, Harry made a Xerox of this newest letter, and sent the original to Julius.

Labor Day was approaching. With a shock, I realized that the summer was almost over. In a week, I'd be back on the Prescott campus, trying to be a teacher again.

It was a seller's market in clams, with everybody wanting to dine out or do clam bakes, so the price of neck soared to $35. Vince and I went out three days running, dug 19 bushels, and made $665. Vince had thrown off his flu, and he worked like a dog. We kept the cherries and chowders for the house, and everybody cooked a Rhode Island chowder and a clam pie. Chino, who'd learned to love fish in Asia, swore he'd never eat another clam.

Saturday night on Labor Day weekend was the great orgasm of the summer's partying.

Harry, Steve and Angel stayed at the Hotel — they were feeling a little under the weather. But Marian and Chino headed for the Casino because they wanted to slow-dance. The rest of us — Bark, Vince and I — rode the beach taxi to The Grove. Vince was content not to dance, just to amble the boardwalks with my arm around him.

When we came home at 2 a.m., Marian and Chino were still gone, and didn't come back till dawn. Their eyes were somber and they had an air of having sat in the dunes, talking, maybe making out a little. The rest of us were at the dining table, deep in a heavy rap about the growing truculence of the religious extremists, and growing violence against gays and lesbians. The room was blue with cigarette smoke. As Marian quietly made herself some tea in the kitchen, Chino sat down at the table, and joined our talk without a beat.

"You wanted us for the summer — the summer's over," he said to me. "Now what?"

"Yeah," said Harry. "We ought to get back to California for a while, and pick up on other business."

A feeling of anticlimax came over me. Almost disappointment that LEV. hadn't showed.

"Well," I said, "I'll carry on alone for a while, and we'll see what happens."

L ater that morning, the two vets and I went for a walk along the bay, so we could have a last private talk. We felt sad to be leaving Fire Island — she was glowing in sunshine. Beach plums were ripening, monarch butterflies already landing in the warm dunes. Harry was a contrast — still dangling a tag-end of flu, off color, out of sorts. He and Chino had little to say about LEV. The fact was — if LEV. had been the second guy in Montreal, so far he had not felt moved to shoot again. He didn't even make threatening phone calls.

What would squeeze his trigger finger?

"We don't know," Harry shrugged.

"Does Vince suspect that we're trying to turn him?" I asked.

"If he does," said Chino, "he's staying cool."

"But we're getting a point across," said Harry. "He's seeing why amateurs don't make it as terrorists. Why the Weathermen aren't around any more. Demons of darkness like us . . . the ones who get paid by the government . . . are gonna rain on his pinko parade."

Gulls wheeled, feeding on butterflies with tattered wings that fell to the water.

"So," Harry added, "he's gotta be a demon of darkness too."

"And," Chino added, "we're saying to him, Hey, man, don't be an amateur or they'll grease you. Get into the paramilitary . . . get trained."

I was shocked at this new twist. My hope had been that they'd simply talk Vince out of his anger. Now they were talking about the organizations and institutions where a private citizen can put together some quasi-military skills. Ranger schools. NRA firearms classes. Academies for pro bodyguards. Mountaineering schools. Sky-divers, scuba-divers. And, as they'd already mentioned, combat vets who tutor civilians for a fat fee.

"And those circles tend to be real conservative," said

Harry. "So he'd have to hack the right-wing shit. Get a new identity — pass as a redneck."

"If he went that route, how long would it take to get trained?" I asked.

"If he works hard, three years . . . maybe," Harry mused.

"He'll need lots of green," Chino said. "Training isn't cheap. Weapons, gear —"

"Vince doesn't have a nickel," I said.

"Julius," said Harry, "has nickels. And he owes me one. I saved his life once. I've asked him if he'd take Vince on. Of course, Vince won't know we have a deal with him. Julius will just happen to cross paths with Vince. And I guarantee our kiddo will jump at Julius' offer. Julius can protect Vince. See that he gets into the right drills."

"Is Julius gay?" I asked.

"Gay as a goose."

Probably Vince would sleep with this guy, as part of the deal. Instantly jealousy showed its Medusa face, with its drag-queen wig of writhing snakes. No wonder Chino and Harry wanted to keep me at arm's length.

"Good plan," I said, choking down my bile. "Except one thing."

"What?"

"You're helping him become a terrorist."

"This way," said Chino, "we have some control over where he is . . . what he learns. If we turn him, we can use that training someday."

"Are you guys crazy?" I exploded.

"No," said Harry patiently. "We're saner than you are. He's set his mind, Harlan. You can't force him to change it."

"We know how you feel about him," Chino added. "But you're acting like some parent, trying to pry your kid out of a student radical group."

"Most important," said Harry, "the plan buys time. Some time for him to cool down."

A battered monarch butterfly had lit on Chino's arm. We all watched as it fanned its wings with slow and dying dignity. I could see the logic of their plan, but I was feeling a deep panic.

"Let Vince be his own man," Harry insisted. "Make his own decision whether he wants to go to the end of the limb."

"Because there's still the big question," added Chino. "Vince talks loco. But can he pull the trigger? None of us know till we go to do it."

There was a dreadful palpitation in my stomach.

"You're playing with people's lives," I said.

"They're playing with *our* lives," Chino said.

"You got a better plan?" Harry challenged.

"What if Vince gets itchy for action before three years is up?" I asked. "What if he goes out of control?"

Chino looked directly into my eyes.

"If things go FUBAR," he said, "you won't want to know."

The message was clear. They might hijack Vince for one last try at turning him, and they'd be kind, if possible. Failing that — if the safety of the gay community hung in the balance — Vince would have a "mysterious accident". I didn't doubt their ruthlessness, or their ability to get away with it. It was a horrible, gut-wrenching moment.

Harry was looking tired. He rubbed his hands over his face, and turned away.

Chino read my mind. He said quietly, "Trust us, Harlan."

He raised his arm, and the butterfly wavered off and landed in the water. A gull scooped it up.

The next day — our last day on the Beach, maybe our last day forever — Vince and I went out in the clam-boat. We found a good spot in the east end of the bay, with no other boats near. The work was an excuse to be alone. I was filled with dread and desire and tenderness — the pain of not having him near. Naked to the waist, our torsos tanned almost black by now, we alternated raking and culling. Nobody worried much about skin cancer in those days. A few oysters came up in the rake, and we ate them right there — sucked them alive out of the half-shell, juice running down our chins.

Vince was silent, bringing me coffee, hovering close. He'd been struggling not to smoke, and he smelled clean. Several times, between grabs, we stripped and dove overboard to swim.

I fondled him in the water — whorls drifting around his thighs like a salmon's milt. Hauling ourselves out, we lay naked in the wet gritty bottom of the boat, on an old army blanket, where nobody could see us. You never knew if a clammer a quarter mile away had binoculars.

"Oh God," he whispered, his face against my belly, "I can't get enough of you."

"Stay with me at the college." I was caressing his neck.

"Please don't ask."

"Why?" I asked.

"Because going back to Prescott is a defeat. I've gotta ... like ... move ahead. You know? Commit to something. I'm 26 ... no future, no money." His warm breath between my thighs, his lips searching. "You called me a whore ... I *am* a fucking whore. Even with you, it's been putting out to have a place to sleep. I feel so lost."

Closing my eyes, I nodded and let my head fall back.

His mouth took me, and the sun poured down on us. I held his head with both hands, feeling his hunger and heartbreak draw my entrails, knowing there was no detour between his age and mine. And was I so wise? Instead, I gave him food more alive than the oyster broth we'd sucked. Afterward he slid up along me, our damp bodies pressing together every way they could, and with eyes closed, he gave me his warm spermy lips and tongue in a long, long kiss. He smelled and tasted like the sea. For a moment, my numbness melted and I was skin to skin with a real person, no image of beauty, but a man whose heat and life were all the more precious to me because I couldn't do anything to protect him. If he died, it would be violently, and far away from me, and I might not ever know how it happened.

Chino and Harry were right. I had to let him go.

He opened his eyes, those amber eyes of a wolf, and looked into mine with a strange calm, and suddenly I remembered how he'd said I would fall for him.

Caressing him, my hands felt his armpits, and he winced.

"What?" I asked.

"Oh ... nodes a little sore. Guess I'm still fighting that flu."

Later that afternoon, our boat thrummed into the Patchogue

marina with six bushels of neck on. We were dressed now, ready for public viewing, hair tight in ponytails, sunglasses on. The post-beatnik drop-out and his rock 'n' roll cull-boy. Vince had his travel bag and jacket in the cabin. From here, he'd walk to the storage place, get his fancy car, and drive to wherever his choices led him.

At the trucks, neck had dropped to $25 — the holiday was over, and it was a buyer's market. No matter. We got $150.

I put half the cash in his hand. He already had the $330 from before Labor Day.

"Thanks," he said.

His beautiful eyes were hidden behind the sunglasses now. No hugs or big dramatic farewells on the quay. But he smiled. "Take care, Harlan. See you."

"Stay in touch," I said.

My next stop would be the boatyard, where I'd park the boat for the winter. I got busy washing her down, so I wouldn't see Vince walking away across the marina parking lot.

TEN

Autumn 1978

A fter Labor Day, Steve and Angel usually stayed on the Island till October. But this year, they closed the Hotel early. Angel wasn't well — lymph glands swollen. Steve was bone-tired himself. I was concerned that he'd contracted some druggie bug from Angel, but Steve shrugged and said he'd stopped using Angel's needles during the summer. The two went home to their Manhattan apartment.

Marian and I drove the two vets to Kennedy. As the L.A. flight was called, Chino kissed my sister gently on the cheek, and said, "I'll write."

To me, he said, "Don't let up. LEV. may be waiting for us to go." Then the two men were gone, down the jetway.

Back in the parking lot, as we got into Marian's car, with the giant jets thundering over our heads, she leaned onto my shoulder, sobbing.

"Why does love hurt so much?" she asked.

I wished I knew, and tried to comfort her.

"What about Joe?" I asked.

"We haven't been husband and wife for a while. His

health is going, and he understands how I feel about Chino. But he's my best friend, and I can't bring myself to —"

Why did I feel just a little bit possessive about Chino?

On the way to Prescott, we stopped at a barber, who shaved my beard and cut my hair back to whitewalls.

E ven with beefed-up security, the college had its familiar back-to-school uproar. Around the brick buildings, the first red glowed in maple trees whose outlines I knew by heart. Behind the athletic center, summer dandelions had gone to seed in the lawns around our beautiful new track. Marian and I were a bit behind, so we plunged into paperwork and meetings. I looked at my campus house with new eyes, and improved security there.

On September 15th we greeted incoming students. A week after that, Betsy and I joined forces with Mike Stella, the associate coach, for track tryouts. Mike had been a straight buddy of Billy's on the '76 Olympic team. In November, the college was going to host its own track meet.

Missing Vince felt like marrow being drawn out of my bones. I missed Harry too, and Chino even more.

Some conservative parents were angry that I was still heading the athletic department, and they withdrew their kids. Because of the school's stand on gay rights, our enrollment and alumni funding had dropped since Montreal. But it looked like my effort to stay out of the public eye was working. Other, more important events had lured the media away. My heart was boggled at the way most of the students were hotly loyal to me. And I was going to field a good track team.

That year, 1978-79, a few more talented college runners did seek us out. I would coach Gary South. And Betsy would coach Linda Crippen, who would just miss a berth on the 1980 Olympic team.

F alcon was a year old on September 2. But we delayed the party a couple of weeks because his grandfather was tied up in court. When the clan finally gathered, Vince came up from New York and John flew in from San Francisco. With John, in his rented airport car, came a surprise — a young family we knew. A young father of 25, with a muscular sprinter's build, china-blue eyes sparkling with antic humor, and frizzy auburn hair held by a hippie headband. His slender blonde wife, and their blonde baby girl.

"Jacques!" I said, opening the car door on his side.

"Hey, coach," said Jacques LaFont. He gave me a tentative kind of straight-he-man hug.

"It's been a while since I yelled at you," I said, hugging him back.

"Goddam dipdunk lazy kid," he said, imitating my Parris Island manner during track practice years ago. "Get those knees up! You run like a goddam girl!"

I winced.

"I don't say stuff like that any more," I said. "The feminists on campus would kill me."

Jacques smiled slyly. This young bird always reminded me of a ringneck pheasant — an artist of evasive flying.

"Well, you'll always be Mr. Knees Up to me," he said. "You remember Eileen. And this is Ana . . ."

I inspected their tow-headed youngster in Eileen's arms. Ana looked at me and screamed. We all laughed. Hearing the uproar, Vince came out of the house, and stopped in his tracks. This was a delicate moment — the two ex-lovers seeing each other for the first time in three years. Vince recovered himself in a split second.

"Heya, Jacques, old buddy," he said, giving Jacques the same kind of sterile hug that Jacques had given me.

Eileen studied Vince with a level stare. Jacques had told Eileen about his relationship with Vince. She had trusted his announcement that he was going straight forever. But her family hadn't trusted it — they hated Jacques. She'd gone over their heads to marry him.

Joe Prescott had cooked up the LaFont surprise. Due to a summer resignation, an assistant's vacancy had opened on the science faculty. The job wasn't much, but better than nothing. A moving van would bring their things in a few days.

The birthday party was held at Betsy's new house, half

a mile off campus. The old two-bedroom stone house stood in a gnarly apple orchard. I wasn't too worried about LEV. watching the party — Betsy had been in the clan for years, and it would be logical for us to celebrate with her, even if the baby's father was a stranger. Marian and her daughter Sara had festooned the living room with yellow crepe streamers and autumn leaves in vases. Jacques and Eileen helped fix hamburgers and baked beans. We wanted an easy cleanup because of early classes in the morning.

Just before it started to rain at dark, Vince and I arrived with the birthday cake we'd made. It was a carrot cake in a big pan, using a supposedly foolproof recipe borrowed from Marian. Some gay men are good cooks — we weren't among them. But the cake hadn't fallen, and it smelled good.

Betsy opened the door into the chill autumn twilight, drenching us with indoor warmth and light. Her face glowed with pride at her new home — the first of her own that she'd ever had. How I wished she had a lover in it!

We hugged her, and gave her the cake.

"*You* guys made this?" she wanted to know.

"By the time we got done, there was flour even on the front gate," Vince joked.

"Fire Island mellowed you two Neanderthals," she said.

Thoughts of security kept crossing my mind. Was it safe, even here? I looked around for bugging devices. Going outside, I walked around in the rainy dark to check the property, then came back, wondering if I was just becoming a psychiatry-textbook paranoid.

Last came John Sive and Joe Prescott, bringing ice cream and candles. Joe had just been diagnosed with emphysema — he came up the walk with slow steps, breathing heavily, wearing the small oxygen tank that his doctor had ordered.

"Happy birthday, dear Falcon . . .
"Happy birthday, dear Falcon . . ."

The baby was held up so he could see the one flickering candle on the cake. As we all blew it out, he gave a shriek of delight. Presents were simple — toddler clothes, gift certificates. John Sive gave Betsy an envelope with the papers for a trust fund that he'd started for Falcon's college education.

Falcon didn't give a hoot about the presents — he was bent on celebrating Year 1 by walking for the first time. With most of us sitting cross-legged in a circle on the worn Oriental rug, we all encouraged his tries. He walked a step or two, and fell. Walked a step or two, and fell. His shock of black hair looked like it was wired for sound. Finally he was up, and going — across the circle, from Auntie Marian over to his mom. Then back across to Daddy Harlan.

We all cheered. Marian was snapping pictures with a flash camera. Joe and Old John beamed from the wing chairs by the fireplace. As Falcon got the idea that I was encouraging him to run, he came charging to me again and again. I loved it, grabbing him up to nuzzle his belly-button. It was the first real flash of Billy that I had seen in him.

"He's going to be a sprinter," I gloated. "Already doing intervals."

"The first gay President of the United States," said Vince. "And he'll sign an emancipation proclamation for gays and lesbians."

"Oh, come on," Betsy cut in. "If he turns out to be a bi anchorman, or a straight chef, and he's happy, that'll be okay."

Ana and Falcon, loose on the floor together, got into a baby brawl, and had to be rescued from each other. As we lingered by the warm fireplace with coffee and tea, our silver-haired old lawyer stared into the fire with his grandson drowsing on a blanket on his lap. His coolness to me had warmed a little in the sentiments of the day. We talked about the baby.

". . . And on my side, Falcon is the third generation of the dynasty," John was saying. "I'm gay, Billy was gay. But the kid here . . . who knows? And I don't believe that genes are everything. But I do think that we're born what we are."

From there, we got into the perennial argument.

"Chino says the whole concept of gay and straight is bullshit," I said. "He thinks we're all bi-sexual on a scale of 1 to 10."

"What about past lives?" Vince put in.

As she listened to us, Eileen's face was expressionless — our blunt talk bothered her. Now and then, she returned my studying look. She had not failed to notice that I was having an affair with the second of the now-infamous "three gay runners". Did she wonder if I would steal Jacques from her? Meanwhile, as she was glaring at me, I noticed that Jacques was staring fixedly at Vince, with an expression that could only mean one thing. My stomach sank. If Vince noticed, he didn't let on — he was talking baby talk and taking Falcon from John Sive.

Steve and Angel hadn't come. Angel didn't feel well enough for the 90-minute drive. But Harry and Chino called from L.A. with birthday wishes.

"Hey, man," Chino told me, "I'm going to AA meetings. And I enrolled at UCLA. Thanks for encouraging me."

The following weekend, I looked in on Steve and Angel. Unshaven, Steve was grouching around his messy apartment. Piles of untouched paperwork littered his desk. Angel was asleep in his own bedroom.

Angel was sweating and feverish at night, Steve said — the boy's bed was drenched in the morning. His lymph nodes were the size of marbles, very sore. Sometimes he seemed confused. Steve was worried. He'd missed a deadline for an *Esquire* fiction piece. "Ten thousand bucks I've lost," he complained.

"Better get Angel to Doc Jacobs," I said. "Knock it out of his system, whatever it is."

"Yeah," Steve agreed. "I dread doctors — he hates being touched. But maybe he's got mono, or something."

My journalist friend Bruce Cayton was also back in town. He'd just completed a postwar update on Vietnam for *Harper's*. Bruce knew that the gay world was the only American fringe with no violent politics yet, so he'd been intrigued at the first wispy rumors of Gay Panthers. He wanted to interview Vince and me. How much had he found out about Vince's new revolutionary activities?

I told Bruce I'd think about it, then called Harry.

Harry mused. "For a reporter, Cayton is pretty sharp. In Vietnam I was always afraid he'd see through my closet door."

"Any problem with Vince or me doing this interview?"

"Not if you keep it a backgrounder . . . off the record."

So, that warm autumn evening, Bruce and I rendez-voused with Vince on Christopher Street by the church. From among the loitering young people and clouds of pot smoke on the church steps, Vince ambled out with his rangy walk. My lover was losing his Fire Island glow — he had been in the city for weeks. He was dressed with surprising conservatism — wrinkled navy blazer and preppie loafers.

"Hi, Harlan," he said to me, as if we'd seen each other yesterday.

Staring at him, I realized how our passion had eroded down to the purely sexual. And, for me, sexual wasn't enough. Respect, and care, and dignity, and discipline, had to be there too.

The three of us walked together. In front of the Bad-lands club, a couple hundred young males in rut were milling around, eyeing one another, cups of beer in their hands. Sweaty tank tops jostled naked torsos, here and there a black leather vest. By contrast, Bruce, in horn-rimmed glasses, looked like a Foreign Service functionary forging through the claustrophobic crowds of some Bangkok avenue. Gay men eyed Bruce suspiciously, thinking he was FBI. Carloads of straight tourists drove slowly by, eyeing the gay men.

The three of us sank down in the dimly lit Cafe Figaro. Bruce and Vince chain-smoked, adding to the haze.

"Vince, you've been a visible activist. Maybe you can tell me . . . where are the *violent* gay radicals?"

"American radicalism has failed," shrugged Vince.

"Gay violence has time-lagged behind other movements. Seems like it's time for Gay Panthers. I mean . . . I've been on this story two weeks, talked to Rayburn and other people, and I feel like I've been fire-hosed with gay anger."

Vince mused his answer. Clearly he was walking the discreet side of honest.

"SDS and Weatherman flopped," he finally said, "because they thought millions of Americans would join them."

The café was crowded, hot, noisy, pressing us into our corner with its noise. Amid the noise, sipping my tea, I realized that I'd never heard Vince be so articulate.

"You're not a Maoist, are you?" Bruce asked.

"Shit no. Communists don't treat fags any better than capitalists do. Look at Castro . . . he treats us like Hitler did. Reinaldo Arenas, their best writer, is in fucking prison. That's . . . like . . . what makes our struggle so unique."

"So what is the alternative to violence, for gay people?" Bruce pursued.

"Guilt, and a good body."

Bruce knew gay humor. "Seriously, now."

"If Gay Panthers were smart, they'd study what happened to all the other violent American fronts," said Vince. "Learn from their mistakes. Nobody wins a war of attrition . . . especially if you're outnumbered. We gays and lesbians are outnumbered. Ten to one, at best. Terrible odds for Panthers, if you ask me."

"Answer my question," said Bruce patiently. "What would *your* non-violent strategy be?"

Vince grinned.

"If I told a reporter my strategy," he said, "I'd be dumb."

Bruce looked at Vince musingly through the smoke.

"Are there any pro-violence groups that I might talk to?" he asked.

"I don't know of any," Vince shrugged.

"George Rayburn said you might know."

"George is out of touch with my thinking."

"What have you been into, these days?" Bruce probed. "Crash and burn on promiscuity, I suppose? Café society? Nothing noble or meaningful?" He was trying another tactic, playing the mindless asshole, trying to sting information out of Vince.

The tactic failed. "Burned out on activism," said Vince gloomily. "I gotta get a capitalist job. Or sell my car and take some film courses at NYU."

I watched Vince try to juju this adroit old investigator off his trail.

"Bruce," Vince added, "don't go looking for commie conspiracies. Some ordinary guy whose lover was beat to death by cops is more likely to fire-bomb the White House."

Bruce turned to me, hoping to use me to open Vince up. "Harlan, what's your view on gay activism these days?"

"I still think the modified Gandhi approach can work for us."

"As I recall," Bruce drawled, "'modified' means that Gandhi carries a loaded .45 in his loincloth."

Like Vince, I wasn't going to tell Bruce my real thoughts either. "I've never fired a shot," I countered. "And there are enough gays in America to make peaceful boycotts work. One in ten still gives us an edge, if we cut where it counts."

A few mornings later, back on campus, I opened my door to find a *National Intelligencer* reporter and his photographer there. They'd eluded campus security, and lurked in my bushes all night. Blood rushed to my head — I'd let my guard down a little. If they'd been LEV., he could have shot me dead on my front step.

"Mr. Brown," the reporter said, "can you tell us if you now have a relationship with Vince Matti? And we understand that Jacques LaFont is back . . . ."

Media scrutiny had started in early 1976, when Billy's and my relationship was exposed. I was 40, Billy was 23. I was his teacher, his coach. Everything about our story hit a pulsing nerve in the rotting tooth of American puritanism. Billy's short, mundane life had offered little juice to the moralists. But my "dark past" offered ripe squeezings. In New York City, after I lost my Penn State job and owed thousands in child-support, I did a thing that even hard-up straight men quietly do — turned tricks for a couple of years. Americans who'd said that hippie boys should be shot because they went barefoot were saying now that I should be slowly roasted to death in public. These people assumed I was carrying on with all three of the boys at once. HARLAN'S HAREM, the *Intelligencer* had called them.

Now, two years later, a few tabloids, gossip columnists, and right-wing commentators were still tracking me.

The next day, I had to reassure Eileen about Jacques. She had been visibly jealous, because he had been running with me every morning, and helping me plan the track meet. All the campus maples were afire with color that day. I sat with Eileen at the picnic table in her back yard. The two of us could hear the traffic on the nearby expressway, as the annual migration of tourists headed for New England to "view the colors". Red and gold leaves fell around us.

Flung on the table between us was the copy of the *Intelligencer*.

"Eileen," I said, "Jacques and I were *never* interested in each other, ever. Can you believe that?"

She fixed me with her intense light-blue eyes. "Jacques admires you so much. He never talks about Vince."

"He's probably afraid of hurting you, by mentioning Vince."

A leaf fell on her hair, and she left it there.

"Jacques and I are going to run together in the 5-K open at our meet," I told her. "Do you think you can hack that? He's going to be my rabbit. I'm aiming for the national masters' mile again this winter."

Eileen sighed, maybe seeing the ridiculousness of her jealous fantasies. I'd seen the silliness of mine with Vince.

"Why don't you help with the race?" I pressed her. "Be there with us. I'd like that."

Mike Stella and my track team sent a letter to the tabloid, stating their support of me. Bruce Cayton wrote too. So did Aldo Franconi, an old Metropolitan AAU ally. The letters were never printed, of course. With Joe failing, it was Marian who dealt with the press. Jacques and I gave no interviews. Meanwhile, with administration approval, I built a fence around the house, and got a big ugly Doberman to put inside it. If the media wanted to do my dog with a silenced .22, let them try.

It was good to have Jacques back. He settled into assisting with advanced biology. His humor made him popular with the students. Now and then he made a quick trip to the city alone, supposedly to do library research, but I had an eerie feeling he was tricking. Had he tried to look Vince up? Knowing the mood Vince was in, my lover had probably brushed him off.

Vince was drifting away from me. I saw him in the city a couple more times — he was surly and restless, and not much fun in bed. It wasn't clear whether Julius had materialized yet. Vince had somehow patched up his differences with Rayburn, and was staying with him. But he barely had enough money to scrape by, and had probably fallen back on dealing ounces of pot. His NYU courses bored him. He did a little running to keep fit.

On October 19, Vince made his second and last visit to the campus, and we had our first fight since Fire Island. Deer season was open, and distant shots in the woods echoed the fact that something was up with him. I tried to talk to him. But he just exploded in my face. The last I saw of Vince, he was in the red car, heading off campus with a screech of tires. I knew he had about $50 to his name.

"Well," I told Harry on the phone, "Vince can sell the car."

"He won't have to," said Harry's voice. "Destiny calls."

My young bird had finally flown away to Julius.

The last Saturday of October, our track meet dawned partly cloudy and cool — the runner's idea of a perfect day. Busloads of athletes arrived from other colleges around the Northeast — fewer than we'd hoped for. But the 5-K open had a good entry, co-sponsored with the Road Runners Club of America. Distance-running fever was hitting America, and the once-tiny RRCA had swelled into a national club with muscle. Our bleachers were actually full. The green field was full of runners, rock music and the echoing voice of the loudspeaker. Mike Stella was our official host, holding forth at the mike with his Italian wit. Betsy was out there with her squad of women runners.

Keeping to my low profile, I stayed behind the scenes. I had put Vince out of my mind.

It was really going to work. I was going to outkick Them.

Quietly, Jacques and I went to the RRCA table, where Eileen was in charge of the entry sheets. She looked like she'd cooled out.

"Hi, guys," she smiled, giving us our numbers. "Good luck."

I was boiling with energy, in good shape from a summer of running on sand and working on the water.

The 5-K was the final event of the afternoon. At the start, 231 motley runners, women and men of all ages, crowded tensely onto the road, behind the white starting-line. Jacques and I were seeded in the front.

My eyes followed the curve of the road ahead. The five-kilometer course followed a paved service road along an uphill loop through our 500 acres of campus woods. It was the last weekend of deer season, and the woods were a magnet for hunters. The drunks and trigger-happy among them had always made stray bullets a hazard. Campus security had already found several dead and dying deer out there. Today people would be gunning avidly for the deer they hadn't got yet. So campus guards were posted along the course, to keep irresponsible shooters off our necks.

I felt a brief pang, wishing Vince were running with us.

"Runners . . . get set," called Mike Stella.

At the starting gun, we sprang forward.

It felt so good.

Running easily together, Jacques and I sat back and let Gary South and the early leaders forge ahead. My young bird moved with the powerful, churning stride so familiar to me.

Biding our time, we stayed in the front of the pack. I moved with the press of bodies, trading nudges of elbows. I loved this rough play. The colorful stream of runners poured into the tree-lined tunnel of woods. Humid smells of leaves filled our lungs. Shadows of tree trunks slipped across us. Falling leaves brushed us. Far off in the neighboring property, came the single echoing shot of somebody's .3030. Here and there, silent guards watched us pass.

Jacques glanced at his stopwatch, tracking our time.

The field was stringing out now. Jacques and I kept a light contact with the leaders, staying in the front of the pack.

At kilometer 3, the six leaders were starting a drive. So Jacques and I picked up our pace, starting to haul them down. We were at the top of the grade now, in the deepest woods. The road ran along the foot of a ridge — it was in bad condition, very potholed, and I made a quick note to talk to Joe about asphalting it. From nearer, somewhere on campus property, came another shot. I noticed the nearest campus guard start off in pursuit of the trespasser.

About 50 seconds later, I heard a strange *phhhhht,* and a slap. It sounded like a hand smacking aginst flesh. A lot of confused echoes were rolling away. Jacques uttered a sharp barking cry, and stumbled.

For a moment, I thought he'd stepped in a pot-hole, and twisted an ankle.

But Jacques was clutching his left shoulder. His face was going pale with pain. Red liquid was springing out between his fingers. At first my brain simply refused to recognize that it was blood, but I did see the need for race safety. As I grabbed him, and swerved us to the side, the next two runners almost collided with us and fell. Then they got their balance, and kept running.

"Jeez," one of them yelled angrily at us.

Jacques stood on the side of the road, groaning with pain. The whole left side of his jersey was soaking red now. Then slowly, with great dignity, he sat down on the gravel shoulder and hung his head in shock. I kneeled by him, and pulled his red slippery fingers away to see an inch-wide hole in his shoulder just below his collarbone, that was spilling dark red. A hiss of violent emotion rushed into the vacuum in my mind. In that moment, I knew.

A campus guard was at our side.

"I think he's been shot," I said.

"Fucking hunters," the guard said violently, grabbing his walkie.

But I knew it wasn't hunters. It was Billy, all over again. It was Montreal. It wasn't ever going to end. Speeding lead had dropped a second young bird of mine. My runner, my kid, my student, who was supposed to be safe with me — so young, warm plumage, bright eyes eager for life. In that moment, I felt as close to insane as I ever did in my life. I wanted to kill, to tear my enemies limb from limb, to shout and rave and accuse, to haul down the whole dry-rotted structure of hate around my own ears and die underneath it — sacrifice my life to end the lie, like Samson.

"Harlan," Jacques whispered shakily, "what happened?"

"Hang on, Billy," I said without thinking. "They're coming."

"Billy?" he said, dazed.

Runners poured on by, glancing at us curiously. A couple stopped. I shielded Jacques from their eyes with my body, so nobody saw the blood. We didn't need panic and a crowd of rubberneckers.

"Keep running, assholes," I yelled at them in the voice of a Parris Island gunny gone mad.

The guard was speaking into his walkie, calling the squad car, the ambulance.

I knew. I knew.

ELEVEN

C hino had grabbed the next nonstop flight from Los Angeles. Harry hadn't come — H-C had landed their first job in a while. As I met Chino by the athletic building, I had done everything possible to calm myself down, after the rage and hysteria and near loss of control of yesterday. But my voice was still unsteady.

"The doctors took a dozen bits of bullet out of Jacques' shoulder," I told him. "The police say it's probably a .22 hollow-point that fragmented."

"Are you surprised, man?" Chino drawled.

Alone, we walked that service road into the woods. It was an unseasonably hot day, so my pants and polo shirt were sticking to me. But Chino, with his old fanaticism about keeping clean in the jungle, looked like he'd just stepped out of the shower. As always, he was dressed to blend in — khaki pants, and a brown T-shirt showing off his strong arms with veins pumped by the heat. His ebony hair was sleeked into a rubber band, and I noticed a white hair or two.

Chino gazed along the crowded tree trunks and thick brush that overshadowed the road.

"The maze of green," he said softly.

We stood listening. At the moment, no police were around.

A late-season bird song rang through the deep woods. Somehow those few notes, and the trickle of falling leaves everywhere, made the woods feel intensely alive, mysterious as an ocean, impenetrable as any cloud forest on the equator. Chino, with his clothing in somber autumn hues, was part of that mystery.

"Rest your eyes," Chino added, "and you can see all the movement there. Everything that moves is something."

My scalp was prickling.

Chino listened to my update. The police swore it was the case of the careless hunter. They had arrested two hunters inside the Prescott property line. One, a kid, was carrying an old .22 rifle and hollow-point ammo. The ballistics people were convinced this would probably be the gun. One local newspaper was in full cry against the evils of firearms.

"There *was* a shot right nearby," I added, "less than a minute before Jacques was hit. But it must have been a hunter. There wasn't an actual *crack, bang,* in the few seconds before Jacques was hit. Just a funny sound, then the slap and the echoes."

Crunching over dead branches and leaves, Chino used my information to locate the hide where the sniper had fired.

It was in a different location than the police had thought — a little natural hole among some granite boulders, under a fallen oak trunk. The site was not a place where hunters would walk through, and was well-camouflaged with brush and fallen leaves. Behind the hide was a ridge piled with more boulders. From here, the sniper commanded a clear view of the service road, 40 yards away. The spot was well within range of a .22 rifle whose performance was cut somewhat by a silencer.

"Very smooth," said Chino. "LEV. planned his 'op' to blend with weekend hunting. He came in here the night before, and parked himself. For camouflage, he probably covered himself with a little net cape with cloth strips sewn on it. Went for the heart shot this time. Probably Jacques made a bobble just then. Avoiding a pothole, or something. When you're shooting that far at a moving target, the tiniest movement out of the pattern can throw you off. He probably analyzed old film footage of you guys running ... each of you has your patterns."

Chino coughed a deep cigarette cough, and added, "He used the boulders to scatter echoes and confuse everybody about his location. After the shot, he probably stuffed the camo net in his knapsack, and just walked right out, using those boulders for cover. He probably wore ordinary hunter's clothing. Nobody would have looked at him twice."

We followed his supposed route, and found that the property line and paved road were just 100 feet away. Hunters parked their vehicles in wide spots on the shoulder. I imagined the sniper getting into a pickup and coolly driving off.

For about 15 minutes, Chino was down in the hole, his brown fingers using a stick to dig around in the dirt and dead leaves. Finally he came up with a brass .22 casing. Carefully, without touching it, he tipped it into a plastic baggie from his pocket.

"This ammo's not new," he said. "Probably bought at a garage sale. You never buy from dealers. You go as anonymous as you can."

"Is he using an old gun?"

"Maybe. One that goes back before they kept good records on gun sales. He's smooth. But not smooth enough, man. He shouldn't have lost this. His first fuck-up. He probably went nuts looking for it. He was pushing his luck to stay any longer, so he scrammed."

"We can prove this came from his gun?" I was trying to think like a trial lawyer.

Chino laughed at me.

"Real life is not the movies. If he's that smooth, he'll do a little re-machining on his barrel now. You can make little changes, so ballistics can't match the markings up. Maybe LEV. does his own gunsmithing. Or his group has a gunsmith. There are lots of tricks. He'll keep moving through his tricks. He won't set a pattern."

"Except one. He likes the .22 rifle."

"Expect him to zig and zag . . . even on that. He shot a rock at you on the Beach."

"Why is he sticking to .22 caliber? It's a kid gun . . . a varmint gun. I plinked with .22s for years. Why not something bigger — high tech?"

"You mean those hot .50 caliber jobs we did in the Nam. Head shots at 3000 feet."

"Yeah."

"This isn't Nam, *compadre*. A .50 caliber hit blows your head off. In the civilian world, an assassin sometimes wants to be more discreet. The .22 has its limits, but it can be a choice little assassin's rifle. Light, easy to customize. If a .22 round hits the head at just the right angle, it whirls inside the brain cavity . . . destroys the brain. Minutes go by before people find the entry-hole and figure out what happened. Gives you more escape time."

I winced.

Chino rested one booted foot on the log, and lit a Tiparillo.

"So, my mate," he said, "this little goat-fuck isn't going to be over tomorrow. Understand?"

I sighed heavily.

"If LEV. was your standard sniper, you'd be dead. When they want to get you, they get you. A sniper has every advantage. But this kind of guy moves into your life and marries you. Harry and I deal with them in L.A. The crazy fan who is nuts about some girl star. Or a photographer who won't let up. LEV. isn't a fan, and he likes to hide in his maze of green. But he's obsessed with you. He wants something."

"What?"

"He shoots into your world during athletic events, and when you make love. That ought to give you a clue."

"Was he aiming at me? Or Jacques?" I asked.

"Jacques. I'm sure of that. And who knows? He may not have intended to kill him." Chino hefted the baggie. "In Montreal, they shot to kill. The Magnum is a hot round that penetrates. This time he used a hollow-point that fragments before it goes deep. That tells me he only wanted to wound . . . maybe to warn you."

"Jacques isn't my lover. If he watches me, he knows that."

"But you're his coach. Maybe in LEV.'s mind, they're the same thing. Notice he hasn't fired at me, and I'm your security. But I'm not your lover, and I'm not your runner."

"What kind of a guy is he?"

"A professional sniper is not your stereotype loco. He's

low-key ... calm ... patient. Good in the woods. Good on detail. Single-minded. Capable of operating on his own for a long time. Detached. But now and then he takes a target personally. He's a surgeon who cuts out human tumors, man. Goes in, targets the disease, goes home and plays golf."

The shock — knowing Chino was right — went right to that flash point of emotion in my sphincter.

"So," I said, "let's say that he and Mech are old sidekicks. Maybe some intense latency there. They go to Montreal to get Billy ... they fuck up and Mech is arrested. So now we have Richie baby in prison and a very angry, heartbroken sidekick outside. That makes me a target that he takes personally."

Chino nodded, looking around thoughtfully.

"If I'm a tumor, why not just kill me?" I asked.

Chino was sucking on the little cigar, which had gone out. "I think he wants to jackal you. Nip you again and again and again. Bleed you slow."

Now the chills were chasing up and down me.

"Harry and me, we both ran our little intel networks in Nam, as part of our jobs, and Harry is a good desk jockey, which I'm not. But basically we're a couple of jungle-bunnies. Julius is the real investigator, and he wants to get serious. This is one of your needle-in-a-haystack things. Dig into Richard Mech's associations, going way back. Cross-check them with police and military records. It might take years, man. Julius has the patience and the connections to do things that Harry and I can't. But we need your okay."

"Jeez ... I don't have that kind of money."

"If you can keep H-C in bullets and beans, we'll hold up the security end. Julius will cover his end, which will be very expensive." He grinned. "Shiiiit, man, I keep hearing about gay money ... let's have it working for us."

"What's my part in this?"

He stared into my eyes. "Go on being your own bodyguard, if you fucking have to. Stay tight with us. And write books."

"Why does Julius care so much?"

"Millions of people saw Billy go down," said Chino quietly. "He was one. He told Harry nobody in this country can kill a good kid like Billy and get away with it."

He carefully put the cold cigar-stub in his pocket instead of flipping it away — an old habit of leaving no traces on his trail. As we headed back to the administration buildings, I looked over my shoulder at the forest. The man who helped kill Billy had just been hiding there.

The maze of green. The tiniest move in its shadows.

My scalp prickled again.

"So I'll send this casing to Julius," Chino was saying. "Maybe there are fingerprints."

He coughed again. "Hear anything from Vince?"

"Not a thing. You smoke too much, my friend."

"Yeah. When I lick the booze, I'm going to quit. My health is not so good. I picked up malaria and other shit in Asia."

"George Rayburn tells me Vince has drifted through New York a couple of times. I figure he and Julius don't want to worry his old movement friends by Vince's dropping out of sight completely. But Vince hasn't been in touch with me."

"Well, Joe and Marian must be freaked out."

"They are. They want to meet with us at noon."

Joe Prescott was sitting behind his big mahogany desk — unusually formal in dark suit and tie. Marian was adjusting his oxygen tank.

Uneasily, I sat down on the visitor side of the desk. Chino prowled the room.

Looking at the sick old man, I remembered a staunch fist-waving liberal who had hauled me out of New York and given me a shot at coaching again. The memory came back, of the snowy morning in December 1974, when he'd come to my office to tell me about three gay boys who'd been kicked off the Oregon State team. Now, this time, Joe called me onto his own turf. I could feel the ax-blade coming.

We went through the ritual. Joe's secretary brought Chino some coffee, and a cup of tea for me. Marian's eyes met Chino's eyes for a split second.

"Harlan," Joe said, "the police want to think it was a hunter. They don't want to think that homosexuals were shot at, because it means they have to protect homosexuals. But just between us, we all know that this is connected to Montreal."

I nodded wearily.

"Marian and I have our responsibility to the students — to parents," said Joe softly. His voice quavered. "We don't want to cater to the moralizing, you understand. But people shooting into the campus is a problem. You're too hot for us right now. Maybe someday, if civil rights get farther ahead, we can start over."

I nodded again.

Now Marian spoke. "You'll give us a letter of resignation today, saying that you want to pursue personal goals as a writer. You can stay on staff till mid-term . . . two months. We'll pay you full salary and a $100,000 parachute. Meanwhile, you can be Mike's consultant. He's taking over, and he values your input. But please keep a *very* low profile. Whoever is doing this, doesn't like you being so public. Our decision is final. Please don't have John Sive talk to us about it. We're . . . sorry."

I stared at my sister, across the gulf opening between us. Tears were standing in her eyes.

For a moment, I felt like throwing their offer in their faces, and quitting. But Marian was right. Why be public, and give LEV. the satisfaction?

"I suppose you have the letter typed already," I said.

They did.

I signed it.

B etsy and the baby were clearly in more danger now. Late that afternoon, as I went by her house, ostensibly to drop off some athletic-department paperwork, I thought about how to approach her.

But she was way ahead of me.

The two of us talked quietly in her back yard, as we weeded around her tomatoes. The lawn under the apple trees was littered with windfalls. Autumn leaf-burning scented the air, and the whole scene was so peaceful. But we kept our heads down, so anyone doing a long-distance visual surveillance couldn't read our lips.

"Falcon and I need to be away from here," she said. "I've been talking to Joe and Marian since that *Intelligencer* story came out, and I sent my résumé around. A community college in northern California wants me. I can start in January."

All my yearnings to have that baby grow up at my side were now crashed.

"Do it," I said, pulling a weed.

"And don't offer to help me. Anything you do calls attention to me and the baby."

I felt a pang. The *familia* (Chino's word was now deep in my brain) was scattering like a covey of quail.

"Chino says . . . if you need him, he'll grab the next plane."

"Thanks," she said, tears rising in her voice. "But whoever they are, they know he's with you. I, uh . . . I'm getting a gun, and I'm taking a firearms safety course. God, if my friends ever find out. Funny, isn't it? The last closet in the gay community is owning a gun."

Suddenly tears streaked down her cheeks.

"Get the bastards, Harlan," she said. "Whoever they are. We shouldn't have to live like this. Get them."

Later that day Chino and I visited Jacques in the local hospital. Our ringneck was sitting up in bed, wearing a huge Earth Day T-shirt in lieu of pajama tops. His wound was a near miss — no damage to bones or the shoulder joint; now it was dressed. Adoring girl students were leaving, and the room was full of flowers and silly gifts.

"Good to meet you, Chino," he said cheerfully, shaking the SEAL's hand. "Heard a lot about you."

We sat down by the bed.

"I don't think this is more Montreal," said Jacques. "Why would they bother with me? I mean, I'm straight now —"

"The police say it was a hunter who missed," said Chino.

"Yeah," I said. "Got you instead of a 12-point buck."

"Good thing my antler isn't decorating somebody's pickup," Jacques commented. "I'm gonna be a father again. Elaine is pregnant." He squeezed my hand. "I wanted you to be the first to know."

Chino and I had already agreed how I'd handle the media questions about leaving Prescott. I'd make the simple offhand comment that it was time for a change. Downshifting out of academe, upshifting into private life as a writer.

Late that night I lay awake in my small bedroom, in the newish Danish-modern bed, still chewing on the rage.

Across the hall, the door to the other, bigger bedroom stood open. It was the guest room now. Chino was sleeping there, curled in the sagging old walnut bed where Billy and I had once slept together. My friend's uneasy, silent sleep filled the house — the sleep of a man who lived his life waiting in ambush. Tomorrow he'd fly back to L.A.

So it had ended. *They* had taken almost everything. Two lovers. My career.

Everything but my life, and my will to outkick Them.

They wouldn't get those.

One Friday morning, as I was waiting out the term, Life balanced out the hurts with healing.

Putting the kettle on for tea, I sat down to read my mail. Since I didn't have much to do on campus now, I could sit back. First, a check for letter-bombs. Then I read. Three moralizing scorchers from clergymen. A psychology professor who wanted to study my gay mind. Seven love letters from men. A straight mother who prayed my example would help her confused boy.

Last was an envelope from the Hames-West Institute for Hemophilia Research in Manhattan.

Reading it, I snapped to attention.

Dear Dad,

It is amazing how the family uptightness has affected me all this time, because deep down I didn't agree with it. If you decide to throw this letter away, and not answer it, I will understand.

It has made me angry to see your personal life spread all over the media. When I saw the latest crap in the *National Intelligencer,* I got mad enough that I decided to try and contact you. If you are interested in seeing me, that would be truly copacetic. Call me at home or the office.

Your son,
Michael

T he teakettle was whistling, forgotten.

Turning off the flame, I re-read the letter many times with heart hammering. From my dresser, I grabbed the old studio-portrait of Michael, 3, and Kevin, 2, and looked at it. Kevin, the extrovert, was as blond as my wife. Michael, the shy one, my firstborn, was dark like me. He would be 25 now.

"Michael Brown's in a meeting," the Hames-West operator said with a Jersey twang. "May I take a message?"

For 82 minutes, I paced around the house, waiting for the return call. John Sive arrived, to talk about parents who were suing Prescott because of me. I couldn't keep my mind on what he was saying. Since Falcon's birthday, John had felt a little closer to me. Smiling wryly, he asked if I had a new lover.

When the phone finally rang, I almost dropped it.

A quiet young tenor voice said, "Dad?"

"Michael."

"Dad. Oh shit," he blurted. "I can't believe I'm talking to you." Then, "Oops. Maybe you don't like four-letter words. I'm a child of the Seventies."

"I'm a child of the ages."

He laughed. "You talk like I thought you would. I . . . can't believe you're not mad at me."

"Let's talk face to face."

"I'll be at the New York Public Library tomorrow to do some research. Meet me at one, by the lions?"

When I hung up, John saluted me with his cup of coffee.

"I knew it," he said. "A lover."

"Guess again, John."

When I told him, his eyes misted, and I realized that my

gain had reminded him of his loss. We sat together in silence for a while, and I held his hand, while the tough trial lawyer cried with the other hand over his face.

After John left, an awful thought came to me. Supposing LEV. had gotten to my kid, and my kid was going to help them kill me? Why not? Michael had been brought up to think I was evil.

Half an hour early, on the library steps, I stood hidden behind the downtown lion.

Nobody noticed the guy in Kangol cap, shabby corduroy jacket, stick-on sideburns and mustache, and horn-rimmed sunglasses. Despite their stains of pigeon shit, the two stone lions stood proud — an interesting symbol for a Leo who was about to find a lost cub. My knees vibrated with tension. Was this the way I'd feel if I was going to see LEV. face to face?

At 12:55 a young man came out, carrying a folder and looking around nervously.

Right away I knew it was my son. In fact, the male chauvinist part of me gloated to see how my genes had overridden my wife's. He was a little shorter than my six feet, but he had my features, bones, eye color — even my contempt for fashion. The wrinkled tweed jacket had homemade elbow-patches. His button-down shirt and fluttering tie didn't match each other or anything else. But had he inherited the gay part? For all his macho vibration, Michael looked desk-job soft, with a curious air of frailty.

I showed myself.

"Dad?" His sea-green eyes were shy. He vibed my wariness, and tensed like a gull about to flush. "Jeez, you look different."

When he went to shake hands awkwardly, his research notes fell everywhere. We ran all over the library steps picking them up. If this fumble-fingers was an assassin's helper, he was a great actor.

"I have to be careful," I told him.

It was a wondrous late-autumn day. As we walked up

Fifth Avenue together, a few last leaves were falling from the sycamores, hitting us gently on the head. I stayed wary, casing the passers-by. At the Plaza, weekending executives were sitting on benches, using foil reflectors to tan their faces. In Central Park, bag-men and bag-ladies dozed on the grass, soaking up the last sunshine before they went underground to the steam pipes. Horse carriages clip-clopped, full of smiling tourists who lived in a sniper-free world.

His eyes met mine. "You were *hiding* . . . checking me out."

"Yeah."

"Do the bigots still bother you that much?"

"It never stopped. There's even a guy who stalks me."

"Why don't you have bodyguards with you?"

"How do you know I don't?"

Michael looked around nervously, getting my point.

"Tell me about yourself," I said.

So he talked, kicking at leaves as we walked. His mother had remarried — a well-to-do real-estate guy that he didn't like. They were living in Albany, putting him through NYU Medical School. He lived in a tiny studio apartment near school, and had a part-time job at Hames-West. Kevin was a senior at Princeton.

Finally we were tired — Michael was soft, I was unbelievably wrought up. So we headed for the East Sixties, and a calming spot I knew, Paley Park. In mid-block, a couple of townhouses had been demolished to create a quiet courtyard. Under the tubbed trees, dozens of New Yorkers sat dreamily at café tables with their bag lunches and take-out coffee. They were mesmerized by sounds of the waterfall that sheeted down the back wall. We picked a table in some sunlight against the wall, where I could see everybody.

"Why Hames-West?" I asked. "You're not a hemophiliac."

"Oh, no. I'm just fascinated with blood. Mom used to talk about bad blood . . . meaning yours. How can blood be bad?"

As he talked about his work, I could see how bright he was. A lot brighter than me.

"You single?" I asked.

"Engaged. You'll meet Astarte. We're going to get married when I finish my internship."

Did this mean he had no gay leanings? Not necessarily.

"Astarte? Quite a name," I said.

"Outrageous name, huh? She's beautiful too . . . a real goddess."

In my most determined woman-dating times, I had never referred to any female as a goddess. Betsy and other young lesbians and New Agers talked a lot about Diana these days. The old dykes I'd known talked mostly about Amelia Earhart.

"You . . . uh . . . live alone now?" he asked.

"Yeah."

Our limping conversation died. He sat staring at the waterfall for a while. Suddenly he said, "You feel so cold."

A silence. "I followed the whole . . . the Olympic thing on TV. What you said to the press after the trial. I felt . . . I really . . . well, I cried. I told Mom I was going to write you. But she gave me such a bad time that I didn't." Another silence. "I don't blame you for being angry at me."

How could I explain that I wasn't angry, just frozen inside?

"Well," he said, "it was great to see you once, anyway."

On the street, my son gave me a last shy forlorn look.

Suddenly my hand sprang out, almost on its own, and gripped his sleeve. His eyes met mine. Instantly, I saw how stupid and paranoid I was being. He could be trusted. I crushed him against me — this warmth, this life that issued from a desperate try at being straight, on the back seat of an old car in 1953. We held each other hard for a couple of minutes, as the warm sun faded over the roofs. This time, Michael managed not to drop his notes. As our hug relaxed, his hand patted down the front of my jacket — he'd discovered the stick I carried inside. He stared at it.

"My world is a dangerous place," I said softly. "If you're going to be in it, you have to get hip."

"Can I visit you a lot?" he said. "Make up for lost time?"

As November passed, and I marked time to mid-term, it was clear that Angel had something besides "mono".

The drive from the college into New York City, along a gray-water Hudson River to the narrow sooty streets of

Greenwich Village, had always depressed me — reminding me of lonely searches for city sex. Parking my car on the street, Michael and I rode the elevator up to the fourth floor and heard Steve unsliding ten different dead-bolts.

A sickroom twilight had gathered in their apartment. Steve had quit writing, and puttered, taking care of his lover. He didn't want his domestic situation aired in the press, so friends and business associates were kept away with the fib that he was writing something big. Angel's weight had dropped to 115 pounds. He had headaches, which he communicated by a new word, "hurt". From the way he stumbled and walked into walls, there were central-nervous problems.

"Doctor Jacobs ordered up a bunch of tests," Steve told us. "Maybe it's a new flu or meningitis or something."

The thought of a nasty new bug, spreading to Prescott, or to Michael and his girlfriend, worried me. But so far Michael and I hadn't caught it. My resistance had always been good.

About this time, LEV. sent me another letter.

KEEP YOUR SON AWAY FROM FAGGOTS. OBEDIENCE WILL BE REWARDED. DEFIANCE IS ALWAYS PUNISHED. FEAR IS HEALTHY.

Wrathfully I mailed it to H-C. They had a whole file of letters now. Julius had gone over them with a fine-toothed comb, Harry said. The pattern coming clear was no pattern at all. LEV. seemed to have culled his materials from every wastebasket in the country.

Harry also mentioned that Julius found no prints on the .22 casing. Nothing to connect the bullet with anything.

The local police had failed to connect the LaFont shooting with that local hunter kid and his old .22. Witnesses placed the kid in the wrong place to take the shot. So charges were dropped.

PART THREE

Rotten Apples

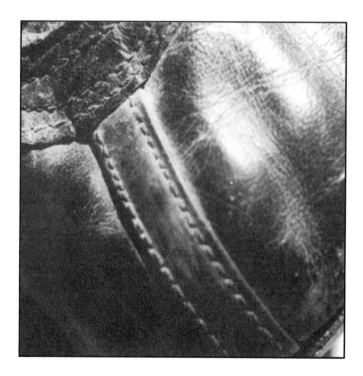

TWELVE

T he next year swung us from light to dark, and back.

For a while, LEV. was inactive. Had he died? Lost interest? Earning money doing something else? Doing other hits? Or just waiting for me to let my guard down?

What would I write? How could I chronicle the terror? Train my own crosshairs on bigotry? Steve's agent, Ernie Glover at Esterhazy & Nebla, read some of my short stuff and thought it was publishable. For the first time since I'd told George Rayburn, "Anything but the podium," I felt embarrassed, and wondered if I should climb back on it.

But chasing words was like chasing that phantom — a kick that fell short.

November 1978

A s the first winter sleets slicked the campus sidewalks, I was still missing Vince — tormented as a druggie. Before Billy, tricking would have solved my problem. But I was tired of believing that a gay man has to chase ass to keep his franchise.

In November, the gay community celebrated Harvey Milk's election to San Francisco supervisor. He was the first gay activist to hold a major office, and optimists took this as a sign we were getting somewhere. The religious fanatics hated Harvey's guts, and I knew from John Sive that he lived like I did — with death threats. But he went around openly with no security, and said in a speech, "If a bullet should enter my brain, let that bullet destroy every closet door."

In mid-November, I met Michael's fiancée.

Astarte Jones was spectacular, all right — a flamingo beside Michael's sea gull. Two years older than Michael, she headed fundraising at Hames-West. She was the "new woman" — liberated, confident, forthright, dedicated to gyms and diet — and her delicately ripped arm-muscles showed through her silk blouse. If she'd been the heroine of that horrifying singles thriller *Looking for Mr. Goodbar,* she'd kick Mr. Goodbar to death with her bare feet.

"Harlan, when I read the crap about you in the press," she said, "I want to *kill* someone."

The two of them had been sleeping together for a while. I figured she'd taught my virginal kid. Their love felt devoted, but quiet, with careers taking most of their energy. She had her own apartment. Why weren't they already living together? Were they carrying '70s independence to the max? Or did Michael have questions about himself?

Tests on Angel showed he had toxoplasmosis. His problems with seeing, speaking and walking meant that the tiny organism was attacking his brain. His immune system was shot too — a complete blood count showed only a few T-helper lymphocytes. I had never heard of T-helper cells, and now learned that they help make antibodies. A normal person has from 500 to 1200 T-helper cells in a cubic milliliter of blood. Striper tested positive for *Toxoplasma.* So the cat was banished to the vet's, and treated.

I junked plans to run in the AAU masters' mile, so I could be with my two friends.

Meanwhile, Michael had me wondering if he was bi. Over Thanksgiving, he and I went to a cocktail party at Marvin Jakes' penthouse apartment on Central Park South.

If Mikey was going to be a doctor, I wanted him to know my rich friends. Fifty guests, cream of the gay New York "A"-list, gathered amid Marvin's collection of Asian art. As the men swallowed hors d'oeuvres, their eyes swallowed Michael. He was wearing an Irish-tweed suit, that I had dragged him to Bergdorf's to buy. It set off his Celt looks and green eyes. Michael was the least vain male I ever met, so he had no idea how good he looked in it.

"Gawd, your kid is cute," Steve's literary agent blurted.

"You're prepotent, Harlan," said socialite Russell Houghton. He was from the horsey set upstate.

"I'm what?"

Russell laughed. "That's a horse-breeding term. The sire puts his stamp on his get. But are you prepotent for gay?"

My son handled the attention with surprising sophistication. When several guys asked for his phone number, he gave them mine.

For Thanksgiving, Michael didn't go home to his mother's. He told Mary Ellen he was seeing me, and she was furious. Michael, Astarte and I planned to cook a turkey for Steve, Angel and friends at his apartment. It was the first time in twenty years that I'd eaten this meal with any blood kin.

Just before the holiday came shattering news from San Francisco. Harvey Milk's forebodings about a bullet had come true. A homophobic politician named Dan White had walked up to Milk in his office, and shot him dead, minutes after shooting George Moscone, the liberal mayor of San Francisco. For days I lived in a frenzy of emotion — after-flashes of Montreal. Somewhere, Vince was weeping, raging, remembering too — pushed that much closer to his breaking point.

December 1978

Just before Christmas, Angel was quietly hospitalized in a Manhattan clinic. When his emaciated form went through the CAT scanner, lesions showed on his brain. His T-cells had dropped to nothing.

Our Prescott friends were scared off from visiting Angel.

"If women get even a trace of toxoplasmosis," Marian said, "it affects the baby. Give Steve and Angel our love."

On Christmas Eve, when I walked into Intensive Care, Vince and George Rayburn were there.

I'd expected Vince to have a boot-camp look. Instead, he was road-stained, sleazy, uncombed, smoking again. He was wearing aviator sunglasses, cowboy boots and a T-shirt that said NUKE A COMMIE TODAY. His battered black jacket had a spread eagle on the back. An energy of straight male feistiness hung around him as he stared at me defiantly. Vince, my Vince, who had marched for peace when he was 15. Now bruises decorated his knuckles.

Ignoring Vince, I sat by Steve, who was hollow-eyed.

Angel was propped on pillows, with his thin hand between Steve's two big hands. He was breathing harshly through the oxygen mask. The right side of his face was twisted — nerves affected by the brain lesions. There was nothing to say. So I just rubbed Steve's shoulder. As Angel mumbled something to Steve, his sunken blue eyes held that spirit clearness of the dying.

An hour later Angel slid into a coma.

Doc Jacobs and I talked sadly in the hall outside.

"It's odd," he said. "So many young gay men that I've tracked through drug use, and STDs, and immune depression, are really sick now."

Steve's lover died just before midnight. It was terrible to see the way Steve cried. I almost wanted to tell him to stop.

The aides tied the boy's hands and feet, strapped his lower jaw in place. Then they wrestled him into a body bag. As all the world was singing "Hark the Herald Angels Sing," the body-bag zipper closed over Angel's once-beautiful face.

For a few days, Vince, Rayburn and I stayed with Steve at his apartment, because our friend was severely dazed. Vince had nothing to say about his new life.

"It would break Billy's heart to see you," I told him.

With his gift for hitting below the belt, Vince retorted, "Yeah, you put Billy on this pedestal of perfect. What if you'd had to live with him day after day, for 20 years? Shit ... you've been with me longer than you were with Billy."

Having said this, he climbed in bed with me. In two minutes I had the upper hand again, and we both behaved like junkies who'd just gotten their hands on some high-grade dope. The next day, we had another fight, and he walked out. I was furious, and called Harry and Chino from a pay phone.

"What the hell is Julius doing?" I barked. "Vince looks like a road-house maggot."

"Our kid needs to do better at passing," Harry said calmly. "Get the lavender spoon out of his mouth, Julius said."

By New Year's, things came to a head between Michael and the family. First Kevin came down from Princeton to "talk sense" to Michael about seeing me. Kevin was six foot two, on the wrestling varsity. They had a confrontation at Michael's apartment. When threats didn't work, he roughed Michael up — broke his nose and cracked two ribs. Next, Kevin's mother and stepfather were on the phone. If Michael didn't stop seeing me, they would terminate payments for school, and sue him to recover what they'd already forked out. My shy first-born said he was having John Sive file assault-and-battery charges against Kevin, and they could keep their fucking money.

Astarte went to war with her own family, who'd been trying to maneuver the pair toward a traditional wedding. Now that they knew who I was, they wanted their daughter to break off with Michael. Since she was 27, and financially independent, she simply said no.

Finally Mary Ellen and her husband agreed not to sue, in exchange for Michael's dropping charges against Kevin. I offered to pay for his schooling. But Michael drew himself up.

"I'll work my way through school, Dad," he said. He grinned past his broken nose. "Thanks, though."

January 1979

During mid-term break, Betsy and the baby made their quiet escape to northern California. She was now the athletic director at Ricelands Community College in the Sacramento Valley.

In the driveway of the emptied house, Betsy and Marian secured the baby's travel seat in the car. The moving van had gone ahead. The two women were driving west together, and Marian would help her settle in. All bundled up, Falcon churned over the snowy lawn, like a tiny blizzard in a red snowsuit. He came running to give me a handful of snow.

"Da," he screeched with delight.

It was the first time he'd called me dad. Feeling a lump in my throat, I picked him up and held him close. He shoved a bit of snow against my face. Even the slight smell of wet diaper seemed wonderful. I prayed that LEV. wasn't watching.

"Don't forget your da," I told him. "Okay?"

His mother scooped him out of my arms. She was desperately eager to be on the road.

"Have a safe trip," I said. "See you when this is . . . over."

"I'll send you snapshots." Betsy gave me a quick hug. "And a studio portrait every Christmas."

"Don't put anything dangerous in your letters," I reminded her, "just in case the wrong people read my mail."

As I got ready to leave Prescott, things of Billy's surfaced from closet and drawers. His suede jacket. His track clothes and the one shoe (Vince still had the other one). Clippings and photos. I couldn't bring myself to destroy them, so they went into a banker's box. The LaFonts were leaving too. Funding had come unexpectedly, so they were moving to Maui, where Jacques would start his wildlife work.

On my last day, as snow fell and I was gloomily clearing my office in the athletic building, Mike Stella came to say a sad goodbye. A few minutes after he left, Jacques wandered in, unzipping his jacket. He looked as gloomy as me.

"Hi." He hung out the COACH IN CONFERENCE sign and closed the door.

"Hi," I said. "You and Eileen all packed?"

"Pretty much," Jacques said, looking around. "I'm trying to come up with a one-liner for the end of an era."

Eyes anxious, he hovered — like a pheasant about to duck into a cornfield. His wound had nearly healed, and he had apparently put the whole thing out of his mind. So the anxiety came from something else.

"I first saw you in this room," I said. "Almost exactly three years ago. You sat in that oak chair. Billy sat there, and Vince sat over there." I pointed.

"God, I was so in love," he murmured, looking at team photos on the wall. One was a 1975 pic of himself, Vince and Billy, grinning like the kids they were.

I said nothing, packing my old Marine track-team photo.

"I couldn't handle Vince," he added. "Now I try handling it other ways."

"Trade, huh? Bathhouses in town?"

"I thought marriage would change me. And I love Eileen. But guess what . . . I still like sex with guys better."

"Does Eileen know?"

"I've been trying to get up courage to tell her."

I shook my head. "It's not smart to lie to your wife."

He shrugged. "Yeah, it doesn't make sense."

"When did you start?"

"When Eileen was pregnant the first time," he said.

"Jesus . . . bathhouses are getting to be unhealthy places. What if you give herpes to Eileen? Herpes can't be cured, you know."

He scowled. "I should have known I can't talk to you."

"This is not about me. It's about you . . . whether people can trust you."

Jacques turned on his heel, and walked out.

As the slam of the door echoed through that cold building, the awful thought crossed my mind that LEV. may have surveilled him too, seen him veer back into gay sex. Maybe that was why LEV. shot at him.

By that evening, at Steve's urging, I had moved into his Village apartment.

February-March 1979

My new address was a quiet street off Washington Square. After years upstate, with real woods to run in, I was back in a ghetto with potted ghinko trees on the balcony. In a changing Manhattan — new glass towers, new thresholds of poverty, new parameters of violence and filth and ethnic mixing — the gay community was ever more truculent, marching toward power under our slanting lavender banners, in a city that traditionally denied power to all but machine politicians.

Steve's comfortable 3-bedroom apartment was furnished with his wild mixture — Spanish colonial heirlooms from ranching relatives, paintings and photographs that celebrated gay male beauty, and art-deco stuff he'd plucked off the sidewalks where people left it for the junkman. The sniper could now do his peeking from the rooftop of the old apartment building across the street. Harry got me a state-of-the-art telephone debugger from somewhere, and I installed it on Steve's phone.

Evidently the sniper was unhappy about my moving in with Steve. Maybe he thought Steve was my new lover. Three days later, a rock shattered Steve's front window on the 4th floor. It had the usual inscription on it. Chino didn't have to tell me that LEV. probably fired it from across the narrow street, using his wrist-rocket.

Naturally, by the time I got to the rooftop, nobody was there. I mailed the rock to H-C, and they started checking new apartment-dwellers in the area. We had heavy wire screens put over the windows.

On the surface, Steve pulled himself together. Angel's death seemed like a thing from outer space that ate him alive before our eyes, like in a movie.

Knowing how much Steve loved company with his paper-shuffling, I helped him sort through his unpublished work. With the old discipline, working late nights, he did the galley-proofing of *Pollen Kisses,* the autobiography that he'd finished on Fire Island. I was the bodyguard now — attentive, efficient, protective. I did some writing too, very laboriously. Steve critiqued my stuff, and I was able to make my first sales — all to the gay press, since my by-line in a straight magazine might draw unwelcome attention.

Steve shared writing secrets. Pornography had taught him about literature.

"Whatever the feeling is . . . if I don't feel it, the reader won't feel it," he said to me.

When Steve's weight dropped and his lymph glands swelled and he had a persistent cough, we called it lingering flu and overwork. By spring, when Steve sent the *Pollen* galleys back to his publisher, he didn't look well. But he refused to go to the doctor. Meanwhile, eerie shop talk kept trickling among gay doctors who worried about STD. When Michael learned about Steve's celibacy, and his reusing Angel's old needles, my son muttered about blood.

"That's the way junkies pass hepatitis B," he reminded us. "It's a wonder Steve doesn't have toxoplasmosis."

Watching my best friend disintegrate was terrible. Angel was pulling him like a magnet, drawing him out of life.

One day, Steve tottered to his desk, and fished out a folder of legal papers.

"Will you promise to do what I ask?" he demanded.

He wanted to give me his power of attorney. He had kept Angel's ashes, and wanted their remains mingled on the Fire Island beach. All income was now in a non-revocable trust — royalties, investments, insurance policies, licenses. His condominium apartment and beach house belonged to the trust. The sole beneficiary was me. The trust would protect me from estate taxes. I could live comfortably off the interest, he said. He hoped I'd publish his manuscripts.

I was devastated, and tried to protest.

"No, no," he said. "You've been my best friend, and you've never had a nickel."

"Your family won't let you leave a dime to a queer. They'll break the will."

"No, they won't — they're all bleeping rich."

Fumbling in his robe pocket, Steve pressed an object into my hand. It was warm with his body heat — the gem of beach glass that Angel had given him, that day in '78.

"Next time you're at the Beach, put this in the jar for us," he said.

On March 20, Steve asked me to meet with his publisher for him. While I was gone, he shot vitamins with one of the old syringes, and managed to mainline air into a vein. It looked like an accident, but I was sure he'd done it on purpose.

The *New York Times* carried the standard obit. Steve

Goodnight, author of ten controversial books, including the bestselling *Rape of the Angel Gabriel,* had died at his Manhattan home, of an apparent accident following a lingering illness. The gay press carried longer notices. That Saturday, a huge memorial service spilled standees onto a Village street. I was one of the speakers; my heart of steel managed to say how much I'd miss him.

Next day, ten of us rode a rental boat over to the Beach.

John Sive, Chino and Harry had flown in. We had no idea where Vince was. Marian and Joe Prescott didn't come either — Joe had just had a stroke. At the Hotel, we stood stupefied on the dunes. While others sobbed and blew noses, the two vets and I dug our hands in the two men's mingled ashes, and sowed them into the surf. Afterwards, we sat silent on that front deck, where we had thrown knives for so many happy hours. It felt like God himself had trained his crosshairs on us.

Before we left, I stood at the jar with the beach glass in my hand.

In every way but physically, as a lover, Steve had been in my world since 1968. Billy had come and gone like a meteor through my skies, and Vince like an asteroid crashing to earth — but Steve shone quietly like a planet, through years of retrogrades. Now he was gone.

The sea-gem dropped with a gentle clink, into the jar.

Spring 1979

The police questioned me briefly about Steve's death. After all, they reasoned, I might have killed him to get his money. Fortunately he'd let himself be seen alive by several people after I left the building. He'd planned it well.

May was always a hard month — Billy and I had been married on May 8.

This May, I got a letter from the L.A. Front Runners. They were one of several new gay and lesbian track clubs — young people running at all levels, for self-improvement, inspired by Billy's example. The very idea of such a club was something I couldn't have imagined in the '60s. They wrote me with their idea for a Billy Sive Memorial 5-K. The event would be held for open amateur runners in Los Angeles every year, on September 9th, the anniversary of his death.

Their letter explained, "We want to attract both gay and straight athletes, to celebrate human rights. Out of respect for you, we're asking your permission to use Billy's name. We also invite you to be involved in the planning, so you can be sure our event will be a credit to Billy's memory."

I wrote back, giving permission and wishing them well. But being there was not something I could face.

That same month, the Dan White trial ended. White got just seven years for the murders of Milk and Moscone. When I read it in the paper, I slammed my fist on the desk so hard I almost broke my hand.

Sickened, we all watched the TV news as San Francisco was shattered by the biggest gay riots in American history. Swarming thousands of women and men sacked City Hall, smashed windows, and battled with police. They torched dozens of police cars, injured 61 officers, scrawled graffiti everywhere. The most interesting part was, that even in this orgy of anger, gay rioters held a last line of liberal ideology — they threw garbage and rocks and bricks, and beat cops with sticks. But not one of them fired a gun at a cop.

I wondered if Vince was there, and had a creepy feeling that he was walking his own lonely road of anger.

Summer 1979

As Steve had predicted, his rich relatives didn't contest the will. I took possession of the apartment and the beach house. That summer, I became the Davis Park "writer in residence". Michael and Astarte spent most of those weekends with me. "Hotel Brown" was the new name. Michael and Astarte learned to listen for tin-can alarms. Most neighbors still thought of me as "that clammer who has a house on the Beach". Nobody bothered me.

Striper traveled grandly to the Beach in her wicker carrier. Nobody bothered her either. She came and went from the dunes with songbirds in her mouth.

But on our first weekend, the two Suffolk County cops showed up. With sinking heart, I heard the boardwalk booby-trap squeak.

"Hi," I said, opening the screen door.

Silently the two entered — blue uniforms, handcuffs, batons, .357 Magnums in holsters. Lance Shirley had replaced Chapman as sergeant. He had a rookie named Bob Enger. Their menace filled the kitchen. Michael and Astarte, who were doing weekend paperwork at the dining table, eyed them nervously.

"My son, Michael," I told them. "And his fiancée, Astarte." Hands were shaken.

"Coffee?" I asked. If it was not a social visit, they'd refuse.

"Uh . . . sure," said Lance. "Lots of cream."

"Black for me," Bob said.

While I filled mugs, Lance looked at the packets of gourmet coffee beans that Astarte had brought out.

"Ey-hey!" he said to Bob. "This coffee is some serious!"

I managed a tight little smile, handing them their mugs.

"Thanks," said Bob. "We get cold diner coffee from Patchogue."

"What can I do for you?" I asked.

"So," said Lance, "Goodnight sold you the house?"

"He willed it to me."

"Why?"

"He didn't have any heirs."

"Thought he had a kid."

"His kid died."

Lance grunted thoughtfully.

"Are you here on police business?" I asked.

Lance met my eyes. "We're just . . . curious."

Both men were South Shore natives. Lance was around 30, out of the old-time bay families known as bonnikers. Six foot three, with a baby face gone hard, Lance had a glow of boozy girlfriends. As a kid, it was said, Lance pirated at night, ghosting his clam-boat into creeks along the South Shore. Illegal clams grew thick there, in the sewage-laden water. He was never caught. Bob was 29, built like a wrestler — married, with one kid. He had inquisitive eyes, and a plaintive voice that was strangely un-cop-like.

The two operated out of the Davis Park marina. Their station was the size of a toll-booth. During summer, between pot busts and Casino brawls, they got to look at pretty girls. In winter, they helped the National Seashore rangers trap stray dogs and cats that vacationers had abandoned. In short, they kept a light hand. After all, the party animals benefited the local economy. Lance and Bob were "cool".

"But not too cool," Lance liked to say.

Now Lance's baby-blue eyes bored into mine.

"So," said Lance, "you're Harlan Brown. *The* Harlan Brown."

Wanting to wring their necks, I stared out the window at the cherry groves, now summer green.

"We've been doing a little checking. You've got quite a history of attracting violence, right?" Bob added.

"Look," I said. "The past is the past. I try to keep a low profile. I'm not a druggie. I don't throw wild parties. Other people's attitudes are their problem."

The two cops' eyes rested on Michael, as if wondering how a notorious gay man could be a father like any other.

"When attitudes go public, they're our problem," said Lance.

How could I keep the police from harassing us?

Then I got an idea. Maybe the light hand would help.

"Tell you what," I said. "Make this your coffee stop and place to get warm. You can get to know us."

Lance hesitated. He'd take a ragging from the bay-men if it got out that he was visiting a queer house. But I could see that somehow my words had touched the outlaw part of him. My two kids being there would make it okay for them. All of a sudden, with that intuition that I'd honed over years of cruising men, horsing around with men, teaching men, breaking men's hearts, I had a feeling that there was more to these two cops than met the eye. They could be valuable allies. They might even turn out to be likable.

Lance was looking questioningly at his sidekick.

"I'd take this guy's coffee over that poison from Patchogue," Bob shrugged.

"Okay," said Lance. "But we keep this very low-key, right?"

August 1979

At Steve's condominium, everything stayed the way it was. I even wore some of Steve's better clothes — jackets, sweaters, his tuxedo. Missing him was not something I wanted to slough off. I was determined to have a new life, and wanted desperately to make my living as a writer. Living off interest income felt too much like being on welfare. But the gay press didn't pay much. And the straight media had softened on gay issues a little bit. Ernie Glover told me, "To get in the money, you have to write a major book. You're so notorious, I could probably sell something off an outline. You do that, we'll be in Fat City."

Now and then, the old idea of writing about Billy crossed my mind. But it was a phantom racing ahead of me.

The old Bible got more crammed with red lines.

Michael, struggling with expenses, had to swallow his pride. "Dad, can I move in with you?"

Having Michael around all the time was wonderful.

"You're soft as a doughnut," I said. "You should run."

The two of us loped across Washington Square, passing the old geezers playing checkers in the sun, taking a different route each time. Michael had natural form — easy and light, the way a gull flies, almost without moving wings. Sometimes Astarte joined us. It was fun to have two kids to train.

The next letter from LEV. was:

FEAR THE WORD OF GOD. KEEP YOUR KID AWAY FROM QUEERS.

Now and then, at the hour of cheapest rates, Chino called. About himself, he said little. He'd stayed sober for a year, so now he was trying to quit smoking.

Then, one time, Harry called.

"Chino isn't doing well," he said sadly. "He's ashamed to tell you, but he dropped out of UCLA."

"I can't hack the attitudes," Chino growled in my ear. "There was a loud noise outside the classroom, and I hit the dirt. The fucking kids laughed at me. There's no respect."

Neither Chino nor Harry said anything about Operation Boomerang. Now and then, they sent me a bill, and I paid it. To make ends meet, they were doing a little bounty-hunting. Harry handled the big predators. Chino was still jittery, afraid he'd shoot somebody for no reason. So our terrible SEAL handled the cases where you walk unarmed into a local beanery and collar somebody who owes lots of parking fines.

Doc Jacobs kept mumbling about gay men's health. But everyone I knew was healthy. Steve's and Angel's deaths seemed like a horrible fluke.

Besides, I was too worried about other things.

September 1979

One worry was Jacques. After an angry silence, my pheasant finally wrote a chatty letter from Hawaii.

Dear Harlan,

Well, it's a different world here. I am a barnie — short for barnacle. Another way of saying *haole* — white man.

Two of my research assistants are Hawaiians who know the uplands really well. One of them, Eric, turns out to be *mahu*. He blurted this pleasantly in front of Eileen, so there was no question of closets. My work has started off well.

Mahu is Hawaiian for gay. "Oh, he's *mahu*," you say about somebody. There are no shadings of *mahu*. None of the obsession with taxonomy that the *haole* gay world is stuck in. No queens, bears, machos, tops, bottoms, dads, nellies, muffins, butches, femmes, kikis, bi's, etc. It's all just *mahu*.

A bigger worry was why Betsy was so out of touch. When she finally sent the first snapshots, she wrote:

Hi Harlan,
'Scuse the delay. So much happening. Buried in practices and meets. A new school year. I do apologize. And I have a lover! I met Marla right here in Marysville, at the spring rice festival. She is living with me, and I think it will be good for Falcon to see two of us in the house.
Gotta run . . . more next time.
Love, Betsy

A couple of times I called her, but our conversations had to be vague because of possible bugging. She never called me. Our warm alliance was struggling to survive the chill of time and distance.

September 9, 1979

The first Billy Sive Memorial 5-K came off. It was held in Griffith Park in Los Angeles. I didn't go, but I sent the race director a telegram that he read to the crowd.

Unlike the elephant, the gay community has a short memory. Maybe it is our slavish devotion to fleeting youthful looks, and our loss of family oral history, that makes us so careless about our posterity. I had already seen a few early-day pioneers dropped by the roadside like used-up tubes of lube, to make room for the porn star of the day, and the activist of the month. Celebrated drag queens came and went like footprints on the beach. So I was surprised when the gay press reported the large entry for the race — 724 runners. And the large crowd, that listened to my words. Straight sports news ignored the event.

So Billy was not forgotten by gay America. His death had stained so deep in the wall of memory, that it couldn't be wiped away like some graffiti.

If only the larger America remembered him too.

THIRTEEN

Autumn 1979

O ne October evening, Vince called me up. He was in town, he said.

We chatted a bit. In his voice was the yearning, so I invited him to dinner the next night. Michael grumbled about my bad taste in lovers, then went to Astarte's for the night, so I could have some privacy.

When Vince came in the door, he didn't kiss me hello, just touched my hand. Then he stood studying the table laid for two, with some of Steve's good linens and silver.

"Living in town brings out the piss-elegant in you, Harlan," he said. "It's a side of you I don't know."

We sat down to beef Wellington and other good stuff that I'd ordered sent over from the Fifth Avenue Hotel a few blocks away, because I didn't want to cook. I was dressed casually. White-on-white shirt, no tie, best jeans, and Steve's favorite beaded belt that I'd found in his closet.

Sitting there in the candlelight, Vince looked magnificent — and it wasn't the look of gym and tanning salon. Clearly he had been mountain-climbing, sky-diving, mud-sucking through swamps. His fitness had the tension, the knife-edge that I recognized. He even held himself differently — that "at ease" manner with neck always braced. Conservative clothes were now his thing — slacks and a blazer that looked like something I'd buy. The only concession to a former sultry image was the half-unbuttoned shirt. His hair was shorn, almost white-walled, but had the same hot luster as before. The clearness in his eyes told me he'd stayed off drugs. Vince did have will — enormous will, like a volcano does.

Yet his rage, his restlessness, made the antique chair creak ominously under him. Last year, Chino and Harry had guessed that he'd be ready in three years. Was he getting impatient? Hungry to spray bullets?

"Still drinking whiskey these days?" I asked.

"No . . . back to wine."

As I leaned to pour his wine into one of Steve's crystal goblets, I drew a deep breath of that after-shave or cologne he was wearing. I couldn't stand most of the stuff that gay men splashed on themselves. The smell of sweat was always best. But Vince's was subtle, like a fragrant wood-essence.

"Chateau Yquem," he mused, looking at the wine label. "You never used to know the difference between Coke and 7-Up."

His way of talking had changed, too, from post-hippie stream of consciousness, with all the "cools" and "likes", to actual complete sentences. I felt a deep tearing sadness, wondering about the disease status of Julius. But I wasn't supposed to know about Julius.

As if reading my mind, Vince asked, "So — who're you boning these days?"

"You've been gone a year. You've got no grounds to ask me."

"Just curious," he shrugged.

Had he seen action yet? Pulled the trigger? He had to know if he could kill people, again and again — do it on orders, do it on his own judgment if necessary. Even I, a peacetime ex-leatherneck who had never killed anybody, knew that. But my training and my feelings were there. If they ever connected, I would pull the trigger. If I'd had the chance to wax Richard Mech as he sighted on Billy, I'd have splattered him, and taken my chances in court.

"Well," I said, sitting down and pouring myself some Perrier, "whoever your new daddy is, he's taking good care of you."

"He's 65." Vince looked up from his plate, into my eyes, from under his long jet-black eyelashes. "And he doesn't fuck me."

"I know. You fuck everybody else."

"You always underestimate me." He sounded bored.

"Maybe I need more convincing than most guys."

He stretched and yawned.

"Oh, I'm not into sex like I was," he said. "At first, being liberated was fun. You know. Meet a cool guy . . . lots of courting, lots of foreplay . . . spend the whole night . . . break-fast in bed." He let his head fall back, and stared at the ceiling. "Now it's ice-cold. The minute you shut the door, the clothes are off and you're in him. Then fisting isn't enough, and you want to tear his heart out . . ."

That sting-ray poison was coursing in my veins.

Striper jumped to my lap, hoping for a taste of beef, and I pushed her back on the floor.

"Rayburn and your old brothers always ask about you," I said.

"Things are good," he said. "Going into a new phase."

"Tell me about it."

He shook his head. "You wouldn't agree, and we'd fight."

"You're still sponging, huh? What about a career?"

"Why do you always pick some point?" he said in a low voice. "Can't you just be with me, Harlan?"

His eyes held such an appeal that I pulled back.

We spent the rest of the meal in chit-chat — what news of Falcon and Betsy, etc. I hoped he wouldn't get drunk, and he didn't — stopped at his second glass. Finally it was 10 p.m. We had coffee and cleared the table. He still hadn't made a move. I wasn't going to beg him for a one-nighter — after all, he was the one who left. I wanted to have him forever, or not see him again.

"I'll call a cab for you," I said, with a lump in the throat.

At the open door, he brushed a kiss on my cheek. As he turned to go out, Betsy's voice spoke in my memory. *He really loves you.*

"Vince," I said.

He looked at me over his broad shoulder, where the tailored cloth and padding rode so easily. His eyes were wet.

The door closed with him still standing there. Our embrace was like a vise, arms crushing each other, thighs locked. I buried my face in his neck, breathing in his fragrance as if I'd been fighting for air underwater. His hand was already sliding down the back of my belt. My hand was already up his jacket, caressing his hard back through the expensive conservative shirt.

"Have you been anywhere that wouldn't look good on a lab report?" I whispered.

"Do I look like I'm dying?" His hand was at my fly.

Steve's old bedroom was luxurious but masculine. The wide bed had an antique headboard carved with naked Greek gymnasts and youths on horseback. Vince's elegant clothes, and my more casual wear, made a trail across the Chinese rug. We yanked off the covers. Naked, he threw himself down prone, looking startlingly bronze against Steve's expensive linen sheets. He wanted to head straight into what he loved most. Bracing his thighs apart, he was trembling violently all over. In the bed-lamp light, his carved runner's buttocks had a metallic sheen. My knees were vibrating like a 16-year-old's, from pure emotion, and need.

I lay down, and kissed the inside of one thigh, letting him feel my warm breath. He groaned — I knew he loved the feel of breath.

"What did you say about foreplay?" I said against his skin.

He smelled like a forest — everything that is natural to a forest, compost and ferns. As I ran my mouth up his spine, he moved like a forest under me — vines twining, fronds unfolding, strange orchids penetrated by strange birds with long bills. For a moment, he was a cloud forest, unexplored, a thousand miles into some lost continent. A hundred thousand kinds of trees and vines and flowers, some poisonous, some with power to heal, none known to me. I was a stranger, feeling baffled and ignorant, like a young botanist with an empty note-pad. I wanted to be a tree, and sink my taproot in his body for a thousand years.

"Turn over," I said. "Make love to me like a man, not a goddam animal."

He obeyed, and swallowed me into the kind of kiss that had haunted my memories. I jujued the foreplay out of him. Then, with pure recklessness and contempt bred of familiarity, I forgot every spooky thought about health, every caution of Doc Jacob's, every question about where this man had been, and both of us went absolutely wild.

Early in the morning, waking to the roar of a sanitation truck outside, the clang of garbage cans, and pigeons cooing on the windowsill, I heard Vince quietly dressing. The feeling that I'd been used came over me. He left without a word. But when I finally got up, a note lay on the dining table. He'd written it on a sheet of my typewriter paper. Standing there naked, I read it over and over:

> Dear Harlan,
> I still love you . . .
> you don't know how much,
> and . . .
> I hope you and I will someday get in synch,
> but . . .
> right now things feel weird.
> Anyway . . .
> I've got my thing happening.
> So . . .
> I'll stay in touch.
> Love, Vince

I went to a pay phone and called Harry and Chino about Vince's visit. "Rich daddy?" said Harry. "Mox nix."

"Who is he? Julius?"

"Come on, you dumb shit. Hang in there."

"But —"

Harry's voice had a cold-steel edge. "Read my lips, mister. Back off. Or I'll be very pissed."

Harry had never called me "mister" before. So I choked down my rage, and said no more. A week later, I was even angrier when it was clear that Vince had given me clap. The whole thing was so embarrassing, that I almost went to a strange doctor for the shots. Instead, I faced Jacobs. He didn't tsk-tsk as he jabbed a needle into me. Instead, he talked about the cases in New York — several dozen now — in which the common factor was swollen nodes and immune-system failure. Jacobs was ticked off about the way a few public-health workers were circulating the phrase "gay disease".

That month, *Pollen Kisses* came out to wildly mixed reviews. More than anything else that Steve wrote, his autobiography made America's toes curl. A couple of bookstores were fire-bombed for selling it.

I got so angry over the lack of understanding for Steve's work that I jumped at a chance to set the record straight. Bruce Cayton was now 55, and tired of globe-trotting after stories. He wanted stories to trot to him. So his gift at yarning and social comment had landed him a late-night talk show, and after the *Pollen* storm broke, he wanted me as a guest. "You were one of the few people who knew Steve well," Bruce pointed out.

It would be my first public appearance since the trial — a testing of the waters. If I were going to publish my own work, I had to be seen.

The day we did the show, the network was a nervous nelly, with extra security in the studio. Bruce and I sat at his spotlit table, with two coffee mugs between us. I talked about Steve as son of the West — pioneer and native-American stock, beatnik in buckskin — the dreamer who wanted to write his own maverick version of the great American novel. Bruce didn't bring up Steve's real-life relationship with Angel — too complicated to handle on a talk show.

"His work was his lover," I told Bruce.

The show pulled Bruce's biggest audience yet. The

switchboards lit up. The following days brought hate calls and hate letters. The letters mostly sounded alike, and it was clear that some evangelist had given his flock a form letter to be copied and sent. Inevitably, there was a letter from LEV., a swat on the knuckles, that said:

I THOUGHT I'D GOTTEN YOU MORE DECENTLY FEARING AND BETTER EDUCATED BY NOW. I FAILED.

Thanks to network twisting of Bruce's arm, the next show featured the Rev. Chuck Chatsworth, just emerging as another spokesman of the religious fanatics. This way, the opposition's view of awful books like *Kisses* could be aired. A few days later, there was a bomb scare in my condominium building. So I sent Michael to stay with Astarte, and called Harry to blow off steam.

"Sounds like you need a little help from your friends," he said.

"I don't need help," I raved. "I need another planet to live on."

"Why don't you babysit Chino for a change?" Harry asked. "He may be half nuts, but he's still good in the woods. And he likes you. Maybe you can help him."

The cormorant did the unexpected and arrived at Westchester County Airport instead of Kennedy — spit-polished and jeans-generic as ever. His little .38 revolver had sneaked past airport security in a crotch holster. But he was thin, depressed and fighting a malaria flare-up. A packet of quinine bark rode in his luggage, that he'd gotten from some *curandera*.

I wasn't in much better shape — three years of harassment was starting to wear.

Chino broke the set pattern immediately. He herded me to a travel shop, made me buy a flight bag and toiletries. He made me put on the hated body-armor vest (he was wearing one himself). An hour later, on tickets bought with his own pocket cash, we were on a flight to Florida.

"*Chingao*, man. This is the best way to be unavailable for comment," the Chicano grinned.

"Where the hell are we going?"

"I always wanted to see Key West. You can call Mikey from there, and tell him to feed your cat."

We were gone a month.

When we got to Key West, Harry wired us $15,000 cash from somewhere, probably Julius, on the proviso that I repay it later. I wasn't going to use credit cards — too easy to trace our movements by purchases.

When I complained bitterly to Chino that he had dragged me far from my desk, where I needed to write, he said,"You're rich now, shithead. Buy a portable typewriter."

So we went to a pawn-shop and paid cash for a used Olivetti. From there to a clothing store, where I got a linen suit and he got a Panama hat. From there to a sleazy beach hotel, where we melded into the herd of sleazy types who infest Florida. There I sat at a table under a palmetto shelter, hiding behind bad-guy sunglasses, growing long hair and a beard again, pecking out short stories and ignoring gay boys who didn't recognize me, but were positive I was some rich daddy ready to be plucked. Chino swam like a barracuda in his ever-more-faded Speedo, looking like a drug-lord's shotgun on holiday, and ignoring boys in his own style. He seemed strangely apathetic to brown asses now.

As the hot humid days passed, my friendship with this brother enemy of LEV. went into a new phase.

Chino kept educating me. He showed me alternate routes in and out of hotels, motels, gay men's houses, stores, bus terminals, that a sewer rat would have missed. He taught me some of his best and dirtiest tricks. Sleight-of-hand with transport, so I'd be a less likely victim of car-bombing. Disguise — not so much wigs and makeup as changing the voice, body movements, even height — everything short of plastic surgery.

"LEV. is a genius at disappearing," he said. "If I could disappear on a boulevard in Saigon, with my gray eyes, you can disappear on the streets of New York. Most celebrities, they're not willing to fucking disappear to escape the danger."

Chino brought a lonely and poignant presence into my lonely life. I chewed him out for quitting school. He chewed me out for not writing the book about Billy. I helped him improve his English and writing skills. He forced me to start learning Spanish by talking it at me. At first this pissed me off. But I got to love the rich bilingual mix that he called Spanglish. Drinking seltzers instead of Singapore slings, we forced favorite authors on each other. I made him read *The Fountainhead*. He made me read *Singing From the Well*, by Reinaldo Arenas. It was a battered second-hand copy that he'd found in Miami. The great gay writer was rotting in a Cuban prison, just seven hours by boat from where we sat. I ditch-dug through it with a little Spanish dictionary that I got in Miami.

We worked our way through the last racial edginess.

He said, "Get hip, *gringo* Marine with eyes of green. Latino gays, black gays, Asian gays . . . we live in a world that's different from yours."

A sad closeness grew around us — a liking of being together, even when it was for hours in silence. It got so we could exchange thoughts, and grin about some stupid little thing without trading words. But underneath the camaraderie, we were both disintegrating slowly, like Steve and Angel had done — not physically, but spiritually. For me, it was some unuttered cry of Billy's name, my inability to get back into the race — even to feel that two words side by side on the page made any sense. For him, it was surely the lover he'd lost in Vietnam. I didn't press Chino to talk about it. He'd probably talk when he was ready.

Days, Chino went for long, long runs with me, both of us getting fitter than we'd ever been in our lives. Nights, he slept with me, shared my bed, .38 handy. He slept with his back to me, silent, never snoring or talking in his sleep. Now and then, like any man, he felt that minimal need. The first time it happened, he unceremoniously put his dark dick in my hand, and made sure I understood that I was the first *pinchi cabrón* white man who'd ever touched it.

Sometimes, when I eased him, he was shivering with malaria. The memory of that month is hot with his smell of quinine, his foreskin in my fingers, and mine in his. Always with his back to me. Never face to face, no real intimacy. The war had maimed his power to be emotionally intimate.

For me, those easings put distance between me and Vince.

I got used to waking up when he jumped out of sleep like a deer, to listen to the tiniest noise.

"Don't take risks," I told him. "My life isn't worth yours."

"If we get LEV., it is."

From Key West, we made rapid and unannounced displacements to other places, and always after we'd mentioned to several people that we were going to somewhere different.

In early November, when things had died down, we made a rapid displacement back to New York, by way of Newark Airport and a long taxi ride.

B ack home, Chino tested my learning by having me do the sweep through the apartment, before he let me and Michael move back in. I passed the test. Everything seemed okay — except Striper, who was pissed off that I'd been gone.

On the assumption that the sniper was surveilling from an apartment across the street, Chino drifted around over there, making lists of tenants and other things. Julius had access to some new databases now, he said. Of course, a smart surveillant would use a fictitious name. Meanwhile, Chino and I parked ourselves on our own roof for several 24-hour periods, with field glasses and a thermos of hot coffee, to see if we could see anything suspicious — curtains drawn, glint of optics, movements on the roof. *Nada.*

"And," he said, "make me a list of everybody in your past who might have a grudge."

It was a long list, starting with Denny Falks, the runner whose lie that I molested him got me dismissed from Penn State. It went from my ex-wife, to a few dissatisfied clients from hustler days. Off went the list, along with Chino's lists, to be cranked through Julius' database.

"Do I get to meet Julius someday?"

"You have to earn meeting Juliusito. He is very weird . . . very hard to please."

I pictured Julius as an old military queen living in a basement somewhere, hard to find in his labyrinth of file cabinets and endless stacks of computer cards, with beautiful young men bringing him coffee, and a direct line to a few other queens in the Pentagon.

Chino went back to L.A. before Thanksgiving. But I missed him.

More and more, thoughts of Chris Shelbourne came to my mind — a deep and hopeless sadness at what could have been. Surely he remembered me. Doing a little elementary investigative work of my own, I got hold of the class reunion committee in Chris' old high school and learned that he was now a stringer for the Associated Press. But they didn't have a current home address for him.

Alone now, I kept up the long, long runs, taking unpredictable routes along miles of city streets, an anonymous bone-lean figure in old sweats, a runner with no race to train for except one of the heart. At night, getting more and more tired, I too was jumping awake like a deer. *Chingao* . . . would I ever sleep well again?

FOURTEEN

Holidays 1979

By December, I was exhausted from overtraining, over-writing, and overthinking about LEV. I brooded about the list of names, and made lots of notes about which of those people LEV. might be. I was through with thinking of Vince and myself as having a "relationship". But it wasn't possible to tell him to his face — he wasn't around.

Then, at mid-December, I got a phone call. Vince wanted to spend the holidays with me — was that cool?

When I called H-C to tell them, Harry said, "Well, our kiddo is up to commencement exercises."

"What's that?"

"Vince still needs to see some live-fire action. So Julius got him into a . . . well, let's say it's a training school for civilians who want to do that. It's run by a Vietnam vet, out in the Carolina boonies somewhere. You pay him mucho bucks and jump through his hoops. If you come out alive, it's the same as a combat ribbon. You can get jobs anywhere in the world."

I sat there in a long silence, digesting this. Finally I said, "You know, part of me can't accept the fact that Vince is carrying it this far. I keep expecting him to come to his senses . . . pull back . . . like most of us do."

"Part of me saw it a thousand times in Southeast Asia," Harry said. "Guys going crazy when their friends were killed."

I almost reminded Harry that I had gone crazy, too, but I wasn't out there with a machine-gun, mowing people down. But the words stuck in my throat. The five thousand San Francisco gays who wrecked City Hall after Dan White was sentenced were women and men who were slowly going crazy. That night, gay leaders had tried in vain to calm them, shouting that violence is how straights solve problems. The mob hooted their leaders down, and put 61 police officers in the hospital.

"Vince could get wasted in Carolina," I said to Harry.

"He could."

"I want to make one more try to stop him. He acts like he still loves me."

"Go ahead and try," rasped Harry's voice in my ear. "But it's risky. You might find out he loves you less than you think."

"**L**ook at all this frivolous bourgeois shit going on," Vince growled, his cold breath blowing over his shoulder.

It was dusk, December 23.

Fifth Avenue was icy, reflecting car lights and frantic shoppers. People were buying, buying. Vince, Michael, John Sive and I were crunching over the ice, heading downtown. We were passing Saks Fifth Avenue, now owned by some foreign company. From the crowded entrance, a warm gust of women's perfume and merry, merry Christmas music came out. We'd been spending, spending on tree ornaments, because Michael wanted a real family Christmas, the kind he'd never had with me around. This morning, Vince had shown up in his Jeep. He was surly, finding fault in straight bourgeois Christmas-making. I was guarded, not wanting to be used again.

A grim foursome, we forged along Fifth Avenue in our warmest clothes. Vince had us all on edge — he was pissed off and restless in the extreme. John was a *GQ* image, shoulders hunched in a Bill Blass overcoat. Michael and I were Village gay hip in jeans, bomber jackets and earmuffs.

I tried to change the subject.

"Jacobs was telling me," I said, "about a couple of gay men in New York with this immune-failure thing . . . who also got some kind of rare cancer."

Vince stared at me.

"The religious right is arming against us," he growled, "and you're staring into test tubes. I think that . . ."

With his power to mutate like field-corn, Vince was wearing jump boots, jeans and a serious goosedown jacket. Under the commando-type wool cap, his hair was severely crew cut. His voice had changed — precise and toneless. His vibe was eerily straight, and he sounded more angry than ever.

". . . And LEV. is only the beginning," Vince was saying. "Too many Americans *want* the queers to disappear. Concentration camps in the desert, like Spiro Agnew said."

As we listened in helpless discomfort, Vince talked about what some gays saw as "the plot to exterminate us". He quoted further from Vice President Agnew's speech about getting rotten apples out of the barrel. His scenario had a horrible logic to it. We were four somber silhouettes trudging past Rockefeller Center, with its magnificent tree, its blaze of lights and music, its skaters sweeping happily around the rink. We ignored the vendors who sold roasted chestnuts — the smoky smell floated past us unenjoyed. Laughing children jostled us. Bogus Santa Clauses collected money for their personal Christmas funds.

"So you really believe all that?" John asked Vince testily. "You're telling me that all the court victories are for nothing?"

Michael stayed silent, looking uncomfortable.

Vince kept his eyes warily moving along the street.

"If I could take Dan White and Anita Bryant and Senator Briggs and a few hundred other people," he added, "and line them up against a wall, I'd —"

He pantomimed holding a heavy machine-gun with his right hand. His body jerked realistically as he mimicked a long burst, letting a long belt of invisible rounds run through the invisible gun.

"Well," John declared, weary of rhetoric, "this old Mary is tired and cold. Let's grab a cab."

In the Village, our neighborhood florist was holding a magnificent spruce tree with a SOLD tag on it.

The Village sparkled with gay holiday spirit. Store windows were decorated with saucy imagination. The famous bakery had its window full of chocolate-covered dicks. As we pushed through the crowds, Vince looked around like he wanted to fix every sound, smell, taste, feel in his memory, as if he was sure he wouldn't see it again. Two women, a butch in custodian's uniform and a femme in suede boots, were wrestling a huge tree onto the top of their car. Now and then, an older male couple passed us — men with careers and money to burn, hampered by glittery gifts in paper bags. A fey mixture of disco music and old carols sluiced the streets.

Vince looked around hungrily.

"God," he whispered. "I love it so much. Why do I love it? There's so much pain here."

Suddenly tears were freezing on his cheeks.

"Are you okay?" I asked him.

"Now and then I get this feeling."

"What?"

"Maybe you understand it —you've been a dad. A feeling like all these men, and all these women, are my kids. And somebody has messed with my kids."

We put up the tree in the corner by the fireplace, where it loosed its pungent scent into the air.

The apartment had a feeling of family overcrowding. Michael had surrendered Angel's old room to John Sive, and was bunking on the sofa for a few days. Vince would share the master bedroom with me. John was planning a traditional roast-goose blowout for tomorrow, so he was busy with cookbooks and checklists.

"In the morning, don't let me forget to call the butcher," he fussed, "to make sure they got my goose order in."

For tonight the old lawyer took charge of our simple dinner.

After dinner, Astarte came, and we all decorated the tree. Amid pleasant arguments about whether the tree should be traditional or piss-elegant, we finished by 10 p.m. The tree was a hybrid of both styles — a silver pyramid of tinsel, glowing with lights in every color of the rainbow. Michael glowed like a kid as he teetered on top of the ladder, hanging the last glass ball by the star.

Vince held the ladder for him. "I can't believe I'm being so bourgeois," he said.

Looking at the finished tree, we all felt overcome by bittersweet memories of childhood holidays. Of the people who weren't there. Steve and Angel. Marian and Joe — it was like they were dead too. Most of all, Betsy and Falcon. We called them up, but Betsy wasn't home. I showed Vince the studio portrait of Falcon that Betsy had just sent. Falcon was a sturdy two years old now.

"You miss him," said Vince, behind me, resting his chin on my shoulder. I could feel a sexual vibe coming from him.

"Yeah." I was on my guard, feeling his body heat.

"He's the real baby Jesus in our cradle, huh."

"Yeah." My mind was moving ahead to our talk.

"If he grows up gay, and you and I do our job, Falcon will have a better world to live in."

Through its windows, the master bedroom glowed like a magic cave, from the holiday lights on apartment windows across the street. Like jukebox hues, color played across the Greek youths in the gilt bedstead, making them move. The fireplace was that New Yorker's joy — a real working fireplace, already flickering with split pine we'd bought at the florist. I pulled the curtains shut, and threw my shirt on the sofa in front of the fireplace. Vince stripped down to his white Jockey briefs, and threw a log on the fire.

My stomach tightened with tension.

While I pulled on a silk robe of Steve's over my boxer shorts, Vince hunkered in front of the fire, watching the flames. Glowing color bathed his nude limbs. I felt armored against his attractiveness, yet he had never looked so good to me. What was the power that this man had, to loot my imagination and hold my emotions hostage for so many years? Now he was 27, less seductive, more poignantly adult and quiet. The little childhood scar under his right eye was deeper. He was even less vain, a scar or two on his lean body.

Vince stood up, and came toward me. "You look tired."

"Working too hard."

"Let me relax you, babe."

Warily, I put my hands on his bare shoulders, and held him away. That was when I noticed that his Lambda tattoo was gone. He'd had it peeled so he could "pass" in Julius' world. The scar was well-healed. More than anything, this told me of the hidden violent world he was moving into.

"You know it was a summer thing," I said. "It's been over for a long time."

Vince looked amused. "It wasn't over two months ago."

He put one hand on my chest, rubbing me gently through the silk robe. His energy told me clearly that he knew he might be killed.

Finally he said, "Look . . . do we have to have this drama about a relationship? Can't we just be friends, and get it on?"

Turning away from him, I leaned against the drawn window curtains. The icy chill coming through the glass bathed me.

"Come on, love. Nobody lives forever," he said quietly.

Pressing against me from behind, he slipped his arms around me. Through the thin silk, his bare arms felt good — not passionate, just good. I was missing touch. So much in his touch called up the emotion and joy of an almost forgotten sunlit past, one without threatening letters. In his warmth, I could catch the new fragrances of his new life, whatever it was. He smelled of castile soap, English Leather and gun oil. For a moment there, I almost lost control.

"Life isn't enough. There has to be honor," I said over my shoulder. "You can sleep on the sofa there."

As Vince let me go, his eyes flooded with a surprisingly intense emotion.

"So Rhett is down to the place in the script where it says *Frankly, my dear, I don't give a damn,*" he said.

"I do give a damn," I said hotly. "But quit trying to use me."

Vince backed away a few steps. The expression in his eyes was not tender now. It was level, cold. No going back now. Time for the most telling lines in the script.

"I can feel where you're at," I said. "You're a step from your revolution, and you're in over your head."

He was silent, standing by his travel bag now, pulling out his combat knife idly. It was a good knife, and it had seen hard use.

"It's not your business," he said.

"It *is* my business," I said to his back. "We have to fight. But fight within the laws, and change the attitudes. If we get violent, *we* will pay. They will be even more violent back."

He frowned. "This is the same shit I've been hearing from you for years."

"You cried over Billy. But you're going to make other people cry?" I persisted. "Bomb airports? Blow the legs off women and children? Kill hostages? Does that make sense?"

He said nothing, flipping the knife and catching it expertly by the handle. His indifference got me angry, an Irish anger that flared somewhere between rage and hysteria. I'd have to trust that last flicker of feeling he still had for me. It was the moment to do the unexpected — break the pattern. The most I could do was use my skill with words, and say something he might remember.

"If you hurt innocent people," I said, my voice trembling, "and drag the whole gay community into total war, you'd be no better than the guy who shot Billy."

The next words poured out of some dark core of will.

"In fact," I added, "if you were about to blow up a plane-load of people, I'd kill you to stop you."

At those words, Vince's eyes went wild.

Suddenly he whipped the knife at me, the way I'd seen him do on the beach-house deck years ago. Only now he was an expert. The knife-point slammed into the wooden fireplace mantel, just one inch from my shoulder. The weapon vibrated like a plucked harpstring. I was shocked at how close he'd come. A wave of adrenaline went over me.

"So turn me in to the FBI," Vince smiled.

He put up his hands in surrender.

Angrily, I yanked the knife out of the wood.

"Go ahead," he urged. "There's the phone. Be the homo hero and save everybody."

I tossed the knife scornfully on the bed between us, with the handle toward him.

"Kid," I said, "here's the benefit of the doubt."

Lowering his arms, Vince gave a cold little laugh. He thrust the knife back in its scabbard.

"You don't have the guts to turn me in," he said.

"And you don't have the heart to blow away innocent people," I said, taking the last shot that I could. "I know you."

In the morning, with a casual "Happy New Year, everybody, see you soon," he went down in the elevator. From the window, I watched him walk away down the street, carrying the travel bag. A light rain was falling, and his reflection followed him on the sidewalk.

My young bird was heading out on the long migration route. He was running the gauntlet of hunters' guns and power-lines.

When I told Harry about the confrontation, he whistled and said, "Risky move."

"I know. I blew off your recommendation. But a guy's gotta do what's in his heart. I had to try something."

"Well, you gave him something to think about, for sure."

New Year's 1979-80

After John Sive left, and Michael buried himself in finals, I did year-end tax stuff, and brooded about the future. I was 44 now, still fit and not exactly hard on the eyes. I had good years ahead yet. The movie with Vince was over. Was I going to kick the habit of passion for men, and get passionate about my work? Was it time to think about dating someone new? To push my search for Chris?

As if Life answered my prayer, a man called me up.

I had met Russell Houghton at Marvin Jakes' party. New York society knew Russell and his wife Cici as art collectors and patrons of the National Horse Show. Russell was an amateur rider, who liked to show his own horses. Cici had died, and now Russell was making widower's moves. He was the kind of gay man that some activists hate — Republican and deep-closet.

Russell had asked me out several times. But I'd put him off. Now he invited me to spend New Year's at his country home, Bel Gard. He said he wouldn't take "no" for an answer. Russell was nearly 20 years older than me. I'd always been the older guy. Maybe it was time to be the young guy.

So I decided what the hell, and packed Steve's shawl-collar tux.

Russell sent his black Cadillac, and I took the two-hour ride north through falling snow, into rural Westchester County. When the car stopped in front of his pillar-fronted home, my Irish poverty was agog at the white sweep of lawns, stables and indoor ring. Russell and his two terriers made three sets of tracks across the snow.

"Welcome to Bel Gard," he said.

The handshake was warm — a hand surprisingly calloused for a gentleman of leisure.

Russell was six foot one, in his mid-60s, with owlish piercing eyes. His florid Anglo face and twice-broken nose suggested a British boxing champion. His walk was stiff: dislocations, sprains, fractures, from falls with horses. When he grinned, he flashed a gold tooth, replacing one knocked out by a polo mallet. That day he was bareheaded, snow melting on his silver curls. Tight riding pants displayed powerful thighs that drove his horses relentlessly. A different sport than mine, but . . . sport was sport.

I asked myself: Would I like driving this guy? Would he demand to drive me?

Russell walked me through the stable, and introduced me

to his hunters and jumpers. "Jaeger . . . Tomcat . . . Ranger . . ." Haltered heads poked out of stall doors. Flaring nostrils blasted me with warm curious breaths.

While caterers set up for the party that night, I was suddenly tired, and napped in the comfortable guest room. That feeling of doors open to new things should have been exciting. But it wasn't. I jumped at every sound in the house.

That night, about 75 of Russell's horsey hard-drinking friends flooded in. As the buffet was demolished, people stood around telling war stories of the show circuit — bad horses, nasty falls at fences. Russell guided me from group to group, introducing me.

"Oh . . . Harlan *Brown*," said Andrea della Ponza, a young pro rider. "God, how great to meet you," she added in a low, conspiratorial tone.

By 3 a.m., several revelers passed out in guest rooms. Russell was a little drunked up himself.

When the house was silent, the two of us lingered in the library talking. What was on his mind?

As Russell threw an oak log in the massive fireplace, firelight played over Asian mementos and photos of the young cavalry officer jumping fences at the 1936 Olympics. The terriers snoozed on the rug. Russell poured himself a whiskey from a decanter, and settled into more stories. His discovery at private school that he was gay — the hiding, the anxiety. Covert doings with another member of the Cornell polo team.

"You and I met years ago," he said suddenly, casually. "You might not remember."

"Where was that?" I said.

Then a chill flushed along my back.

"The hotel room was dark," he added.

That client had felt like a man of 40-something. He had paid $1000 for an aggressive active's time. He hadn't wanted games or role-playing. He wanted to get to an edge. In the dark, without whips or other aids, I took him there.

I was aghast. The worst kind of small-world scenario.

"I see you do remember," said Russell.

He opened an antique safe in the wall. Out came a morocco photograph album. When I opened it, a deep shock ripped through me. Russell had known the photographs must exist, so he had gotten them. The nude poses of a working professional in the gay sex industry. There I was — looking like a young, angry, hot-eyed Michael, with my schlong dangling down my thigh. The poses were created by Marty Ekstein, noted gay photographer of the '60s. I had destroyed the negatives and my portfolio when I left New York to go to Prescott. But a few prints were still blowing around the city like dead leaves — worth money now.

"You aren't ashamed of those years," Russell mused.

I swallowed the anger, and slapped the album shut.

"No," I said, trying to sound casual. "I was young, dumb and full of cum."

Why had he pulled this move? To convince me that a relationship was foregone, since I'd already had him? He'd just made me feel young indeed — vulnerably young, and violated.

Russell got up, and poured himself more whiskey.

"You keep crossing my path," he said. "The next time was the Montreal Olympics. Jaeger was on loan to the U.S. team. Next, Marvin's party. I wanted to see you, close up, in the daylight."

"I don't understand," I said.

"You're out in a way that's . . . inconceivable to me."

"Not by choice."

"Cici is gone, my children grown, less reason to hide. No, I am not going to . . ." He waved one hand dramatically. ". . . *Come out,* walk down Fifth Avenue carrying a sign. I think that kind of thing is so common."

I'd already heard his horsey friends use that word. To them, common meant "not well-bred".

"How will things change, if some of us common folk don't show our faces in public?" I asked.

Unsteadily, because he was really drunk now, Russell put away the album, and locked the safe. In his blunt boot-leather way, like he was driving a high-powered horse at a big fence, Russell was proposing to me. He stood by the window looking out into the dark. It was snowing again — large flakes blew softly against the pane.

"I'd like to have you in my world," he said. "You're not discreet company. But I can manage that."

"Why not some dewy young stud?"

"I've had my fill of the young studs."

The fire popped in the silence. As I put my empty tea mug on the coffee table, I thought of Vince.

"These days, I go to bed only with people I love," I said. "And love has worn a little thin."

Russell's eyes went to my gold wedding band, no doubt wondering how he could get me to take it off. But I was on edge about the way he'd handled the photo thing. I didn't feel any quiver of interest in him. His world didn't feel comfortable to me. I'd be a bird, all right — a canary in a gilded cage.

When we retired, I locked my bedroom door.

Next day, the limo swept me back toward New York City.

On the back-seat bar, I found a manila envelope containing the photographs. Maybe he knew he'd overstepped, and wanted to recoup by returning them. I'd have to assume he kept copies.

A t home, depression closed in again. No new thing. Love was a crematorium with Billy's body in it. Having Billy, then Vince, had insulated me briefly from the homosexual's terror of having nobody. Would I wind up being the old guy cruising bars again for five minutes of skin contact with another living human being? Haunting the tenderloin and paying the young guys like I'd been? Who cared about an old guy?

About to burn the photographs wrathfully in my own fireplace, I remembered the grand statement that I wasn't ashamed. And I wasn't, dammit. So the photos went into that banker's box of mementos that I called The Box.

I wrote a note on the stuffiest-looking card I could find:

Dear Russell,
        Thanks for a special time. I'm glad to know you.
In the long run, friends matter as much as lovers.
                Best always,
                Harlan

FIFTEEN

Winter 1980

The visit with Russell was the start of several months where I stepped off into deep space, into strange and scary worlds.

Prescott College had folded. With intense emotion, I read in the January 20 *Times* about a leveraged take-over of Joe's software company. Joe had lost his means to underwrite the college, and too many alumni had backed off from "immorality on campus". Eyes filled with tears, I was sure that religious fascists were behind this move to cut the school's throat. When I'd calmed down, I called Marian and Joe at their home number.

They didn't have much to say. But Joe wasn't starchy now — just sad.

"They gave me a golden parachute," he said. "We're selling the property to a developer. Financially, I should be happy, because my health isn't up to it any more. But . . ." He paused. "I, uh, I kind of miss having morning tea with you. Hey . . . remember those foul shots with our tea bags and your wastebasket?"

"You were always high-score man." My eyes misted.

Then Marian got on the phone. "My daughter Sara is going to Ghana to study herbal medicine," she said. "Joe and I are moving to California. He needs the climate."

The Prescotts were embarrassed at the way they'd fired me. I was ready to swallow my pride, sad about losing them. We could have gotten together for dinner before they left. But neither side budged.

"Well," I said, "send me your new address."

Once upon a time, I was the man born without tear ducts. Now it seemed like anything at all could get me weeping. As I sat over my dog-eared Bible, crossing out more passages, it occurred to me that I was having a delayed breakdown over Billy's death. Like a moray eel, I dealt social shocks, till people started avoiding me. Michael tried to give good advice about a therapist. When I barked that I thought humanity were fools for running to shrinks, my son backed off too.

Now and then, I got out my .45 automatic and stared at it.

If life was a race, I had run thousands of miles since Montreal, and gone nowhere. The dark Front Runner loomed ahead with every stride. My efforts to beat him to some vague finish-line were a joke. I was losing. And I was judging myself into a personal hell for losing a no-win race. Why hadn't I killed myself yet? The old Harlan believed that suicide was a sin against God. But if I set my heart as the heart of God, it meant that I owned my life, and had the right to dispose of it any way I chose.

I did put the gun away.

But, for the first time since high school, it was suddenly too much effort to get out there in the morning and run a few miles. Time to break the pattern. So I quit.

George Rayburn had just been diagnosed with a funny kind of pneumonia, caused by a little organism called *Pneumocystis* that is usually harmless. He had the immune system ticking down too.

Doc Jacobs kept muttering about the patterns he was seeing. Several gay men had died of immune failure now. Some unhealthy men shared a profile. They'd had amoebas, hepatitis B, mononucleosis, every kind of STD, plus a fondness for poppers, alcohol, drug abuse, tricking and passive anal sex. Now and then, listening to Doc, I felt a chill. Thank God I didn't fit the profile. But George didn't fit the profile of bathhouse warrior either. He'd been monogamous for two years. So was his lover, Earle. Neither of them used drugs or booze. The only thing George ever did to himself was work to death in the gay-rights movement; he was 36, and his health had been frail for years.

Through February I visited George as he got thinner, coughed like crazy. But he was being medicated with the standard thing for *Pneumocystis,* and seemed to be getting better.

I yearned to live alone on Fire Island. But the weather had turned cold and stormy. Getting myself out there, making the beach house livable in winter, seemed like a huge task. Nights, I sat in the apartment and tried to write. The damp Manhattan air made me cough. When I thought about Vince, about Chino and Chris, my heart felt like a lump of dirty Manhattan ice. Even making love to myself was too much effort. Sexual tides of old had ebbed to the barest of wet dreams.

It had been months since LEV. was in touch. Had he gotten bored with the whole thing?

On February 19, I came down with flu. Vitamin C, herb tea, and cough medicine didn't help. Michael was alarmed at how my flu dragged on, complete with swollen glands and graveyard cough and a profound dragginess, and he pestered me to go see Doc Jacobs. But I was the Neanderthal, toughing it out.

"It's no big deal," I told him.

One evening Harry called. Vince was in some kind of trouble, and Chino was extracting him. My morale was so low that I didn't give a hoot what happened to my ex-lover.

By February 28, the flu seemed to be gone, except for a cough. No word on Vince.

That day, feeling guilty about physical inactivity, I bundled up and took a one-mile run down toward Wall Street. When I got home, my body felt dead-flat and achy.

For the next two days, I hardly stirred out of bed. The cough got worse, and my lungs gurgled. On the third night, when my temperature hit 105, the thought went through my thick head that I was in big trouble. Was I developing the *Pneumocystis* thing that George had? Steve had coughed too. Jacobs kept raving about sexual contagion, but I hadn't been in bed with either man.

Michael sensed my distress, woke up and came to my room. "Dad, enough of this shit. I'm calling your doctor."

The ambulance ride was a blur.

At St. Luke's-Roosevelt Hospital, I waited three hours in the emergency room, watching the human wreckage of New York stream past. Early that morning, somebody died, or was released, and I was wheeled to a freshly made bed in a private room. The next day was another blur of oxygen mask, blood work, bronchoscopy, sputum test.

When I woke up, Chino was sitting by the bed, wearing a surgical facemask. Seeing his grave eyes over that mask gave me a shock. People wore masks for heavy contagion, didn't they? My mind was going wild.

"Hey, *loco*," he said.

He took my hand in his strong warm hand, and squeezed it hard. One tiny drop of melt trickled down the side of my icy heart. Why wasn't I in love with this maimed but loyal friend?

Doc Jacobs, also masked, stood over me in his white coat, with clipboard and fistful of X-rays.

"I suppose I've got what George has, huh?" I croaked.

"What you've got is bacterial pneumonia, and bronchitis. And," Jacobs added, "you've got tuberculosis."

"Come on. TB went out with the horse and buggy."

"Glad to see you arguing with me," said Doc. "It's a good sign." He was writing stuff on his clipboard.

"So now I sit in some sanatorium?" I croaked. "Like in a goddam Victorian novel?"

"Oh, no," Jacobs chuckled. "Today treatment is medication . . . six months. Once we get your pneumonia under control, you can handle it as an outpatient."

When the doctor left the room, Chino said, "You've had the bad news. Want to know about Vince?"

"Only if it's good news," I whispered.

Sleep slid over me for a few minutes, and when I woke up again, Chino had left the room. Another pair of eyes, beautiful, but haggard and sad, were looking at me over another white mask. They belonged to Vince. Gone was his military drag. His clothes were bottom-drawer leavings from somewhere — faded jeans, torn ski jacket, old Adidas and an ancient Watergate T-shirt. He was clean-shaven, with an air of a quick spit-polish for viewing.

Slowly he sat down by the bed.

"So your little adventure is over . . . is that it?" I croaked.

He chose his words carefully, in case we were being over-heard.

"Yeah," he said hoarsely, looking down. That shame was glowing in him again, the way it always did when he felt or imagined my judgment. "I got to the training camp and it was like . . . I don't know . . ." He drew a deep sigh of exasperation. "I looked around at the other guys, felt their vibe, and for the first time I . . . really saw where I was heading. Suddenly I just . . . flamed out. There's got to be a better way."

"I tried to tell you that," I whispered.

He jumped up, and his eyes went black with emotion.

"Why in the fucking hell," he burst out, "do you always have to be the big know-it-all? Just because you're older doesn't give you the right to belittle me! So I made a mistake. Didn't you ever make a mistake?"

He towered over me, and poured a scalding soliloquy through the mask, onto the bed.

"Jesus, Harlan, where's your heart? Emotionally, with you, I feel like . . . I don't know. You make me feel like when I was 17 and had my sacred dream about loving men. It was going to be . . . a ceremony or something. And wonderful . . . if I could get up the guts. Then I got fucked for the first time. Yeah, I lied . . . somebody had me before you. I was hanging out on Melrose Boulevard. This college guy, he was from Texas Christian . . . fed me a line and took me to a motel on Sunset, and he did me till I was raw, and then he left. I cried all night and felt like some girl who'd been raped. After that, I believed that being gay meant being used. Being the most alone that a person could be. So I used people. Fucked people. Until I met Billy. What a revelation. Wow, man . . . another human being who still had the dream. And . . . guess what. Billy didn't love me. But that was okay, because Billy was my first gay friend, and that was something."

With a wrenching movement, he turned away, and leaned against the cold window. His breath steamed the glass.

"Then we met you, and we both fell for you. And guess what . . . you didn't love me. But that was okay, because you and Billy got together, and it was like . . . the two of you had found the golden romance that every dyke and every faggot dreams about. The ceremony. Maybe the Goddesses and the Gods put you out there so we could see the golden thing was real. So I could go on hoping."

His tears were spilling down behind the mask. Incredibly, one tear made it to his neck, where it spotted his collar.

"But . . . you're not golden with me, man. Emotionally, you have me and walk, like that first guy did. And I wish to God I could hate you. But I can't, because you were the golden thing for me."

There was a long silence. Down the hall, the hospital intercom was calling out a code blue — somebody was on the edge of death. I knew I was supposed to feel sorry, so sorry. I tried to feel sorry. But it seemed like my heart had been replaced by a knot of mucous.

"Come here," I whispered.

Weakly I held out my hand.

"Fuck you . . . cold-hearted son of a bitch," Vince raved. "No wonder women talk about male chauvinist pigs. You're a *gay* chauvinist pig, man. You're the worst there is."

"Come over here."

My hand lay open on the white coverlet.

Slowly he sat down in the chair again, bent over the bed, pressed his face in my palm. His hot tears trickled through the surgical mask, onto my fingers. He cried into my hand, smelling like soap and tears. With my other hand, I stroked his feverish head. Finally I felt around for the Kleenex box, handed him some.

After a few minutes, he sat up and blew his nose.

"So what happened there at the camp?" I whispered.

His eyelashes were stuck together with tears, as he stared out the window.

"The night I got there, I had this weird dream. There was this dark hole into a wall, really creepy looking, and Billy was saying, 'No, no, don't go in there'. I hadn't dreamed about Billy for years. I woke up in my tent, really freaked out, and suddenly I knew I'd come to the end of it. So I left my gear, and sneaked out."

"They must have had sentries posted."

"Yeah. I almost got my buns shot off. Then I was stranded in some no-nuts little town, no money, nothing I could sell. The cops arrested me for vagrancy. So I called Harry and Chino, and Chino came and bailed me out, and they loaned me a little bread."

"What are you going to do now?"

He wiped his eyes with the Kleenex.

"Get the Testarossa out of storage and sell it. I can get twenty-five thousand for it, maybe. Go home to California. Get a job. H-C says I can crash on their sofa till I get my shit together."

I tried hard to feel something, but I couldn't, and exhaustion was swallowing me again.

When I woke up, Vince was gone, and Chino was sitting there holding my hand again.

"I respect him for going that far," Chino said. "I went to Vietnam sick inside about a lot of things, and I did pull the trigger. And it wasn't more gutsy than what Vince did. Not many people ever make a real decision. He did, and he's a changed man."

"I suppose I can meet a certain person now," I croaked.

Chino knew I meant Julius. "Cool out for a while," he said.

A nurse came bustling in with a little paper cup of pills.

"This is your medication that Doctor ordered," she said.

As I swallowed down the pills, Chino asked:

"So . . . you gonna live?"

"Why not? Things can only get better."

"No shit. So far, LEV. has made a fool of us. We're stuck in a pattern. It's gotta change."

"You going back to California?"

"I'll stay a few days. Michael and Astarte are going to help me keep an eye on you. A hospital is an easy place to get somebody."

Suddenly, for no reason and every reason I could think of, I was the one who was sobbing now. What had I done to deserve a friend like this? I turned my face away from pure shame. Chino didn't say anything. As the horrible sobs racked my sick lungs, his hand was still rubbing mine gently.

E very day, the nurse brought the drugs with mysterious names — isoniazid, rifampin, pyrazinamide. Sitting up, I stared out the window, where Vince's tear-streaks still showed — at the depressing vista of power-plant smokestacks and bridges. The hospital air was a recycled miasma of other people's breath, medicines, body fluids, despair and suffocating pain. I had time to think how the losing race had impacted my own immune system.

Terrible dreams hounded me. I found Billy's body laying forgotten on a gurney, in some empty corridor. The corpse was tied up in green garbage bags, with twine wrapped around it. I remembered trying to wrestle it into the seat of my old pickup, and failing. The limp corpse had a will of its own — one long sinewy leg kept sliding out, blocking the door. Then, all of a sudden, the corpse got away from me and ran off down a rainy street. I was chasing it, trying to throw a kick. "Stop! You're mine!" I was yelling at it. But it stayed ahead of me, not turning its shattered head, powering along with jerky bounds.

I woke into the hot silence, with nurses rustling down the corridor outside, and was afraid to sleep.

As the days passed, my beard and hair grew long again. One day, when Michael brought my mail, there was a home-made get-well card and a letter from LEV. — the longest one yet. He must have spent days clipping and pasting.

APOLOGIES FOR NEGLECTING YOU ... I
HAVE BEEN AWAY ... NICE TO SEE YOU RIGHT
WHERE I WANT YOU ... HOW DOES IT FEEL
TO HAVE YOUR LIFE GOING NOWHERE ... LIKE
MINE DID ... FEAR THE STRONGER MEDICINE
... I AM CLOSE ... SO CLOSE
    LOVE,
    LEV.

"God," said Michael, reading it. "He knows you're here."

"This is so creepy." Astarte shivered.

Chino read it. "Definitely someone who knew you."

"He could be anybody ... an orderly right in this hospital," Michael added.

"Did Julius ever finish running through the list of old grudges?" I asked.

"Yeah. Of the 19 men on the list who are your age or younger, 4 of them are veterans. Including your friend Denny Falks. But ... maybe our guy isn't a vet. So far, Julius hasn't connected any of them with Richard Mech."

I sighed, as Chino put the letter in his jacket pocket.

The same batch of mail brought a sad letter from Jacques. Their second baby had died at six months, of a stubborn ear infection. Eileen was flat on her back from exhaustion.

Russell came down from Westchester, bearing a book for me to read. It felt like an apology about the photographs.

"When you get out, come recuperate at my place in Puerto Vallarta," he said.

To my surprise, Vince called from L.A. I had the oxygen mask off now, and talked with him while propped on pillows. It was surprising how distant I felt.

"Are you okay?" I asked.

"Yeah, I am."

He was putting on a good front — trying to sound like the cocky old Vince.

"I've paid H-C back — got a place of my own." By his tone, he was anxious to show me how responsible he was being. "And I've finally got a job in films. It's a dy-no-mite job."

"How'd you manage that? Find a camouflage casting couch?"

Vince ignored my barb. "I start next week at Valhalla Productions."

"Never heard of them."

"If you were in TV ads, you would. They've won all kinds of awards for commercials. Paul Eckhardt's the producer-director, and Darryl Fiske is the DP. They go to Dorothy's church, Harlan. They want to be out in Hollywood . . . move over to long format — documentaries and features with serious gay themes."

"Why the hell would they hire a freshman like you?"

"Because I made an appointment and charmed their butts off. They need somebody who can . . . do what I do. Make juju. Evolve into a casting director . . . executive producer . . . . Anyway, it's the first time I've ever been wanted for my mind, instead of my body. I'm gonna shoot, but it's going to be film, man. Diamond bullets . . . into people's minds."

This statement was touching.

"What's your title?" I asked.

"Assistant producer."

"Sounds impressive."

Vince laughed. "It's not. I'm a script reader, editing assistant, gofer and best boy. But I get to learn on the job."

"Good for you," I said, sounding like a father.

"You should come to L.A. and visit the studio," he said. "Paul and Darryl would love to meet you."

But he didn't say he wanted to see me again. And I didn't care to see him. Screw golden romance. Screw passion. No more 20-something guys for me. Better somebody my age, who was halfway sane and had some common sense — if there was such a man. My old high-school flame Chris would be my age. He'd seemed pretty sane in those days. Maybe I should summon the energy to look him up.

Two weeks later, the hospital sent me home, and Chino went back to L.A. Dutifully I kept up the program of TB medication.

My life was at a turning point. For the moment, my lungs were too weak for running. I felt strangely lost without running . . . spirits empty and flat. And right now, roughing it on Fire Island, or socializing in L.A., would tax me too much. So I dug up my passport — hadn't used it since the European track tour with the three boys in '75 — and flew to Puerto Vallarta, Mexico.

For three weeks, Russell and I sat in the hot sun at his villa. I soaked in the healing rays, and swam in the pool, and ate wonderful Mexican food. We actually did get to be friends. Russell respected the line I'd drawn. Besides, he had broken some ribs in a fall with a horse, so he wasn't in shape to wrestle anybody into bed.

One day he leaned painfully from his deck-chair and fingered my gold ring.

"You still with what's his name — Vince?" he asked.

I didn't feel like explaining that it was Billy's ring. "No. That's over."

"Then why the ring?"

I forced a grin. "Social protection."

Russell guffawed. "From what? You look like some married man who's out for trade."

As spring neared, I felt strong enough to think about Los Angeles. I suspected that Vince wanted to improve his status at the studio by bringing me in. But then Paul Eckhardt himself called me at the villa — expressed interest in my writing, invited me to a get-acquainted meeting. I'd never written a screenplay, but wondered if I could learn.

So Russell had his Lear jet fly me to Los Angeles.

SIXTEEN

Spring 1980

At Los Angeles airport, Vince was waiting in the boarding area — a dark, quiet figure in the crisscross of
passengers.

His eyes met mine, with the accusations still alive in them.
Ever the shape-shifter, 28 now, he looked like a serious film-
industry professional. Tote briefcase slung over his shoulder,
heavy with scripts, reels, people's head shots and what-not. He
wore sunglasses, running shoes and slacks, and a designer T-
shirt. His dark hair was yuppie short. And he looked very fit.

As we left the terminal, there was edgy small-talk.

"You look good," I said. "Been running?"

"Yeah. I've missed it."

"Run for fun?"

"I belong to the gay track club. You know . . . the L.A.
Front Runners. The ones who've been asking for your help
for years."

I ignored his dig.

"Some people in the community are disgusted with you
because you don't take the podium," Vince persisted. "You don't
lead. You don't even help."

"I'm no good on the podium if I don't have anything to say."

As we crossed the street, Vince frowned at my own fashion look. "Coach chic" was now "bay-man casual". Steve's old Abercrombie & Fitch jacket. Spit-polished cowboy boots. The beaded belt of Steve's that I loved. My hair and beard were trimmed, but pirate-length.

"Your sugar daddy is fucking you over," Vince ragged me. "He isn't buying you a new wardrobe."

"Russell's just a friend."

"Tell me another one, honey."

"Nothing to tell."

"You look like a beach bum."

"I *am* a beach bum."

"Stop wearing Steve's clothes. It's unhealthy."

As Vince's Jeep raced along the freeway into West Hollywood, I sat behind my dark glasses, feeling empty and flat. Our hair blew wildly in the warm morning air. All those palm trees and tile roofs felt alien. I knew L.A. only from track meets in the distant past, and had never been in a mood to explore its pleasures. Vince yelled some local history over the wind. West Hollywood had been a retreat of "bohemians" from the earliest movie days. Gay life centered around the "strip" on Santa Monica Boulevard. And yes, there were rumors about sick men out here, too.

"You'll like the West Coast," Vince insisted. "Gays and lesbians are swinging a little political power here — the kind we don't have in New York."

Just then, an LAPD police cruiser pulled us over. We had to submit to a registration check.

"Pig-fuckers," Vince said when they left. "We still don't swing the police. They like to pull over gay guys in Jeeps."

First, we went to the Santa Monica strip to find Harry and Chino. In the balmy spring morning, not much was happening. Boulevard boys and panhandlers had called it a night. Studio One and the Blue Parrot and other bars and discos were closed. At cafés, people drank coffee and read papers. Shoppers milled the sidewalks, past flower stalls, where vendors arranged roses and birds-of-paradise. At the Hamburger Haven, Harry was brooding over coffee alone. He looked L.A. butch, with blond hair in a little ponytail, and a gold earring on the side that said top.

"Where's Chino?" I asked.

"You might see him at the Valhalla soirée tonight. Chino is doing less and less good. He moved out of our place."

This was bad news. "You two had a fight?"

"No. But he's been . . . remote. He sleeps in his vehicle like he's homeless, and showers at the Athletic Club. I gave him a membership for his birthday, so he'd have somewhere to clean up. I've tried, Harlan. Tried to be the older brother he never had. Therapy, these new 12-step programs for PTSD. Nothing works. Maybe you can do something. I'm afraid he's giving up."

Harry's eyes misted — the most emotion I'd seen him show.

"PTSD?" I asked.

"Post trauma stress disorder. New word for shell shock."

After Harry left us, Vince dragged me to his favorite clothier on the Boulevard. Fortunately it sold my kind of casual. As we looked through clothes racks, my mind was flooded with worry about Chino. To make more conversation, I said:

"Well, you look like you're doing fine."

"I am. Finally on the right track."

"You dating anybody?"

"Too busy. I'm into friendship and ideas."

"What? No partying?"

"*Moi?* Hey, babe, I'm a workaholic now."

Honey, I thought. *Babe.* In New York, it was getting so nobody but old queens said *darling* any more.

"What about you?" he ragged me. "Seriously . . . are you going to feather a nest with Russell Houghton?"

"He's more your type," I ragged back. "He's got all kinds of money. I'll introduce you."

Quickly I chose slacks, pullover, a corduroy jacket. The cowboy boots and Steve's belt looked good with them.

Valhalla Productions was located in a funky old soundstage on Sunset Boulevard, not far from the Paramount lot. At

11 a.m., Paul and Darryl gave me a grand tour of the little office. The staff numbered six, including the secretary. I met the two other associates, a black lesbian couple — CFO Rose Bass and casting director Vivian Woodruffe. Then they gave me a private screening of their first documentary. *Night and Fog* was about the 200,000 gay men and lesbians killed in Nazi Germany. Valhalla had taken a deep breath and entered it in the Cannes Film Festival. Vince was credited as executive producer. I was impressed.

Later, at a sun-splashed restaurant table, Paul said:

"Why don't you take a shot at a script? The market for serious gay films is going to explode."

Darryl added, "We'll even do the big no-no. We'll give you — gasp! — creative control. On a screenplay of *Rape of the Angel Gabriel*. We understand you control the rights."

The thought of Hollywood backed me off, but they kept hammering. "The things you know . . . the perspective that you have," said Paul. "We young queers need the gay men and lesbians like you."

"I'll think about it," I hedged.

They were all working hard to shoot diamond bullets. What was I doing? Still running from that .22 Magnum.

Vince had his own tiny apartment, in a duplex next door to Paul's and Darryl's house on Rosewood Avenue. This was a quiet West Hollywood residential street, with modest stucco homes jammed side by side. I'd be sleeping at Paul's and Darryl's. That evening, their patio "soirée" was crowded with film people aged 20 to 35, all bright-eyed as baby kittens. Everybody was eating in the new health style — drinking juice and spritzers, noisy with shop talk. As I walked in, everyone went quiet, like I was a wild bull elephant looming into their space.

The reception nonplused me. "Uh . . . hi, everybody," I said.

"Hi, Harlan," they all chorused.

My old pirate eyes roved their eager young faces. In 1974, six years ago, when I had fallen in love with Billy, many of these kids were in high school. A lump swelled in my throat.

Chino called to say tersely that he wasn't coming.

"But I'll pick you up at 8 tomorrow morning," he said.

Late, after everyone else left, Vince lingered to talk with me, briefcase slung over his shoulder. From the darkened patio deck where the two of us stood, Paul's and Darryl's silhouettes could be seen through the kitchen window. They'd sent home the caterers, and were doing some last cleanup themselves. Paul gave Darryl a peck on the cheek. Darryl rubbed Paul's back.

I felt cold as ice. Vince shuffled his feet like a kid.

"Hey," he said, "why don't you go out with the Front Runners tomorrow morning? We run together in Griffith Park."

"I'm not in shape."

"The next Memorial 5-K is going to be bigger and better. I'm race director, and I want to make it a primo event. Maybe you'd get involved this time. The club would love that."

"Another time," I said.

He shrugged, looking down. A sudden wind had come up, and the palms gnashed their fronds together in that strange night sky so full of color and sound. Slowly Vince's hand reached into his briefcase, and pulled out Billy's track shoe.

"You were right," he said softly. "I would have made a terrible terrorist."

He put the shoe in my hand.

I stood there turning it over and over, feeling numb at this surprise victory. What did he want to do — grab a lifejacket from the sinking *Titanic* of our affair? The moment passed, and he turned away.

Did he hope I'd call him back again? I didn't.

He walked away into the swaying palm shadows.

Next morning, over coffee, Paul said, "Don't forget us. You have family to step into, here in L.A."

"Thanks," I said. "I'll think about your offer."

About a quarter of nine, Chino braked his Land Rover at the curb with a screech. He was unshaven, hollow-eyed. Blankets and clothes were stowed neatly in the back. As I climbed in, I could feel how my best friend was hanging on by fingers that were trembling and tired. One slip, a theft that cost him the vehicle and weapons, and he might let go — plummet away from us, down into the river of homeless vets on the L.A. streets.

We went to the West Hollywood Athletic Club, where he put in a hard workout — too hard. It felt like he wanted to melt down thought in the fire of effort. From there, cleaned up, we went to Venice Beach, his favorite place to get away from everybody. We sat in an outdoor restaurant on the strand, and ate steak and eggs and salsa and fries, then stared at the ocean, past the skate-boarders and ladies walking their dogs. I wondered if he'd open up to me, about Vietnam. A tense and tender silence shimmered between us. Those energies around him, that ate the sunlight, were enough to drive away anybody — even an old buddy like Harry. I was another black hole. How could I do anything for him?

We walked on the beach, and he complained about his scalp feeling tight. So I had him sit on the sand, and I kneeled behind him and massaged his head for a while, till his tense burning scalp loosened up a little.

He didn't close his eyes, or relax his neck into my hands, but he did murmur, "*Caramba* . . . you're good."

"As a coach, I was a licensed masseur . . . I'd better be good."

"Where are you going from L.A.?"

"Back to the Beach."

"Why are you hanging onto Fire Island?"

"I need to be alone. Have some things out with myself. Billy's death. The way I've been so addicted to love." The feel of his glossy hair was getting me hot.

"Yeah, you *pobre loco* . . . you're always hearing those wedding bells." He pulled his head away, and looked around at me. "What if LEV. makes a move on you out there?"

"You've taught me what you can."

I sat down by him, and we gazed out across the bright water.

He changed the subject to *familia*. "Marian and Joe live in Malibu now. Joe's had a stroke — right side paralyzed. She nurses him. You hear from our Betsy?"

"At Christmas. She and Marla are fine."

"Why don't you take a run up north . . . see them and Falcon?"

"Oh, I don't know . . ."

He stood up. "Let's drive up. I got nothing else to do."

From a pay phone, I caught Betsy grading papers at home. She was reluctant, but finally agreed that she and Marla would meet us next morning, at the Colusa Wildlife Refuge. And they'd bring Falcon. She said that Marla knew a little about the security problems, and they weren't eager to have me visit their home. With a new energy, my sidekick and I crossed the city, finally striking Los Feliz Boulevard on our way to the Interstate 5 north. Chino was zigging and zagging, making sure nobody was following us.

Finally he took a right off Los Feliz.

"We'll zag through my old *barrio*," he said. "Silver Lake is mostly Latino. Some Anglos and Asians. Gays and lesbians moving in too. That's a new thing since I was a kid."

We took a quick detour over Silver Lake's breezy hills, past the small lake, through a maze of old fixer-upper houses where gays and professional people lived. A grim grid of streets on the hotter flat was where poorer Latinos lived. Along Hyperion Avenue, he pointed out a few gay bars, bookstores and restaurants.

"Any *familia* still here?" I asked.

"No. My uncle and cousins moved to Santa Barbara. My grandma lives near the Santa Ynez reservation. I call now and then, but I haven't seen them in a long time."

A few blocks further, he zagged left into a hilly park, as beautiful and big as Central Park. The more civilized vistas had noble old shade trees and lawns planted a century ago, that drank up precious California water. Above us reared the wild wooded ridges — natural, tangled and brushy, almost like a dry tropical forest. The maze of green.

"This is Griffith Park," he said.

As we drove along the curving roadway, we passed dozens of runners and race-walkers and joggers and bicyclists. Some wore Front Runner T-shirts — stragglers from the run that Vince invited me to. Vince was up there somewhere ahead, moving along with that miler's stride. Suddenly I felt a pang of missing the sport.

"So the Memorial is run right here," I said.

"It is."

"Good course for a 5-K."

"In the daylight it is," he said dryly.

"Is it cruisy at night?"

"Very cruisy. When I was a kid, I biked over here sometimes to hide in the bushes and watch guys *haciéndolo*. These days, paramilitary groups sometimes come in here at night to train. Black power groups . . . right-wing Anglos. Sometimes they hunt each other. Sometimes they hunt the gay guys. Yeah, it gets pretty *loco* in here at night."

He gave me the first faint grin of the day.

"Let's hope LEV. doesn't attend the Memorial," I said.

"Yeah," said Chino. "The thought has already crossed my mind."

Soon we were on Interstate 5, racing north over the Grapevine pass, into the desert. We shared the driving, talking Spanglish. He was relaxing a little. By nine that night, we were north of Sacramento, pulling off the I-5 into a truck-stop. The motel room had two beds, but need flashed between us, unspoken, so we lay down on one bed. The thought of what organisms we might be trading did cross my mind, but only for a second. After all, I knew him, didn't I? We'd never given each other crabs or clap — there was something to be said for that. As usual, he kept his back to me, but his warm cock filled my hand, and he reached around for mine. His rich skin tasted of chilis and unshed tears.

Billy's shoe glowed in my suitcase.

N ext morning, we gazed over the incandescent flat of the Central Valley. Its engineered squares of rice-lands and wheat-fields were a hot green. Here and there, distant grain elevators broke a smoggy horizon that was straight as a slide rule. Along brimming irrigation ditches, snowy egrets stalked for frogs — reminding me of Vince. Vibrating with excitement, I wanted to come out of this visit with Betsy's concession that I could somehow be closer to Billy's child.

East of the I-5, near the town of Colusa, we found the wildlife refuge. It was several thousand acres of rushes and ponds, once part of a vast swamp that was now rice-lands. From a distance, the water was white with snow geese, resting and feeding in their spring migration. As we stopped in the small parking lot, a pheasant ducked away into some grass. Half an hour late, the two women drove up. Marla was driving. I remembered Betsy's wish for the butch who'd take her home, and was expecting a big strong woman who looked like a trucker. Marla was a surprise — a dancer, long-necked and graceful as a heron, with leg-warmers on her legs, and hair in a bun.

Betsy looked fit and buff — bright in California colors. But she wasn't happy to see Chino with me.

"Are you sure it's safe?" she asked him, frowning through the passenger window of the battered compact car.

"Everything looks okay," he shrugged.

"Then why are you two iron warriors together?"

"Misery loves company," I said.

I was looking past her, at my spirit son, strapped in his car seat. Billy's boy stared back with sharp, suspicious eyes. He was three now, comically broad-shouldered. And his hair was still dark. He didn't look like Billy at all. He felt like a baby cowbird who'd hatched in a songbird's nest. Did Doc Jacobs get the damn semen samples mixed up with somebody else's?

The two women got out of the car. Falcon was tugging at their hands like a balloon ready to soar. Maybe his home was all female, but he clearly knew he was a male, and a rowdy one at that.

"Falkie, you remember Uncle Harlan? Say 'hi'."

Falcon was silent, staring up at me.

"And this is . . . Uncle Chino."

Falcon stared at Chino, then jerked loose and ran off. His mother sprinted after him in a 1-second, 5-yard dash.

"Well, *you're* in shape," I said as she dragged him back.

"We can hardly wait for him to start driving," she said dryly.

Subtle tensions surrounded us, as we sat at a picnic table

by a nearby rice-field. We ate some homemade apple cobbler that the women had brought. Falcon didn't want to be held, though he climbed briefly into my lap, only to decide that Chino was more interesting because he had a long ponytail to yank.

Meanwhile, Betsy and Marla chattered about their lives. Betsy was proud of regional NCAA wins for her women's track team. Marla taught modern dance at nearby Sutter Community College — she was divorced, no children. They were having to be discreet, pretending to be just roommates. Strong biases against gay teachers had been kicked up in some California schools by the 1978 Briggs Initiative.

Falcon jumped off Chino's knees, swooped around, gave a heart attack to a pheasant or two in the grass. Marla grabbed him when he got too near the water.

"Still go to church?" I asked Betsy.

"There's no gay church in Marysville. Marla and I met at the rice festival . . . I went to the temple in Marysville to pray to the Rice Goddess," Betsy grinned.

"Now and then we go to straight church," Marla added. "If only they'd take half the time they blah blah blah about money and Male, and talk about Female. Don't they get it? They offer *nothing* for women to identify with . . ."

There we were — two unhappy men, and two happy women. I was touched by the two of them — sunlight on their hair, heads bending together over Falcon. The feeling between them was very strong, and clean, and fiery-bright. My fading moon-glow was able to see how beautiful they were together. What did it feel like to give pleasure to another woman? I loved giving pleasure to a man — whether it was making Vince faint, or the one little grunt I'd squeezed out of Chino last night. But I'd never given a thing to a woman. Was I too busy worrying about performing? What the hell did two women feel like together? I'd never asked myself.

Marla was Betsy's opposite in every way — talkative, sunny, openly affectionate. Now and then they burst into uproarious laughter — some lesbian in-group joke that went over the heads of us men. Had they found the golden romance that Vince talked about?

While Marla and Chino took Falcon for a short walk, Betsy and I talked privately.

"Are you happy, Bets?"

"You can't tell?" she parried.

"Lucky woman."

"I waited for years for this. Passed up women who didn't feel right. Sometimes I almost gave up hope."

Silence.

"Wish I could say *you* look lucky," she said. "But you look sad. Still carrying a torch for Vince?"

"Oh no . . . that's over."

"Where's Vince's head at?"

"Calmed down. No more gay Panther. He even gave back Billy's shoe."

Betsy was dubious. "Really?"

"He's settling into a serious career. Films, like he always wanted to do. You should get in touch with him. He asked about you."

She looked doubtful. "Vince is like a pit bull . . . he doesn't let go once he takes hold. I'll keep my distance a while longer."

"How are you doing with Falcon . . . really?" I asked.

Between the lines was my real question. How do two lesbians raise a son? And how would two gay men raise a daughter?

"Okay . . . I guess." She shrugged. "He's a wild child, as you can see. The day-care center wants him put on Ritalin, but I won't. Much as it grates on our feminist sensibilities, we keep men in his world. Universal men. Now and then, we find one. There aren't many around. One male babysitter — a couple of students of mine — a couple of faculty friends. Gawd, I'll never forget how Falcon hurt Marla's feelings one day. A faculty guy came to visit, and Marla and Falcon were playing with a ball in the back yard. And Falcon told her to go in the house. He wanted to play with *him.*"

Anxiety made me push it now.

"When Falcon's older, if things ever quiet down," I said, "let him come visit me."

She looked at me sharply. "We'll see. The decision is half Marla's."

Her meaning was clear — the answer to my question, between the lines. She still honored my deep emotional tie to this child. But she was saying, *Marla is as much his mother as you are his father.*

Just then, Marla shouted, "Betsy! Harlan! Look!"

Betsy's lover was pointing at the sky.

From the ponds, a white spiral of geese was lazily winding into the heavens. The air was humming with sound.

"Aw-right!" Betsy shouted. "They're on their way!"

The three of us ran into the refuge, along a narrow road between two ponds. Betsy kept a tight hold on Falcon. Now the ecstatic clamor filled the sky — voices of migrating birds, thousands of them. The snow geese circled upwards in that slow-turning spiral, till they were at maybe a thousand feet altitude. Then they began stringing into V's, heading north into an arctic springtime with a single mind.

"Where are the geese going?" Chino asked.

"Canada, I guess," said Betsy.

She had her arm around Marla's waist, and kissed her gently on the cheek.

Soon the ponds were empty — nothing left but floating white feathers, and a few ducks.

When Chino stopped the Land Rover in front of the United terminal at L.A. airport, he shoved a small leather case in my overnight bag. "My bug detector," he said. "You haven't been in the beach house for a while . . . better do a good sweep."

"Thanks."

Our eyes met for the good-bye. "You going to make it?" I asked.

"With a friend like you, I will."

That magnetic tension pulled us ever stronger, and we gave each other a long hug. Our unshaven cheeks grated together. Then he felt like he was edging away from me. I didn't want to leave him. And I felt aroused. *He's so crazy he's sane, and you'll fall for him,* Steve's voice said in my memory.

"You want to tell me something," I said against his hair.

"Maybe. If things go FUBAR."

"When you decide to talk, I'll listen."

"Yeah, maybe you would."

"When you decide, come see me on the Beach."

The car behind us honked.

"Goddam faggots," the driver behind us yelled. "Move it!"

O n the flight back to New York, I fought with myself about it. The passion with Vince was over, and good riddance. But were my best friend and I heading for something? I felt like an alcoholic asking himself if he could have a drink. Maybe it was time to get another bodyguard, so Chino and I could have this thing. The feeling had been building like lightning — time for a jarring flash to jump between the two clouds. But Chino still seemed edgy. Was it some lingering racial or ethnic thing that I was still too insensitive to see? And why did we need caresses? We were so close already — closer than sex, closer than love. Making love with Chino seemed almost incestuous. Restraint can be as precious as passion.

What had Harry called it? PTSD? Post traumatic stress disorder? First time I'd heard the term. Was this a $64 word (the Fifties phrase dated me) for what had happened to my own life?

Maybe I should get on with locating Chris Shelbourne. For all I knew, he was the solution to my problem — the missing piece that changed the puzzle into a perfect pattern.

M ichael met me at La Guardia Airport. His eyes showed me fear that he was losing his dad again. I spent several days trying to show him that I was sane and loved him. But Michael was being emotional about something, wanting to cling. I was too shaky a post to cling to.

"You still haven't gone to a therapist," Michael insisted.

"I think therapy is a lot of crap," I barked. "A guy ought to be able to figure out his own problem, and deal with it."

"That's why you're such a mess," he barked back. "Christ
. . . and I thought you were the strongest guy in the world!"

"I have to be alone for a while."

"Tell you what," he said bitterly. "When you want me
around, *you* write me the letter next time."

There was a mound of mail to deal with. No new missive
from LEV. But there was another letter from the past —
and it was from Chris. My heart almost stopped as I read
his name on the envelope. He'd sent it care of the Bruce
Cayton Show, who forwarded it. It was odd that I'd been
thinking of him. Like we were both psychic. The letter was
hand-written under an AP letterhead, with a home address
in Santa Barbara, CA.

Dear Harlan,

I suppose you get lots of letters from people who
say they knew you when. It's hard not to be reminded
that I knew you once — you seem to be everywhere
these days. I saw you on the Bruce Cayton Show —
you haven't changed much, still locking horns with
everything that comes down the pike. I'm married
these days, got a lovely wife and two kids, pretty
successful career — can't complain, I guess. I come
to New York once a month on business. Maybe we
could get together for dinner, talk about old times. If
you call and I'm away, just tell her who called, and
leave a message. Hope to hear from you.

All the best,
Chris

The hopeful hints were all there in the letter. Did I want
to see him? With Vince in the past, and Chino in a holding
pattern? Did he want something from me? Who knew if the
spark could flare up again?

That night, not surprisingly, a dream ambushed me with
a memory from 1952. Chris and I were running together. I was
following him along a deer trail through the Pennsylvania
woods. Autumn leaves fell golden around us. He kept looking
back over his shoulder, as if he knew the devastating effect he

had on me. I loved that shy radiance in his face, his smile that revealed a tooth chipped in a scuffle we'd had. He wasn't as strong as I was — I'd beaten him easily. Close on his heels, I was the male in rut.

We passed a road sign. Then we were in the cab of an old blue Chevy pickup, panting and sweaty, and I had him trapped against the passenger door — his back was against the window. He was hot for me, but his sky-blue eyes were nervous. I kept trying to kiss him. He kept turning his face away. Finally, for a moment, he let me — lips parting to me. Then his eyes flashed with fear, and he was pushing me away. "No, no, please," he was saying. "Stop . . . it's a sin." I was wild with love, and woke up in the struggle to convince him it was all right.

I lay there, in New York in 1980, deep in the spell of that dream. How could Chris be so warm and alive, so unchanged inside of me, after 25 years? Memory tricks us.

The next morning, my hand shook as I dialed the number.

"This is his wife, Helen," said a woman's voice. "He's out of town on business. May I ask who's calling?"

We chatted for a bit, and I told her I was an old school friend. She'd never heard him speak of me, but willingly took a message that Chris could find me in Davis Park, Fire Island.

When I hung up, I was shaking nervously all over.

With a few clothes, my typewriter and Bible, and Striper in a carrier, I took a cab to a Long Island used car lot. There I slid into anonymity again, and bought a blue Chevy truck for cash. An hour later, I was on the Long Island Expressway. The need that I felt, to be out on the water in my clam-boat, was a starving as strong as any I'd ever felt for sex.

Fire Island was pulling me back — to that curve of shore where the dark Front Runner still waited to challenge my kick.

SEVENTEEN

Summer of 1980

In the South Shore boatyard, I got the clam-boat out of dry dock, and checked her for security. After a trip to the supermarket, not forgetting coffee beans for the cops, I loaded the boat.

By late afternoon my boat was thrumming slowly, cautiously into the Hotel Brown cove.

When I tied up, a silence closed around me. The area was alive with birds feeding. I walked around on the dunes. In the warm level rays, the cherry brush was filled with gentle flitterings of tiny finches. A male warbler sat on some bayberry, and poured his song everywhere. The contrast between all that vibrant life and my own battered spirit was so stark that I just stood there, stunned. The song pierced my heart, and I knew that I'd come to the Beach to have something unexpected and unutterable happen to me.

Something winked at my feet. A bit of sea-smoothed glass.

Feeling a twinge about Steve, I dropped it in the jar.

The house stood dark and silent as a tomb, closed up since last autumn. But I felt positive that someone had been inside. Why? To place a bug? While Striper stalked her first mice, I went nuts with the bug detector, checking everywhere. Some-one had definitely been there — things were knocked over, drawers open. Had LEV. done this just to give me jitters? Or was a little surveillance transmitter going to appear — nestled behind a beam or inside my desk, where it could tap its tiny wire into the phone line for power? I didn't find a thing. But my nerves were screaming as I unloaded the boat, and furi-ously planned how to re-do all the old booby traps.

When night came, lights in other beach houses felt as far away as stars in deep space.

At 9 p.m., I was startled by the boardwalk squeak. It was the two cops. Their Jeep was parked on the beach.

"We saw your light," they said. "Wanted to make sure it was you."

Glad to see them, for some reason, I put coffee on. They weren't such bad guys after all — crass, but good-hearted. They seemed glad to see me too. When they found out some-body had broken in, they got somber. They'd kept an eye on the place, they said, but hadn't seen anything suspicious. So I broke down and told them the bare minimum about my prob-lem with harassment. They didn't ask naïve questions about why the FBI and other authorities weren't concerned. For the first time, I had the full attention of the FIPD.

"A weirdo coming on our Beach," Bob said, "it's some bad."

"No one needs to know but the three of us, right?" Lance added.

After they left, I spent a nervous night, jumping at every sound.

Around 3 a.m., I finally slept, and had another of those recurring dreams.

This time, the dead man and I were running through the night, along starlit dunes, with slow-motion strides. I threw a tremendous kick, and drew even with him. He surged, to get ahead of me again. So I did something I'd never done before: grabbed him by the arm, tried to spike his ankle with my track shoe — any dirty trick to take command. He spun on his heel, and seized me in his arms. His mouth took mine in a long terrible tongue-twining kiss. He was streaming with blood, bathing me in that hot smell that I remembered from Montreal.

I was berserk, wanting to get him off me. We went down, rolling over and over in splashes of sand. I had my stick, and pounded him with it. He screamed with pain. I was about to crush his head with an awful blow, and stopped myself just in time. Under the stick, there was now a strange handsome boy, maybe 13, with dark hair. Calmly, he stared up at me.

"Don't hurt me," he said. "I'm your pacing partner."

I awoke with a gasp, trembling and sweating.

A s soon as it was light, my clam-boat was putt-putting across the bay to work.

It was a magnificent morning — the water glassy calm, the island laying under an opal mist. But that dream haunted me. My nerves were screwed as tight as a miler's spike. Driving here and there aimlessly, I couldn't decide where to dig. Rage drove me, at this stupid, deadly, soap-opera thriller scenario where I was trapped — driven crazy by the thought of a voice-activated bug in my house, transmitting every confidential word, every breath of love-making, to a receiver hidden some-where outside, maybe in a neighboring house or a boat, with long-play tape reels that turned and turned, capturing my life. NICE TO SEE YOU RIGHT WHERE I WANT YOU . . . HOW DOES IT FEEL TO HAVE YOUR LIFE GOING NOWHERE . . . LIKE YOU HAD MINE DO. Where he had me was celi-bate and alone. What had I done to make him feel like that?

Suddenly my self-control snapped. I cut the engine, flung my anchor overboard and started raving at the sky.

"Fuck you," I was screaming like a lunatic. "Fuck you, God. Fuck you, Billy. Fuck you, LEV. I've had it. Come on — it's you or me. Let's get it over with!"

Startled, a couple of gulls flew up off the water.

I was striding back and forth in my boat, tipping her gently.

"Come on, God — get your ass down here!"

On another boat, a couple hundred feet away, a clammer was staring in my direction. Then he started his engine and drove hurriedly off.

Part of my mind stood aside, coldly, and watched me walk

off the edge. Hard to believe that poor stupid piece of shit was going bonkers. He was supposed to be the perfect Marine standing guard at the White House.

Then slowly my rage and grief blew itself out.

Feeling empty, I sat slumped on the prow.

There were sea birds, and cloud shadows dappling the bay, and sea grass drifting past on the current. Into my emptiness came a deep quiet of prayer. Not praying to anyone — no words, just a being there. Hot sun beat down, penetrating to my icy bones. I wanted to soak all that radiant life into me. I wanted to make love to that life, and be loved by it.

Suddenly the water roiled around the boat.

Puffs of breath exploded. Dolphins — six of them. They played with the boat, making little squealing and clicking sounds. Filled with tenderness, I lay prone on the prow, trailing a hand into the water. One mother dolphin actually brushed her slick rubbery back under my fingers. A thrill jarred me, hotter than anything I'd ever felt during sex. Then her young one lingered under my hand, blow-hole working, rolling his eye up at me. It felt like Billy was there among them — his life so at one with the universe, that I could touch it again. His voice echoed in my mind, like it did now and then, saying, *Hey, Harlan, it's simple. We're alive. We love being alive. The water loves to be alive. The Earth and the whole universe are alive, alive. Our Deity is Love of Life. And you're still alive . . . barely. The question is, how much do you love life?*

Now the water filled with fish, glancing light off their mass like a vast sheet of silver foil. The fish said, *Alive, alive,* as the dolphins ate them.

Suddenly I felt dreamy, heavy-limbed. The bottom of the boat, a pile of burlap bags there, looked eminently comfortable. So I stretched out and nodded off, floating in prayer and dolphin squeals. For the first time, I wasn't afraid to dream. Let's go, Deity. Hit me with your worst.

A breeze woke me, nudging the boat against the end of her anchor rope. I hadn't dreamed.

The sun was directly overhead, so warm that I was wet and glowing inside my clothes. The clam-rake handle against my arm was stove-hot. Blinking, I sat up and looked around. The dolphins were gone. Colors were intense — rainbows wavering on the ripples, in the boat's shadow on the water. The bay smelled strong — like composting seaweed and pure iodine. I felt better than I had in years — strong, and really well. A good meal was in order — take care of myself better, put on a little weight. Somehow I needed to take action — find some way to end LEV.'s control over my life. To do that, I needed to write. And what I needed to write was about Billy.

Throwing the rake over, I dug a grab of clams for my dinner. Ravenous, opening a few with a clam-knife, I swallowed them. *Alive,* they said as they slid down my throat.

Back home, scooping Striper out of the desk-chair, I rolled a sheet into the typewriter.

The first lines that came into my head were:

I can be precise about the day it began. It was December 10, 1974. That was the day I met Billy Sive, and he asked me to coach him.

The thud of typewriter keys felt like it traveled through the desk, down into the pilings, and into the dunes. It deafened the ears of whoever might be listening on the bug.

As the days passed, I pulled out Steve's writing secrets. "If I don't feel it, the reader doesn't feel it," he'd said to me. Now I started where he'd started, and found that his secret had wings.

What bird was I? Maybe the albatross, riding out a thousand gales. This book would finally teach me how to fly, and write.

Days were healthy work on the water. My lungs, still delicate, didn't fill the way they used to. But Doc Jacobs had told me they'd heal. Evenings at the typewriter, I raced in a wondrous frenzy, not stopping to fix typos. As Billy had said, it was simple. I had broken the set pattern, demanded change. Life is change, and growth. Death is part of change. Like pieces of sharp glass polished into gems by the patient waves, Billy's death had worn into something that could heal me. This miracle came to me not from the pages of somebody's book of rules, but through my own slippery life.

A new psych had struggled into life. But that boy I'd seen in the dream was young, delicate, his wings still wet and crumpled. I had to get him in shape. The loaded .45 lay by my typewriter — starting pistol in a new race.

A s the days passed, I made phone calls to see if others were healing.

"*Harlanito* . . . what's happening, man?"

"Things. Are you okay?"

"Haven't reached FUBAR yet. I got a little work . . . made some money. You sound good."

"Finally started that book."

"About time. I miss you, *pinchi*. You calm me down."

"You crazy sea snake, I miss you too. When are you going to come talk to me?"

"If I go FUBAR, I will. By the way . . . on the two cops there. I talked to Harry, and we agree it's okay for them to know a little, as long as you just describe us as private eyes. And don't mention Julius."

"H i, Mikey."

"H'lo, Dad." His voice in the phone was subdued, cautious.

"How you doing?"

"Oh . . . okay."

"Me too. Things looking up a little."

"Yeah?" Cautiously.

"Weekdays alone is okay. Weekends, it'd be good to have my boy underfoot."

"No kidding," he said dryly.

"You want me to send you an engraved invitation?"

The next Friday evening, Michael came out alone, and we mended the fences. He opened up about what was bothering him. Running had given him more energy. But he wasn't very

interested in sex. He felt he didn't measure up as a macho —
especially to my example. With Astarte it was a special friendship, he said. If he ever felt that feeling for a guy, maybe he'd
be in a gay relationship. But he didn't. "Jesus," he added, "all
I hear is sex, sex, sex. My passion is my work. Is there something wrong with me?"

"No. And I envy you, kid. Passion almost killed me."

On the cherry-shaded deck, I showed him The Box for
the first time. He gingerly inspected the re-united track
shoes, flipped through the July 1976 issue of *Time,* with
Billy's and my faces on the cover. Billy's suede jacket, crushed
flat. The shorts, and the singlet with the Olympic rings on
it, already looking old-fashioned — athletic styles were
changing. I'd laundered them several times, but a few grayed
blood-stains still endured.

Michael held the shoes, with tears in his eyes.

"Why are you keeping this stuff?" he asked.

"So people won't forget. So Falcon can know someday that
his father was a real flesh-and-blood man."

Michael shuffled through the Epstein photos.

"Passion for your work, huh?" he said.

I flushed.

"Dad, this stuff is weighing you down," he said briskly.
"Let me take it back to the city. It's probably safer with me
anyway."

H otel Brown needed repairs. As July and August passed,
Michael and Astarte and I went to work with a rented
gas generator and a do-it-yourself book. A Patchogue con-
tractor put new shakes on the roof. Window-seat cushions
got new covers. We kept up security, and set as few patterns as possible.

I wondered when, and if, Chris would visit me.

But the summer stayed quiet.

My low profile had worked — since 1976, there'd been a
turnover of house owners, and few in Davis Park even remembered Steve. The cops called me Har, and people went
from there to "Harold," and I didn't correct them. Even

conservative families knew me as the bearded loner who worked the bay and dabbled in writing. It was such a relief. It was also a lie, because I wasn't being myself.

My celibacy didn't fit the cops' picture of sex-crazed homosexuals. So they figured I was prime to be turned. Now and then they dragged me to the Casino, or the Friday-evening "sixish" by the ferry dock, where singles mingled to drink Harvey Wallbangers and hit on each other. I had a good time studying the straight social scene. After I let an art-gallery owner who looked like Farrah Fawcett slip through my fingers, Lance said despairingly, "That's it, Har. That's it, then. You're a hard case."

Valhalla Productions stayed in touch. I still didn't commit to working with them. But they got a year's option on *Angel,* with me approving the script that Paul was writing.

The sun burned reddish tints into my shoulder-length hair. My feet grew hard as clamshell from working barefoot in the boat.

It was the era of notorious people publishing their memoirs. Even the Watergate felons got to do theirs. So the notorious track coach was going to do his. I wanted my book to "tell it with dignity," as Steve had said.

"Are you guys prepared to protect my ass if I publish this?" I asked H-C on the pay phone one day.

"Hey, sweet thing . . . absolutely," Harry said.

My writing-room in the Tower was fresh with repairs. The desk had a favorite *Pollen* poem of Steve's push-pinned to the wall beside Falcon's picture. I even slept here now — had put a low double bed in front of the Franklin stove, to dream with the flames. The four windows gave a magnificent overview. Across the dunes, bending grasses always told me which way the wind was blowing.

One day, I was struggling with the chapter where Billy and I made love for the first time. Dreaming with my eyes open, I allowed myself to call back the feelings of that extraordinary half hour, and wrestled them into words. Did the rewrite work? Was it honest? Did it reveal too much?

Beside me, the window was open. Just then, Steve's poem drew attention with its fluttering.

"Steve, what do you think?" I asked out loud.

Suddenly the poem blew down on top of my typewriter. It lay there, moving its sun-yellowed edges like the wings of a giant butterfly.

On other nights, I struggled with the chapter where Billy was killed, and cried every time I rewrote it.

By Labor Day, the first draft was done.

Now and then, for R & R, I wrote erotic poems. Like a thunderhead towering into a summer sky, that handsome boy of my dream grew to a man in my daydreams. He didn't look like any real man I had ever fantasized about. Like an advancing storm, this lover lit himself with erotic lightning. He was older too — not a flawless 20-something jock out of *Runner's World*. His scars said he'd been around. *My name is Muse,* he said, talking in my mind the way Billy sometimes did.

But, like Billy, my Muse lived in the world of spirit. I couldn't touch him, except by touching my own body.

J ust before Labor Day weekend, a strange man came walking along the beach from the west. He looked like the Village bohemians I used to see in the '50s — French beret, soft tie knotted loose, jacket slung over his shoulder. A handsome sandy-haired man in his 40s, with a tense Irish-English thoroughbred look. He was barefoot, trousers rolled up, carrying tennis shoes over his arm tied by the shoelaces.

Nothing moved in the area that I didn't notice. So I watched him through binoculars, as he passed the house. He had the lean build that I liked, and straight, silky hair that ruffled in the wind. He headed on down the beach — probably on his way to some straight house.

"Oh well," I thought.

An hour later, the stranger came in sight again — walking along the boardwalk to the Hotel, putting a bare foot squarely on the squeaking board. Michael and Astarte were still in town, and I was alone on the dock, working on my boat engine.

The visitor looked at me shyly.

"Harlan?" he said in a quiet tenor.

"Who's looking for him?" I growled.

"I'm Chris Shelbourne."

After my initial surprise, instead of getting shivery knees, I found myself strangely calm. Chris and I sat alone on the front deck. Up close, his silky temples were gray. Hard lines etched his face, and shadows filled those sky-blue eyes I remembered. Was this really him? The Chris I remembered was wired, high-spirited, full of laughter, boy silliness, and flash — the perfect mate for sober-sided me. This man was quiet, sad, wary. I couldn't fit him into those volatile memories that had been my deepest, most precious secret.

He said, "My wife gave me your message."

"You've been on a helluva long trip."

"I'm an AP stringer, so I travel forever. I'm like the Flying Dutchman."

"How the hell did you find the right house? Most people around here just know me as Har," I said.

"Oh," he laughed, "I was discreet. I asked for a dark-haired 40-something loner. Everybody knew who that was." The laugh was dry, without the old sparkle.

"You came from The Grove?"

"Yeah."

"So . . . you're out?"

"My wife doesn't know. I still feel a lot of conflict."

"How'd you manage in the service? Guys must have been all over you."

He laughed. "I managed to avoid the military. The only overseas shooting I do is with overseas guys — my favorites being French guys. I was based in Paris in the late Sixties."

His eyes were sparkling a little, so we both got to dishing.

"So you like frog legs," I said.

"French men are more natural. I felt less guilty. When I wasn't doing that, I bicycled around the country. It was a wonderful time of freedom. I almost didn't come back."

"So that's why you look so fit," I teased. "You still run?"

"Running is boring. How do you stand it, Harlan? Now soccer . . ."

After we shared dinner, I invited him to overnight in a guest room. Late that night, the two of us were in the Tower Room, talking. He showed me wallet pictures of his wife and kids. He was curious about my loves, the public scrutiny. I was feeling a mild attraction, more like an old loyalty, but definitely not what Vince called the "juju". It shocked me to see my capacity for disillusion.

Sometime after midnight, Chris and I were sitting on the roof outside the Tower Room window. Under full moonlight, the ocean was a sheet of neon silver. On the bay nearby, a boat was drifting with engine off, running lights dark, rocking gently. The occupants were probably making wild love. In the moonlight, I noticed his hands — lean, strong, well-made. Sexy hands. Chris steered the talk around to the summer of '52. The last day of vacation together before school started. Crazy stunts we'd done. Running in the woods together. Plinking at targets with my .22. The shy kiss. He'd never forgotten it. He'd been sorry that he hadn't written — he was too scared and guilty to write. But the kiss had changed his life forever.

He was sitting right behind me, and his warm hands closed on my shoulders, squeezing gently.

"Harlan, you can unbend a little with me," he urged softly. "I finally unbent."

It felt too sudden.

"I'm not that easy anymore, Chris," I said.

"Come on." His lips were on the back of my neck, searching in my hair, which was down to my shoulders now. His warm breath found my bare skin. Those lips that had changed my own life forever. "Old times' sake. Who knows . . . maybe it was meant to be, after all this time."

For a moment, I almost let it happen. Then I moved my head away from him and said, as kindly as I could, "We'd need to know each other again."

As Chris went down the spiral staircase to his bedroom, his eyes showed hurt. Next morning when I got up, Chris was already gone. His tracks angled across the dunes to the beach — heading west toward Cherry Grove.

For a few days I felt bad, wondering if I'd been insensitive about a chance at love. But then I pulled myself together. It hadn't felt right to plunge in like a fool, and I had to trust that. Maybe he'd think it over, and agree with me, and call again. If not, loving life had to include letting the past die.

Another person who walked back into my world that summer was an old enemy — my ex-wife. She'd been in touch with John Sive about Michael. But now she'd changed her tune. The three-Kleenex approach. Begging and pleading to see her son. Heartbroken. Wouldn't I see her, and work out our differences, so that Michael would be in touch with her again? She had in mind a summit meeting at a restaurant in Lake George, halfway between our two homes, no lawyers present, no lovers or spouses, no security — just the two of us.

I talked to John from the marina pay phone. John had gone on being my lawyer, but the distance was still there.

"I strongly advise against the meeting," he said crisply. "It isn't your job to be a go-between between her and Michael."

Harry and Chino agreed.

"If Kevin was that violent," said Chino, "it tells you where she's at. She might pull a Saturday-night special on you."

"You think LEV. might be connected to her?"

"We can't assume LEV. is a man. There's nothing in the letters that gives us a fix on sex. She could be paying some guy to do her dirty work. Julius is going to give her a once-over."

At that, I really felt a shiver.

When John Sive relayed my refusal to Mary Ellen, she went wild into his ear, threatening endless lawsuits and revenge. Later Michael told me she'd tried to call his office, and he'd hung up on her.

After Labor Day, I was revising the book, and couldn't tear myself away from the Beach.

One day in September, I heard excited shouts. The first bluefish run was on — millions of the fighting fish pouring their way south to the Carolina Banks. I grabbed my waders and pole, and raced to the beach, along with a couple dozen other people from the beach houses. The wash was alive with ravenous blues feeding on tiny smelt. Just as I made the first cast, the police Jeep pulled up, poles sticking out the back. Lance and Bob had their waders on, too.

"We just got a squeal that a *big* run's on at Mastic," shouted Lance. "Hop in!"

My pole flung in with theirs, we careened down the beach.

The diehard Island lovers enjoyed the pungent autumn days. Wild creatures were in urgent flight. Monarch butterflies. Ducks and geese and snowy egrets. One day, Striper joined the great migration — she disappeared. At first I got all paranoid, thinking she was the victim of another hate crime. But a couple days later, I found her half-eaten body. Evidently she'd been killed by a wild animal. I missed my little cat spy — the last living link with Steve and Angel.

Autumn was abandoned-pet season again. One day the two cops showed up with a thin Black Labrador pup that they'd found wandering around. She pranced all over my deck on her big feet. Lance produced two cans of dog food to get me started.

"If you're not gonna have a boyfriend," Bob said, "you gotta have a dog. You gotta!"

The pup named herself Jess.

Finally I committed to wintering on the Beach, so I could finish the book without a break. Non-perishable groceries and firewood arrived from the mainland. That year, winter came early to the South Shore. People closed their beach houses. Ferries stopped running. Only the hard-core clammers went out on the bay now. Such a normal end to a good year. It never occurred to me that I was looking at a fragile moment in time, that would soon be gone.

By mid-November I'd turned the manuscript over to Steve's old agent. Ernie sold hardcover and paperback rights for $150,000. It was one of those lucrative contracts of the '80s, and a staggering amount for a jock who'd never made more than $40,000 a year. My book would be published in October 1981.

Chris didn't contact me again.

Neither did Vince. It appeared that the door between us, like the one between me and Chris, had finally closed.

On December 14, when I picked up my mail on the mainland, I got the first letter from LEV. in months. This one baffled me. It said,

> BAD BOY — RUNNING AGAIN — HAVEN'T YOU LEARNED TO FEAR — SPORTS ARE HOLY — OFF LIMITS TO FAG SCUM — DESIST OR I'LL WHIP YOU.

The letter didn't make sense — I wasn't running now.

Suddenly impatience and rage almost choked me. With the book done, it was time for me to take LEV. by the throat. Chino was right — he was making fools of us. It was time to kick. Time to blow the menace off our track.

That night, I wanted to discuss it with H-C, but couldn't reach them, so left a message. For some reason, I was feeling worried about Chino. Then I started worrying about other family, and made a few calls. Outside, as I talked, a chill wind was sweeping the bay. The Beach was dark, with only a few lights along its 30-mile sweep. Around the corners of the house, the wind sighed, moaned, talked softly, like a lover outside who was trying to sweet-talk his way in. The first drops of winter rain flicked against the panes. Jess lay on her side by the warm stove, dreaming of raccoons.

Betsy and Marla didn't answer. Evidently they had gone somewhere for the holiday.

John Sive's voice softened a little. He groused about his gall-stone pains, and a case that wasn't going well.

Russell sounded insufferably cheerful, and wondered if I'd spend the holidays with him.

"Did you know George Rayburn died?" Doc Jacobs asked.

As I sat there, stunned, my doctor told me that George had developed a rare cancer that usually wasn't fatal. He'd heard of a few other gay men with the same problem.

After 11 p.m., Chino finally called me. He'd gotten the message. He sounded terrible — lifeless, no energy.

"Call me back in a few minutes," he said.

That was my cue to call him on a secure line. So I threw on a rain poncho, and jogged the half-mile past rows of dark beach houses to the marina pay phone. The only lights in Davis Park were a house boat in the marina, and the tiny police station.

Chino answered right away, and I said, "Look . . . I just got another letter. We've got to make a breakthrough on LEV."

"You vibed me, man. I was about to call you and say that."

"You don't sound good, buddy."

"I'm not," he said bluntly. "My malaria flared up. And my morale is down to FUBAR. Read me the letter."

I did.

"Well," he said, "it makes sense if Vince got the same letter. And Vince got it after he announced that he's going to compete seriously again."

This was an ominous development. LEV. had never written to anyone but me.

"You need to come talk to me," I said.

"I know. And I've got a new theory about LEV. Don't meet the plane. I'll jump down your chimney the night of the 17th."

EIGHTEEN

December 17-19, 1980

O n the morning of the 17th, a winter storm moved across the South Shore. I cooked some good food that could be re-heated, and watched the winds picking up, the bay getting choppier. How the hell was Chino going to come onto the Beach? My emotions were running like high tides as I got ready. The cops came by for coffee, and I casually mentioned a visit by James Cabrera, ex-SEAL, now a private investigator on the harassment case. In case they happened to see Chino arriving, they needed to know he was on our side.

The cops had their own ability to read vibes, and they smiled craftily.

"So you finally got a boyfriend, right?" Bob demanded.

"We're the cool Fire Island cops," said Lance. "You can tell us."

"Strictly business," I said.

Late that night, during a lull, as I sat nervously by the downstairs stove with a book, some tin cans in the perimeter booby trap clanked insistently. It must be him — using the cans as a doorbell, to make sure I didn't shoot him. Hackles bristling, Jess barked. When I opened the door, his wet figure loomed out of the dark in a blowing poncho. He had a back-pack over his shoulder, wrapped in a plastic garbage bag to keep it dry.

"Jess, it's okay," I said.

My dog's hackles lay down. Smelling of rain and willows, Chino gave me a tense abrazo.

When he started to rove the house to check security, I said, "Don't. Not this time."

He nodded curtly — he could see I'd kept a tight ship. While I warmed some food, he stripped by the stove and yanked dry clothes out of the backpack. He looked gray and drawn-down, overtrained, with hard new lines in his face. The old combat stare had turned in on itself. This was his last shot. He'd tried everything else.

"Throw your gear up in the Tower Room," I said.

When he sat down to the steaming plate, Jess dozed off across his foot.

"At some point, the two cops might check on us," I said.

"They brothers?" He was putting lots of super-hot salsa on his food.

"Maybe. It might be a good move to invite them to dinner tomorrow."

"As long as they don't mess with us."

"How'd you get here?"

"I rode a chartered ferry over to The Grove yesterday." He was starved, enjoying the good meat and salad, talking with his mouth full. "There's a holiday social thing going on. After dark, I sneaked out a service entrance, and hiked up the Burma Road. Have you heard anything from our two lesbian lovebirds?"

"No. They must be away. But they mailed me the pic for the year," I said, reaching a manila envelope from the counter.

Chino studied the color photo. Falcon looked ready to burst his little T-shirt. His black hair sprang up in a willful cowlick.

"Quite a kid, man."

His eyes lingered briefly on the picture. Then, going to the sink, he swallowed his quinine pills.

"Before we talk about LEV.," he said softly with his back

still turned, "I did some thinking on Venice Beach one night, with my .38 up my mouth. Maybe there's a way to unfuck my situation. *¿Qué tu dices a eso?* What do you think?"

It was now 1 a.m. The storm was really hitting — gusts slamming the house. Up in the Tower Room, we lit a kerosene lamp and piled more wood into the open Franklin stove. The thick drapes were already drawn, so the room would hold heat. Jess flopped down on the rug. Chino sat slumped on the edge of my bed, elbows on knees, staring into the fire. Trying to ease his neck, he turned his head from side to side. When he shrugged his tense shoulders to loosen them, his vertebrae crackled. The enormity of his life hanging by a thread was before my face — I felt a little short on profound wisdom.

So I said, "How about a full-body massage . . . loosen you up?"

He considered it, hovering in the old edginess. Then he nodded, and undressed in the warm firelight. While I warmed a jar of almond oil, he stretched out on the bed, with a towel over his middle. He kept one arm over his eyes, showing the swatch of ebony hair in his strong armpit. His thighs were trembling — malaria and cold and sex and a sudden shyness, all at once. His ponytail lay flared across the sheet.

My own body was feeling a deep trembling. Could I be dispassionate for once — do this for his healing? Or was I just grabbing at any human driftwood the sea carried in?

With the kerosene lamp turned out, only firelight lit the room. Sitting on the edge of the bed, I took his feet in my hands. They were well-made, hard, calloused, with mutilated toe-nails and lingering dermatitis from old trench foot. The soles were scarred — he'd gone barefoot in the jungle. Ankles and calves were scarred by the few phosphorus burns, where flesh had grown back in. I flexed his stiff instep, tried to work some love into those hard toes.

Chino stirred jumpily. His energies were fighting me.

"*Carajo* . . . I never knew my feet were so sensitive," he murmured.

As his physical scars passed under my fingers, I wished I

could find the old spirit scars, and ease them. Feet done, I kneaded his calves and thighs, feeling holes in the muscles where shrapnel had punched. My cravings stirred, and I fought to be disciplined. He had to ask for intimacy — I wasn't going to take advantage. Where was that place of deep prayer that always came over me in the boat? *Alive,* my hands said to him. Taking his right arm off his face, I tenderly worked that hand that had pulled triggers and cut throats and broken necks. Remembering about swollen lymph nodes, I contrived to feel his. They felt normal.

Undoing his ponytail, I spread his long hair in my hands. It was clean, strong and heavy like horsehair, and glossy as a crow's back. Working his tight scalp, I pulled locks of his hair slowly, gently through my fingers. Soon, enriched with the plant-oil from my fingers, his hair caught the firelight like it was golden foil. *Alive, alive.*

He laughed a little, his strong stomach jerking. "Is playing with my hair part of the deal?"

"Part of the deal," I said softly.

Right under his right breast, was the gnarled old scar — the pec muscle felt fossilized in a spasm. When I worked it gently, his whole body moved strangely, in sudden distress. Then, to my amazement, tears welled in his eyes. He put his hand over mine, and helped me rub the place.

I bent over him. "Want to talk to me?"

For a while, Chino stared up past me, at the firelit ceiling. The tears ran and ran — out of the corners of his eyes, down his temples, into his hair. He swallowed convulsively, his Adam's apple working, and talked in a muffled voice.

"Ever since I got out of the hospital, I thought . . . if I just deal with stuff . . . you know, the morphine addiction, the drinking, hold a job, get through school, do something with my life . . . if I could just do that, I'd forget."

I had an idea what this was about.

"How did he get it?" I asked.

"Friendly fire. A sniper."

Chino clenched my hand so hard that it hurt.

"The .50 caliber round blew off the whole front of his head. The back of his skull was left on his neck. It looked like a red dish. I can't get it out of my mind. I dream about it, man. This red dish staring at me. But I can't forget. What I did forget is what he really looked like."

"The sniper knew you were friendlies?"

"I think somebody higher up knew about us."

"You get hit too? This?" I touched his chest.

"Yeah. A smaller caliber round. I crawled to a stream, drifted down. A Navy patrol found me. The open wound in the water . . ."

Chino kept rubbing my hand on the old scar. His eyes asked me to say something. I was beginning to understand some things. His bonding with me after Billy's death, his determination to get LEV.

"You tried to find out later who the shooters were?"

"I tried. Before I met Harry."

Suddenly I knew I didn't want to know if he'd succeeded.

"When you love that deep," I said, "you don't forget."

"I did."

"Stop punishing yourself — let it come naturally."

"What makes you think so?"

"You've set a pattern of how you see him. Break it."

His eyes held mine. He swallowed again, nodded.

A deep booming came up through the sand under the house — the surf must be tremendous now. I kept working, felt him shifting a little under my fingers — hardened muscles yielding ever so slightly. He was so hungry to feel touch — to feel life, like every human, even a baby. New Age talk about "seeing energies" had always sounded like a lot of crap. But I swore there was a fragile glow of blue, like northern lights, in the air around him. As I worked deep in the contracted muscle-strands along his back and thighs, he started groaning softly with pain and relief. All of a sudden I felt the hoarded pain of his life flowing into my hands and arms. Now and then, a hologram flashed around him, as if I was dreaming with my eyes open — burned children, helicopters exploding, gunfire blowing men's bodies apart.

"I'll watch your back while you sleep," I said. "Have the worst of my own dreams along with you. Will that help?"

"Maybe. Release me, will you? Get me relaxed."

"Only if you face me."

In the dark room, a pyramid of embers glowed in the open stove, licked by blue flames. Quickly, not to lose the feeling around us, I shed clothes and lay facing him, our bodies barely grazing in the radiant heat. His knees were quivering— he was like a boy about to have his first time. Working with one hand, I kept up the slow, loving pace, letting massage become caressing. After a while, his hand lay shyly on my hip. He was vibrating like a blossom about to fly apart in the tiniest breeze. Little by little, he let me press against him, slide my arms around him. As my hand finally slid under the towel, and took hold of his cock, his forehead was barely touching mine.

"Cariñito . . ." he murmured. Our firelit faces were bathed in each other's rough breathing. Then his lips searched for mine — that terrible jungle-fighter giving me the shyest kiss that I'd ever had, saying that he trusted me.

Gently I kissed him back, stroked him, felt him gather courage and will, move against me — that ocean of his giving up the first of its drowned ships. I helped him drive the surge as high and intense as we could. Jesus, how I wanted to go into him, but his psyche was too fragile for that. So I held back, and let my hands and my mouth say *Alive*. The house shuddered with waves breaking just beyond the barrier dune. He was fighting for his life against me, panting. Our breaths, bursting together, were lost in the hot wave of release.

Heavy against me, he fell asleep first, eyelids twitching in REM sleep. His Mary medal slid back over his shoulder.

The fire had gone out, but our bodies glowed under the covers. I was in his dreams. Or he was in mine. A dark body loomed at me, roiling like a river, muscles sheeting over the bones like water over rocks. Hot for him, I tried to go into him, but he simply flowed over me and swallowed me like a waterfall. Deep underwater, the current tumbled me along the bottom, through clouds of war debris, and flashing silver fish. Mutilated corpses bumped past me. Getting my footing, I started to run against the current. He was there again, just ahead of me, running in light that rayed down through the water. His strides were infinitely slow. The long hair streamed back, over a torso dappled in shadow. I pulled up my kick and overtook him for the first time. He turned his head to look at me. I saw his face. He was Chris.

As I reached for Chris, he dissolved into a swirl of silver fish.

A gray dawn lit the ice-cold room.

Dressing, we yanked open the emergency-exit window. Wet wind filled the room, blowing papers off my desk. A changed world met our eyes. Three inches of wet snow had fallen on Fire Island. The white shore curved away into a stormy indigo distance. Willows bent into white arcs. Blinking dazedly, we climbed out the window, onto the snowy roof. Down below, a buck deer stared up at us, with willow bark hanging from his mouth. When Jess scrambled out too, the deer bounced away into the brush, with snow cascading over his antlers.

Chino stood there boldly on the roof, in plain view, loose hair blowing, and I suddenly realized we were no longer a target here.

Why was I still dreaming about Chris? That boyhood myth was dead. Maybe the healing would take me longer than I thought.

On the beach below, ice-green breakers moved in slowly like mountain-ranges, with spume blowing off their peaks. They crashed right at the foot of the barrier dune. We sat on the dune, bathed in blowing mist and thunder, our intimacy coiled between us, like the sound in a conch shell. The newness and youngness, like a scent of bruised willows, trembled around us both. We looked at each other's transfigured faces. His eyes were still red from crying. I was glad to see a little color in his skin, a fragile light in his eyes. As he slid his arm around my waist, I slid mine over his shoulders, shelteringly, and pressed him against my side. He leaned into me, our unshaven cheeks grating together.

"Did you dream?" I asked, loud enough to be heard.

"*Nada*. But I slept good."

"Keep trying."

He laughed a little.

"My muscles are so fucking sore," he said, "it feels like you took that stick of yours and beat me all over."

With a comb from my pocket, I was smoothing his mist-wet hair, till it shone like a cormorant wing again.

"The pain is lactic acid in your muscles," I said. "If you jog a little, that'll help flush it out."

I was twisting a lock around his hair, to make a ponytail, when suddenly Chino turned his head. Two dark-blue figures were striding along the boardwalk. Even through the noise, Chino had heard that loose board squeak.

Without saying a word, we agreed that to hell with the cops, we would keep our arms around each other's waists. I could feel the old *barrio* hatred of Anglo police surging inside my friend, but he kept his cool. The two cops walked up, with their own brief glow of Anglo bay-man edginess about brown-skinned Spanish-speakers.

"Sergeant Lance Shirley, Suffolk County Police . . . Bob Enger . . ." I made introductions.

Everybody shook hands. Lance and Bob took their reading on the lithe hard-eyed man before them, and decided to be very cool.

"You guys are the only people on the Beach besides us," Lance shouted over the roar. "No waves topping the dune yet, right?"

"We're watching it. Thanks for checking on us," Chino said.

To defuse the tension, I said, "If you two don't have cold burgers coming over from Patchogue, why don't you join us for turkey tonight? We promise not to recruit you."

A fter the cops left, Chino and I started stuffing the turkey. "So what's your new angle on LEV.?" I was washing the bird in the sink.

He was chopping onions. "We've been running up the wrong trail."

My stomach plunged. "How do you know?"

Chino rubbed an onion-tear off his cheek, and tossed me a letter from the backpack. The familiar generic envelope was addressed to Vincent Matti, at Valhalla Productions. The familiar paste-up letter unfolded. It was identical to the one I'd just received.

BAD BOY — RUNNING AGAIN — HAVEN'T YOU LEARNED TO FEAR — SPORTS ARE HOLY — OFF LIMITS TO FAG SCUM — DESIST OR I'LL WHIP YOU.

Chino said, "Vince got this after the *Advocate* interviewed him about next year's Memorial. You didn't see the story?"

"I haven't read a gay paper in months." I shut off the water.

"The story was about how he's involved in the race promotion . . . training seriously. He's going to run the Memorial, to launch his comeback in track."

Why this sudden dedication? Vince had dropped the sport for years.

"So LEV. tracks the gay press," I said. "And it ticked him off."

"I've got a feeling this is our first break. One of those things that you wonder why you missed it before."

Out of the backpack, Chino took a paper bag and emptied it noisily on the table beside a few unpeeled onions. Out came baggies containing the rocks, and the .22 hollow-point casing fired at the Prescott track meet. With his brown finger, Chino lined them out on the table.

"Look at the pattern," he said. "First, the bullet at Montreal. Then the rock through the window. Then the bullet at Prescott. Then a rock . . . a rock . . . another rock. Why no more bullets? Why did he switch?"

I stared into his eyes.

"Think about *where* he fired these two kinds of projectiles," said Chino.

"The rounds were . . . at athletic events. The rocks weren't."

"No shit, mate. But why?"

"We were good boys and stayed away from track."

"You're missing my fucking point," Chino barked at me. "All this time, LEV. has never fired a shot at *you*. Only at your lovers competing. Or guys he believed were your lovers. He shot at Jacques because he was taken in by the tabloids. But notice he never even shot at me."

"What makes you think LEV. won't shoot at me?"

"Because I think he likes you," Chino said flatly.

Chills went up and down my spine. There was a long silence. I stood listening to the surf roaring outside. Suddenly, the turkey's raw meaty smell reminded me of Montreal, and I retched.

"What can we do to turn this around?" I whispered.

"Two years we've been on the defensive. Harry and me were trained to be offensive. I say let's *offend* this guy."

"Great idea. But how?"

"Piss him off! Lure him out!"

Down on the beach, the boom of breakers was getting louder. Chino's idea was riskier and more hair-raising than what I'd had in mind. Luring could mean only one thing — providing LEV. with a target.

"You mean . . . that Vince should be a decoy in the Memorial?" I asked. "We try to grab this guy before he shoots Vince?"

"Vince and I have already talked about it."

My mind was pushing away the picture of Vince's head in the crosshairs. A deep, scared, horrified trembling spread through me.

Chino had sliced onions spread on the chopping-board, and his knife diced them with hair-raising energy.

"My God, man," I said. "This is not Vietnam! Vince could be . . ."

"That's the problem with you goddam faggots," he retorted, dumping the chopped onions into a skillet. "Too many of you believe you're not in Vietnam."

I slammed the dripping turkey on the table.

"Bullshit! You're home now! There's lawyers, and courts, and what civilians call ethics. A bunch of civilians could get shot. A gay 5-K is full of targets for this guy."

His eyes blazed. I'd never seen Chino so angry.

"*Caray* . . . why won't you understand me, you gutless Mary?" he shouted. His deep raspy voice filled the house. "Vince is going to run anyway. I'm frigging talking about being ready! No different than when the President rides in a motorcade. The Secret Service *knows* he can get smoked. They *know* civilians could die in the crossfire. But the President fucking goes out fucking anyway, because that's what fucking Presidents do. And fucking runners run."

For once, he was cursing like a sailor.

"Bad example. Kennedy got blown away," I said.

"We have an advantage. We know a few things about our shooter. I know Griffith Park like I know my own dick. We can grab this guy's *nalgas* before he pulls the trigger!"

"No! No! There's no way I'd be a party to this! If we fuck up, Vince is gonna die!"

Chino's gray eyes bored into mine.

"You've got eight months to get in shape," he said. "You can be Vince's rabbit in training. That will piss LEV. really good, man."

Dinner in the oven, dough rising for rolls, Chino and I went out on the front deck. The tide had pulled out, but huge turbid waves were still crumpling down, making sounds like bombs exploding. The sand was piled with wreckage — seaweed, lumber, broken sea-creatures. Jess was down there chewing on a dying horseshoe crab. Helpless fury still filled me. Chino was somber, full of thought.

"What else is on your mind?" I barked.

He faced me. "You and Vince."

"What the hell do you care? You want to get Vince's head blown off!"

"He may be a candidate for the ... uh, the thing that Jacobs is so *loco* about."

I felt my body go cold.

"Don't get me wrong. He's strong ... looks good," Chino said. "But he's got the swollen glands. And the thing is this. Remember that guy Mario that Vince was shooting speed with?"

"Yeah?"

"Mario just died."

There was a roaring in my ears.

"Thirty years old, man, and he died of some rare skin cancer that nobody ever heard of," Chino went on. "Vince told me. He was kind of shook up, because they'd shared needles. I talked to Jacobs about it, and I talked to Michael. We've all seen junkies pass the hepatitis B around when they share needles. Steve shared needles with Angel, and he died. Jacobs thinks there's some new thing being transmitted. Vince went for some blood work. His T-cells look okay, so far . . . 900 something."

After all the times I'd said *Screw Vince* to myself, the news was a shock.

"I've watched the two of you go through all your crazy shit," Chino added. "And I think you both still care."

I stared out over the sea. The thought of Vince suffering like Steve, Angel and George had suffered was more than my mind could hold. And I'd been exposed too. That image of suffering kicked hard at the door to Vince that I'd thought was shut, and locked, for good.

"Why didn't you tell me this right away?" I exploded. "If I have it too, I've given it to you."

Chino shrugged. He had picked up a piece of beach glass and was playing with it. "You got swollen glands?"

"No."

"You vibe healthy to me. And who knows what I have?"

"Did Vince ask you to talk to me?"

"No."

As on the day I saw the dolphins, my wrath collapsed into an eerie silence of inner truth.

"So that's why he's so willing to be the rabbit in your crazy plan," I whispered.

"That's why."

A steel-gray twilight was coming on. Chino dropped the glass in the Mexican jar.

"Listen, *puto* Marine," he said. "Vince is no different than me and Harry. The three of us know we're living on borrowed time. The question is — do you?"

The vulnerable Chino of last night had vanished. He was now the officer, standing straight. "With you, or without you," he went on, "we're going to do the crazy thing. Because the alternative is to go on eating shit. I don't eat shit. Harry doesn't. Vince doesn't. But I'm not *ordering* you to help. If you do, it's strictly volunteer."

I could feel him maneuvering me. "You fucking sea snake — damn you to hell!"

"Are you really going to let Vince be out there alone?"

I was silent, agonizing.

"Are you?" he insisted.

I met his eyes.

He grinned. "What the fuck, Harlan. Break the pattern and be crazy for once."

Decision bit deep in my mind like a miler's spikes. My eyes fell to the jar. I noticed that it was full. Chino read my mind. We grabbed the heavy jar, and wrestled it down to the beach. There, we both went wild, flinging the gems as far out as we could. When the jar was empty, I grabbed a piece of driftwood and beat the jar to pieces. We hurled the pieces into the sea.

"Time to move to California," I said.

"I'll help you pack."

While Chino set the table, I made phone calls. Michael and Astarte were astonished by the decision, but told me I should go. It was 1:30 p.m. in L.A. When I told Valhalla they had a new writer, Paul yelled to the staff, and I could hear them cheer.

Then Darryl said, "Come spend New Year's with us."

Vince was out. Paul said he'd give Vince the message.

At 5 p.m., when the two cops came trampling in, the downstairs glowed with candlelight and stove-heat. Good food disappeared into four male stomachs. As Jess lapped up some scraps from the foil roasting pan, the cops talked gay harassment with us, and took the measure of Chino's intelligence and heart. The last of their edginess faded.

"So that's it, then," said Bob sadly. "That's it. You gotta go."

"We gotta," I said, falling into bay parlance.

"Harlan's selling the house furnished," said Chino. "We're bugging out tomorrow with a few boxes of stuff."

"Houses on the Beach always sell fast in the spring," Lance said. He was standing behind Bob, rubbing his partner's shoulders.

"What time you going off the Beach?" Bob asked.

"About two, so we get to the mainland by dark."

"We'll come by to see you off."

When dishes were done, the cops headed back to their tiny heater-warmed station. Chino and I went up the spiral stairway and we slid into a deep, dreamless sleep.

N ext morning, we got a dozen empty liquor cartons from under the Casino deck. While I packed up my office, Chino sat reading some of my book.

"I always hoped you'd write something like this," he said.

As I packed personal stuff, I noticed that the gold wedding band had gotten tight. My hands were an older man's hands now — stronger, nurturing, more capable. Soaping my finger, using almond oil, I wrestled with the ring. After a terrible struggle, it slipped over my knuckle, and I put it in my pocket.

Steve's clothes were boxed for a thrift store in Patchogue. His tuxedo was still in good shape — I gave it to Chino. The beaded belt would go to Harry.

"Why do you think I need a tux?" Chino asked. The tuxedo made him look dramatically broader in the shoulders. Jerking the cummerbund, he tested to see how easily it broke away if someone grabbed him.

"Because you're going to be a great man. Like your *mamita* said."

The old Bible fell apart in my hands one last time. Chino helped me pick up pages, peering curiously at red deletions.

"Not much left," he said.

"Whatever I wind up with," I said, "it'll be mine. Not somebody else's."

That afternoon, at 2 sharp, when the police boat roared into the cove, the clam-boat was already loaded, and Chino and I were just tearing up the last trip-wires. We gave the cops a gift box we'd packed. It was full of good coffee beans, and all my oldie tapes from the boat. The card read, "To FIPD with love and kisses from two queers."

Lance checked the coffee. "Woo-ee," he said. "Colombian that ain't pot."

He hugged me — a drinking-buddy hug, slamming me on the back. We had closet-type, he-man hugs all around.

"Stay cool," Chino said.

"Right," said Lance.

"But not too cool." added Bob.

"If you . . . uh . . ." Lance cleared his throat. ". . . If you run into your bad guy out there, and you need a couple of off-duty shooters, let us know."

Engine thrumming, the clam-boat moved away from the dock. Chino leaned beside me. I felt a lump in my throat. Outside the cove, I opened the throttle and the 150-horsepower engine lunged forward. The bay was still choppy — cold spray dashed over us. Jess put her front paws up on the prow, and barked excitedly, ears flapping in the breeze.

For a moment, I thought of the gold wedding band in my pocket. It could be slipped overboard into our bow wave, given back to the sea. But this didn't feel like the right thing to do.

If we failed in our coming mission, the strangers would take what they didn't already have.

Behind us, Fire Island drew away. Soon there was only a misty line on the horizon — the longest sandbar in America.

In Patchogue, just before offices closed, I placed the house with a real-estate agent, while Chino sold the boat. My boxes went in the back of the truck, under a tarp. When we left town, my friend insisted on taking the wheel. As I looked at the darkening countryside — harvested potato fields patched with snow — I felt close to tears, holding my dog, remembering that miserable Christmas last year.

Chino suddenly said, "You've earned meeting Julius."

"It's about time. Does the old weirdo live around here?"

"You can ask him all your burning questions about Vince. And he can help us with the Memorial planning."

"Sounds good."

"But you can't know the route. So blindfold yourself, mate."

Feeling uneasy, I pulled my wool cap down over my eyes.

NINETEEN

Holidays 1980

M y old truck slowed onto a gravel drive, then stopped. Jess burst into wild barking, half-standing in my lap. My scalp prickled. "You can look now," said Chino.

We were parked in front of Russell's house at Bel Gard. What Jess wanted to kill was Russell's two terriers. Russell and Harry leaned against the driver's door. The screaming eagle had scuttled his wild West Hollywood look — hair cut short now, earring put away. First Chino chuckled. Then Russell guffawed, and slammed Harry's shoulder.

I was open-mouthed at the way I'd been taken in.

"Julius?" I asked Russell, just to make sure.

"The very same — at your service."

"You devious snake-eater," I said to Chino.

"Oh God." Chino was bent over the wheel, laughing like a boy. "Harlan was so good . . . he didn't peek once."

L ater that day, the four of us were in Russell's Jaguar, heading for a holiday dinner at our host's favorite restaurant in South Salem. I was practically out of clothes again, and had to borrow a spare tux from Russell. Harry was driving, with Russell in the passenger seat. Both men had divined that Chino and I were sleeping together. My best friend and I were in the back, and I couldn't help noticing that Russell had his hand on Harry's thigh.

"Well, Mr. Harlan, I guess you want to know how I met Mr. Harry and Mr. Chino here," Russell said.

"No shit, Mr. Russell," I said.

Harry explained:

"Russell was one of the old Asia hands who got sent into Nam early, as an advisor. I was a young pup, and Russell housebroke me. But after I came out of the jungle, I didn't want to be in touch with anybody for fuckin' years, so I lost track of him."

"Years later," Russell added, "winter of '76 it was ... Harry looked me up. Told me about your problem, Harlan."

"And about Vince," I said.

"Delicate subject for you?" asked Russell.

I shrugged. "If I'd put my jealous energy into writing books, I'd have a whole shelf in print. And I'd probably still have Vince."

Russell chuckled. "Mr. Harry painted an irresistible picture of your young man," he said.

Harry's eyes calmly met mine in the rear-view mirror, reminding me of my long-ago promise to keep my temper.

"He did?" I said, as casually as possible.

"Said Vince was a gorgeous animal ... hot as a pistol ... no money, but lots of potential," Russell went on. "Said he'd left you. Well, I thought it was a damn good idea for a gay activist to get mud on his boots. And it sounded like this one needed a daddy."

"Then ... by fall of '78, Vince was already here with you?" I asked.

"Oh, he was in and out, doing his homework. He never lived here. Cici was in the hospital by then. My old life was coming to an end. I was looking for somebody. But —"

Russell sighed, and rubbed Harry's thigh.

"— I didn't appeal to Mr. Pistol," he added. "He told me he was sick of trading on his looks. He wanted me to *respect* him. I told him he'd have to earn my respect by working like a fatherfucker. So he did. And I never got him to bed either."

Russell's remark about young studs came back to me. Vince, my Vince, always full of surprises, ambushing me with unsuspected maturity. I had to feel a surge of pride.

Inside The Arch, the maitre d' led us through a genteel glow of candlelight and hum of voices to a table in a corner — two walls at our back, a nearby window that we could crash through, and a good view of everybody else in the restaurant. There we were, four gay mustangs in black tie and tux, surrounded by Westchester society ladies wearing big hats, and members of the South Salem fox-hunt, and holiday decorations straight out of Dickens' *Christmas Carol*. A few people stared at Chino's ponytail.

"So you fell for Vince," I said to Russell.

"Like Rome fell." He threw down the wine menu. "Fuck the piss-elegance. Let's have some strong drink. Harry?"

"Wild Turkey on the rocks."

"Harlan?"

"Perrier straight up."

"Make that two," Chino said.

Russell ordered a Bombay gin for himself, and said, "My own kids turned out so common and stuffy. Gawd. Vince burrowed under my skin like one of those goddam little tropical insects. Harlan, what happened to the two of you, anyway? If you don't mind my asking?"

I shrugged. "We both had some ... I believe they call it attitude problems now."

The drinks came, and Russell gave me a reproachful look. "I listened to him talk about you, and finally wondered if I should be bird-dogging *you*."

"We all love a Vincent once," I said. "Somehow we survive."

Russell raised his glass.

"To the Vinces," he said.

In due course, Russell had to go to the head. When we were alone, Chino didn't look at me, just stared down into his glass of Perrier. But Harry was studying me, his smooth blond hair looking silvery under the restaurant lights. Harry was 40 now, and looked every bit a mature Andover preppie — except for that hard sultry stare in his hazel eyes. I stared back.

"Hot as a pistol, huh?" I said.

"Smoke and mirrors," he smiled.

When Chino went to the bathroom, Harry asked me, "He's a changed man. What'd you do to him?"

"Smoke and mirrors," I said.

After turkey with oyster stuffing, and deciding we'd pass on the chocolate mousse, we wound up at some roadhouse on the Connecticut line, with a pro football game blasting on the TV. We sat in a corner booth, and Harry and Russell had more drinks while we told more Boomerang stories.

"Brucie Wucie almos' screwed things f'r us," Harry said.

"Bruce Cayton? How?"

"Brucito was hot on the trail of those pansy Panthers," Chino said. "Even after that interview, he still thought Vince was hiding something. He thought the trail would lead to the Nelly Cell. Instead, the trail was about to lead to Russell's boudoir. Russell got pretty scared."

"How did you guys take care of Bruce?"

Harry grinned. "You don' wanna know. But later on, Russie Wussie greased Bruce a li'l bit by using his media pull and getting Bruce th' talk show."

"Boomerang was slippery, all right," I said. "We could have failed."

"You've seen too many movies, Harlan. Spook work is always slippery," said Chino.

"Harln," mumbled Russell, "y' know, I nevr unnerstood th' additude that homosekshuals r 'ntelligence risks. We're bedder at deep cover'n anybuddy. I shudda had a Medal uv Honr for somma the shit I pulled in Soweast Asia. Az it is, nobuddy knows but tha fly onna wall."

Chino and I drove the Jaguar home, with the two happy drunks in the back. Russell was busy quoting some Chinese general I'd never heard of, named Sun Tzu.

We went our ways to separate bedrooms. Russell was still cautious about letting his household staff know.

This time, my guest room was a goddam king's chamber, all gold ormolu and Oriental brocade, warm and fire-lit, drapes closed. Cedar boughs were fragrant on a vast marble mantel supported by two naked marble maidens. It connected discreetly with Chino's room through a shared bathroom. When I'd turned out the light, Chino's dark form appeared in front of the blazing fire. He shed tux and cummerbund, flicked on the bedside radio, found a Latin station in New York. A pulsing rumba filled the room softly.

Shucking his boxer shorts, he looked so different already — firelight bathing his limbs, movements slow with muscle-pain but more relaxed. When he kneeled beside me, his eyes were already wanting touch.

"*?Te gusta vivir?*" I asked, running my hands up his thighs. "You like being alive?"

"*Cada día más.* More every day."

He gave me the first deep kiss. "I hope you're not hearing any wedding bells," he whispered.

"Not with you, buddy. I know better."

I was the ultimate hustler, paying him for my life by helping him sieze his own back. My hands, fingers, tongue, went deeper than before. I gave him a *kissito* that lasted an hour, all over his body, loving him with his language, sexy talk in Spanglish against his skin. His dead silence broke and he was gasping quietly. "My heart . . . more . . . *así* . . . like that . . . *ayyyy* . . ." I wrung the first deep cry out of him.

Sometime toward dawn, I was dreaming again. That mystery athlete turned his head as I drew even with his shoulder. In place of that face of death that I'd always seen — Billy's face, Chris' face — the face was a man I didn't know. We were matched stride for stride, immensely long strides that took us across wooded hills, and green lakes nestled deep in laurel glens. Suddenly, I jumped awake.

Chino had started up on one elbow beside me. He was breathing like he'd been running. The radio was still playing static-y music, and he shut it off.

"What?" I whispered into the silence, heart racing.

Had he heard something? Were they coming to get us? My hand reached to my .45, on my side of the bed. But Chino just lay there. His eyes looked at nothing, full of wondrous dread.

"Did you dream?" I asked quietly.

"It only lasted a second. But it was so real," he murmured. "He was just standing there. That's all. But it was so real."

"Did you get a good look at him?"

"Oh, yeah."

Chino lay back down, into my arms. His eyes were wet. "He must have been hiding inside of me all this time," he said.

N ext morning, at breakfast, Russell silently handed me several bulging files. I had noticed how careful the old spy-master was, about discussing Operation LEV. in his own house. Flipping, I saw photo-copied and hand-written pages on the narrowed field of LEV. possibilities — all collected by himself and by dirtbag gumshoes that he'd hired without telling them the whole story.

His commitment to helping us get justice for Billy was impressive.

The first file was tabbed MARY ELLEN. Russell had found out that my ex-wife had hired private detectives and bodyguards herself, and was keeping close tabs on Michael. He'd been unable to determine if the deal included a hit on me or not.

Second file was UNC. This person was conjectured to be unconnected to my past life, but morally and mightily offended by Billy's and my existence on Earth — enough to team up with Mech. Russell had found little to flesh out the file.

The GROUP file held reports on right-wing extremists who had shown anti-gay bias. Some of these groups were public, political, and well-known. Others, of a more paramilitary nature, were covert. Russell had just discovered that Mech was connected with one such shadowy group, Joshua Force, based in California. Russell was trying to put one of his own men in place right in the Joshua Force, but the group was wary about new members.

The fattest folder was DENNY FALKS, my Penn State runner. He'd wanted me, then turned on me when I rejected him. The file told me new things. Denny's fingering me had made the dean suspect him as well. In a second round of muffled homophobia, Denny was removed from the team. He dropped out of school, did a hitch in Nam, got himself into police work. Now he was a California SWAT man, with a rep as a sniper. He'd been married, divorced, treated for on-the-job stress. And he'd been in and out of New York a couple of times when I was being harassed. Spookiest of all, Russell learned that Denny knew the Joshua Force leader.

Other files contained all the abortive efforts to connect Mech with other old grudges from my past.

Breakfast over, Russell put away the files. We strolled outside and played with the terriers on the lawn, where we couldn't be overheard. I had my unhappy Jess on a leash.

"What do you think about the files, Harlan?" Russell asked.

"Joshua Force," I said with a shiver.

"Yeah," said Russell. "We're going to see more and more like them. That kind of guy doesn't like free love, uppity liberated women, or fags. America is what the Bible says, to them. What about your ex-wife?"

"She hates me, all right," I admitted. "Especially because of Michael. And she's rich enough to afford a hit man. But Chino has this theory that LEV. likes me. Mary Ellen doesn't like me. She'd dust me in a minute."

"The way she talked to John Sive, she'd torture you first."

"Maybe."

"Denny?"

"I think he's the strongest candidate. Denny's a *loco* and a plotter . . . always was. Wonder if he's connected to Joshua Force."

"I'm checking it out," said Russell.

Strolling across the meadow, we came to an old tree stump. Chino used it as a conference table, spreading out a Los Angeles Parks Department map of Griffith Park.

"Jeez, the park is big," I said. "Bigger than Central Park."

"Almost sixty square miles," said Chino. "Bounded by the 5 freeway on the east here. Forest Lawn Cemetery and the L.A. Zoo on the north. To the west is the 101, and Los Feliz Boulevard on the south here. Griffith is a real maze of green for our shooter to lose himself in."

A winding loop was marked through the park, in red ink. "The course?" I asked.

"It starts here, at the ranger station near Los Feliz. It ends near the start." Chino's brown finger moved expertly over the map. "Here ... and here ... a few places that I remember, overlooking the course. Good hides. When we get back to L.A., I'll sneak and peek."

"Let's hope Vince's health holds up," Russell said.

I looked at Russell. "You've spent a helluva lot of money and time doing this. Why?"

Russell's pale blue eyes went briefly dark. Clearly his personal motive had little to do with an hour in a hotel room long ago. I realized he had been in the stands in Montreal that day. He'd passed up watching his horse go in the grand prix, so he could watch a boy that he secretly admired go in the 5000-meter.

New Year's 1980-1981

C hino and I took Interstate 80 west. Nights in motels were consumed with fierce therapy. We thought we'd try to see Betsy and Marla and Falcon. But to our surprise, when we called them from Reno, their number was disconnected. The Ricelands College switchboard told us Betsy was no longer with the school. This was a disturbing development. I was starting to feel like a father pursuing an ex-wife across state lines in a child-custody fight.

"What'll you bet," I said, "that Betsy and Marla read the *Advocate* piece too? Maybe they got scared."

Wanting to find out more, we stopped at the campus in Marysville, pretending to be friends passing through. In the personnel office, we were aghast when a woman took us aside and said quietly that Marla had been killed in a car accident right after Thanksgiving. Marla's family, who knew she was a lesbian, swooped in to take the body, and barred Betsy from the funeral.

Briefly, our two minds saw the work of LEV. here. But the woman kept talking. The accident had happened on

Business 80 in Sacramento, in one of those dense fogs that
blanket the Valley in winter. Five cars were involved, and
three other people were killed. Betsy had been devastated,
the woman said. It seemed like she had vanished overnight.
She had left no forwarding address.

I wrote a sorrowful note to Betsy and left it to be forwarded, in case she was in touch.

As Chino and I drove on, we were choked into silence. We
detoured onto Business 80, and saw where the guardrail had
been crumpled everywhere by the pile-up. We parked there a
while, then drove on across the Central Valley. In our mind's
eye, we could see the two women among the snow geese, with
their hair shining in the sun. Marla's spirit had joined the
great migration.

"Jeez," Chino finally said, "it's like we're jinxed."

"And you know what? In the middle of all that, Betsy
remembered to send me Falcon's picture."

"Yeah," said Chino. "She won't forget her *familia*. We'll
find her."

The thought of Marla's crumpled bloody body made me
think of Vince, and the Memorial threat. I'd have to move
heaven and earth to keep him from being hurt.

On the 31st, just as the sun came up blood-red into the
smog, we raced into the Los Angeles Basin. I could feel
Chino starting to put a little distance between us, and I did
the same. At a boarding kennel we dropped Jess off for a
few days. I hated to do this to my dog, but Paul and Darryl
had a cat.

"Are you going to see Vince right away?" Chino asked
me.

"If he's home. Valhalla isn't working today."

I felt off-balance, thinking about Betsy's loss, armoring
myself against old feelings about Vince, quivering with new
feelings for Chino.

At Paul's and Darryl's house, the Land Rover was parked
on the street where Chino left it. Breakfast and hugs wel-
comed us. Famished, we ate with them. California food —

waffles heaped with sun-ripened fruit, toast spread with avocado from their patio tree. Over the plates, Paul and Darryl raised the question of security with me around. On my suggestion, they hired Chino on the spot — as studio security chief. The deal included a room at their house.

After breakfast, Chino stretched and said he was dying to work out. I hadn't called Vince yet, and finally decided to just go over.

Outside, a wind was kicking up, and Chino's ponytail blew as he faced me on the sidewalk and took me by the lapels. Emotion roiled — I felt such a deep thing for him, and knew I had to kick past it.

"Things are looking up for you," I said.

"Yeah . . . thanks to you."

"You going to be okay?"

He gave me a slow, ceremonious Latin kiss on the cheek. In West Hollywood, we could stand there on the street and do this. It felt like a kind of good-bye.

"Don't worry about me," he said. "I'm going to have my time. Go take care of our kid."

Chino jumped in his Land Rover, and headed off to the Athletic Club, leaving me standing there on the empty street.

Vince's half-wild little patio was overgrown with bougainvillea and palmetto.

Stopping there for a moment, I felt the blood pounding in my temples. Partly it was the idea of confronting him. Partly it was knowing that LEV. had targeted him right here in West Hollywood. All around me, that winter wind buffeted the trees — the santa ana wind that I'd heard about all my life. My skin felt shuddery and sensitive, as if I were an Atlantic dolphin tossed into strange Pacific waters. For better or worse, this vast city was my new home, the place where we'd make our stand. Everything was alien — crowded Spanish-style houses, palm fronds clashing together. A few winter roses (such a shocking surprise for a Yankee) bloomed in the patio.

Vince was home, and buzzed me through the security gate.

The apartment was a sunny, one-room bachelor digs, living space and office combined, with a tiny kitchenette and bathroom to the side. The bed rolled away into a sofa. His dresser looked like an altar — a candle burning, and a little bronze statue of Mercury hung with rosaries. On the wall was a *Night and Fog* poster. The room smelled of warm beeswax, of flowers in the sun.

Vince was standing by his desk, flipping through a script. He was barefoot, wearing snug white slacks and pullover. As he turned, his eyes met mine with a new anxiety.

"Funny ... just before you came, I was thinking about you," he said, trying to keep his voice even.

"Juju," I said.

He didn't invite me to sit, so I leaned against the wall. I felt like I was seeing him for the first time.

He looked and felt so different. Vanity, arrogance and self-ishness were fading. These days, he didn't care how beautiful his eyes were. The young wolf was older, with the knowings of leg-hold traps and the murderous ways of men. If ever he was a male who carried within him a world of hidden magic and power, it was now. Billy had shown me love can exist between two men. Vince had been showing me — the hard way — what love really is. He was now the same age as I was when I first started having sex with men. For the first time, it struck me how much like me he'd become — somber, restrained. And how much like him I had become — younger, more open, less judgmental. Loving myself, trusting myself, was now possible. So was trusting Vince, even loving him. I felt such regret at the way jealous passion had blinded me.

"Why are you here?" he asked.

"To apologize," I said.

"Why should you apologize? You're always right."

I ignored the barb. "For going so crazy. Thinking you were getting it on with Russell."

"So H-C finally told you the whole story, huh."

We were silent for a minute.

"Weird," he said. "I mean ... here I'm worrying about some yahoo with a gun, and maybe I've got the ... whatever."

"Chino told me about Mario."

He shrugged again.

"When I talked to Doctor Jacobs, he was *adamant* that gay men should stop having sex till we find out what it is. Like . . . the sun should stop shining, right? Then I called Michael — *he* goes on and on about blood, and needles. And, you know, I did get this creepy feeling 'cause I'd shared needles with Mario."

"How'd you find out he died?"

"I happened to notice Harold Fairbanks' obit in *Update*. I hadn't seen Mario since the summer of '78. He was in real estate in San Diego."

"You look good."

"I feel great. Just out of curiosity, I had a CBC done. My T-cell level is 900 something."

A long silence.

"How's your health?" he asked.

"I'm healthy as a horse. I dug clams all summer."

"You look really good."

"What's your plan?" I asked.

He shrugged. "Live on the edge."

"Live alone?" I asked.

"Yeah . . . I'm alone, all right. I've been a mercenary with men's hearts, haven't I?"

The old Vince — the one I'd broken up with — wasn't that honest. Neither was the old Harlan. It was time for me to be that honest.

"Chino and I have been together," I said.

"I could see *that* coming. Well, he's a good man."

"We're not a couple."

"Why not?"

"Both of us need to handle some old stuff."

Vince nodded. He didn't seem to give a hell what I'd done. "Chino has earned some slack from life."

Head bent sorrowfully, he turned away. Suddenly he said in a hoarse voice:

"God . . . there's so much I want to do!"

He slammed his fist down on his desk. The shock of energy jolted down through his body, right into his strong buttock muscles. It was the athlete's rage that sweeps into a world class effort. My memory leaped back to three college boys who'd just reached my office at Prescott — tired hitch-hikers, so desperate and determined, their eyes asking me for help. This last boy was asking me one last time.

"Then why," I wanted to know, "are you so ready to risk your life in the Memorial?"

Suddenly, in one of those mercurial shifts of his, he grinned. "If I go out, I'd rather go like that than the way Angel did. Anyway, I feel this good juju all around us. I trust Chino and Harry. I think we'll win."

I had to grin back. "That's a good psych for a runner to have."

Eyes alight that I'd mentioned running, he made a dramatic fist in the air. "Right on! The grandest kick!" he said. "Hauling down Death. Yeah!"

"Go for broke," I said. "With me."

"Are you serious? You're going to be involved?"

"There's no way I'll let you do this alone."

Now his face was glowing, anxious — the volatile emotion. Words tumbled from his lips.

"Harlan, look, we were hard on each other. But . . . do you think that we — I mean, I *can* go it training alone. But —"

"Yes," I said.

"You'll coach me again?"

"No drugs or anything else that cuts your performance."

"I don't do drugs any more."

My heart glowed to hear that. "I'll be your pacing partner, too. What the hell . . . I'd like to run again. With all the new training technology, an old dog like me can do a 4-minute mile."

Our gazes held each other. Now the air between us was bathed in sheet-lightning of questions. The last time we'd been together, we'd hurt each other. Trust is delicate, and we'd shattered it. Could it be built again? Could there be intimacy again? His grin faded a little.

"But let's —" He hesitated. "Let's not —"

"Not rush into things this time?"

"Yeah," he said with relief. "Let's — I don't know . . ."

"Let's get to know each other."

"Court me, Harlan. I'd love that. Everybody always wanted

my body, but nobody ever courted me first. Except Russell, who wanted to shower me with diamonds and caviar. But you . . . just dragged me off to your cave."

"What'd you have in mind? Sleigh rides in the moonlight?"

"Mr. Brown finally has a sense of humor. Unbelievable."

"Carry you up the stairs?"

He looked down with pain in his eyes. "Yeah — we never got to the stairs, did we? We fucked on the door mat."

I studied his expression. In it was the heartbreak of every man's hunger for love, warring with every man's hunger for pure napalm sex.

"How about starting out with a run together?" I said.

It was good — running at an easy pace along Rosewood Avenue, with the santa ana in our faces. Watching that magnificent young human being in motion beside me. Seeing his sweat slowly stain the back of his faded Watergate T-shirt. His feet striking so decisively onto the concrete. His long burnished legs with their bandage-wrapped knees, striding with the rangy ease of a wolf's. Genitals jarring gently in the front of his shorts.

At mid-afternoon, Vince and I walked up the alley to Paul's and Darryl's.

As the house prepared to celebrate New Year's, Harry was helping Chino move in. The gay caterer almost had a heart attack as he went out to his van for another tray, and met Chino coming in with his shoulder harness and gun holsters. The caterer asked Paul quaveringly if he expected trouble at the party.

Out in back, on the sheltered deck, six gay men luxuriated in the warm afternoon sun, celebrating the New Year. Paul's and Darryl's Abyssinian cat went from lap to lap. The *Fame* sound track was blasting out of the stereo. We traded raunchy jokes, and laughed till our sides hurt. I'd been sad for so many years, I had almost forgotten how to laugh.

At sunset there was a wonderful surprise — Michael and Astarte arrived from LAX. Paul and Darryl had flown them from New York. Russell arrived later. The laughter got louder, as Vince started clowning. Holding Nefertari, the cat, in the air, he was disco-dancing around the patio with her. The cat hung in his hands with bored trust, paws dangling limp, yellow eyes staring down at him. People were falling over laughing as they watched.

Moi? I prowled around feeling the warm sun on my skin, holding a goblet of orange juice like it was the Holy Grail.

Was it possible that I was starting to *like* being gay?

The patio was crowded with friends and associates of Valhalla, people I'd be working with. A toast was proposed.

"To Harlan's move," Paul yelled above the music.

"Hear, hear," everyone yelled back, and drank.

Raising my own glass, I saluted them. But as evening came, and the party got even louder, a shadow came over me. I got to thinking of holidays past, and family lost, and went indoors, to the quiet, empty TV den. There I sat at the phone, got Marian and Joe's number from Information, and called them up.

"Hello." Marian's familiar voice sounded sad and heavy.

"Hi, sis," I said.

"Bro!" Her voice wavered between glad surprise and embarrassment.

"Happy New Year. How's Joe?"

"Not good. He's dying slowly. Where are you calling from?"

"West Hollywood. I just moved out here."

"Wonderful," she said with false brightness. Then her voice broke. For a minute, all I heard was muffled sobs.

Finally she said, "Bro, I've missed you for years. I burned my bridges with you, and I'm so sorry."

"Well, maybe we should talk about new bridges."

Marian didn't know that Betsy's lover had been killed, and she was shocked. Betsy had been out of touch with her, too.

At midnight, as everybody sang "Auld Lang Syne," Harry, Chino, Vince and I traded looks, and touched our glasses together. The challenge that faced us in the coming year — the Memorial 5-K, eight months away — passed over us like the shadow of a great wing.

PART FOUR

Coming Home

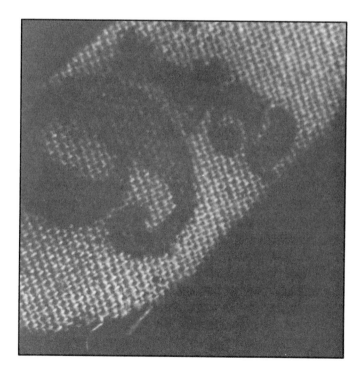

TWENTY

First months in 1981
Readying for the race

V alhalla had surprised everybody — the upstart whose *Night and Fog* had taken the documentary prize at Cannes. Now Paul was pitching the *Angel* development to potential investors. But suffering homos in Nazi death camps was a safer subject that Steve Goodnight's tale of abused youth. Tinseltown, even the rich closet gays in it, wouldn't touch *Angel.*

My office was as spartan as any coach digs — a view of the Paramount parking lot, an earthquake crack down the wall, and my old black Remington typewriter parked on the desk. As I pounded out a memo on the *Angel* script, Paul was wrestling the same script on one of those new-fangled personal computers coming into American life — a VIC 20 that put typescript on a TV screen.

At Paul's, unpacking some gear in my guest room, I happened on my old pair of track shoes. The black Tigers that I'd worn in the masters' mile in early 1978. They looked as worn-out and antiquated as a World War II bomber jacket.

In fact, everything I'd used in Billy's training felt behind the times. In just a few years, a lot had changed in shoes, sports medicine and training technology.

Before turning off the light, I read the current issue of *Runner's World*, to start catching up.

Vince and I lasted one week without "rushing things". Next Sunday, we went to Griffith Park and met three dozen other Front Runners. The club president accepted my membership cooly, as if not believing that I was finally going to get involved. Vince and I did the Memorial course. Now and then, his eyes met mine. I reached over and smacked him on his hard butt. He smacked me on my hard butt.

As we were warming down, I told him between breaths, "When the AAU threw you out, they thought they'd rob you of your chance. Well, you're only 29. So aim high."

He nodded, his eyes still holding mine. As we stood there in the smell of each other's wet hair and hot sweat, the first hint of blue lightning was licking the air between us.

"First we get a good foundation under you again," I added. "And John says he will tackle the AAU — get your card back."

We were at the Jeep, pulling out our sweats.

"The Mr. Brown pep talk. I remember it well." He flashed his sexiest grin at me, pulling on his sweat pants.

His hard frame looked so filled out, so mature and defined. No kid blurriness any more. Why had I ever thought kids were so attractive?

"Some good runners don't mature till late." I was still trying to be serious. "So we'll take it a step at a time."

"That's me . . . the late bloomer," he laughed, giving my arm a slow, warm squeeze.

The Front Runners gathered around us, panting, laughing, sharing war stories of their training and psych problems. Gay boys and lesbians of assorted ages and skin colors. Struggling actors, students, professional people fleeing stresses of desk jobs. This was my team now. They'd asked me if I could design programs for them. Of course I could.

For the rest of the day, Vince and I had a good time doing nothing. We ate brunch with the other Front Runners at a

Silver Lake restaurant. We went on a slight shopping spree, to get me a few decent clothes. Finally we sat in an outdoor café on Sunset Boulevard — the kind of thing I hadn't done since the European track tour in '75. We stretched out our legs and talked. I was getting to *like* my hellion. It was fun to argue with him — made me figure out what I really thought.

An urge to do the unexpected was there. I made a phone call.

That evening, after Vince left me at Paul's door, I went to my guest room wishing I could see his face when he found the surprise.

In five minutes, the phone rang beside my bed.

"Rhett Brown," said his voice, "get your ass over here."

When I walked in his door, I wondered if I'd blundered into some pagan shrine. The darkened room was a magic cave, ablaze with votive candles. He'd lit candles everywhere — on his cluttered desk, on the bedside table by his fold-out sofa bed, in the galley kitchen, even the tiny bathroom. Candles blazed on his dresser, around the Mercury and the bouquet of long-stemmed American Beauty red roses. He'd found the florist box at the door, with a note that said: "Hey, late bloomer . . . call me if you're ready to be carried up the stairs."

Vince was just sticking the last rose in a vase. His eyes met mine with that wondrous flash of sensuality, sinew, mischief, mayhem and macho vulnerability that was who he was.

"What's up, Scarlett O'Matti?" I asked.

His voice went hoarse and serious. "Are you sure you want to do this? I mean —"

I touched his cheek, rubbing his five-o'clock shadow.

"Whatever I'm going to get from you," I said, "I've got already. Is that a reckless statement?"

"Doctor Jacobs would have a fit."

With an explosive breath of relief, he slid into my arms and hugged me hard. He felt like home — his smell, the feel of his skin. For a long, long time we embraced in that sea of light. From the stiff way he felt, he hadn't made love in a while. I wanted to give up the old control, let this new mature being haul me down like a wolf, let him open up my guts and feed on me.

His bed was king-size, sheltered in a corner, far from the windows. For a moment, we both remembered that glass shattering over us. Then we forgot it as the candles burned low. Huge shadows leaped around us as we moved almost like running, fighting to live, muffling our groans against each other. A bluish dizzy glow spread across my vision, around our two surging pelvises. Then we both exploded with one voice and a hot blue star of ecstasy. I was the one fainting this time, falling into that blue light.

In the quiet aftermath of that renewed trust, we lay side by side, listening to the santa ana's roaring and lashing in the palms outside. I had a rose, and was caressing him with it. He stretched his muscles luxuriously under the touch of those velvet petals.

"I'm going to tell you something," he said.

"Uh oh. Dark secrets of the past."

"Before the Games, Billy told me if anything happened to him, he wanted me to stick with you."

This didn't surprise me. For the first time, I didn't feel angry or sad that he'd brought Billy up. For the first time, we could both broach certain subjects without any angry passions.

"You were in love with Billy," I said.

"I still am. And you've got a thing for our snake-eater, huh."

I nodded.

"But Billy's blown, and Chino's too hurt. And you and me . . . we belong together like a pair of track shoes."

He gave me that earnest young wolf look, head cocked a little. Vince would let me be free to have that one deep place in my heart for Chino. I could finally heal the pain of my own possessiveness.

"This place will be too small for the two of us," I said.

Vince rolled on his stomach, half onto me, and took the rose away from me. "I suppose you'll hate living in West Hollywood. That'd be like you."

"Maybe we should look for a place in Silver Lake."

"I've got a better idea," he said, holding the flower to my nose. "The other unit on this floor is for rent. It's just like mine. Four hundred a month."

The rose was teasing my belly now.

"Your place, my place," he murmured. "We can slam the door when we have fights. Humongous Irish-Italian fights, with the neighbors calling the police. Hmm?"

He drifted to sleep with his head on my chest, rose wilting in his hand.

A wild, fierce, new truculence now drove my life. We *had* to win at the Memorial. We couldn't fail. Harry and Chino let us have a week's honeymoon, then pushed to start our planning. So the four of us rode around West Hollywood for an hour in Chino's Land Rover.

"Okay, gentlemen," said Harry. "Here's the deal."

Harry would be in command, with Russell as advisor. No one else could know — not Paul and Darryl, not even John Sive. While we'd operate in civilian clothes, we would maintain discipline and security. All preparations would be camouflaged, so Vince and I looked like two jocks getting ready for a local race.

"What about money?" I asked.

"This time, Russell is laying the green on," Harry said. "We shall not want."

That same week I had a strong urge to call Marian. It was time for her and Joe and me to mend fences. So I got my dog, and drove up Pacific Coast Highway to Matador Beach, about 10 minutes from her house, and called from a phone booth. Her voice sounded terrible.

"What's up?" I asked her.

"Joe had another stroke. He's in Century Hospital. I just came home from there and I was just . . . going out to do . . . something. I cabled Sara in Ghana, but haven't heard yet. She's probably in-country in a village somewhere. I . . ."

Her words were racing, voice shaky.

"Marian," I said, "we should see each other."

"My thoughts, exactly. Where are you?"

When the white Mercedes turned off the Coast Highway, her familiar figure was at the wheel. What bird was she? Maybe a wild swan, strong enough to break a man's arm with her wing. She had struck at me, her own, out of fear for her students, also her own. Hands in windbreaker pockets, I waited quietly by the old truck. My hair and Jess' ears stirred in the stiff breeze.

She parked right by my truck, and slid from the driver's seat, eyes guarded.

How would we get through the first awkward moments?

As always, her clothes were tasteful. But this time, in haste, she'd pulled a sport jacket over flowing tunic and pants that were more keyed to dining. Hair unkempt, no makeup, she showed the years of strain and nursing.

"Hi, sis," I said quietly.

My windbreaker blew open, and she glimpsed my stick rigged on my left suspender. All around us, the strong wind hissed and shushed in the tall shrubby chaparral around the lot. Perching on top of a tall dead yucca stalk nearby, a mockingbird poured his song onto the wind. I was learning the names and songs of California birds.

She touched the stick.

"Things are still that bad?" she asked.

"Yeah."

Her unsmiling eyes met mine.

"I apologize for the cruel thing we did to you," she said. "I'm not just sorry — I'm embarrassed."

"I was as *loco* as you were," I said.

We walked slowly down the weathered flight of steps. It was a weekday, so we were the only people on the beach. The wind was on-shore, surf noisy, and a fine mist blew against us. We left a sedate double line of prints in the sand, with Jess' galloping prints looping back and forth crazily.

After I'd updated her on everybody, including Vince and his planned comeback in the Memorial 5-K, she said, "God, sometimes I feel like we've all lived forever."

"Has Betsy been in touch with you yet?"

"No."

"Me neither."

"I think of Betsy every day," said Marian. "Marla's death must have absolutely crushed her. And I think she's still terrified that someone will hurt Falcon."

A wave came sweeping up close to us.

"You ever see Chino?" I asked.

"Now and then. He's been a . . . a close friend."

I thought of my best friend in my sister's arms, and felt just a twinge of spurious jealousy. Poor Marian hadn't let herself have sex for years. She was looking away, eyes suddenly haunted.

"Harlan," she whispered, "this is a terrible thing to say. I feel so wicked. But . . . I wish Joe would die. He's almost completely paralyzed."

"It's not wicked to want mercy for someone you love."

The tide caught up with us, so we moved higher up the beach. The wind was getting colder, and some Pacific storm-front clouds loomed on the horizon.

"What are you going to do when Joe goes?" I asked.

"Get involved again. Politics, maybe." She gave a small sad smile. "When a GOP brat like me starts worrying where the country is heading, America's in trouble. I don't like this new wave of rightist fanatics who want to shove their values down everybody else's throats."

"The gay and lesbian vote is becoming important . . . in California, anyway."

"Indeed," she said with a starchy tone coming into her voice. "I wish that Joe —"

Suddenly, unbidden, her tears welled up, and she put her hands over her face and began to sob. I held her tightly against my stick, arms all the way around her as she shuddered with grief. A big cold wave gushed up past us, wetting our feet.

"So many women today have horrible marriages," she said against my windbreaker. "I was so lucky. Joe is one of a kind . . . ."

If anything ended the sting of that whiplash that drove me away from Prescott, it was that hug.

An hour later, we were in the intensive-care unit at Century Hospital. Joe was propped up in bed and fumblingly tried the old basketball game that he and I always played in my Prescott office. With his one functional hand, he tried to flip a wadded Kleenex in the trash-basket. He missed again and again, and looked profoundly depressed. But when I told him about the Memorial 5-K, his tired old eyes lit up briefly.

"Teh Vis t' b'n 'm," he mumbled with his drooling half-paralyzed lips.

Marian wiped away the drool, and translated sadly. "He says, tell Vince to burn 'em."

J anuary 1981 became February.

I checked the publisher's copy edit of my book.

Vince and I were training with teeth-bared fierceness, coming back to racing trim fast. As my lungs got 100 percent functional again, we wore a groove across town to Griffith Park. That urban forest became home, like Sherwood Forest was home to Robin Hood's outlaws. Chino and Harry joined the Front Runners, patiently went to the brunches and other drills, so they could logically be seen running with us, spending time in the park, being race security — just in case LEV. was watching.

The first day that Chino ran with us, Vince, as race director, went over the logistics with him.

"It'll start here at 7:30 a.m. . . . and finish here," the race director said between breaths, pointing. "Timers and officials here . . . the platform there on the lawn, for the awards . . . portable toilets over there . . . picnic tables over there . . . we'll feed people a light breakfast afterward . . ."

"Do me a detailed map," said Chino. "I may want to change some locations."

"Yessir."

"You aiming for a win? Break everybody else's hearts?" I asked Vince.

"Naw," he panted. "I wouldn't do that. There's going to be divisions . . . age groups . . . sex . . . ability . . . handicapped. So lots of people can win something. No vulgar bowling trophies either. I've got somebody donating nice medals. Billy's profile on them."

"The city give you hassles about a permit?" Chino asked.

"They did at first. But everything's all set."

"It's an open race?" I asked.

"We don't have AAU sanction, so I can have anybody enter. I want joggers ... vets in wheelchairs ... old ladies ... little kids. Anybody who cares about freedom."

Chino frowned.

"Security nightmare," he panted. "But ... okay. Harlan, those walkies from the beach house ..."

"Yeah."

"Get them to me. We'll finally use the fucking things. What about the L.A. police?"

"The LAPD is not thrilled about babysitting a gay-sponsored event. Especially because Harlan and I are involved. But they've got to give us the legal minimum."

"Not a fucking word to them. All the LAPD needs to know is ... you and Harlan will have your licensed personal security at the race. Like any celebrity in town would do. If anything happens, our official story is that we handled it in the moment. Understand?"

"Yessir, boss."

"Let's get our Fire Island cops in on this. They offered some help. If we need to get the LAPD's full attention, they can do that better than us. Harlan, you contact them. Tell them as little as possible till they get here."

"Got it."

"What about publicity?" Chino asked Vince.

"Lots," Vince said. "Valhalla is donating 30- and 60-second TV spots. We'll target sports publications and gay media. Cities with big gay populations ... the Southland especially. So we get a good entry. I'd love to get a thousand runners."

"The more publicity, the more LEV. will want to shoot and loot," Chino grinned.

Finally neither Chino nor I could hold Vince's pace.

"Whatsa matter with you old farts?" Vince ragged us.

He accelerated to a 4:30 mile, and left us in his dust, with that electrifying burst of speed that he still had.

Suddenly the cormorant and I were jogging alone on the narrow drive. Wild young eucalyptus trees crowded on either side, hissing and rustling ominously in the santa ana wind. It gave an eerie feeling, as if we were in some tropical war a thousand miles from anywhere, deep in the maze of green, and LEV. was watching us from his hide. *He likes you,* Chino's voice said in my memory. Was it really possible that LEV. was Denny? Denny had liked me. Why would a grudge last so long? It didn't make sense.

Chino caught my spooky feeling.

"Yeah . . . I feel him around too," he panted. "Fuck a duck, man — that *joto* boy of yours can run."

"You're doing all right," I said.

Our eyes met briefly, and I could sense him feeling the flash of tender nostalgia, the same as I did. But "therapy" had to be in the past. Our present was the mission.

He flashed one of his rare white-teeth grins. It wasn't a sexy grin —just eager for action.

"The Memorial is gonna be a no-shitter," he said. "I better be ready to run like a rabbit myself."

March 1981

The fierce drive made me want to pull my family closer around me.

Chino did a little investigative legwork, and located Betsy. She was living quietly in Costa Mesa, just two hours south of L.A., teaching athletics at Orange Shore College. Falcon was in kindergarten there. I wondered what had possessed her to move to Orange County. We did not intrude on her wish to be left alone. But I wrote her a letter, care of Ricelands College, hoping she'd get it. *Never give up,* I wanted to tell her. *Take care of yourself. You're all that the boy has. If there's anything you need, get in touch. You know I'd move heaven and earth for the two of you.*

I was lonely for Michael and Astarte, and they were lonely for me. So the two of them decided to move to L.A. They put the Village condo on the market. When Hotel Brown sold too, I felt it was only fair to plunk all the real-estate sales proceeds into development for *Angel*. Steve deserved that kind of payback from me.

Lance and Bob told me on the phone that the Beach was quiet — too quiet. Come September, they were looking forward to an L.A. vacation.

April

Early April, Michael and Astarte made their move to L.A., and we had a wonderful reunion. The two found a place to live not far from us. Astarte landed a fundraising job, and my son got a new internship in L.A. They'd kept up their running, so they joined Front Runners right away. Both of them had surprising potential in long distance, and I encouraged them to think of serious competition.

"Gawd, Harlan," said the Front Runners president. He'd started warming up to me. "Half the club is your family!"

Later in April, John Sive had a sudden gall-bladder operation. Our cutthroat lawyer was getting old.

Chino was actually finishing his UCLA sophomore year in political science. I helped him write his papers. Now and then that sharp yearning for him came over me, and a nostalgia for those two stormy days on the Beach. But I kept it to myself, because I wasn't going to jeopardize the new psych with Vince. We'd need that psych at the Memorial.

May

One day in the park, Chino and I had a crucial talk about the race.

On the pretense of a little cross-country run, we took off through that mile-wide disk of woods and ravines bounded by the circular course. Chino wanted to show me some topographical features. At about the 3-K mark, we passed a rocky wooded promontory that overlooked a major curve on the course. It was forested with young eucalyptus and thick brush, right up to the edge of a 30-foot bluff, that fell to the edge of the paved two-lane road. The drop-off was typical of the dramatic broken terrain in the park.

Chino said quietly, "Just sneak a peek at that spot."

A hundred feet farther, we slowed to a walk, so Chino could talk freely.

"We'll call it Hide A," he said. "It's the spot I'd pick."

"Why?"

"Because it's far enough into the race that Vince will be moving to the front by then. And it's the least obvious. Our shooter can make his approach through all that brush, and nestle down in the rocks and bushes just above the drop. The brush is so thick that he probably won't be disturbed by spectators. The position dominates the area. He can shoot downhill. He'll have rocks at his back too — scatter his echoes. A wide field of view . . . he can fire as the target is approaching, or going away."

"Why isn't the position obvious?"

"Because it's so risky. It's inside the course loop. He could be trapped here. He'll have to cross the road if he plans to escape north, east or west. I doubt he'd evade south . . . that'd take him right into the race command area and Los Feliz. *I* wouldn't do that. There's a couple of safer positions outside the loop. But he'll know I'd spot them."

Just looking at Hide A gave me a feeling of choking paranoia.

I said, "He'll fire over the longest distance, won't he?"

"Yeah. Seventy-five yards is about maximum, if he uses the silencer. That's another reason I think he'd pick this spot . . . when the runners first come in sight around that curve, he has a direct line of fire over about 70 yards."

"And he probably won't shoot when the runners are passing right in front of him, because that exposes his position more."

"Why Harlan, you're starting to think like a sniper," Chino said dryly.

I smiled a little, but nothing was funny. "What are his chances of a one-shot hit at 70 yards?"

"With a running target, 65 percent, maybe. And he has

to compensate for shooting downhill . . . and the up-and-down motion of the target. My guess is . . . he'll try for the approaching shot, because the target is getting bigger, not smaller, and he won't know if he'll get another opening."

"Once Vince kicks," I said, "chances are he'll be running alone. Unless a couple other guys kick with him."

"Yeah, this bothers me. I want Vince to be more protected out there. We want to dangle him like a lure . . . nothing more. I want Vince to wear a T-shirt with Kevlar panels in it. Harry and I will be wearing them too. They're light . . . just a few ounces. Russell will get them made up for us."

My stomach clenched with tension.

"A body-armor shirt doesn't stop a head shot," I said.

Chino looked pained. "You can't ever eliminate all the risk, Harlan. Only some of it."

"I know. That's what spooks me."

"Got any other ideas how we can cut risk?"

I looked back through the trees at Hide A. What he'd said about the line of fire gave me an idea.

"I'll run with Vince," I said. "Pace him the whole way."

Chino narrowed his eyes and looked at me.

"If your hunch about LEV. liking me is right," I said, "I could block the head shot, and he won't hit me. As we come into view of Hide A, I'd be ahead of Vince, on the line of fire. As we come even with him, I drift back to his side. As we pass, I fall back more, staying on the line of fire. I'm taller than Vince — that handles the downhill angle."

"You can stay up with your *joto* boy?"

"He's going to run a conservative race. I could handle it."

"You spent three years trying to disappear . . . now you're ready to jump in front of the crosshairs?"

I grinned. "Hey, skipper . . . never set a pattern, right?"

Chino grinned back. "Okay. You're on."

If Vince was going to be in the crosshairs, I wanted to be there with him.

"Everything depends on how the race develops," I said. "If I block his shot, or if a bunch of guys kick with us and LEV. just can't get a clear shot, will he have a plan B?"

"He won't have time to take another position during the race. But the awards ceremony worries me."

"He can't assume that Vince will be in the awards."

"But he'll know Vince is race director. And the race director will probably get up on the platform."

"LEV.'s disguise will have to be real good," I said.

"Something that looks normal in a park on Sunday. Even a mother with a baby buggy . . ."

"Think he'll have a spotter?"

"We have to assume he will."

"Will he shoot just once?"

"One shot, one kill. The first shot gives you away, and you have to bug out."

It was sinking in that I had volunteered to stick my own head in the path of that speeding .22 round. I could almost feel it spiraling through my brain. Life was sweeter, suddenly — as fragile as those roses I'd laid on Vince.

That night, when Vince found out I was going to run the Memorial with him, he was very shook up at first.

"Listen," I said. "I've always been the kind of coach who does what his runners do. I don't stand around on the sidelines in a suit and tie. I never ask somebody to bust quarter miles if I can't bust them myself."

Vince looked into my eyes for a minute. "Chino and Harry okayed it?"

"They're professionals. They won't argue with a volunteer."

I hit him gently on the shoulder, and said, "Hey . . . we're a pair of shoes, remember?"

Slowly he nodded. Finally he hit me back, very gently.

About this time, my ex-wife discovered that Michael and I had moved to the West Coast. She was more desperate than ever to win her war with me over Michael's love. Now Mary Ellen showed up in L.A. First she checked into the Beverly Hilton. Next, her chauffeured car was parked across the street from the duplex where Michael and Astarte were living. Her own bodyguard rode shotgun in the car. She left spooky tearful messages taped to Michael's security gate.

We took her new move very seriously — her stalking us, her open display of armed readiness. Russell still believed she was a contender, and I had to agree.

June

Michael and Astarte tried to ignore his mother. They were gung ho to run the Memorial, and asked me to train them. Astarte was ambitious enough to talk of winning her age-group. Feeling queasy about my inability to tell them what was afoot, I put them both on a program.

Russell was also in and out of L.A. He and Harry weren't openly squiring each other, but they were tight. The old soldier had his network going, tracking the movements of Denny and my ex-wife, still trying to spot if she too had any connections to Joshua Force. And he was going to help us tell some of the noble gay war stories. He sold a few of his high-priced horses, and put the money into Valhalla.

We hoped to start shooting *Angel* in 1982.

That same month I finally figured out what to do with Billy's gold ring. Nothing else had seemed right. Vince heard my plan, and agreed. So one day he and I drove together to the Santa Clara Mint, who was going to donate the 30 medals for the race — gold, silver and bronze for each division.

In the office, we sat with Vince's contact, Burt, a young executive who was gay. Burt proudly laid out the proofs on the desk for us to look at. Vince had picked Billy's best profile photo, and the mint's artist had turned it into a beautiful low relief. Billy's brave eyes and windblown curls looked just right. It was strange, seeing my lover turn into a monument before my very eyes. When Vince and I looked up at each other, our eyes were wet.

"We're proud of this," Burt said. "It's one of the nicest we've done."

Feeling apprehensive, Vince and I accompanied him into the foundry, where they had a "melt" going and were about to gold-plate the first 10 of the medals. The place shook with the roar of the gas-fired furnace. As its door slid open and I stared into its heart of light, a blast of heat rolled out over me. A claustrophobic flash of the past almost suffocated me at that moment — I expected to see Billy's ashes in a gray heap. Now, a small crucible sat there. As a worker in insulated suit and safety glasses lifted the crucible out with tongs, the melted gold, dull red, trembled with the movement.

For a moment, the old grief splashed me, like hot metal.

Another worker handed me a metal-cutting tool.

Pulling myself together, I gritted my teeth and nipped the ring in three pieces. Billy's death had to transform into power and healing for as many people as possible.

The biggest piece I tossed into the crucible. The others, tiny bits, I gave to Burt for the silver and bronze melts.

TWENTY-ONE

A s the summer of 1981 moved on, we started counting down to the Memorial 5-K.

Vince and I settled ouchily into life together. Usually the door between our duplexes stood open, making what he called the "simplex". Now and then, it slammed shut — to be creaked open later by him or me, and an apology offered like a rose. With spooky caution, I let myself love the simple daily things that I'd had with Billy, and lost. The sounds of another man in the house. His footsteps behind me, a warm kiss on the neck, his smell in my pillow, the clink of dishes in the kitchen. Could we survive long enough to have two wheelchairs in the sun? Two old men with liver spots on their hands, still arguing about gay politics?

July

T he New York *Times* and other papers jarred the country with the first headlines: RARE CANCER SEEN IN 41 HOMOSEXUALS. Rumor spiked into arguments. Was it sexually transmitted? Should the men stop being so free with sex? The gay community would split deeper than the

Grand Canyon on these issues. But the religious extremists would all agree — it was God's judgment on sodomites.

The news left Vince and me staring at each other. Mario had died of that rare cancer. It was called Kaposi's sarcoma.

Meanwhile, the month of July saw Chino still sneaking and peeking in Griffith Park. He was hoping to catch sight of LEV. doing the same.

Now and then, Chino did a stake-out, sitting quietly behind dark glasses in somebody's van, a different one every time, with a camera and zoom lens, binoculars, a thermos of coffee and a porta-potty in the back. Or he rambled around unrecognizable, disguised as a homeless dirtbag with his bedroll of stuff, watching the flow of people through the park. A couple of times, he spent the night, and we could only imagine his adventures during those hours when the main cruising areas were rustling with horny men and gay-bashers.

August

G ay men and lesbians were nervously handing around another news story. The *Wall Street Journal* said that new research linked "gay cancer" to some cases among women and heterosexual males. Jacques called me from Hawaii, and nervously asked what I thought. I knew he was afraid he might have given something to Eileen, and maybe to the baby that died.

"Well," I said, "until they find out what it is, and develop a test, we're all in the dark."

Marian was in a panic that Chino had given her something. "It was only ... er ... heavy petting, but ..." She couldn't discuss the matter with her straight gynecologist. He didn't know anything about gay sex, and didn't want to know. I told her to call Doc Jacobs. All Doc could tell her was to go for a complete blood count, to see what her T-cells were doing. Her count was a little over 700. But that in itself didn't tell us much.

Chino was so shell-shocked on health that it was hard to get him really worried about this. But because it was Marian, he went grumpily to a West Hollywood doctor. His T-cell count was around 600 — the low side of normal.

If I had the thing, did I get it from Vince? Or did it go back farther in time? Already some conservative gays were talking about "hustler's disease". It was all the fault of those loose men in the community, they said. Maybe I had it already, and gave something to Billy. If I did, Betsy might have been infected. And if she was, what about Falcon?

My 46th birthday was that month, and Chino gave me a strange gift. It was a votive candle, in a glass holder with the Virgin of Guadalupe painted on it. Lingering Protestant ghosts in my brain started yelling protests at the sight of it.

"What the hell is this?" I tried to say in a ragging tone. "You trying to make a Catholic out of me?"

"*La Virgencita* isn't Catholic. She's the sea . . . Life. That's what my granny always told me."

"So you're trying to make a pagan out of me."

"Notice how her hands are open?" he said. "Open for everybody, man. Even queers."

I put the candle on the new dresser in my new bedroom — all new furniture, the first I'd owned since I was married. Vince had his altar. Mine had always been in the front of somebody else's church, with some minister of God between it and me. I could have my own altar, goddam it. Next thing I knew, I was lighting the candle now and then. Only to humor my best friend, mind you. And the *Virgencita* helped me feel closer to Betsy, wherever she was, poor lonely soul . . . and Falcon. Beside it, went the pair of old Tiger shoes. Now and then, a flower or two. If I could give roses to Vince, I could damn well court myself a little bit too.

Most of all, I prayed like a bastard that none of us would die in the Memorial.

Mid-August

There were burning questions about how we would actually get LEV. in custody. One Saturday in the park, Chino and I were jogging along quietly, alone, while Vince busted through his workout up ahead. Jess was happily galloping along with us, tongue hanging out.

I asked Chino, "When will LEV. move into the hide? The night before?"

"That'd be the obvious thing to do. I'm going to spend that night in the area, just in case. Or he might ease in next morning, with the spectators."

"Let's say we spot him . . . we're in hot pursuit. I assume he'll be carrying a hand gun for self-defense?"

"A small gun, that he can reach quick. But he might not use it unless his back's to the wall. A shot brings every cop in L.A."

"Think he'll have a getaway car?"

"If he can do it without police pursuit. Movie stuff. Too risky. My guess is — being he's a genius at fading away — he'll evade and escape on foot. Lose himself in the crowd. Or head north through the park, where he's got 60 square miles to lose himself in. Trees, brush, canyons, isolated streets. If he gets to the north side, to Forest Lawn or the L.A. Zoo, he might have a car in a parking lot. So we have to grab him in the first few minutes."

"But if we are actually chasing him on foot, how is he going to move?"

"That's a good question. There's a whole art of escape and evade in the woods, if you're a sniper being pursued."

We crossed the road into the woods that formed the northern perimeter of the course.

About an eighth of a mile in, we crashed out of thick brush into bright sun, and found ourselves on the edge of another steep drop-off. It was a deep winding ravine with gravelly unstable sides. In the bottom, 50 feet below, was a dry rocky wash with soda-pop cans glimmering and a couple of half-dead sycamores. A raven flew across it, stirring desolate echoes with its call.

"Jeez," I said. "What a hairy place."

"Yeah," Chino said. "I played down there as a *chavalito*."

"He'll have to get across this. How far does it run?"

"About one K in our direction, two K in the other."

"Hard to get into, hard to get out of."

I was walking along the edge when suddenly the unstable soil crumbled under my feet. Chino grabbed my arm just in time, before I slid over the edge. A few little rocks rained spookily down, down to the bottom.

"Oops," said Chino.

"No shit," I said. "Thanks."

Later, at brunch in the Silver Lake restaurant, Chino drew escape diagrams on a paper napkin.

"Running straight away from us is *not* what he'll do," the cormorant said. "If he gets to some dense brush, he might jump into it and crawl for a while, on a zigzag pattern. Best one is — he might run full speed and straight for a ways, to make us think he'll keep on like that. Then all of a sudden, in a spot where he's out of our sight, he'll slow down and veer right or left, and double back around, like this . . . and leave the park on a different heading entirely."

"Hey, Chino," Vince asked, "let's say you grab him first. What are you gonna do?"

"Oh . . . make a citizen's arrest," said the SEAL blandly. "If he's still alive."

"Gotcha," Vince smiled.

I frowned. That was still the difference between Chino and me. I still had the hope of the bad guy standing trial in shackles.

Chino rubbed his fingers on his eyes and yawned.

"*Chingao* . . ." he wondered. "How much longer can LEV. push this thing?"

"If he's as tired of it as we are," I said, "it's a question of who makes the first mistake."

"Yeah. I still don't like our odds. We're spread so thin. We're still feeling around for that needle in a haystack. Especially on surveillance in the park — watching for him to show up. I'd like to saturate the area with professional security. But I can't do that . . . our guy would probably spot them. We don't want that. So the boss and I are thinking how to get better surveillance another way."

We were quiet for a few minutes.

"Have we done everything we can to lure LEV. in?" I asked.

"Who knows?" said Chino.

"I know one thing we haven't done," Vince said. "Be a lot more blatant about Harlan being there. He should get as much coverage as me. The widowed lover who is now saying up yours to the world . . . determined to go on doing his thing. He should speak at the awards. Hey — that would really piss LEV." Chino nodded agreement.

Speak at the awards? No. I'd probably cry in public.

"No speeches," I said. "But we can announce I'm running."

So we got a story about me into the gay press, hoping that LEV. would spot them.

B ut by the end of August, there was still no sign of life from LEV.

No letters from him, no rocks through windows. Nobody had tried to kill our dog. In fact, life was curiously back to normal — what I'd dreamed of. At times, I felt silly, like on Fire Island. Maybe this was all a wasted exercise. But never mind — it felt good to be taking action.

Vince and I were running 4:10 miles and 16:00 5-Ks in time trials, and his knees were holding up. Russell delivered the four T-shirts, made of mesh with a Kevlar insert that covered our chests front and back. The shirts were wonderful — they weighed only 19 ounces. To get used to our shirts, Vince and I started wearing them on workouts. We wore light loose pullovers over the top, so the inserts wouldn't be visible.

In between, we made movies, and laughed with our *familia*, and played games with Chino and Harry — backyard practice at stick-fighting and knife-throwing to keep ourselves sharp. Vince's health stayed good. He glowed. His T-cell count had actually climbed a bit. Michael and Astarte were looking good too. Michael was surprisingly dedicated to his running, starting to talk about going for a medal in the Memorial, maybe serious competition.

Running the rolling course again and again, we determined that the men's fastest winning time would be around 14 minutes, a few seconds more, depending on how hot it was that day. The women's fastest winning time might be around 15:30.

The first few days of September were the final countdown. It was also Falcon's fourth birthday on September 2.

Vince was handling his own nervousness by applying line-producer skills to race director.

"You promised to donate a thousand pounds of bananas for the breakfast," I heard him on the phone. "Not sell. Give."

September 5

H arry and Chino were working out their "saturation" plan. They contacted the local gay veterans' association, and got ten volunteers who'd be watchers for us. They'd park themselves around the course for a few hours, like idle Sunday visitors. They'd have tiny walkies the size of cigarette packs, which had cost Russell a bundle. If anything suspicious moved in the maze of green, they would radio Chino.

September 6

O ver 700 mail-in entries came from as far away as New York, Canada, Hawaii. More would enter on race morning. TV ads were running, and a good crowd was expected. Right-wingers declared they'd picket our race. Grudgingly, the LAPD assigned a few extra cops.

John Sive flew into town. He was still shaky from his operation, and trying to get enthusiastic about fighting the AAU over Vince's card. John was getting seriously burned out after his long years of fighting. He still didn't know about our plan, and I dreaded having to tell him if things went wrong.

September 7

V ince and I were physically ready. But emotionally, mentally, spiritually, we felt the race looming — just two days away now.

That morning, local ABC news got wind of Michael Brown's presence in the race. They asked to do a joint interview with Michael and me. Chino and Harry okayed it. In the afternoon, during workouts at the park, the ABC van showed up, and my stomach churned as I went before the cameras for the first time since the trial. It was just the chance that we'd wanted — to be blatant.

Then the interviewer turned to Michael.

"Why are *you* running?" he asked.

Michael drew himself up.

"I'm running in Billy's memory too. I never knew him, but I know he was a helluva guy . . . and I think he was an incredible example to sport. If anybody ever won against all odds, Billy did. And I'm also running as a gesture of love and support for my dad."

That night at home, we watched Michael's face on the TV screen, as he spoke. I felt a little uneasy at seeing him out in the open like that. His mother was surely watching it on her TV in the Beverly Hilton, and she was surely furious. If she was behind LEV., and she needed one last spur, this would surely be it.

September 8

In the morning, our two bonniker cops showed up. They had their off-duty .38s, and were ready to rock and roll. They checked in with LAPD and let them know that two Suffolk County police officers were in town for a little vacation, possibly a few of those wonderful California girls. Then they checked into a motel on Sunset. We had a feeling that the two of them were more interested in California boys, and would slip discreetly over to the Santa Monica strip, maybe just walk the street and breathe the air freely for the first time. We hoped they'd stay out of trouble.

That evening, we all ate at Paul's and Darryl's — they made a spread for us, so we didn't have to cook. Weather report for tomorrow: early-morning fog for the race, clearing to hot by noon. Runner's weather.

At around 7 p.m., Harry, Chino, Vince and I had a final update. We stood in the dark alley behind the duplex, where we wouldn't be overheard. The air was warm and still, and fragrance of night-blooming jasmine hung on the air. No santa anas this time of year — no blowing winds to move a speeding .22 round a hair off its course.

"Here's Russell's latest on our suspects," Harry said. "Denny Falks is on police business in Fresno. Mary Ellen is still at the Hilton — Russell's guy overheard her in the bar, telling someone she was in town to see her son."

Fresno was uncomfortably close. The Beverly Hilton was closer yet.

"Well, this is it," Chino said. "Tomorrow we hop and pop."

"Get some sleep," Harry said. "Harlan and Vince, meet me at your door at 0600."

Then Chino left to go across town for his night watch in Griffith Park. He was wearing colors that would blend in the dark — jeans, black-dyed Adidas and a dark gray windbreaker. When Griffith closed at 10 p.m., and all visitors were supposedly gone, Chino would already be a shadow in the maze of green, waiting and watching to see if a shooter would move into position. He was willing to be charged with the misdemeanor of trespassing in the park, if he could jump LEV. that way.

"God, wouldn't it be great," Vince said as we walked home, "if we could wake up tomorrow and find out that Chino collared him?"

That night, without even discussing it, Vince and I weren't going to make love. We both felt superstitious, remembering last embraces in Montreal before the 5000-meter run. So Vince gave me a kiss, and fell into the new bed in my duplex.

Still awake in the dark room, I found myself jittery — getting up and lighting the candle. The pair of shoes cast a long fitful shadow. Vince had picked a rose in the back garden, and put it there, in a water glass. At the sight of it, tears almost came. Looking up in the mirror, I saw a

graying burnished man with a combat stare and a lion tat-
tooed on his shoulder.

"Come to bed, ya dumb shit," murmured Vince.

We lay there for a few minutes, both of us ridiculously
awake and jittery now. Finally he rolled half onto me, and
hugged me, arms trembling. I wanted to run my hands down
him, to feel the wonder of that highly conditioned body at its
first peak of a comeback, but I didn't, because of a horrible fear
of remembering how Billy's body had felt.

"So," he said, "are you falling for me yet?"

"Maybe."

His weight on me, he let his warm lips travel over my face
for a while. "I warned you that would happen. Remember?"

"I remember."

"So I'll do something for you that I never did for any other
man."

His eyes sparkled, hinting at some unimaginable sex thing.

"What?" I asked.

"I'll . . . fix you some hot milk."

We both laughed. He was gone a few minutes, clinking
things quietly in the kitchen, then came back with that magic
potion that he knew always knocked me into sleep. We shared
it, then lay down again. The next kiss tasted like milk, and we
wound up making love a little bit anyway. Then, still close
with me in the hot and the wet, he said in a barely audible
voice, "In fact, I never get tired of you . . . you know that?
Nobody ever made me feel like you do."

I, the writer, was always short on words after love.

He kept talking dreamily in my arms. "All of a sudden I
don't understand the age thing. I wouldn't take a day away
from you . . . you know that?"

"I wouldn't take a day away from you either," I murmured.
"Now go to sleep."

But we tossed and turned, with the sounds of the
Montreal stadium in our heads. Knees and elbows jostling,
sheet tangled around us. Through the screams and cheers,
my life was running.

Then I was in a car, driving in Pennsylvania, where I'd
grown up. It was late afternoon. Red autumn light slanted

across the mountain ridges, and crumbling outcrops of unmined coal. Trees cast long shadows across stubble-fields of corn. Every hue of color, every smell was so familiar that it hurt.

Passing a farm, I knew it was my Uncle Nat's farm, where I'd spent every summer through high school. Beyond the toppling barn, there was a thicket in the woods — my private boyhood place. There, while my dog Jess pointed at birds, I hid and dreamed my secret daydreams of Chris. Glimpses of his body when grownups weren't looking. Remembered grazes of touching. Gay fantasies ripened untaught in my imagination as naturally as the red berries on the dogwood. My boy erections flung seed like milkweed pods. The daydreams were never long, because I had too much energy. Eager and afire, I was up and off, buttoning my fly, shouting at Jess, racing like the wind along the stubble-fields in my corduroy jacket and tennis shoes.

Voices and pictures rose from the land like mist. Voices of Sunday School children singing:

> *Jesus loves me, this I know*
> *For the Bible tells me so . . .*

My father strode out of the print shop, his voice roaring, strong ink-stained fingers hurting my arm as he yanked me out of the tub where he had caught me taking a bath with another 8-year-old boy. His shaving-strap cracked on my wet body, raising deep welts.

My mother's eerily soft voice hissed in my ear: "The lake of fire is where you'll go, if you touch other boys."

Fire spread around her, over the land. Into it, she threw my little trove of battered books. *Atlas Shrugged,* by Ayn Rand. *Catcher in the Rye.* The writings of Jack Kerouac. "These evil books have taught you that you have some kind of right to put yourself first," she said. But the fire drained away, taking her with it, and that secret sunlit thicket survived, as plants always do, coming up from the charred roots, thriving on the ashes.

Now the highway led me along a wooded slope. Up ahead, a faded blue '50s Chevy pickup was parked on the shoulder.

Two high-school boys in flannel shirts and caps were walking down the slope, away from me. They were carrying old-model .22s. They paused, and plinked a few shots at a nearby road sign. The sign already had a few rusted bullet holes in it. The boys were laughing, competing, arguing about who hit closer to the mark.

Then the boys slid their guns into scabbards, and climbed in the cab. They were laughing, shoving in horseplay. One boy got his arms around the other, and kissed him playfully. Right away the kiss went deep and serious, their hands squeezing on each other's shoulders, before one boy jerked away with a sharp cry about sin and Hell. That was when I finally saw their faces. They were Chris and I.

I struggled awake, in a spell of deep anguish, to find Vince's body laying reassuringly beside me. I lay there thinking. Something about the old Chris thing, the adolescent guilt and secrecy, the moral conflict, still went so deep in me, that I hadn't healed it yet. What had I missed? What could I do?

Vince stirred, hand going to the alarm clock, just before it went off at 5:30 a.m.

TWENTY-TWO

September 9, 1981
The Memorial 5-K

At 6 a.m., Harry knocked on our door.

"Well?" we asked him, hoping against hope that an arrest had been made during the night.

"Chino hasn't been in touch," Harry shrugged.

Harry was ready to run, if he had to — in woodsy colors, old jeans and Pumas, his own favorite running shoes. Today was a no-shit security day. But as licensed bodyguards, he and Chino had to be more discerning than cops about whether they'd pull a gun. And both of them liked to keep things simple. Today, all that Harry carried was a knife, and his smallest-size automatic. He wore the gun concealed inside a light windbreaker, in a holster positioned where he could draw it fast.

Vince hadn't learned as much as I about real-life "professional security experts". So he was shocked at what he thought was Harry's casual approach to the danger ahead.

"Jeez, Harry . . . is that all you're carrying?" my lover demanded as he pulled his Kevlar T-shirt over his head.

Harry gave him a small, tense, patient smile.

"Kid, if a single shot is fired today, we've failed," he said. "And it's always over in a couple of shots anyway. Move it, guys."

We threw our gear into Harry's old VW van, and headed across town. By this hour, Chino would be out of hiding at Griffith Park, and over at the race command area, making sure that our gay vet Watchers were in place. Russell wasn't going to be there — the old barn owl had judged it better to be discreetly out of sight. So he was in Palm Springs, staying in touch with his field guys by phone. He would come up to L.A. tonight.

As we wove through the light traffic, Harry gave us more of an update.

"Denny Falks has made a move closer," he said. "Russell's guy says he's right outside of town, near Gorman. He's supposedly attending a SWAT clinic at some rifle range there."

Vince was cracking his knuckles — something he never did except before a big race.

Me, I felt like I was sweating molten gold.

Suddenly the old friction grated between me and Vince.

"So you won't speak at the awards?" Vince asked.

"No. But I'll make sure you survive to get one," I growled.

"Sure, sure," Vince mumbled, disgusted.

6:45 a.m.

At the park, we drove past the big banner reading BILLY SIVE MEMORIAL 5-K. Like a windsock at an airport, it hung dead quiet in the drifting fog. No wind meant that the shooter, if he showed up, had a few more digits of percentage for a hit.

This intimate little road race was nothing like the Olympic Games. Pavement and lawn teemed with a growing crowd where athletes and spectators mingled, laughing and horsing around. Those were the days when the national running craze was getting off, and major road races just starting to pull big entries. As I recall, the Boston Marathon was pulling several thousand by then, and the New York City Marathon was close behind. The crowd was bigger than we'd hoped — maybe we'd go over 1000 entries after all.

Placards shook jubilantly in the air. WE REMEMBER BILLY and SIVE LIVES and GAY IS GOOD. A few religious rightists stood behind police barricades, silent, grim — we'd see more of them in the future, as they picketed abortion clinics and Gay Pride events. Their signs said GAY IS <u>BAD</u>, NOT GOOD, etc. Near the picnic tables, where runners sipped free herb tea and coffee, a sound van with a bullhorn was blasting those damned disco rhythms that seemed to be the gay anthem by now. A Valhalla video crew was walking around — Paul and Darryl wanted footage for the record.

As we passed the empty awards platform, two club members were at a table, laying out those beautiful medals — 30 of them. Today the gold from Billy's ring would come alive on the warm breasts of boys and girls, seniors, handicapped, anybody who needed hope. A lump filled my throat.

Vince was simmering with anger at me.

Beyond, about 75 feet away, the Front Runners' food concession and the row of portable toilets were doing brisk business. Farther still, the lawn rolled uphill to the maze of green and a rocky crest.

My eye lingered on the crest. A good sniper hide.

As cold fog drifted across the tree tops, people wore heavy sweats, held steaming cups close. The dank chill would cut our crowd a little, keep some thin-blooded spectators away. But the morning was a delight for Southland runners, who often have to perform in the heat.

An eerie quiet filled me.

6:50 a.m.

The VW van nosed through the crowd, and parked behind the Front Runner tent, among the race crew's cars. We got out with Harry right in front of us.

Chino met us there, armed as casually as Harry. He was carrying his little old .38 revolver that he'd used as a side arm in Vietnam. From his eyes, we knew right away that the night's wait had been a *nada*. He noticed our mood but said nothing.

Chino pulled the three of us aside for a quick update.

"The night was so quiet, I could hear the bats fucking. Only nine of our Watchers showed. One's sick. They're out there with their walkies. Johnny Pufescu is watching Hide A — he was the sharpest this morning. Our two cops are hanging out in the center woods — best place to help with an arrest."

As he spoke, he and Harry were scanning everything around us, noticing every movement.

Chino went on, "Mary Ellen is here. And guess what ... Denny Falks is here. He drove in and parked, like he's just another spectator. Russell's guys are on the radio, tracking them both."

Harry kept a blank face as Chino discreetly pointed the two people out.

My stomach tightened at the sight of a white limo in the parking area, with a shadowy woman's shape inside, wearing a hat — my estranged wife. She was always big on hats. This was the first time I'd seen her in over 20 years.

On the other side of the lawn, a stocky fit-looking guy in a baseball cap was sipping a coffee alone, looking around with hard cop eyes — that ex-half-miler of my Penn track team. If our suspect was Mary Ellen, she'd have her shooter on the grounds somewhere. If it was Denny, he was probably carrying an off-duty gun, and might plan to walk up and fire point-blank like Dan White did at Harvey Milk.

If neither two was our elusive quarry, it meant they were both drawn here by old pain and compulsive curiosity. And it meant we were left looking at that spookiest possibility of all — a sniper who was completely unknown to us.

Suddenly my fists clenched with rage.

7:00 a.m.

Marian arrived and hugged us. "Joe says 'smoke 'em, babies'. He wishes he could be here."

"Band-Aids," I barked at Vince.

"Don't yell at me," he barked back.

My lover yanked up his psychedelic print pullover and Kevlar singlet, being careful not to display it, and I taped Band-Aids over his nipples — they were tender and bled easy with the sweat and rubbing. He looked disco-flashy, in the new style lycra running-tights. His Saucony racing flats were custom-made, with a new kind of insole that ensured minimum stress on his knees.

I looked more old-style, in a plain pullover and shorts, and my own choice of Sauconys.

Now, as entries closed and Rick, the assistant race director, came up to Vince with the entry sheets, Vince brusquely handed me my number 8 and two safety pins. Vince was 9.

Vince looked at the entry sheets. His eyes widened a little.

"What?" I said.

"I got my thousand runners. We pulled 1126 entries," he said.

"How does the field look?" I asked Rick.

"Not too loaded," Rick said. "A few hot collegiates and opens. Joe Park is here. Marta Breagy's here."

Joe Park, a Korean immigrant boy, and Marta Breagy, a Berkeley student, were hot new faces in West Coast distance running, and the experts were watching them.

"The rest?" Vince asked.

"Lots and lots of open runners," said Rick. "Joggers. Gay, straight, young, old. Fifteen wheelchairs. One hundred and forty people over 65. And about three hundred people who want to run with their dogs on a leash."

"Make sure the wheelchairs feel welcome," Vince said tensely. "Let the paramedics know we've got beaucoup seniors."

Feeling my anger isolate me, I stood and looked over that heaving, exuberant crowd. Runners warming up, runners stretching, laughing and talking and trading tips on training. Everywhere I saw the young eager faces, the older eager faces, hair bright in the sun, a glow of health and striving. They hadn't forgotten Billy. His life, and his death, and what he stood for, had drawn them here.

Vince was beside me. Scowling, he looked at the people too. "Beautiful sight, huh?" he said. "Outrageous."

"Screw you, Vince."

He wasn't leaving it alone.

"You'd rather be shot in the head in the closet," he blazed at me, "than get up in public and say two gutsy words! Our strong but oh-so-silent Marine."

"Cool it, time to go," said Harry, coming up.

With Harry flanking him, my angry egret turned on his heel and went off to warm up. A local TV news crew homed in on him, and he talked into the mike as he walked, with many eyes following him.

"Watch your butts, guys," somebody sang out. "Matti is back."

"Oooo . . . watch Matti's butt," somebody else added.

Everybody laughed.

"Go, Vince, go!" a bunch of gay guys were chanting.

"Joe, Joe, he's our man," chanted Park's young Korean fans.

". . . This is a training run for me . . ." Vince was frowning at the TV reporter. It was his hint that he wasn't going to showboat in his own race.

Just then, Michael and Astarte found me. Their eyes were filled with anxiety at Mary Ellen's presence, and I tried to calm them down. "Harry and Chino are on top of things. You kids just run."

Hadn't I said that to Billy in Montreal?

Michael enveloped me in one of his emotional kid hugs. He, too, was looking more grown-up — 28 now, more hardened, eager for his future. I held him hard, then hugged my unofficial daughter-in-law. "Kill 'em, girl."

"Yeah!" Astarte made a fist.

Chino looked at his watch, then me. It was 7:10. I did my warm-up stretching there behind the tent.

"What's with you and Vince?" he asked.

"The usual piss-off about the podium."

"It'll make you both run better," Chino said heartlessly.

At 7:25, Chino, Marian and I eased down to the start. Runners were racing up from last flying visits to the toilets. Vince and I were seeded in the first row at the starting line. Joe Park was there too, a short wiry guy in a white headband, trying to psych Vince by looking fearless. Behind us, the street was a solid mass of humanity forming up — slower runners seeded into their divisions, wheelchairs and pet people to the rear. Poker-faced Griffith Park rangers stood by to help direct traffic. The LAPD men looked like they wished they were elsewhere. Squad cars and the ambulance were parked, ready.

"Everything's set," the cormorant said into my ear. "If anything moves out there, we're going to know it."

At 7:28, Chino's hand squeezed my arm, and he left.

Vince and I exchanged an angry look.

For a moment, that dream invaded my thoughts. This morning Chris was a million miles from here, helping his wife get the kids ready to go back to school. Here, Vince and I were off to a bad start. It *was* my job to lead, to be the example.

At 7:29, our Front Runners president, Mason McMeel, stood by the start with a bull-horn.

"Ladies and gentlemen," Mason said, "welcome to the third edition of the Billy Sive Memorial 5-K!"

The roaring cheer that went up from that mob of runners made chills run up and down my back. Whistles were blowing and tambourines beating wildly like we were in some big outdoor disco. I wrestled with my loneliness and rage.

"Okay . . . attention everybody," Mason said.

The mass of runners quieted.

"For the newcomers to the sport," Mason said, "we have people along the course with Gatorade and juice. We have first aid available. We have everything you need today, except maybe —" He paused, and laughter went up at the unsaid joke. "So take care of yourselves. This is a day that we celebrate caring for people. Everybody's a winner here. That's what this race is about."

More cheers went up. The rightists were stony-faced.

As I looked at the course curving away into the maze of green, I felt an unutterable paranoia and terror.

"You don't have anything to say to me?" Vince dug at me.

"Yeah," I snapped. "You'd rather have your head shot off in public than keep your mind on the race. Let's get together here, or we're fucked."

"I'll count to three," Mason announced. "On three, I'm going to fire the starting pistol. When you hear that sound, run like hell."

Everybody laughed. Vince stared at me. Our stomachs were churning. His elbow nudged mine unfeelingly.

"One . . . Two . . ." Everybody tensed forward, toes on the line. ". . . Three . . ."

CRACK! went Mason's pistol.

We leaders surged forward like a breaking dam, with that river of people rolling after us.

T he 5-K course meant that a little more than 3.06 miles lay ahead. We'd be running counterclockwise around the loop. Now and then I glanced at my watch, tracking our pace. We were already sweating in those Kevlar shirts, running easy, at the head of the men's pack. That thunder of shoes on pavement was behind us. We were riding just ahead of it, like surfers on the slope of a giant wave. Already the field was breaking up into the men's pack, then the women's pack, then a mixed pack of slower women and men, and the plodders and wheelchairs and oldsters stringing out in the rear.

My knees felt quivery. Suddenly, as I remembered to think of my psych, Muse was there inside of me, running light and effortless, like a boy. He steadied me. I was Muse now. Efficient breathing. Smooth movement. Adrenaline pumping. Relentless purpose. The good sweat sleeking me.

So much to think about. Eyes scanning a little to track Vince and Michael and Joe Park and other runners. Michael was in the pack behind us. Everybody's breaths were exploding rhythmically around us, like a huge herd of dolphins. Vince and I were running a gauntlet — a thousand sniper hides going by that Chino had missed. The hit could come from anywhere. That maze of green pressed on us suffocatingly, from both sides of the road. It teemed with ominous movement. I forced my mind to focus, here and there seeing a man sitting slumped or standing slouched — our Watchers.

We went through the first mile in 4:20.

"Too fast," I panted.

Vince ignored me.

"Back off, stupid," I barked.

This time, he eased off. Now he was moving like a wolf on the hunt, steady in his rage, sitting back in that mental place where he nursed his kick.

Hide A was just ahead, around the next bend. Vince and I found ourselves running at the front of the men's pack — everybody else was hanging back and letting us set the pace. For once, we were front runners by default.

As we rounded that curve, just short of the two-mile mark, Hide A came into sight.

Piss-off or no piss-off, I wasn't going to fail in my duty to Vince. So I moved ahead of him — right on the line of fire, between Vince and the gun muzzle that I assumed was there, 70 yards away. Were the crosshairs centered on my temple, my heart, the finger squeezing the trigger? The shooter swinging the gun barrel slowly, tracking us along with frustration, hoping for the opening to Vince's head, so he could drop him like a deer? Was it my imagination? Would the shooter get pissed off, and decide to dump me instead? Would my world suddenly go dark?

As we approached the rocky promontory, sweat rolled down me. I drifted back, little by little, staying on that deadly line. As we passed the hide, I was right at Vince's side.

Then we were past Hide A, and I was drifting back farther, staying on the line of fire, staying on it. I counted our strides till I knew we were well out of rifle range.

Joe Park made his move now — he pulled ahead of us. Michael and two boys in UCLA shirts went with him. Michael was looking good, moving with his gull ease. Vince and I made the decision to stay right where we were.

The second mile was a 9:01.

As we rounded the next curve, and Hide A went out of sight behind us, I felt a rush of relief, and pulled up to

Vince's side again. We exchanged quick looks, but didn't waste effort talking. I was feeling the effort of keeping up with a world-class 29-year-old. The extra 19 ounces of the Kevlar shirt was dragging me down. Passionately I drew on Muse's strength.

One mile and a sixth to go.

Suddenly Michael and the two UCLAs looked ragged. Park had burned them off, and we were reeling them in. More and more spectators crowded here, and we raised a bow-wave of applause as we went through.

"Vince . . . hey, get going!"

"Hang in there, Joe!"

"¡Qué rico, mamí!" from some Latino.

Was LEV. waiting here somewhere?

The crowd was thicker, applause louder. All those innocent people didn't have a clue what a few of us feared. I prayed none of them would die in some insane firefight. Was it my imagination, or did I see Denny's baseball cap somewhere?

Michael and the UCLAs fell back to join Vince and me. Then the UCLAs came unglued completely, and dropped behind us. Michael was running right on the other side of Vince, struggling to hold himself together.

I didn't want Michael anywhere near us, so I snapped, "Mikey . . . pick up . . . take second."

He couldn't, or wouldn't, respond.

"Damn you, Mikey! Blitz!"

My voice galvanized him, and he pulled ahead.

Ahead, Park was going out of sight around the final turn. He threw a paranoid glance over his shoulder, wondering where the famous Matti kick was. Vince and I were just sitting in, with the men's pack trailing broken behind us. Park knew he had it. So he bolted the last stretch, wanting to come in looking good.

With every second remaining, the possibility of a hit soared.

Mile three. Our time was 13:59.

We rounded that last curve, and the banner loomed into view. I saw it blearily, through sweat in my eyes. One sixth mile to go. Down to the finish between two walls of clamoring, yelling people. Here and there, an LAPD cop. Ahead, Park was hitting the tape.

At the last moment, a black man from the men's pack pulled up to Vince's shoulder, to challenge us for third place. But we surged, and the black guy faded. Michael crossed the line second. I slowed a little to let the electric timer see Vince as third.

Applauding spectators flooded around us. A sweaty Park was being hugged by Asian buddies and girlfriends.

Vince walked around, panting, to warm down slowly. Harry stayed with him, in case our shooter might walk up and try that point-blank shot. Vince's fancy tights were deep-hued with sweat. My lover looked hardly tired. Me, I bent over and gagged — maybe from the tension and anger.

Michael hugged me. He was shaking all over with exhaustion.

"Next time, move your ass when I tell you," I panted.

"Right. Sorry, Dad."

"You went out too fast, but that's how we learn."

But Chino's and Harry's eyes said we weren't out of the woods yet.

"This makes the awards a primo target now," Chino said to me quietly.

"I know," I said. "That's why I want to get up to the mike first, and say a few words. That okay with you, boss?"

"So you're finally going to do it. Why?"

"Because they've come here to see a living example," I said savagely. "Not a dead one."

Runners kept streaming across the line. At 15:29, 19-year-old Marta Breagy crossed to be the fastest woman overall. Third was Astarte, looking happy as hell, to take the women's 20-30 age-group with a 16:06.

The sound van cranked up volume, and the whole area started thumping like the Ice Palace on a Saturday night. Gay and lesbian couples danced exuberant free-style on the lawn. Religious picketers lowered their eyes, or pantomimed a barf to one another, and left hurriedly. As the fog lifted, tired runners straggled to the latrines and picnic tables. Hands grabbed oranges, granola bars, cups of juice.

Vince and I did our warm-down. Feeling a slight twitching in my thigh muscles, I ate two bananas for potassium. The media, disappointed at no Matti fireworks, flocked around Joe Park. Meanwhile, people kept crossing the finish line. The first sweaty senior — a blue-haired lesbian. The first wheelchair. The first old geezer with his collie on a leash.

Finally, as our group sat at one picnic table, Harry went off to check on Mary Ellen and Denny, and Vince drank a big cup of Gatorade. He and I kept on our Kevlar shirts. Gay male runners came by to schmooze and slap our backs, but Chino was planted in front of us, his eyes cold. Any of those guys could be LEV.

"Mary Ellen's limo left," Harry reported. "Denny is over there shooting the breeze with LAPD."

Chino's walkie crackled, as one of the Watchers radioed. "Chino? Johnny here. You read me? Over."

"Loud and clear," said Chino.

"That hippie cyclist is headed your way."

"We'll watch for him. Do your Phase 2 now."

"That's a ten-four, boss."

Chino leaned and spoke in my ear.

"Johnny is at Hide A. He spotted a cyclist with a backpack. After the race, the guy wandered out of the brush at Hide A. Johnny's freaked — he didn't see the guy go in there. I'm having some Watchers make a cordon along the tree line, for the awards."

Our eyes met. With so many people crowding around, and so many places to shoot from — the crowd, vehicles, toilets, the tree line above — a bullet could come from almost anywhere.

Half an hour later, all finishers were in.

Now I could see a Watcher or two loitering along the tree line. Pretending to relax, I watched the two vets' eyes. They were scanning, scanning — now and then pausing on the cyclist who was ambling down the slope from the tree line. He was pushing his bike along. Lean and professional looking, he was wearing goggles, light gloves, like he was training for the Tour de France. But his long loose dark hair and mustache gave him a Frank Zappa look, and he walked with counterculture artlessness. His outfit was tights and pullover that were tie-dyed, hippie-style, into greens and browns.

"Looks like he's heading for the latrines," Harry said.

"Denny is coming this way," Chino added.

Chino got up and kept his eyes on the SWAT man, whose baseball cap was working its way through the crowd.

Harry got up too, and walked casually toward the end of the row of toilets, his eyes fixed, like a cat's, on the hippie.

But the cyclist stopped in the crowd, and just stood there, gawking around, as if waiting for the awards to start.

Just then, Mason went to the mike. The disco volume went down. Chino stood in front of me and Vince, eyes scanning the crowd, pausing on Denny. The cyclist was still where he'd stopped.

"Ladies and gentlemen," Mason said into the silence, "before we go to the awards, it gives me great pleasure to introduce a Front Runners member who is also our guest of honor today. Harlan Brown . . ."

I got up on the platform and went to the mike.

As sun broke through the fog, that crowd of glowing faces and colorful runners' gear lit up, bathed in blessing. Their eyes were fixed on me. Some people sat at tables, while the rest relaxed on the grass. Bare arms and legs sprawled everywhere. Sunlit heads lay on lovers' shoulders, or in lovers' laps. There were even a few straight lovers and married couples — arms across shoulders, pairs of hands tightly held. And the usual singles with the usual questions about love in their eyes. Probably the youngest runners had only a hazy idea who Billy Sive was. In 1976, they'd been in grade school. Some just wanted to get their medals, and go home.

Was LEV. listening? From that maze of green somewhere? For all I knew, he might be so pissed off by now, that he'd finally squeeze the trigger on me. If so, then the next five minutes would be my last chance to say something to the world. This wasn't a funeral service. And a certain kind of gay wit — bitchy, campy — had never been my forte. But a laugh or two was in order, so things wouldn't get too heavy. Above all, my words had to be honest.

I cleared my throat, and adjusted the mike.

"I've always been a private kind of guy. So today," I said, "it's time to do something I've avoided doing for five years. Talk personal about Billy Sive in public."

My voice felt like it was filling the whole park. Echoes came back from the wooded ridges to the north of us.

"He'd want us to remember him by talking about life, not death. Beyond all his passionate idealism, Billy had a passion for being practical. He'd say, Harlan, it's kinda dumb to go on and on about my death, when everybody dies sometime. Life is what really matters."

People's gazes met mine — directly, personally. The cyclist was looking down thoughtfully. Vince's face, at the edge of the platform, already sparkled with tears. For years, I'd been so afraid that I'd fall apart weeping in front of a crowd. But now, there was relief at draining this old infected wound.

"When I first met Billy, I'd known I was gay for many years. But I didn't like being gay, and I prayed to God every night that I'd wake up straight some morning. It didn't happen, and I was 39 and a passionate knothead, and adrift. Billy was 22, and he'd set his course. He looked at the Olympics two years ahead, and said, *Yeah, the double gold in the five and ten thousand meters.* He looked at me and said, *Yeah, him . . ."*

A little ripple of laughter went over the crowd.

". . . I looked at him, and said, *Omigod . . ."*

More laughter.

Chino and Harry weren't listening — their eyes were scanning, scanning.

"No, I wasn't very proud. And I was tangled in the myths that trip so many of us passionate gay knotheads. It took me a while to figure out the difference between passions that enslave me, and passions that free me. Somehow Billy didn't get his feet tangled there. Don't get me wrong — he had his heartbreaks, and made his mistakes, like all of us do. To Billy, love was wonderful. But other things were wonderful too. The beauty of our Earth. Friends. A meaningful career. One day a guy was hanging around who had passion on the brain — you know the kind of guy I'm talking about — and he asked Billy how many inches, and Billy said, 'Ten thousand meters . . .'"

A big laugh burst from the crowd.

For a moment, the thought of LEV. went away. The crosshairs went away. There was only what I felt.

I noticed a few couples hugging each other. One TV news camera was pointed at me. *Screw the media.* Doggedly, I went on.

"Billy knew there was a risk, that day in Montreal, five years ago today. But he ran, anyway — passionately. He died in the moment he was pulling on everything he was, to win."

A few tears were crawling down people's faces, glistening in the sunlight. My honesty had touched them. Now their emotion touched me, and swept me into my own tears. My throat filled, and I could hardly speak. *Damn — I was going to cry anyway. Screw it — don't give up. Keep going, Marine. Take the fucking hill.*

"Victory is a passion. It isn't here —" I showed them my stopwatch. "It's here —" I touched my heart.

Tears were running down my face. *Keep going, Marine. This time it's your tears, not your rifle, that is your best friend.*

"That's why no one can defeat us — as runners — as members of the gay community — as members of the *human* community — unless we're being our own worst enemy. Unless we sabotage our own passionate efforts inside our own hearts."

My voice was failing, but from somewhere inside of me, I pulled a kick and pushed strength into it. It felt like all of Los Angeles was hanging on my next words.

"The real enemy is inside of us, and it's the thing we dread the most. In my case, the thing I've dreaded most passionately for five years is standing here in front of you and crying. So now it's time for me to have that victory and let you see my tears."

There was a long stunned silence. Then I became aware of Vince getting up on the platform beside me, putting his arms around me. I put my arms around him, too, and the whole world got to stare at us for a few seconds. *What the hell, Marine. Break the fucking pattern.*

Finally, I was able to get my voice clear, and finish up.

"So . . . thanks for coming today. You all do honor to Billy's memory."

A s the loud applause died, I was finally off the platform, with Vince's arms still around me. My lover didn't say a thing, just held me, with his chest heaving. It was hard to tell whether he was laughing now with relief, or still crying. The podium hadn't been so bad. I had actually survived it — passionately. The way I'd survived everything else.

"That was worth all the shit we've put each other through," Vince said against my neck.

People's hands squeezed my arm. "Thanks, Harlan." "Right on, man."

As the awards got under way, Harry and Chino were right at our elbows.

TWENTY-THREE

"In our handicapped division," said club president Mason, "the bronze medal goes to . . ."

A grinning paraplegic gunned his wheelchair up the ramp that Vince had so thoughtfully built. As he parked on the platform, that lovely medal settled around his neck on its rainbow ribbon. Vince had wanted the slower winners to be honored first. One by one, those medals went off into the crowd, with their trace of Billy's life inside, to be oohed and ahhed over.

Chino whispered in my ear, "Harry's still watching the hippie cyclist. Denny is about 15 feet away, to your three o'clock."

Our tension grew. Only three medals remained on the table.

"And now," Mason intoned, "for our top three overall, in the men's division. The bronze medal goes to Vince Matti . . ."

My knees started shivering, and not with sex. From where Denny stood, to the mike, was about 25 feet—an easy shot. Harry had moved out of the cyclist's sight, and watched him lean his bike on a tree and enter one of the latrines.

As Vince got up on the platform, tremendous applause went up, mixed with exuberant gay wolf-calls, digs and wisecracks. In the summer of '78, he'd been the flavor of the month,

then dropped from sight. Now he had seized community attention again. He acknowledged the tribute to his charisma with
a knowing grin, that probably gave hard-ons to half the men
in the crowd. I had actually matured to the point where this
kind of thing amused me instead of driving me crazy.

Vince walked to the mike. Our tiny security force had their
energies stretched to breaking.

I almost closed my eyes — and didn't, because the bronze
medal was on Vince's neck now. Nothing had happened.

He walked off the platform, and nothing happened.

Was it possible that LEV. had turned his attention elsewhere? Or died? That we had put in the effort for nothing?

". . . Second-place man, overall, is Michael Brown," the club
president was saying.

Radiant with pride, my son stepped up on the platform to
claim his first trophy. If I hadn't been so baffled about LEV.,
I might have felt insufferably proud.

Then, as Mason's loudspeaker voice was filling the air,
and the silver medal slipped around Michael's neck, things
happened.

To everyone else, it looked like the two security professionals had suddenly gone berserk.

Harry bolted along the row of latrines. My eye traveled
past him, and saw a door that was barely ajar, toward the
platform. Chino flew across the stage and shoved Michael
down on the platform, with himself on top. Simultaneously,
Harry hurled himself against the toilet door, slamming it so
hard that the whole unit toppled over on its side.

Screams went up. People fell this way and that.

In a fury, Harry was on the latrine, yanking the door. It
was locked and we could hear the occupant thrashing inside.
Finally the door-latch gave, and Harry dragged the shaken
occupant out. The cyclist's backpack was askew, his tights now
tie-dyed ridiculously with blue chemicals and a little shit. Up
close, he looked like an older hippie — mid-40s, with a broad
nose over that Frank Zappa mustache.

"Jeez," he was yelling in indignation.

Harry grabbed the man by the shirt, and slammed him against the next toilet like an enemy prisoner he was about to interrogate.

"Where's the gun?" he barked.

"Jeez!" the guy shouted. "I was just taking a crap!"

With that expert speed that Angelenos have when violence shatters their world, everybody stampeded away from the area. Two LAPD men ran to the latrine, shoving Harry away from the cyclist. These were cops who didn't like faggots or private security, and Harry was both. Harry wisely didn't resist.

"Lay off, gumshoe," said one cop. "This is our gig."

"He had a weapon," Harry insisted.

The cops did a quick pat-down on the cyclist, glanced inside the toppled latrine. They looked inside the backpack and saw a half-eaten sandwich, a few bicycle parts and repair tools, a rusty old bicycle pump. They gave Harry a disgusted look.

"Beat it," they told the cyclist. "You're clean."

"Listen, fag," the other cop said to Harry, "we could take you in for assault."

Harry was controlling himself. "I saw a weapon, man. Search the fucking latrine."

"If you argue with us and F us," the first cop said, "we'll add charges of obstructing."

I was staring at Michael, who left the platform with Chino. My son looked shaken and mystified. Suddenly my whole body became one pulse of adrenaline. If there was anything I trusted, it was the two vets' intuition and powers of observation. "They" had really done the unexpected this time — put the crosshairs on my kid. After the news show, the hit shifted to Michael. The sniper planned it at Hide A — couldn't get an opening because Michael was buried in the pack. So he made a last-ditch decision to try it later . . . walked cooly into the area with the gun broken down in his backpack, and assembled it inside the toilet. The loudspeaker and applause would swallow the *pfffft!* By the time the tiny bullet-hole in Michael's head was discovered, the cyclist would have jammed the gun into the latrine and walked off into the crowd.

Vince and I looked at each other. He swallowed hard.

The cyclist calmly zipped his backpack, grabbed his bike, and walked off.

Harry's eyes were black with rage. He watched the hippie walk away up the sloping lawn, toward the trees.

While this was going on, Chino caught my eye. The same thought crossed all our minds. The hippie shooter had just bluffed his way out. We couldn't let him get away.

Still arguing, Harry walked after the cops. The cops were yelling back. Now Denny had actually walked over, and gotten into the discussion. Taking advantage of the diversion, Chino quietly told Michael to go join Harry. Vince gave his medal to Michael. Then the three of us eased away through the gawking crowd. Chino's move would be interpreted as moving his two clients to safety.

We slipped past the latrines, out of the cops' sight. The cyclist was almost to the tree line now, ambling along like a druggie, looking in his backpack for something.

"Lance, Bob, Johnny," Chino said into his walkie. "Hippie coming from your 5 o'clock. I'm in pursuit."

The three of us ambled after him, trying to look casual. Spotting a stout two-foot piece of limb on the ground, I scooped it up, so I'd have a weapon. Vince picked up a rock.

"The bicycle pump is the gun," said Chino.

"You're kidding," I said.

"It looks like a single-shot weapon, and he's still got the round chambered. He's hoping we'll follow him. That's why he didn't just lose himself in the crowd. He's going to try something."

Suddenly, when we were well into the trees, our quarry ditched his backpack and bike, and bolted into the brush.

Chino jammed his walkie in his pocket and the three of us blitzed after him. Adrenaline and rage amped a new blast of energy into Vince and me.

The forested center of the course was now empty of spectators. Lance and Bob were out there somewhere.

Ahead, we heard our quarry racing, slashing through the young eucalyptus trees and foliage. Here, no trees were big enough to hide behind, so he just kept going. Now and then we got fleeting glimpses — he was carrying the rusty barrel of the bicycle pump like it was a pistol. No silencer was visible. His footfalls crashed on the dried leaves and bark. As we crashed after him, we could barely hear him over our own noise. Tree trunks, branches, went slashing by. Chino hand-signalled Vince to break to the right, me to the left — the man might try the evasion trick of slowing and doubling back. If we were more spread out, we could catch him doing this.

So we obeyed, and kept running.

Chino stayed unerringly on the track, following the broken branches, foliage stirring, fresh footsteps in the fallen leaves and bark. He had not drawn his .38. There was so much foliage in the way, that a shot was out of the question. And the sound of a shot would have the LAPD all over us.

The circle of forest was a little over a mile across. Where was the cyclist trying to get to? His car?

Two minutes into our run, we came to some huge old eucalyptus, their trunks magnificently twisted by decades of beating santa anas. Chino stopped dead behind one of them, and we both did the same.

We tried to stifle the sound of our own panting, to hear him running somewhere. But there was only silence. Our quarry had hidden somewhere too, behind one of those trees, maybe inside a hollow one, wanting to get behind us. It was eerie. No music or announcer could be heard here — just the distant sound of planes going into LAX. Amid the eucalyptus leaves, we waited. The scent of eucalyptus filled our laboring lungs. Sweat was pouring over me now, from the Kevlar shirt in the midday September heat.

We waited. Waited. And waited. Vince almost moved, but Chino, behind his tree a yard away, made a "quiet" signal with his hand.

Quietly Chino picked up a pebble and made a soft overhand throw toward a massive half-dead tree. It stood 15 yards from where I believed the quarry had stopped. The pebble hit the dry leaves, and we heard a rustle as our man flinched, there behind the tree. With Vince and me still flanking, we

worked from tree to tree toward him. When our quarry saw
our maneuver, he broke and ran straight ahead in a different
direction.

Now he was heading past the belt of brush at Hide A.
Again we fanned out to keep him from angling again. Damn,
he was fast. We were faltering, floundering, falling behind,
fighting our way through brush — losing sight of him. His
tie-dye was a good camouflage. Now and then, we lost his
sound entirely — he must be finding bare places or rocks to
put his feet. Vince and I were exhausted from the race and
the sudden heat, and Chino wasn't as trained as we. But
somehow we pulled energy out of nothing.

Three minutes later, the road was ahead.

Our quarry dashed across it. Traffic was moving nor-
mally now, and a car missed hitting him by inches.

We crossed the road, too, past some staring cyclists, and
charged on.

As we were crashing down into a little swale, he was way
ahead of us — going up the slope on the other side, out of
sight, into the brush.

Just beyond was the deep ravine. Did our quarry know
about it? Way to my right, Chino pointed ahead, reminding me
about the ravine.

We were laboring, legs bending, lungs hurting, scrambling up the slope. Vince's and my racing flats were sliding
on dry leaves. This was the worst I'd ever felt. It seemed as
if I'd been running like a lunatic all my life — chasing
images of terror and repression. Now America even had us
chasing a monstrous image of a new disease. The race would
never end. It was all of history. It was millenniums of human time. The cross-country race from Hell.

Pulling on a last shredded glimpse of my Muse inside
me, I surged ahead. Chino was out of sight somewhere,
plunging through the brush like a stag. Clear sky showed
ahead — the ravine. I'd have to be careful not to run off the
edge.

Then I was out of the brush, on the edge. From behind
a tree, the cyclist stepped out, holding that strange little
gun on me.

He was about 20 feet away. I could see the gun clearly now — the bore-hole in the barrel, and a rubber bicycle handle screwed into it for him to hold it by. That .22 high-velocity round, meant for Vince or Michael, now was aimed at me. His finger was on the simple little trigger, no trigger guard, that unlocked out of the barrel.

Sweaty, panting, we faced each other, right on the brink of the dizzy drop. Up closer, I could see that his dark hair was a good dye job. Something in his build was familiar — and that lean, well-made sexy hand, fingers bared by the bicycle glove, now holding the gun. Where had I seen that hand?

There I was, with nothing but a stick in my own hand. Instinctively, I raised my arms in surrender.

His face was frozen with a cold, intelligent, yet freaky rage — teeth showing, nostrils white.

"Satan's beauty!" he rasped in a deep strange voice. "You pushed me — now you suffer my judgment!"

Even with the rage in it, the voice was somehow familiar.

"Chris?" I gasped.

"I'm taking you with me this time!" he shouted.

He tore off his goggles and mustache with his left hand. Even with the brown contact lenses and nostril inserts that made his nose look wider, I could see that it was him. Behind Chris, our cormorant had emerged from the brush and saw the situation at a glance. He'd put his .38 down. I knew he could hardly use it without endangering me.

"Chris, are you crazy?" I shouted back. "Cool out!"

"Put the gun down, *amigo*, and we'll talk this out!" Chino called in a calming tone. "I'm not armed."

But we were talking to a lunatic. He laughed — that boyish laugh gone bad.

"Come on, Harlan, you and I are going to fuck in Hell!"

His finger tightened on the trigger.

Almost before I could register the thought of death, there was the high crack of the .22 and the blow on my left breast. It felt like someone hitting me hard with a hammer. As I staggered a little, Chino rushed Chris, knowing he'd fired his one and only round.

As our quarry whirled to face the new assailant, holding

the gun like he intended to club Chino with it, Chris' sudden movement loosed the unstable ground at the edge. I threw the stick at him hard, like a knife, hitting his upper arm, making him drop the gun. Vince was there too, racing up, hurling the rock, hitting him in the shoulder with deadly force, getting him off balance.

Suddenly, a whole section of the edge — loose, light soil and gravel — gave way under him. Strangely silent, as if he accepted his fate, he plunged down the cliff in a plume of dust, hit a rock, bounced horribly and fell again.

As the clatter of echoes died away along the ravine and the dust cleared, we saw Chris laying motionless in the rocky wash, 50 feet below.

Chino sprang to me, and ripped up my shirt. Right over my heart, a fierce little hematoma was welling up rapidly. The body armor had stopped the bullet. Vince found it in the dust at my feet — flattened due to the muzzle velocity of almost 2000 feet per second.

"Don't touch it," Chino said. "It's evidence."

My passionate sidekick stared into my eyes.

"If I hadn't made you wear the fucking Kevlar, man," he snapped, "you'd be dead."

Grabbing his little walkie, one of the very ones that we'd bought years ago for the beach house, he called the police and paramedics.

Meanwhile, Vince was bending over. He'd run so hard that now he was puking up the juice he'd drunk, like a sick dog. I was shaking all over, feeling the stings where branches had ripped my skin.

Then Chino picked up his .38 and found an old path he knew, down the drop. Scrambling, sliding down the steep slope, braking by hanging onto tree trunks, the two of us reached the bottom. It was hot down there, and full of echoes and trash.

When we got to Chris, he was still breathing. His head was bloody, the red trickles just starting from his mouth and nose and ears. We approached him cautiously, Chino with his gun drawn. There was no underestimating this man. But he didn't spring to life. His eyes stared up at us, sick with serious injury. His face was pale with shock.

Panting, Chino kneeled and grabbed him savagely by his shirt. The man winced with internal injuries. "Go on — kill me," he groaned, "please kill me."

"Where's your spotter?" Chino barked.

"Alone," came the gasp from bloody lips.

I was riven with emotion, unable to believe more than that Chris had snapped after I rejected him last summer. That this was just the rare and extreme case of faggot looniness and pique. But Chino's face was convulsed with cold fury. He was about to finish Chris with a hand chop, a pressure. The autopsy would probably reveal nothing inconsistent with injuries suffered during the fall.

"Don't," I panted, grabbing my friend's arm.

"Fuck you, man." Chino threw me off. "Don't protect this piece of shit."

I grabbed him again. "I'm protecting you. You don't know who's watching. You want to do time for this? Why?" We grappled briefly. "Look at him ... The fucker's dying ..." I kept panting.

Biting his lip, Chino suddenly pulled himself together and let Chris go. Tears were running down his face.

"Yeah," he said.

Up above, we could hear squad car sirens. When the cops finally reached the bottom of the ravine, Lance and Bob were among them.

B y the time we all got back to the platform, most of the crowd had left. A few rubberneckers hung around smelling trouble. President Mason had clawed things together again, and poor Joe Park had gotten his gold medal with little attention. The sound van had left, and Front Runners clean-up crews were clearing the trampled lawn of trash.

Denny Falks walked over to me and commented dryly, "Goddam, Harlan. A guy comes over to you to say hi, after ... how many years is it? ... and all hell breaks loose."

If two gutsy "real cops" hadn't taken our side, the Front Runners race security might have been collared by the LAPD. As it was, evidence forced the LAPD to pay serious attention.

Finally they had to grudgingly commend the two queer body-guards for their restraint and their handling of the situation, without firing a shot.

When Lance and Bob had yelled enough bay-man obscenities, and the LAPD had searched the bottom of the ravine and emptied out that latrine, they found the parts for a strange-looking little .22 custom rifle. It was made to be quickly assembled from four pieces. The short gun-barrel and silencer, when it entered the park so openly that morning, had resembled a rusted, old bicycle pump. The rust ensured no glint. The stock had fitted inside the bicycle seat. And the scope looked like a water bottle — the kind that cyclists strap to their bikes. In the latrine, the sniper had managed to take the gun down and jam the scope and silencer out of sight in the shit. When Chris left the area, he still had the parts to reassemble it into a hand gun.

The flattened round, laying in the dust where I'd stood, was a .22 Magnum, like the one used to kill Billy.

As Chino had said once, spook work is slippery. So is what people believe to be truth. Like my red lines in the Bible, the day's events had left us staring into deep space, where up is down and straight is curved. By that night, Chino and Harry had stripped me of my illusion that Chris had acted out of simple aggravated queer spite. A call to Russell in Palm Springs had activated Russell's network, and our keen-eyed old owl already had learned that Chris knew Richard Mech. A monstrous war story of radical rightist politics, blackmail, guilt and obsession began to unfold.

John Sive, Chino and I rode to the hospital in a detective lieutenant's car. In spite of serious injuries, Chris was still conscious. He'd insisted that his wife not be called. He'd told the LAPD that he'd talk, but only to me. The LAPD was somewhat embarrassed about their fumbles that day, so they agreed.

A tormenting hunger to understand was overwhelming me. What had possessed Chris? Why had I let a personal myth blind me to danger? Why hadn't I questioned his motive in writing to me?

The ride was silent. Headlights streamed past us on the freeways, planes and choppers crisscrossing overhead, under the lurid mauve glow that was L.A.'s sky-color at night. The hematoma on my chest was throbbing. All I could think of was Michael, and the news interview we'd stupidly let him do. Michael stating his loyalty to his dad. It gave Chris the idea for the perfect unexpected move.

As we went up in the hospital elevator, John told the lieutenant, "I don't trust this situation. Our security man stays with my client."

The lieutenant frowned. "Police protection should be enough."

"Bullshit," said John. "It wasn't enough in Griffith Park this morning. In fact . . . the LAPD almost obstructed a legitimate citizen's arrest for an attempt at murder."

"Okay, okay." Politically, the lieutenant could see where this was heading. "So you think there's a group of religious nuts behind this, huh? Tell me more."

At Intensive Care, several police and detectives were talking, and two cops were standing guard outside the room. In their eyes was the old admiration for any man who was man enough to shoot queers, and the dislike for us queers who'd taken him down.

"You've got five minutes," the police sergeant growled. "He refused surgery, and he can't stand much."

In the room, Chris was flat in the bed, with oxygen mask on his bandaged head. He was breathing with deep strange dragging sounds, like some alien fallen to earth, whose bones were grinding together inside of him. Around him, life-support machines did their electronic dances on their displays.

At bedside, Chino stood right beside me. I looked down at this man whose threat had levered our every move for five long years.

"Chris," I said.

After a few moments, Chris half-opened his eyes and looked at me through a fog of painkillers. They'd removed his brown contact lenses. In his familiar blue eyes, I finally saw the real Chris — not the one I'd kissed long ago, and remembered as golden romance, or even the one who'd visited me on the Beach last summer. This man was a pure hologram of belief — little left in him that was not someone else's idea of gay, or someone else's idea of straight. He'd pushed me away from the kiss. For the rest of his life, he tried to push away the thought of me, and all men like me. He had spent a lifetime moving in the human spirit's maze of green. He knew how to be the perfect sexual shadow. Like a bullet, his look of love and hate struck so deep in me, that I had to armor my own spirit against it.

Through the oxygen mask, his voice had an eerie inhuman tone.

"Ah, Satan's lover," he croaked.

His eyes closed from the effort.

The detective lieutenant's eyes widened a little at these words. My hair stood on end. At that moment, I was very far from Christian forgiveness. I wanted to grab Chris, and drag him out of bed, tear him loose from the IV, slam him against the wall like Chino had done.

"So LEV. is *Leviticus*, huh?" I asked.

His eyes fluttered open again. A faint smile hovered on his lips, still flaked with blood. The horrible voice was clearer now.

"Stupid man . . . I dangled it in front of you . . . sometimes I prayed you'd remember."

"Remember what?"

His eyes held mine. His breath rattled deep in his lungs. From somewhere, he pulled the last of his strength.

"The road sign. LEVEL ROAD. We always shot at the O . . . you always hit it . . . I always hit by the V, so it looked like LEV. You gave me such a bad time. You were always smarter . . . faster . . . knew it all. And a better shot. How could you forget the sign?"

His chest moved jerkily with what might have been a laugh. "Well, I outshot you, didn't I?"

Suddenly his voice faded, and he seemed to sink down, and grow smaller. His eyes misted, but he was too weak to cry.

"So much pain . . . Glad it's over . . . Stay with me."

His hand, that fine hand, bruised now, groped for mine.

I pulled my hand away.

"Chris," I said, "I'm sorry I was a heartless little asshole. But you took a life. You helped kill Billy, didn't you?"

"Of course I did."

"And you want me to hold your hand?"

Chris was gasping with the effort. He croaked, "Give me something of yours . . . to take to Hell with me."

"You saw me cry this morning," I burst out bitterly. "Let it be for both of us."

"Five minutes is up," said a cop.

The detective lieutenant started in on Chris.

"Were you working for somebody? You tell us, maybe we can go to bat for you with the D.A."

But Chris' eyes had closed. He was past plea bargains and D.A.s. His eyes didn't open again.

A t midnight, when the detective lieutenant let us off on Rosewood Avenue and drove away, Chino and I stood looking at each other for a moment. The hot September night was dead still. We were both exhausted from the long day of danger and emotion. I was dropping in my tracks.

"Russell says he'll go on investigating," Chino said. "The questions are huge."

"So last summer," I said hoarsely, "he did the most unexpected thing of all. He fucking put a move on me."

Chino's eyes were full of his own pain. "Why didn't you tell me about him?"

"He was that secret, guilty, magic, kid love. I trusted it."

"You should have told me he came to see you. It would have saved us all the hassle," he said.

"The dreams I kept having," I said. "Somehow I knew."

"Yeah, you did. A fighter learns to trust that."

"If it hadn't been for you getting me so spooky," I added, "I might have taken him to bed."

"And," Chino said softly, "he might have cut your throat when you got him there."

A t about 2 a.m. that morning, the whole family was sitting around slumped in Vince's back garden. Enough chairs had been dragged from both houses. Coffee mugs and pop cans stood around. Even Paul's cat looked limp, laying on top of the garden wall.

For five of us — Harry, Chino, Russell, Vince, myself — it was "mission complete". We should have been feeling elated. The ritual wild party to unwind. Hadn't we done something that homos dream of doing? Hadn't I drawn my sword against the strangers who killed Billy? But I felt sad beyond expression. So did everyone else — deeply depressed, profoundly introspective, full of questions. John Sive, Marian, Michael, Astarte, Paul and Darryl were also there, and they'd caught our mood. Michael and Astarte were still in shock that someone had tried to kill Michael.

John's angry eyes told me that he sensed things had happened behind his back.

I was the only one on my feet — prowling around, walking this way and that, listening to the sounds of the L.A. night, possessed by the questions. Whining uncertainly, my dog trailed after me. A faint hot breeze was rustling the palm fronds and bamboos around us. For the rest of my life, I would never hear foliage rustling with innocence of old. Always and forever, it would bring up the maze of green.

Lance and Bob had just arrived in their rental car — they'd brought the news that Chris had died at midnight.

"Guys," I told them, "we owe you one."

"No sweat," said Lance. "Small favor for all the coffee, right?"

"Look at it this way," added Bob. "We coulda spent the day trapping stray cats. Right?"

The two redneck bonniker cops seemed to have adjusted to the company of queers. Lance had his gorilla arm draped across Bob's shoulders.

"So this Shelbourne was some kind of special-warfare guy who went bad?" said Lance, trying to be helpful.

Russell and Harry had brought several bottles of bourbon, and they were already half-plowed. Chino was on the verge of falling off the wagon. He had his first glass of bourbon in one hand, but he hadn't chugged it yet.

Suddenly Chino hurled his shot glass against the patio wall. It shattered into ten thousand bits.

Then he left, and we heard the engine of his Land Rover

cough into life. He would probably drive over to Venice and sit on the beach in the dark for a while, and pull himself together. Everybody else watched the bourbon running down the wall, into the rose-bed.

"By the way," Harry said. "One loose end."

He handed Michael the latest note found taped to his gate.

CONGRATULATIONS ON YOUR WIN, DARLING. I'M GOING BACK TO NEW YORK, BUT I'LL BE IN TOUCH. LOVE, MOM

For a few minutes, we were all silent, listening to the bamboos clacking together.

Finally I stood up. My mind roared with the questions.

"Always do the unexpected, right?" I said.

As the family stared at me, I picked up the bottle of bourbon that Chino had poured from. I hunted around for a clean glass.

"Tonight," I said, "I'm going to get drunk."

Vince got a glass, too.

"Whither thou goest," he said.

TWENTY-FOUR

July 1990
Great South Bay, New York

S itting in the boat, remembering, I drew my mind back to the present.

The dead dolphin's shadow was longer. A cloud of flies hung around it.

By the gunwhale, my wavering reflection looked back from the water. A mature man of 55 was there — an old albatross — gun-metal hair receding a bit, crows-feet and mouth-lines deeper. The eyes were more human, less sure of the answers, more courageous about questions. Maturity had to be a desirable thing, if it helped me see life in the face of death, and a poem in the mask of writ:

> *Because we have set our hearts as our own before heaven and earth,*
> *Behold, we stand strong before strangers, the terrible of the nations, who war upon us:*
> *And they will break their swords on the beauty of our wisdom,*
> *And they will fail to defile our brightness . . .*

Some old questions still ate at my spirit.

The LAPD and the California attorney general and our family had all investigated Chris Shelbourne. Law-enforcement authorities were damn well aware that violence today was more likely to come from right-wing, not left-wing, groups. But the law failed to get Chris' wife to admit she knew of his secret life. Eventually the authorities gave up an active investigation. After all, the system wasn't really motivated to stem the violence directed at gays and lesbians.

It was our old barn owl, Russell, patient and silent, hunting mice in the dark, who finally located an ex-member of Joshua Force. The man had done time for rightist violence. He was tired of the whole thing, willing to talk provided it was off the record.

Yeah, he said, Richard was the old hand who took the lost kid under his wing. He met Chris in the '60s while being staged in and out of Vietnam, from a French base. Chris was working in Paris — ready to explode with guilt, belief and hunger for virile action. In 1970, after they both got back to California, Mech recruited Chris into a tiny nucleus of militants who were deeply disgusted with hippies, dope, uppity women's libbers, polymorphous perverts and the general fall from grace of "their" America.

Mech trained Chris himself, said our informant. Chris was eager to prove himself — took to it like a duck takes to water. The kid worshipped the ground Mech walked on. Relationship? Our informant didn't think so. Mech was a hard-ass on moral purity. Chris always seemed just as hard. The Force chaplain learned that Chris knew Harlan Brown when. So Chris was, you know, under a lot of pressure to show the guys he was okay. When the Billy Sive scandal boiled up, it was the perfect chance for a hit that would make a moral statement. The two were the perfect sniper team.

The snafus started with a Canadian trial, he told us. They'd counted on Mech being extradited, getting a very light sentence in an American prison. Later, they'd withdrawn support from Chris' ongoing harassment of me, considering that he'd gotten a bit mental and "tetched by the Lord". It wasn't their MO to put that much effort into harassing one person. Wham

and scram was their style, like they'd done with Billy. Joshua
Force had other fish to fry. Like a planned campaign of esca-
lating violence against abortion clinics. So Chris had funded
Operation LEV. with great difficulty and tenacity, hitting me
between AP assignments. The informant was surprised to learn
that Chris was a homosexual. Chris did a good job of fooling
everybody in the Force, he said. The Joshua men believed they
could smell a pansy a mile away.

We learned nothing from Richard Mech, who was released
from Canadian prison in 1988. After Mech returned to the
U.S., he dropped out of sight. I didn't want to know why.

The years had passed so fast.

In late 1981, my book sprinted onto the bestseller lists. Old
controversies exploded again. I seized the opening to get the
rest of Steve's work published too.

One major studio did approach me about film rights. I
listened to their jitters about the love scenes. Dammit, I *wanted*
Billy and me to kiss on the silver screen. But however liberal
Hollywood may have gotten, there was still one command-
ment. *Thou mayest portray homo misfits and drag queens. But
thou shalt not film two butch males in the throes of passion.*
Valhalla was hot to do it, and I'd have trusted them. But I
couldn't hack the close personal involvement. Like hearing the
director say, "Hey, in the closeup here, let's have more blood
on his head."

As the '80s moved on, anti-gay sentiment grew stronger.
The AAU refused to give Vince a new card, and the courts
upheld the refusal. It wasn't till the union folded, and a new
athletic body took over, that Vince could compete. But open
gay men don't last in American "he-man" sports. Gay ballplayer
David Kopay and gay umpire Dave Pallone were both forced
to quit. Vince finally got tired of the hassles, and his health
was starting to fail.

So we turned our efforts to Front Runner clubs and movies
that were "diamond bullets". Two wins at the Sundance Film
Festival, a win at Cannes for *Angel*, and a reputation for Vince
and Paul as a top young producer-director team, with Darryl
as the "eye" of their vision. And a growing list of screenplay
credits for me. In fact, Valhalla films had a bigger following in

Europe than in the U.S., where we were known mainly on the film festival circuit. The movie mainstream still denied that gay men and lesbians are fully human.

But, even as right-wing extremists were making things steadily worse, some things did change for the better.

The LAPD, for example. These days, the department had a recruiting table at Gay Pride events.

As I started the engine, a magpie flew up from the dolphin's carcass.

Ahead was the first meeting with Betsy in ten years. We hadn't seen her since that day of the snow geese in 1980. My stomach tightened with the old resentment. I'd tried and tried with her. Why had she cut herself and Falcon off from us? Even with the loss of her lover?

The boat headed toward the rebuilt Davis Park marina. Pulling out my cellular phone, I punched the number of Chino's phone, that he wore at his belt.

"I'll be at the marina in five minutes," I told him.

"See you there," came his voice.

Wonderful new thing — the cellular phone.

Five of my family were waiting on the ferry dock.

In his fluttering windbreaker and baseball cap, Vince looked tired, alarmingly thin, from a week's shoot at the Gay Games. He was 38 now, still striking, his eyes deep-sunk but compelling, frame pared to the bone by three years of active symptoms. He was gun-metal gray as me, staying alive out of sheer will, a veteran of alternative treatments — he hadn't wanted all the drugs. His eyes were sad at what he'd seen.

Chino had his arm around Vince, with that quiet new fire in his own eyes. The cormorant was wearing his "out and proud" vet clothes — a camo beret, a frayed eagle-and-trident SEAL patch on one jacket shoulder. He was 41 now, still single but not worried about it — healing steadily, inch by inch. Lately Chino had finished his masters in political science. He'd been in touch with his blood *familia* again, and was helping Project 10 with gay Latino kids in some L.A. high schools.

At Chino's elbow was John Sive. At 66 he was our white-haired curmudgeon, and walked with a cane. John and I had finally made our peace.

Michael and Astarte were trying to deal with John's two dizzy little spaniels on leashes. My son's career as a hemophilia researcher had put him ringside on the massacre we were all living through. After years of unrelenting cohabitation, he and Astarte had finally decided to get married and make me a grandfather. My daughter-in-law's slender form showed she was six months pregnant. Who knew what sexual mysteries her genes, and Michael's, would carry?

"God," exclaimed Michael, as he climbed into the boat, "coming back here is like landing on the moon."

"The ghost of decadence past," John proclaimed as Michael helped him into the boat.

"We didn't think we were decadent," Vince retorted. "We thought we were normal."

My lover refused a hand from Michael — he didn't like being coddled — and sank on a seat beside me. I was still old-fashioned, and liked to call him "lover". Nineties terms, like "significant other," seemed a little cold. While Chino drove the boat, I put my own jacket on Vince, because his thinness couldn't stand up to eastern chill any more.

With time, Vince and I had grown together like two trees, rubbing together in the wind so long that our bruised bark grafted as one. We were a good sniper team for the community — shooter and spotter, each covering the other's back. One shot, one kill on the lies and ignorance. Our voices were heard from podiums at Congressional hearings, our voices echoing along the Capitol Mall, over the heads of a vast crowd. We were one of the golden gay pairs that lived in America's face. This time, the strangers hadn't been able to destroy us, or silence us.

Nine miles farther, another change waited — one that we'd dreaded to see.

Here was Fire Island Pines, once so rich in men. The men had come like a storm of pollen on the wind, like monarch butterflies going south. They came in search of liberation, sensation, dignity, sleaze, a lifetime love, a summer thing. Now the Pines skyline had changed — gaps where houses had been torn out, like missing teeth. Hurricane Gloria had swept away houses and boardwalks.

Farther, beyond the scrub forest, Cherry Grove loomed into view. The image of Vince go-go dancing on the bar was still so powerful in my brain that I could smell his sweat.

But today it was mostly lesbians who filled the two towns on weekends and holidays.

The men were gone because they were dead. Their migration cut short, lives fallen to the sea, wings shredded by the mystery disease that we now know as AIDS. The sickness had stalked us singly, the ultimate sniper, invisible as Chris had been — one shot, one kill. We'd unwittingly put our own bodies right where the crosshairs meet. Two hundred five names of men I'd known personally were on a list in my desk drawer.

The family now realized that Angel's and Steve's deaths were probably among the earliest from AIDS. And Steve, like Vince, had probably contracted the virus through shared needles. My bout with TB probably came about through exposure to Steve and George — the *Pneumocystis* pneumonia sometimes had TB complications.

The test, when it came out in 1985, told us what we'd already suspected: Vince was positive for the HIV virus that causes AIDS. So were Harry, Russell, and Jacques. Through some quirk of immunity, I was still negative. Chino was negative too, and so were Marian and John. I didn't know if Betsy had tested herself, but she and Falcon were probably okay. Something called "safe sex" was now part of our lives.

TV newscasts told me that millions of people worldwide had AIDS — most of them heterosexuals. But I had not experienced those millions of deaths. All I knew was that our own government had done little to combat AIDS, and far too many Americans were pretending it was a "gay disease". All I knew was the exhausting work that so many of us had done to help rouse some honesty and humanity about AIDS in non-gay Americans. All I knew was that most of the men I'd ever known, and a few of the women, were gone.

Coming here told me how a survivor of Hiroshima felt, seeing the flatland of ashes. Standing here dazed, asking how and why I'd been spared.

W hat was missing from my understanding of those years?

Like most men, I'd been hot to unload my virginity when I was young. All the authorities told me that innocence and virginity are the same thing. One time only, I'd lose them both, as a coming of age. Today the authorities tell us that the Seventies were a depraved time, when the weeds of disease went to seed. But I had to disagree. The Seventies were a case of innocence without virginity.

Innocence has little to do with sex, I thought.

Real innocence is more like sea-water — comes and goes with the tides of hope. Mine ebbed by degrees, through my years of loose sex. It came surging back with Billy's love. After his death, my innocence was heavily polluted by the years of harassment. Innocence was won again with Vince. It was tinged red by Chino's pain, and Chris' hate.

Men, women and children alike lose their innocence to hate. A nation can lose its innocence with a single crash of gunfire. For the U.S., I think, this dreadful moment came in 1969, with the massacres of students at Kent State and Jackson State. Uniformed American men marched onto campuses, and shot at young people, both colored and white, to make them bow the knee.

The Seventies were a desperate try at forgetting these slaughters happened.

Many still believed in our own goodness, our American dream — in jobs for every graduate, in elbow room for every immigrant. We believed that peace and love could be found, that justice would be done, that the system could work, that holocausts were over, that green revolution would feed the world, that rain forests could be saved. After all, we still believed that condoms were for birth control. We believed that government microbe-fighters would march on every disease the way they'd marched on TB.

I was 30-something then. I too believed — till I saw Billy die.

Today Kent State cancer had metastasized in the American body politic. People who'd screamed that their own daughters should be shot for not wearing bras, were now screaming that church and state should be one. Among the dying innocents were the 30 percent of teen suicides who are gay boys and lesbian girls.

Moi — I still carried the loaded .45 in my loincloth. If I ever had to use it to protect my own, I would.

Pulling out my wallet, I flipped it open to the school photo of Falcon. All those years, Betsy hadn't failed to send the picture, though the envelope never carried a return address. My boy was 12 now, and looked 16, in his first flush of handsome, with his first spots of acne. He had slanted hazel eyes, flooded with embattled innocence and teen edginess. They were his mom's eyes, with her Elizabeth Taylor eyelashes, and on him they looked just as good.

As I'd always known, he didn't look anything like Billy. He looked more like his mother, like his Granddad Sive.

Grabbing the phone, I punched the number that Marian had given me, of a house in The Pines.

Betsy's voice answered.

"Hi, it's us," I said. "We're in a boat outside the marina."

Her voice was tense.

"I'll meet you on the ferry dock in 15 minutes," she said.

Tying up in the marina, we watched Betsy and Marian walking down the boardwalk. Betsy was 37 now, silver showing in her cap of dark curls. Solemn, proud, apprehensive, she stopped and stared back at me. She was more muscular than I remembered, dressed simply — jeans creased from the heat, a silk-print shirt that was sticking to her, a straw boater to keep off the sun. In her eyes was Marla's sudden death, and all the loneliness of her self-willed exile.

Marian was wearing her typical L. L. Bean seersucker slacks, that she'd never given up. She, too, had joined the AIDS war, as Malibu councilwoman and tireless fundraiser.

The two women friends had gotten back in touch again by meeting at the Gay Games. There, they'd met some lesbians who had a house in The Pines.

Alone, I climbed up on the dock, and waited for Betsy and Marian. The muggy autumn air was alive with the sounds of a resort — radios blasting on boats, women shouting from house to house.

Betsy and I didn't hug. But we did cautiously shake hands.

"Why didn't you bring my boy?" I demanded.

"He's staying with neighbor friends in Costa Mesa," she said brusquely.

"Why didn't you bring him?"

"I won't answer to you, dammit, Harlan. He's only 12. He doesn't understand yet."

"Isn't that our job . . . to help him understand?" I barked. The old rancor in me was boiling.

"Look . . . have some patience," she burst out. "You'll see him when the time is right. He's still alive . . . and he might have died if I hung around you guys."

"Let's not argue," Marian said. "Life is too short."

Always the peacemaker, my sis put her hand on my arm. I choked down the rancor.

Now Betsy was looking down in the boat, at the three men. Vince, sitting on a cushion because his butt was so thin, wordlessly held up his arms. She climbed down into the boat, and went into his arms. It was Vince who cried, sobbing silently, holding her tight. Betsy, who had the same kind of problem I did with tears, just held his graying head against her shoulder. A single tear squeezed out between her long eyelashes.

Then she hugged old John Sive, amid wiggling spaniels, and shook hands cooly with Chino.

In another moment, our full boat was putt-putting out of the marina. We passed hundreds of gulls resting on the water, the biggest flock I'd seen all day — wings folded, bobbing gently up and down. The birds even looked reasonably healthy.

Way out, Chino cut the engine, and we drifted. Betsy and I sat apart on the seats. In the shade of her straw brim,

Betsy's eyes pondered as she looked back at the Island. Chino's strong hand rubbed my shoulder absently. I put my hand over his. More gulls flew in from somewhere, till we were surrounded by floating birds, eyeing us.

Marian cleared her throat.

"We walked on the beach," she said. "Look what we found."

Her hand came out of a pocket, and showered some bits of beach glass into my palm. A hurricane of feeling swept over us all. Memories of those who were gone, threats to those still alive, challenges to the young among us — their fates written in the wavering ripples all around us, as if the bay were a beryl wall of names.

I gently tossed a bit of glass into the water. The nearest gull thought it was a tidbit, and lunged toward it.

"Poor Jacques," I said.

"I can't believe he's dead," Betsy said. "Marian told me a little. What's the story?"

"Well ... Eileen left Jacques after they found out they were both positive," I said. "At first she hated him, hated gays ... So she took Ana and went home to Michigan. Her parents punished Jacques by paying for treatment only for Eileen ... Jacques had no money. Finally Eileen was turned off by the attitudes, and she came and found us in L.A."

"And her parents are still trying to get custody of Ana," John growled. "On grounds that Eileen is an unfit mother because she has AIDS. My firm is handling the case. And Ana's negative."

"So what happened to Jacques?" Betsy asked.

"After Eileen left," I said, "he stayed at his field camp on Maui, working. Vince and I paid for his treatment. Finally, we hadn't heard from him in a while, so I flew to Maui. I'll never forget it — this dying man laying in his filthy tent ... brilliant-colored birds everywhere in the forest around him ... the sound of their calls. His assistants had left, scared. I brought him back to L.A. He'd wanted to do something for the Earth, and he felt like he'd FUBARed everything. I spent three weeks trying to help him forgive himself. He was in a lot of pain, so the doctor put him on a morphine drip, and he went to sleep in my arms."

My eyes welled, remembering.

"His Hawaiian assistant, Eric, wrote up the study," Michael added. "He presented it at the next IUCN conference."

"How's Eileen doing?" Betsy asked.

"Hanging in there. She's gotten tight with us. Ana is a great kid. She's Falcon's age," I said.

Sixteen years ago, three lost boys had come winging to me for help. Two of them had died in my arms. In time, the third one might die in my arms as well. Where was the wisdom and beauty in this? Whatever it was, it was making me hard. So hard that their swords would break in half over my shoulders.

"We lost Harry," Chino said sadly. He tossed a bit of glass in the water.

"And Russell," John added. "Too bad you didn't know him."

"Doctor Jacobs," Vince put in. "Died of the thing he tried to warn us about."

"I knew about Joe," said Betsy. "I read the obit."

Marian gently tossed a bit over the side.

"I still miss him," she said softly.

Astarte, silently dreaming with the baby inside her, took Marian's hand.

Without speaking, I let another wild gem slide in the water.

Billy, you're not such a young bird any more. You've grown old lingering here with me. Time for you to fly.

And one more beach diamond — the last.

Chris, I'll give you one more thing. Freedom from my judgment. I don't have time to be angry or sad anymore. There's more important things to do.

The glass sank out of sight.

My palm was still full of wild jewels. Precious lives to be guarded, precious days to be spent together. Wisdom and beauty to be shared. Wars to be fought. Races to run.

"Well," Vince said dryly, "I'm too fucking busy to die."

Betsy smiled crookedly, her arm around Vince's neck. They were sitting close now, like two teenagers on a campus lawn, talking homework. She tweaked Vince's nose.

"None of us," she said, "believed you and the Neanderthal would last the summer."

As Vince slid me a loving look out of the corners of his narrowed eyes, a passing speedboat flushed the gulls into the humid sky. All those wings caught the light, as they lofted higher and higher.

Clearly remembering Marla, Betsy bit her lips. We all caught her emotion.

"Feels like you've run that 100-miler," I said to her.

"I hope I have a friend waiting at the finish," she retorted.

After hesitating, Betsy put out her tiny hand — a hummingbird's talon. I put some of the beach glass in her palm, and closed her fingers around it. Right away, she put a gem in the water for Marla.

"How do you know I'm not about to blister you with my kick?" I asked.

Betsy tossed me a grim little grin.

"Because," she said, "I already reeled you in, ten miles back."

Moving with one mind, that galaxy of wings made a stately rotation above the marina, commanding the entire horizon. They dwarfed even the distant towers of Manhattan, far out of sight beyond the sulphurous wall of smog to the west. Now and then, each gull yawed to a knife-edge, disappearing into the blue. Then, with one easy rowing stroke of the wings, the creature rolled into view again. The dance of the whole flock was like a glimmer of slow white lightning moving away across the bay.

Our eyes followed the gulls.

Somehow, like them, we would stay alive.

Like them, we belong to a certain sky, that is ever our refuge and our home.

About This Book

*H*arlan's Race was created "hands on" with computer print technology.

I wrote it on an Apple MacIntosh SE and Apple PowerBook 170. My double-density disks traveled to the Mac SE of Barbara Brown Desktop Publishing, where they were reformatted and typeset using Aldus PageMaker. Fonts: Century Schoolbook and Radiant.

Jacket art and illustrations were created by Laguna Beach artist Jay Fraley, on an IBM Compatible. He used the Aldus PhotoStyler program to manipulate his photographs of the exact model Tiger track shoes mentioned in the book.

Disks containing finished text and art went to service bureaus in L.A., with the end product being high-resolution laser copies of text and color separations for the cover. These went directly into make-ready at Patterson Printing in Michigan.

To me — who first smelled printer's ink in 1956 in a traditional composing room filled with clattering Linotype machines and splatters of lead — the relative ease and cleanness of desktop book production is a wonder.

P.N.W.